Readers love Anton Du Beke's sparkling fiction...

'Beautifully written'

'What a triumph'

'A story full of true emotion, heart, poise
and survival'

'I was enthralled from start to finish'

'Anton Du Beke has done it again'

'A truly fabulous read'

'The story of The Buckingham just gets better
and better. Couldn't put it down'

ANTON DU BEKE

The ROYAL SHOW

ORION

First published in Great Britain in 2023 by Orion Fiction
an imprint of The Orion Publishing Group Ltd
Carmelite House, 50 Victoria Embankment
London EC4Y 0DZ

An Hachette UK Company

1 3 5 7 9 10 8 6 4 2

A CIP catalogue record for this book is
available from the British Library.

ISBN (Hardback) 978 1 3987 1016 0
ISBN (eBook) 978 1 3987 1018 4
ISBN (Audio) 978 1 3987 1019 1

Typeset at The Spartan Press Ltd,
Lymington, Hants

Printed and bound in Great Britain by Clays Ltd,
Elcograf S.p.A.

www.orionbooks.co.uk

To the mums – Mum, Hannah and Beryl.

Thank you for everything.

The Royal Performance

in the presence of

Her Majesty the Queen
His Royal Highness, the Duke of Edinburgh

on the evening of

Monday 29th October 1962

at

The Palladium, London

and featuring...

Norman Vaughan, Eartha Kitt, Cleo Laine,
Cliff Richard & The Shadows, Bob Hope, Bill
Martin – and the spectacular return of the
FORSYTH VARIETIES!

29th October, 1962

The whispers spread through the building: the royal procession has arrived.

It is what they are gathered for, here in the London Palladium. Outside, winter is coming on. Darkness has settled over the city. But, in the Palladium, there is only magic and light. All day the backstage halls have heaved with the comings and goings of dancers and musicians, jugglers and comics, a troop of prancing corgis, master illusionists and comics beyond compare. Guitars ring out; technicians make magic out of flickering lights; projectionists, carpenters, stage-dressers and engineers – all of them are working together, towards this grand ideal: for one night only, to put on a show by royal command.

'She's here,' the dancers gathered around the black-and-white television in the corner of the chorus dressing room all say. 'She's really here.'

'Her Majesty, and all of her guests, up in the royal box…'

To sing, to dance, to conjure illusions for the Queen and her consort – it has been the dream of so many performing lives, and none more so than Ed Forsyth, leader of the feted Forsyth Varieties. Alone among the performers in the Palladium tonight, only handsome, grand Ed Forsyth has played for a king or a queen before. Fifty years ago, he took to the stage for the very first Royal Command Performance, lifting his golden voice to serenade the King. Ever since that day, he has been dreaming of a return. Anticipating the honour of an evening just like this. Picturing how it might feel, to perform for the Queen.

But in none of his imaginings has he been standing here, gazing down upon a body lying on the floor.

The crimson blood pooled around the head.

The lifeless eyes, gazing vacantly upwards, windows to a soul that is no longer there.

His eyes flash around, taking in first the other performers around him – his oldest friend, the master of illusion; the dancer who has brought him here – and then, at last, to the sign on the dressing-room door.

Two simple words, etched in bronze and put there by his own hand.

The name of his beloved son:

CAL FORSYTH

Ed Forsyth looks back down, at the bloodied body on the dressing-room floor.

Her Majesty might be in the royal box tonight, enjoying the rapture of this spectacular show – but, backstage at the London Palladium, a murderer is on the loose.

Two Weeks Earlier...

I

Black-Sheep Boy

The Tanner Hop was not a public house of particular note. Its bar was neither big nor small; its back room, where old men hunched over dominoes and pints of Mackeson's Old Stout, was neither slovenly nor grand; even its landlord – who had worked in the Hop since he was knee-high, rolling the barrels with his father who'd owned the pub before him – was an unremarkable fellow. Whether you were a visitor to the small Seaford town, or one of its long-time inhabitants, there were livelier, more enticing places to frequent on a Saturday night. Right now, a rhythm-and-blues three-piece was playing at the Peggy Sue. The little ballroom by the pier was hosting the final heat in a county competition. Beyond the homely comforts of this back-street boozer, life was a riot of colour and music; lovers were catching each other's eyes for the very first time; hearts were being variously healed, broken, and then healed all over again.

But for the dark-haired man who occupied the table by the window, nursing his pint of Watney's Red, the Tanner Hop was the only place to be.

The regulars hadn't seen him in the Tanner Hop before. He was younger than most who drank here – if he was thirty years old, it was only by a few short days – and he wore his coiled black hair in the way young men sometimes did: as if it hadn't

7

seen a brush in days, longer than it ought to be, wild and unruly, as if there was something aspirational in looking as if you'd just got out of bed. By the way the wives in the bar kept looking over at him, then whispering among each other, it was clear he was good-looking. But youth was always good-looking to those who had left it behind.

Maria, who had the night off from the chippie down by the pier, remarked on his green eyes and took the chair opposite him. He was polite enough when she started chatting, listened attentively to her talk of King Edwards and her mean-spirited boss, who had, by some strange mercy, bought a travelling burger van and took himself off, sometimes, hawking to lorry drivers in lay-bys. He even offered to stand her a drink at one point – though, to the confusion (and not to say the chagrin) of Maria's friends, who were watching intently from the corner by the old jukebox, he sent her to the bar to fetch it, with a handful of coins from his pocket.

'I'm sorry, darling,' he said, the tone of his smooth, bass voice only deepening the pub's sense that he was an outsider. 'I've got to keep at this window. I can't move an inch.'

By now, some of the older men were balancing their wives and daughters' sense of intrigue with an equal sense of resent-ment and distrust. But if the young man noticed, he did nothing to either deter or provoke it. Until Maria returned from the bar, he kept his gaze on the windows and the seafront street beyond.

'Here you are then. A tomato juice, just like you asked for.'

Some of the men crowding the dartboard on the other side of the bar started guffawing at the idea of a man with a tomato juice. Maria flushed scarlet – she knew one of those men – and was making her apologies when the young man said, 'I already drank my fill. There's no shame in knowing that. See, that lot over there – they only know when they've had enough when they're bunching their fists up and getting into a scrap. Me? I know better.'

As he took the tomato juice from her, his hand closed over hers. It was, thought Maria, the thrill not just of her evening but of the last several months. Well, there was hardly any excitement at all in plaice and chips, mushy peas and a jar of pickled eggs.

'You know, you still haven't told me your name.'

The young man stiffened at the question. That only set more tongues wagging. What kind of a man didn't want to give his name?

'I'm Cal,' he told her.

'Well, Cal, I'm pleased to make your acquaintance.' She scattered his coins back on the table. 'And that tomato juice is on me. I'm not like that lot over there,' she said, leaning in conspiratorially. 'That's my uncle and the boys from the Conservative club. They couldn't possibly imagine a girl having a bit of,' she raised her voice dramatically, 'FUN AROUND HERE.'

'Keep it down in that corner,' came a voice from behind the bar. 'There's money riding on this dartboard.'

'Cal, tell me,' said Maria, certain now that they had reached some common ground. 'Why are you staring out of that window? What's going on out there, when there's a perfectly lovely young woman, right here, who's trying to get your attention?'

Cal was about to answer when suddenly a flash of colour split apart the darkness. He leapt out of his seat, draining the tomato juice in one fluid motion.

'It's the best seat in town,' he said, reaching up and fumbling with the window clasp. 'That's the main road out of town. The Newhaven road. The last of the ferries came in two hours ago, over the sea from Dieppe.'

'What – what are you talking about?'

The clasp clicked in Cal's hand. The window opened up. A gust of rain whipped within, soaking the net curtains, upsetting the newspaper in the hands of the man at the neighbouring table, setting up exclamations of shock and frustration from everyone around. 'Close that up!' the barman was shouting, wiping his hands on a rag as he came around the bar, ready to remonstrate with Cal. 'Here, you. Are you listening to me? It's nigh on winter out there. I'll not have—'

Half a dozen voices might have been cursing his name, but Cal didn't seem to hear any of it. He was craning his head out of the open window, watching the Newhaven road.

Maria saw what he had been waiting for.

A bright red double-decker bus was cutting its course through the night. Shining in scarlet, more vivid yet than the ones that plied London's roads, it came past them in great arcs of rain-water, followed by a fleet of black taxicabs, a blue-and-white Volkswagen microbus – and a canary-yellow Ford Anglia, which Maria noticed seemed to catch Cal quite by surprise. Regardless, it was on the double-decker leading the procession – a Union Jack proudly flying from its upper storey – that Cal's eyes were fixed when the barman's meaty hand yanked him back inside.

'What do you think you're doing, you crazy sod?' the barman snapped, and wrestled with the latch to close the window. 'I've a mind to get you a mop – it's rained all over my bar.'

Maria watched Cal as he seemed to cogitate on this for a moment. Then, clearly deciding that the barman was probably due some sort of restitution, he scattered the coins meant for the tomato juice on the tabletop and inclined his head, as if doffing an invisible cap. 'I'm grateful,' he said, then, snatching a brown leather jacket from where it had been slung across the back of a chair, bounded for the door.

He was already there when he remembered her. She sat at the

rainswept table, feeling quite as discombobulated as the rest of the bar. He tugged an imaginary cap towards her too.

'I owe you that drink,' he said, and, when he smiled, all of the bewilderment she'd been feeling somehow melted away.

But Maria did not get to say another word to Cal, for he was already gone.

Rain. She'd quite forgotten the sight, the sound, the smell of English rain. For two months, and, in spite of the time of year, it had been balmy evenings and scorching afternoons, the scents of olive groves and oranges, seventy-five degrees even in the shade. And now... *this.* Evie knew that some of the Company were thrilled to be back in these familiar surrounds – and, of course, there was always a certain nostalgia that came with the return from a Continental tour – but, really, this wasn't the welcome she'd been hoping for.

This *rain*, it was like an omen.

The ferry ride had been one of those interminable ones, the sea hardly fit for a crossing – though of course the authorities at the terminal wouldn't dream of cancelling. Evie understood that; the Company of which she was an integral part – the Company to which she had been born, and in which she had worked for all the twenty-nine years of her life – had never cancelled a show in all the decades of its existence, except in those war-torn days when the provincial theatres were closed behind the blackout curtains, or the playhouses of London buried beneath bombs. But, at least, when a variety show wasn't quite timed to perfection, it didn't end up with a riot of seasickness, a troupe of dancers all looking green around the gills, two performing dogs barking in wild panic in the hold, and Evie's sixty-six-year-old father, Ed – a man almost as seasoned in travel as he was in variety theatre – declaring he'd never go to sea again.

It was to her father that Evie went now.

The double-decker bus in which she was riding was one of the old AEC Regents. Decommissioned in 1945, having served its tour of duty ferrying shoppers, day-trippers, city clerks and engineers – all the wild gamut of London life – around the war-torn city, in its retirement it had taken the Forsyth Varieties around the English counties, across the channel into France and along the sun-kissed coast of the Mediterranean: to Paris and Naples, Rome and Milan; to Monaco and Antibes, Valencia and Seville. Well, there was romance, of a sort, in the wartime buses – and, even in Europe, when people saw that flash of bright scarlet, some frisson of excitement moved in them; it had seemed churlish to change that. But inside, where the folk of London once sat with their shopping, everything was different. The seats of the lower deck remained – though spaced out more widely now, allowing corners where members of the Company might gather, play cards and drink tea together as they travelled – but the upper storey had been stripped bare. Where banks of seats once sat, now there were two private chambers: one, behind black curtains, a nook for sleeping the long journeys away, and the other, to which Evie now picked her way, an office of utilitarian but cramped design. She knocked on its door now.

'Come in,' came the voice from the other side.

Evie opened the door.

There sat her father, Ed. A tall, broad man, he had started to shrink in the last few years – though whether that was his body reacting to the slow encroachment of age, or the after-effects of grief, Evie had never been sure. The only thing she was certain of was that her father had not been the same in the years since her mother had died. It was only his single-minded devotion to the Company that bore his name that had carried him through. A consummate performer – compère, comic, singer – he had given his life to the Forsyth Varieties, just as his father and grandfather, the darlings of the music halls, had before him. And if in these latter years he was not often to be seen in the heart of the stage – for how difficult was it to recapture the joys you once shared with your lover, when you walked out to meet the spotlight alone? – that had only made him more fastidious in plotting the Forsyth fortunes behind the scenes: each commission hunted down assiduously, each tour planned to perfection, each blitz of publicity masterminded from this little desk at which he now sat. He was, Evie was heartened to see, wearing the same brown woollen suit that he always wore when he was taking care of business. 'Evie, my sweet,' he had often declared, 'a man should take his work no less seriously, even if it is behind closed doors. Only half of a theatre's work is done in front of a crowd.' Even so, he looked grateful for the opportunity to set down his papers. He had taken to wearing spectacles – unheard of, in an earlier time – and he lifted them from the bridge of his nose.

Evie did not share many of her father's looks – the crowd used to say that she had the look of her grandfather about her, tall and statuesque, a presence that could fill a stage – but, in their green eyes, they were startlingly alike. Ed's had faded with the years, but they still glittered when Evie looked at him. It could be like looking into a mirror – a mirror, perhaps, that foretold the future.

'We're here, Dad. We came into Seaford just a few moments ago. The theatre can't be far.'

Ed stacked up his papers, straightened his lapels, and got to his feet. 'About time as well. By my reckoning we're two hours behind schedule, thanks to that blasted crossing.' There was a little mirror hanging over the cramped desk at which he'd been sitting. He stretched open each eye in front of it and dabbed at his lips with a corner of a handkerchief. 'Well, Evie,' he said, and took her by the hand. 'Tonight's the night. The beginning.'

She grinned. She always loved it when her father spoke like this: with hope for the future, with the frisson of excitement for victories yet to come. 'It's been fifty years,' he said, still considering himself in the mirror. 'I don't suppose, even at twenty-nine, you can imagine what it's like to have fifty years of memories stored up here.' He tapped the side of his head. 'Fifty years of performances. All of those hundreds of thousands who've watched us. Who've watched me. All of the thousands of opening numbers. The thousands of curtain calls and bows. But there's none that sticks in my mind like that summer's day. July, nineteen twelve. By God, I was sixteen years old. Sixteen years old, Evie, and to sing before the King.'

Of course, it wasn't the first time Evie had heard this story. Indeed, it was one of the founding myths upon which her father's life had been built and the older he got, the more it seemed part of the legend of the Forsyth Varieties itself. Ed Forsyth, headstrong and with the voice of an angel, had been part of the contingent from the Company invited to take to the stage at the Palace Theatre. *By Royal Command*, the papers had said, *the finest, most talented entertainers in the Empire will come together to celebrate the coronation of King George V*. And there had been Ed Forsyth, singing among them.

'They tell you not to look in the monarch's eye, of course,' Ed said, harking back to the occasion once again. 'But I was just a slip of a lad. I hardly knew about temptation. So I did. I looked up, and saw the good Queen Mary gazing back down. Her eyes were glittering for me. I'd never felt such purpose. I'd never felt such pride.'

There was no measure by which the inaugural Royal Command Performance hadn't been a success. The funds it raised for the

Variety Artistes' Benevolent Fund was only the start of it. Its true success had been the start of a movement. The celebration of variety theatre. The benediction granted to dancers, singers, comedians, acrobats and other, wilder entertainers; the blessing of a king. From that moment on – and though he was about to be dragged into a war that would churn up the Continent, and keep him away from the stage for years to come – Ed Forsyth knew where he was meant to be: at the centre of the stage, singing, by royal command.

And now, half a century later, the Company he had inherited from his father – the Company that, one day soon, he would need to pass on for stewardship to the next generation – was to return. In two short weeks, The Royal Variety Performance, as it had become called, was summoning them home.

Beneath Evie and Ed, the double-decker suddenly slowed. 'We're here.' Evie reached across her father's desk to peel back the curtain blind and look out on the rain-streaked night. Through its shapeless blur, she saw the hulk of the small theatre waiting. Few lights lit up its windows, for this particular theatre rarely hosted performances out of season, but she could see the rest of the Company flotilla already arraying itself around the doors. The old taxicabs were disgorging the dancers, the musicians, the acrobatic crew, while the blue-and-white microbus hunted down its own parking spot.

'Dad,' she said with a grin, 'it's time.'

But when she looked around, she saw that her father – always silent on his feet, a talent drilled into him by his mother, whose lightness of touch in the ballrooms had been something of legend – had already gone. *Well*, she thought, *at least he was energised*. There'd been a time when he'd been like that every hour of the day; to see it, even fleetingly, reminded her what a force of nature her parents had been.

Evie locked up the office and picked her way through the now static double-decker, down the stairs to where the rest of the passengers were stirring. She saw Ed talking to the bus driver – Hugo used to be a talented mimic and had on various occasions performed with his ventriloquist act among the Forsyths, though now preferred setting up the rigging, marshalling logistics and generally bossing his younger crew about – before striding out into the pouring rain. Slinging bags over their shoulders, brandishing umbrellas and raincoats – and generally murmuring that rain over the seaside was, at least, better than rain over the Channel – the rest of the Company began to follow.

Evie was about to follow when she felt a presence on her shoulder. There, waiting quietly in her wake, stood Max. Of all the dancers who Evie marshalled for the Company, Max had absorbed the sunshine of the Mediterranean coast the most. His mop of blonde hair was almost white and, against the bronze of his skin, it made him look as if he was already wearing stage makeup. A dancer of rare talent, Max was one of the newest additions to the Forsyth Varieties, and indeed was just returning from his very first Continental tour.

Having first made certain they were alone on the bus, Evie took his hand.

It had been a few nights since she'd lain in his arms. It wasn't that romance was outlawed among the members of the Company – if that were the tradition, Evie herself would never have existed, for it was backstage after one of their defining pre-war performances that her parents had first fallen in love – but something in Evie disliked the idea of being watched, being *seen*, being *known*, before she truly understood this herself. Max was six years her junior, and – especially in these latter years, as her father took more of a backseat with the Company – directly in her employ. Companies like this might have been breeding grounds for romance, but they were also breeding grounds for professional jealousies, mistrusts and more. Secrecy, for now, was the better option.

Of course, when she looked into his golden eyes, part of her wanted to shout it from the rooftops. Part of her wanted to kiss him right now. She stepped a little nearer, closing the gap between them. He reached up, stroked her hair – as dark as his was light, she had often thought, like each was the photographic negative of the other. There was beauty in that image. A song-writer might have taken it and crafted some ballad that echoed through time.

'We'd better go,' Evie said, though it was taking all her strength to tear herself away. She'd had to rely on that inner strength so much in recent years; she'd found a steel, an endurance, she hadn't known she was capable of. But the best dancers were made of stern stuff, her mother had always told her. *I've seen you hang one-handed from the trapeze, Evie, dear. Don't tell me there's anything you can't do.* 'There's so much work to do. All of the kit to be unloaded. The lodgings to attend. It's already past nine o'clock. If we're in bed before midnight, it will be a miracle.'

'I'd like to be in bed before midnight,' said Max, with the barest hint of a smile.

They lingered over that thought for a heartbeat. Then Evie, still stroking his hand, said, 'Come on, my father will be gathering everyone. He's been up there ever since the ferry, and don't tell me he's been going through the profits and payslips. No, he's been preparing some great homecoming speech. I just know it.'

She was about to walk away when Max tightened his hold on her hand. 'But perhaps that means he's got an announcement. Perhaps that means he's making *the* announcement.' He paused, but when Evie did not immediately reply, he pushed on. 'His retirement, Evie. What if he's about to announce his retirement? And his successor? The next lead of the Forsyth Varieties.'

Evie was still. To say it was to jinx it. To speak about it was, in some way, to will it into being – which had only, in the past, left her with a feeling of treachery, Evie herself the betrayer to the father who'd raised her. And yet – hadn't her father raised the subject, on more than one occasion? Of how hard it was to keep going, with his wife no longer at his side? He'd assumed the mantle of the Forsyth Varieties from his own father when he'd been only a little bit older than Evie. The year she'd been born, her grandfather going off to the coast to live out his days – and Ed Forsyth, becoming the spearhead of the Company that bore his name.

'It's been written in the stars since you were born,' said Max, his eyes eager and expectant.

'It's more complicated than that,' Evie ventured.

But was it? For a fleeting moment, she allowed herself to dream. Her father was growing older. He was slowing down. If he wasn't quite the ghost he'd become in the months after her mother had passed away, he had not yet reclaimed his stature as the head of the Company. The dancers, musicians, acrobats, singers and comics – they loved him, but did they look to him for leadership any longer?

It had to happen sooner or later. And all of the old fears she'd grown up with – not one of the variety theatres she'd encountered over the years had been run by a woman – seemed suddenly obsolete. This was the sixties, by God. Anything a man could do, so could a woman. The world was seeing that, at last. She'd grown up in the Company. She'd lived and breathed it every year of her life. Even in those girlhood days, when the country had been at war and the Forsyths temporarily disbanded, she'd spent her summers performing. Her evenings, her holidays, her weekends. And in the last years, since her mother... Well, Evie was practically running the Company anyway, wasn't she? She'd won her father's respect in that. If there was anyone who could lead the Forsyth Varieties into a new era, surely it was her?

'It's yours, Evie. He's making that announcement tonight. I'm sure of it. Fifty years since he stepped on stage for the King. At the end of the month, he'll do it again. Mark my words: he's bookending his career. He's going out in the way it began. *By royal command.*'

Their fingers untwined and, together, they picked their way to the doors of the bus. Outside, in the rain-lashed car park in front of the Seagate Theatre – that tumbledown old place where all their preparations would be made – the rest of the Company were bringing packs and travelling trunks out of their vehicles.

'Do you know,' she ventured. 'I've been so swept up in getting back to Blighty that, until this moment, I haven't thought about how it might *feel*. To soar through the air on the trapeze, and be looked upon by the Queen. Dad used to talk about the wonder of it. To be just a slip of a lad, singing for his supper – and then, suddenly, to be singing for royalty.' She found she wanted to take Max's hand again – and perhaps she might have risked it, for the doors to the Seagate Theatre were opening up and the Company was flocking inside, leaving so few of them to see her. But caution was the better part of valour; there would be time enough for that later tonight, whether her father made a dramatic announcement or not.

'At least I've got one thing going in my favour,' Evie laughed as they hurried together across the broken asphalt.

'What's that?'

'Well,' she said with a grin, 'I'm the only true Forsyth left. There's only me here!'

But, as they rushed to follow the rest of the Company into

the theatre's inviting doors, neither saw the shadowy figure who watched them from the halo of one of the streetlights further down the road.

They just rushed, oblivious, into the shelter of the theatre.

But they would find out soon enough.

Some moments before Evie and Max had emerged from the double-decker, Ed Forsyth hammered at its side stage door and cried out to be admitted within. If he could not project his voice like he'd been able to do in the prime of his years, there was still something dramatic about its quality. Yes, there was something suitably dramatic about a thundery night and the neglected little theatre at which his Company had arrived.

'Ed,' came the gruff voice as it drew back. 'You always did know how to make an entrance. Where in hell have you been, old chap?'

The rotund, curmudgeonly figure standing in the doorway was none other than John Lauder, the Forsyth Varieties' resident mystic, mesmerist and shadowgrapher. At least John was dressed for a night like this, covering his not-inconsiderable girth with a chunky knit cardigan. The cap on his head, which hid greying curls, was not the sort he wore on stage – when he cut a much more debonair figure

'John, I have need of you, old friend. The hour is almost nigh.'

The theatre's dusty interior might have looked neglected and disused to some, but there was little Ed liked more than an off-season theatre. Somehow, the emptiness of it just pulsed with promise. To Ed, it smelt like home. He'd performed here once or twice across the years – if he remembered correctly, this had been the first stage he'd invited Evie out onto, back when she had just learned the unicycle and was keen to perform alongside her mother in the old acrobatic routines. To spend the next weeks here, lost in rehearsals and new routines, pulling together the show that would crown this year's Royal Variety Performance, was the sort of thing of which every entertainer dreamed. A whole theatre, a playground in which the Company could create. He'd been anticipating it every bit as much as he was anticipating stepping out into the Palladium.

'How was Monaco?' John asked, as he led Ed into the theatre's galleried auditorium, with its vacant stage like a blank canvas waiting for the Forsyths to do their thing.

'Much as you'd remember, John. They turned out for us, of course. How long has it been? Ten years? Twelve? The air's different out there, John. It fills you up. And Evie was just spectacular. The stage at the Fort Antoine – the rigging, and the lights! You can't perform in the open air here in Blighty. England has its joys, but it isn't like singing and dancing in the balmy Mediterranean air, midnight on the approach, and the *life* still buzzing around you.' He stopped; perhaps he was getting carried away. 'It's a younger man's city, John – but it was a shame you weren't there with me. I should have enjoyed your company, if it's to be the last time.'

John mumbled something incoherent. Then he said, 'You know my thoughts on that, Ed. I'm just glad you made it home in one piece. My dreams foretold otherwise.'

Ed smiled. 'Let's leave prophecy for the stage, John. Here I am. What do you see before you? Your old friend, or his ghost, come back to haunt you?' Ed made the most strangled howl, imitating some wraith from beyond the grave. 'You worried unnecessarily, old man. The trip was a joy. Whatever dreams you were having, John, they were just dreams. Here I am, in the flesh and blood, and about to lead us all out for the Queen's reception.'

John sighed. 'I'm glad you're back, Ed. I've been sick out of my skin.'

'Well, you don't need to worry any more, John. We made it back, every last one of us. All that *feeling* of yours has really done is cheat you out of three months in the sun.'

'Yes,' John grumbled. 'Well, perhaps someone had to keep the home fires burning. Come on through – there was a stack of post waiting for us when I arrived. I trust you don't mind but, given you were late getting in from Dieppe, I had a sift through it.' He paused at Ed's curious look. 'I didn't open any of it, Ed. You know me. I'm just a common work-a-day illusionist. A bit of shadow theatre on the side. You're head of this Company, and will be until…'

His eyes drifted up and Ed followed his gaze. Yes, there was Evie, coming into the theatre – and that tousle-haired Adonis of a dancer traipsing behind her. What was his name? Yes, *Max*. Sometimes, it seemed he followed her like a dog.

'They're yours to open, Ed. You're the leader here. Most of it looks like the same old insurance fluff, and there's a few en-quiries of interest forwarded on from the digs in London. But there's one letter in particular…'

John let that thought linger as Ed followed him into the warren of dressing rooms backstage, and to the little director's study at the theatre's furthest end. Here, by the three buzzing bars of an electric fire, John seemed to have made himself at home. Preposterously, a fat black cat was curled up on a rug; Ed supposed it had been mewling to get in, out of the rain, or perhaps it was resident here in the theatre, keeping itself fed on the mice that always riddled places like these.

The letters were splayed out on a desk sitting under the small study window. Yes, thought Ed as his eyes ran over them, just the usual insurance and taxation demands. There was so much more to running a variety company than just getting up on stage and belting out the standards. You had to be consummate performer, yes, but you had to fulfil so many other roles: a man of business, an army general, navigator, salesman – and, far too often for Ed's liking, now that he was getting on in years, a wise counsellor to the troupe around you. His poor wife, Bella, had been better at that; there wasn't a person in the Company, man, woman or child, who didn't think of her as a second mother. Evie had struggled with that, once upon a time. So had…

Ed's eyes lit upon the final letter.

He darted a look at John.

'You old rascal,' he said. 'You know what this is.'

John sank down into a chair by the fire. The black cat lifted its head to consider him disdainfully, then decided it didn't want to be disturbed from its rest, and lay back down again.

'I haven't opened it, Ed.'

John's grin was wide and toad-like. Ed shook his head ruefully. He'd known John since they were boys, and John had auditioned to apprentice the last illusionist who'd worked for the Forsyth Varieties. Ed had seen him read minds, divine histories, even summon the dead – but all of that was an act, just something that happened on stage, skills learnt from his old master. All the rest – the prophetic dreams of which he sometimes spoke, his 'second sight', which he claimed allowed him access to a person's most private, innermost thoughts – was just bluster. Ed didn't mind indulging it, because of course a bit of mystery, a bit of a *reputation*, always helped in the promotion of the Varieties – but, of course, it was hokum. There was no *real* way that John knew what was in that letter. He was just playing on Ed's expectations. Just taunting his sensibilities. Just prodding at his *hope*.

And, of course, it was an airmail envelope.

The postmark itself said that it came from California.

You could infer so much from that.

'It's good news, Ed. Open it up. Then you'll see.'

Ed brandished the envelope wildly. 'It had better be, John. Don't go playing tricks with an old man's heart.' He slid a finger into the envelope and prepared to open it. The paper tore. 'You better have the right of this, John. I'll expose you as a bloody fraud if you don't.'

John reclined in the seat, to the cat's further disdain, and spread his arms magnanimously. Just two old friends, taunting each other – was there any richer joy in the world?

Ed tore the envelope open, unfolded the pale, eggshell-blue paper and started scouring its words.

He looked from the paper to John and back again. Ed might have been sixty-six years old – but in that moment he had the joy of the sixteen-year-old lad who'd strode out onto the Palace stage and sung, as sweet as a bird.

'He's coming, isn't he?' John beamed.

'You old dog!' Ed roared, laughter turning his voice towards shrillness. He didn't mind; on reading the words of this letter, he suddenly felt like a boy at Christmastime. The world was full of wonder. Possibilities extended in every direction. 'He said yes.' He guffawed. 'By God, he said yes.'

'I can only remember you being as excited one other time, Ed. And that was when Bella said she'd marry you. *She said yes.*' Laughing, John imitated the Ed of old. *'Yes, yes, yes!'*

Sometimes, it was bittersweet to think of Bella, but not tonight, not in this moment. In this moment, had she been here, Bella would have been as animated with joy as Ed himself.

'John,' he declared. 'Rally the Company. Have them gather by the stage. I'm going to tell them this myself. Tell them … tell them I have an announcement to make.'

*

The rain was still coursing across Seaford as Cal made his approach. By now, every other soul had disappeared through the theatre doors, so there was no longer any need to slink in the shadows. Heedless of the rain – which had already matted his wild curls, running down the inside collar of his leather jacket – he strode across the car park. In the same moment that he reached the double-decker, lightning rent the sky. *Well*, he thought wryly, *that was suitably dramatic*. He lingered for a little while over the double-decker's shimmering scarlet sides. He lifted himself onto the points of his toes to peer within. Then he drifted on, past the microbus, past the old taxicabs, past the canary-yellow Ford Anglia – and into the shadow of the theatre itself.

At least, here, the rain did not drive into him.

Momentarily, he felt calm.

He reached for the door handle.

And, of course – trusting fools that they were – they had left it unlocked.

Evie was rallying the dancing girls to lead them to the lodging house. Billeting a company the size of the Forsyth Varieties – with its twelvefold troupe of dancers, its musicians, its dog trainer and comics, backstage staff and more – always proved a logistical challenge, but at least in Seaford the solution had been clear. Seaside towns always had enough accommodation, especially out of season, when the hostelries and hotels slashed their prices to encourage whatever guests they could. The row of lodgings on the other side of the pier, round the back of the theatre and overlooking the storm-thrashed sea, was more than adequate for the Company – without even needing to trouble the accommodation in the theatre basements, where generations of stage managers and travelling artistes had variously made up their beds. She was preparing to march the girls through the storm when Max burst in and said, 'It's Mr Forsyth,' with an air of formality he only ever used when they were in the company of others. 'He wants all hands.'

If there was a collective groan from the dancers – all except flame-haired Lily who, at twenty-two years old, still had the curiosity and *joie de vivre* she'd had when she'd auditioned for the Company six short years ago – it did not negate the secret look that flickered between Evie and Max.

Hovering in the corridor without, Max reached again for Evie's hand. 'This is it, isn't it? He's going to talk about his retirement.'

Even now, she didn't want to jinx it. It was not out of the ordinary for her father to make some rallying address to the Company. That was what all good leaders did. The thing that preyed on her mind was that she hadn't expected it to be tonight. Her father was weary; the Company had been travelling, by road and sea, for a week of long days and nights. Tonight was for setting up camp, for resting, for making that mental transition – so crucial for a performer – from one season to the next. One run of shows was over; on the horizon, something spectacular loomed.

'I just don't know,' she said, and was about to follow her dancers through the doors when Max drew her back.

'You *do*, Evie. You just don't dare to believe. But you should. You *should*. You're leading the Forsyths already. All he's going to do tonight is tell it to the world.'

By the time they stepped through the doors, the rest of the Company were gathered in front of the stage. It wasn't often that the Forsyth Varieties looked like the audience in a theatre like this, but so it was tonight. Lily and the other dancers were crowded into the front row, as raucous now as they were ever elegant and disciplined on stage. Davith Harvard and his dogs, Tinky and Tiny – who had been plying a lonely trade, from summer fayre to village fete in the valleys of Wales, when Ed had made Davith an offer he couldn't refuse – were occupying the aisle. The three acrobatic performers, who worked with Evie and often supplemented the show's dance routines, were sitting in the shadows some way back, while the musicians (always a particular lot) formed their own huddle on the left-hand wing. Evie could not help but feel warm at seeing John Lauder lounging in one of the seats behind her dancers. It had been some time since she'd last seen the old mesmerist, and the longing to sit in his quiet company had been resurgent in her as they'd travelled north across the Continent; Lauder had been like an uncle to her growing up and a rock in the years after her mother had passed away. Without him to support her, she had often thought, the Forsyths might not have survived the years of her father's depression.

Lauder caught her eye as the theatre filled up. Here came the stagehands now. There were only three dedicated hands, for in a company like this, everyone mucked in; the bigger man was honing a clowning act that he had, for years, been hopeful Ed might put on the bill.

'John's smiling at you,' Max whispered. 'He *knows*, Evie. I'm telling you – he *knows*.'

'Oh, John knows *everything*,' Evie said, remembering all those times she'd sat on John's knee as a girl, and let him plumb all the secrets of her mind. 'If anyone knows what my father's thinking, it's John. But, Max…' She was about to admonish him – there seemed something too treacherous in speaking of it so openly. But she saw the smouldering look in his eyes, and immediately she melted. It was only Max. He only wanted what was best for her. And he wasn't shackled by the familial guilt of it. He was only acting out of love.

Yes, she thought. *Love*. That was what it was. It had started out as – what, some fun? Lust, of course – but then … She returned his smile. Of course, she loved him too. The real, lasting kind of love. She knew it as fact, because she'd never felt this ridiculous before. Love, then. In a tight-knit Company like this, it was probably going to be a problem.

'You better go to the other dancers,' she whispered. 'Before somebody starts suspecting—'

Footsteps tolled on the stage.

The familiar click of the walking cane her father had started to use.

Evie heaved a sigh. Her heart was hammering – not just because of Max, but because of what was about to come.

It was too late. Her father had already begun. Now, all she could do was take a sidestep from Max, if only to mitigate whatever whispers were already ricocheting around the Company, and listen.

Up on stage, her father took in the Company like he was about to introduce a show. By God, he was a professional. Even as his old age approached, it seemed he could hold a room spellbound. That smile of his. And the way his eyes, coursing across the audience, seemed to pick out every individual in turn – making each of them feel special, like they were the only ones in the room. It was bewitching to see him use these tricks on the Company itself. When Evie had been a girl, she had sometimes been jealous that her father seemed to love a stranger as much as his own child. Now that she was grown, she could see it for what it was: just another piece of illusory magic to make a theatre come alive. But how powerful it was!

'We've come a long way, my friends,' Ed began. 'Through

the stormiest seas together. Through hail and driving wind.' He didn't just mean the Channel crossing, thought Evie. 'But here we are, almost at journey's end – and all of us together, as it was meant to be. Odysseus made it back to Ithaca, but he did not bring all his companions with him. So many were lost along the way. But you and I, my friends? We have come *together*.' He paused, but only for effect. Then he went on, 'As you all know, in only a short time, we will leave this place for the sights and sounds of London. Fifty years ago, I set foot on the stage of the Palace Theatre for the very first time. Sixteen years old, and I sang for the King. And now I return, and you will all accompany me there – this time, to the London Palladium, and this time for that good King's granddaughter, our Queen for many years to come. Together, we will celebrate her tenth year on the throne. We will exemplify all that is proud and great about the variety theatre to which we each devote our lives.' He glanced, again, across every face in the room. 'But, my friends, we will not do it alone…'

At this point, her father produced a leaf of eggshell-blue paper – it could only be a letter, thought Evie, that had come from overseas.

Some new curiosity was being piqued in the theatre.

'Some time ago, upon first learning that the Forsyth Varieties had been invited to return to the Royal Variety Performance, I took a chance. What, I wondered, might make our show resonate through the ages? So that they carried it, in their hearts, long after the curtains had closed? A star, my friends. Somebody to ride out with us, and fill the Palladium with such bright, vivid light that, for years to come, the Royal Variety might pale in comparison. Of course, by then, I already knew the kind of luminaries with whom we would be sharing a stage. Cleo Laine. Eartha Kitt. Bob Hope…

'But, my friends, I have one such star of my own. An old friend, whose path diverted from mine many years ago. A friend who started out a variety performer just like us, but leapt upon an opportunity and chanced his arm in California. A friend who became one of the greats. A friend who, upon receiving a summons from his old compatriot, is to do us the honour of joining the Forsyth Varieties for this very special night. His name?' And here Ed lingered in silence for some time, building the anticipation and thrill in the room. 'Do any of you know the name *Bill Martin?*'

There was a pregnant pause before the clamour and cheering began. Among the dancers, Lily in particular, seemed to be effervescent with enthusiasm – though there was every chance she was less than a third of Bill Martin's age. Alongside Evie, Max froze, his face a rictus – of shock, awe, perhaps even horror? Disbelief was echoing in a dozen different ways all through the theatre.

Bill Martin: the name was known the world over. Star of the silver screen. Singer of some of the mid-twentieth century's greatest ballads. His soaring voice could fill both television studios and stadiums alike. He'd been a star for MGM. He'd spent years on every American talk show, and even ended up compèring his own Saturday night spectacular, *The Bill Martin Show*, for six long years immediately after the war. His debut movie, *The Man With the Silver Eyes*, had broken box-office records. He'd have been the star of *Guys and Dolls* if only Sinatra hadn't pulled some strings at the studio. No, not even Sinatra could hold a torch to Bill Martin at his best.

And he had started out, just like everyone in this room, in the varieties.

The cheering was dying down. With a roving look, Evie's father recaptured the attention of the room.

'I received word, not one hour ago, that Mr Martin will be joining us for our appearance before Her Majesty the Queen. But, more than that, my friends. As you are all aware, we come to the Seagate Theatre, this proud provincial auditorium, to prepare for the greatest night of our lives. And I am proud – effervescent with pride, no less! – to announce that Bill Martin will be joining us here as well, to aid in our preparations, and so that we might find the right place in our show for him to shine. Yes, my friends, Bill is to devote several days of his time to devising this show with us. He is to coach us and prepare us. To shower us with a little of his starriness, so that we all might triumph. I daresay we will, each of us, be a little more vibrant, simply for his presence.' Ed folded the letter again and slipped it into his back pocket. Then, when next he spoke, it was with a quieter, more thoughtful, more reflective air. 'My friends, you know what this performance means to me. I am, some of you will have noticed – though none, of course, have dared to say – not quite the performer I once was. I know what my Bella was to each and every one of you who knew her. You know what she was to me. I have been proud to keep the flame of the Forsyth Varieties burning in her absence from this world. But it seems to me that ours is a world of portents and omens. The world of the theatre is filled with such magic that it is not beyond the realm of possibility that, every now and again, we are sent signs from on high.'

Evie could feel that Max had drawn near again. The rest of the theatre were rapt, still basking in the afterglow of the Bill Martin announcement and suddenly anticipating some even more significant announcement to come, so she did not send him away. He only wanted to be close. Close for when the moment came.

Her heart was beating some wild thunder, resonating with

the storm drumming on the theatre roof. She'd been denying it so long, but suddenly she could deny it no longer. The Forsyth Varieties really was going to be hers. She saw her father's eyes lift from the crowd to pick her out – and, yes, this time she was certain: it was not one of his bewitching tricks of the stage. This time his eyes really were for her alone.

'My friends, the feeling has been creeping upon me, of late, that I have been offered a climax to my fifty years on the stage like no other. A chance to live my first day on the stage once more. To do it among all of you, my old friend Bill Martin to serenade me, and my daughter, Evie, to dance in time. My friends, we all come to a point in our careers where we realise—'

A door slammed shut.

Up on stage, her father paused. His eyes, which had been fixed so intently on Evie, lifted to pick out a fresh shadow at the back of the stalls. Soon, every eye was following his.

Footsteps, and then footsteps again.

Then the whispers began.

Out of the darkness at the back of the stalls, a drenched figure slouched. There he stood, coils of black hair matted to the line of his jaw, the brown leather of his jacket shimmering in the stall lights.

Evie froze.

Up on stage, Ed's eyes grew wide.

And John Lauder, who'd presaged such disaster before the Company had embarked for the Continent, hung his head in devastation – for he'd realised, a moment too late, that the impending tragedy he'd foreseen hadn't been about the Continent before: it was about what would happen on the Company's return; about what would happen in this very moment.

'Bill Martin, huh?' said the drenched figure coolly, bobbing his head. 'That's quite something. Quite a show-stealer, I'm sure.'

The figure paused, slinking further through the stalls, coming at last into the full light. 'If you have Bill Martin, you mightn't be in need of another star singer after all.' He inclined his head, seemingly aware – and perhaps even inviting – the startled looks of the Company. 'But I'm here all the same.'

In the stalls, Max reached for Evie's hand, but Evie, more startled than any in the Seagate, ripped it away. She wrapped her arms around herself, disbelieving as the new arrival reached the stage.

'Hello, Father,' said Cal. 'Believe it or not, I've missed you all.'

2

Brothers and Lovers

'My *brother*,' Evie said, lacing the word with as much poison as she could. 'He always did know how to steal a moment. He's been doing it ever since we were children. A little show for our mother, dancing and singing for our neighbours – over in Suffolk, back when the war was on. We'd have it planned to perfection. We'd have rehearsed it, over and over, just like our mother and father used to say. But then some idea would pop into his head. He'd change it up, without any warning. Improvise over the top of everything we'd planned. And here's the thing, Max. Here's the thing that frustrated me, most of all. It was always better. It was always *good*. My brother had an instinct for a moment.'

The lodging house was just a short walk away from the Seagate's back entrance. At least the rain had let up long enough for Evie to get here, hurrying all the girls along with her. By rights, Max oughtn't to be here at all – there were two other male dancers with the Forsyth Varieties, and they were lodged in a different house, all for propriety's sake. Not that propriety seemed to be on Evie's mind right now. After Cal's sudden appearance, the all-hands meeting had quickly ended, with Ed shepherding Cal off, while the stalls filled up with gossip and innuendo. To Evie's horror, it had fallen to her to wind it all down – when all she wanted, in that moment, was to flounce away and bury her head in a pillow, the better to absorb her screams. Cal. The black-sheep Forsyth. The brother she'd loved, and of whom she'd seen neither hide nor hair since the year after their mother passed on. He'd picked his moment well. Whatever preternatural talent he had for making a statement, it had been on full show tonight.

Evie had thrown her bags down, but hadn't yet cast herself onto the bed. She was distinctly aware of the girls through the walls. Surely they knew that Max had followed her in here. He'd been carrying her suitcase – acting the gentleman, as he always did – but, of course, there would be whispers. There always were.

She paced up and down, looking out of the window on the darkling night. From here, she could just about make out the dome at the top of the Seagate Theatre. She tried not to picture her father, communing with her brother somewhere in the theatre walls, but the image just kept reappearing in her head. Cal. He'd looked different, of course; nearly five years would change anyone. Of course, she'd seen his image since then. There'd been that feature in the *Melody Maker*. She'd seen the hoardings outside the Cavern Club in Liverpool, that time the Forsyths had been performing at the little theatre on the Wirral. Or there'd been the time when they'd been at the City Varieties, up in Leeds…

No. She shook the image out of her mind. 'He's heard about the Royal Variety. That's what it is. So he wants to sashay back into the Company, sit at our father's right hand again. Act as if the last five years of our lives didn't happen. But where was he when we needed him? Where was Cal, when my father was in the pits of his despair? Where was he, when the Homburgs started poaching our talent? You weren't here, Max. You didn't see it. The Forsyths might have… *ended.*' Evie's voice cracked, and in seconds Max was rushing to her. That she fended him off was not because she didn't need him: it was only because of the ears she was certain were pressed against the walls, Lily and the rest of the dancers intrigued at what their principal was doing in the privacy of her own room.

'Do you think he knew?' Max whispered, at first upset – and only after she sent him a mellowing look, understanding – that she had brushed him aside.

'About the Royal Variety? Max, it's common knowledge.'

'I mean about ... your father's retirement. You, in line to take over the Company.'

Evie bristled. 'You mean: did he come back, because he thinks it's his right?'

'I never knew your brother, Evie. But is it really so far-fetched? If he knew about the Royal Variety, it's a decent bet he'd think your father had his eye on the end of his career. Like I said – to bookend things, singing for King and Queen. If he thought the Forsyths might need a leader ...'

Evie frowned. 'My brother was always more interested in himself than he was in the Company. We're in it for each other. He was in it for himself. Just look at what he's been doing all these years. God, he fancied himself ... he fancied himself a new Bill Martin!'

'Well, maybe that's it,' said Max baldly. 'He found out about ... *Bill Martin.*'

The way Max said the word seemed to suggest that he was not over-awed at the idea of Bill Martin joining the Company as an honorary Forsyth. The rest of the troupe seemed thrilled at the prospect. But Max seemed harder to win over. Perhaps he was only trying to console Evie, in some oblique way – finding reasons that Cal had just turned up, out of the blue. And perhaps there was truth in it: Cal's voice had once been the heart of their shows. He had their father's talent for capturing a room, and their mother's range. It was a formidable coupling. He'd have been jealous if he'd caught some sniff of Bill Martin. Perhaps that might have driven him back, to try and reclaim his throne. And yet... how could he have known, when their father had found out only an hour previously? No, why ever he was here, it was for some other, ulterior purpose.

'You never met him,' Evie said, more sadly now, and at last crashed onto the bed. 'It's so difficult to explain. He was my brother. He *is* my brother. But he's...' Her voice cracked again. 'He's not a Forsyth. Not any more. How could he be, when he abandoned us all?'

'Bill Martin, then, Dad? You've pulled another rabbit out of the hat. What are you, now? Sixty-six years old, but not out of tricks yet. Now, *that* should be a show.'

The little stage-manager's office at the back of the Seagate was hardly the setting for a reunion like this. Only a couple of short hours ago, he'd stood here and opened a letter that had filled him with untold joy. Bill Martin. *For one night only.* Now, he looked at the young man in front of him and tried to remember: *he's my son.*

Cal always knew how to make an entrance, but he'd outdone himself tonight. 'Like that time you were late to the stage in Lyon. Off with that girl from the hotel, and running out of time. We all thought you were a lost cause – but then you barrelled in, guitar in hand, and stole the damn show.'

There were some among the Company, Bella included, who had looked back on that moment fondly – Cal was a wild one, they said; he ploughed his own furrow, sang his own song – but Ed had always been of a mind that it was a damn fool move, and pure indulgence to entertain it. 'The audience *knew*,' Bella had said. 'They were in on the act. Part of the thrill.' Well, there'd been no audience to manipulate or hoodwink tonight. Just the Forsyth Varieties, filled with all the folks he'd walked out on.

There was nothing else for it. No preamble, no skirting around the horror, no way of avoiding conflict instead of confronting it face on. 'Cal, what in hell are you doing here?'

Cal had heard the venom in his voice. Ed hadn't meant to manifest it, but how could he not? How could he sit here and offer to pour tea, after all the bile that had been spilled, after the rows of Bella's funeral, after those months of agony and indecision that came after? To his credit, the younger man absorbed the blow with scarcely a flinch; Ed supposed he knew he deserved it.

'I wanted to see you,' was all Cal said. 'I know you'll find it difficult to comprehend. But it isn't that I've forgotten you, *any* of you, over the years. It isn't like I've forgotten *her*. Belle of the Ball. My mother. I loved her too, Dad. But ...' He started faltering as he tried to explain. 'It's been hard for me, too. I'm not saying it to detract from everything that happened. I'm not saying it thinking you might just forget. I'm saying it because it's true. It hasn't all been girls and glamour. I've been out there on my own. I've worked hard, and I've done it without a soul at my side.' He stopped. 'I'm tired, Dad. I wanted to come home.'

'Home,' said Ed. He had to ruminate on the word. Of course, for the players in a variety troupe like the Forsyths, 'home' had a different connotation than it had to so many. Lots of the players, dancers and musicians had a place they might retreat to – the home of a loved one, a family member, their mother and father, if they were lucky enough that they were still alive. But others had no home except for the double-decker bus in front of the Seagate, the fleet of vehicles that took the Company from place to place, the hostels and digs they wound up in, the common rooms and clubs where they congregated each night. Ed had lived his life like that. By the time he was born, the Forsyth Varieties had moved on from their music-hall beginnings, and the little theatre in Manchester where they had been resident performers, and taken to the road. Ed's father had been of the first generation to live transiently like that, squirreling away little nest eggs across the years so that, one day, they might retire in comfort, or else find a place at one of the homes for retired artistes that proliferated in cities like London, or even Paris. Ed, then, had known no other home but the road.

He supposed that this was what Cal was saying as well: that it was this spirit of home that had brought him to the Seagate tonight. But Ed remembered the arguments about the direction the Company should take; he remembered a younger Cal scoffing at the old sets and standards, bringing out his guitar to play one of the new rock-and-roll anthems, caterwauling as if 'rockabilly' could ever rival the music of old. Benny Goodman and Glenn Miller. Frank Sinatra, Sarah Vaughan. *Bill Martin* himself.

Ed had even understood – at first. Cal was a burning talent. His thirst for something new might be just the thing the Company needed.

But then ... Bella was gone, eaten from the inside out by the illness that took her, and suddenly all that was 'new' seemed treacherous to Ed.

'Cal,' Ed intoned. 'We've travelled a long way to get here. The Company's been on the road for a week. We've got a task ahead of us. A Royal Command. I mean for this to be the best show the Forsyths have put on. But you walked out on us, almost five years to the day. Left us, as I remember, when the run in Nice had barely begun. I had a hole in the middle of our act as wide as a bloody ocean, Cal!' For the first time, Ed's voice rose in controlled fury. No longer was he standing in the cosy, poky little office at the back of the Seagate Theatre; now he was back on a stage in Nice, about to compère a show missing its defining star. 'Your mother was barely a year in the ground. We needed you. I needed you. And I don't give a blast what Evie's done since – sought you out in those bloody clubs, read the *Melody Maker* and the *New Musical Express* and whatever other rags you went courting. You left us when it *mattered*, off to do your own bloody thing – and now you waltz back in here like the last five years didn't happen, like we can just pick up where we left off! It's madness, Cal. It's – it's …'

The fury had been too much for Ed. 'You have to help me out here, Cal. I don't know why you're here. If it's the Royal Variety you're after, well—'

'I don't care about the Royal Variety, Dad. I just wanted to come home.'

Ed had prided himself, across a long life, on being an inestimably good judge of character. A company like the Forsyth Varieties demanded such of its leader. Dancers ordinarily lasted only a few seasons. Singers thought of the varieties not as a lifestyle but as a leaping board from which they might reach some higher stratosphere in the showbusiness world. Jugglers and acrobats, magicians and mesmerists – these were often the mainstay of a variety theatre, but in the modern world even they had opportunities beyond the provinces. Television beckoned. The proliferation of summer festivals was almost enough for a man to go it alone. To keep a variety company alive, you needed to pick not just the best performers, but the acts you were sure had staying power.

The problem was, he'd lost that with Cal. He thought he'd understood him, once upon a time. Cal had the burning ambition of youth, like all young men did; like Ed himself. Yet, somewhere along the way, all that had changed. The ambitions of Ed's generation had been doused, of course, in the fields of Flanders and France. Scarcely two years after he'd sung for the King, Ed had been carrying a bayonet in his name, digging in somewhere around Verdun. He'd seen the same for a new generation when war returned to the Continent for a second time. Ed had been too old to wage war by then, but, with the Forsyths abandoned for the duration of hostilities, he and a few other acts, John Lauder among them, had gone to entertain the troops whenever the opportunity arose. Now that he thought of it, that had been the first time he'd seen Bill Martin in twenty years as well – the great shining light of California, formerly the club singer of Uxbridge, had come to do his part for morale as well. And perhaps that was the problem with young men like Cal: for them, the realities of the world had never brought a hammer down to fell their ambitions.

That had been Cal. Too bright for the Forsyth Varieties, without the steadying influence of his mother, he'd burned with more and more potency – until, at last, an inferno raged. After that had come the drinking; after that, the affairs with the local girls, the fight in the bar in Dieppe, the missed ferry in Calais. Now, when Ed looked at him, he wasn't sure if this was the same man whose hand he'd held as a boy, who'd sat at the piano with him and learned his first faltering arpeggios and chords.

'You put me in an invidious position, Cal. Perhaps even more so than the night you walked out.'

'This isn't my decision,' Ed whispered, at last.

Cal looked forlorn.

'No.' Finding new strength, Ed got to his feet again. 'Things are different here, Cal. I couldn't do it alone, not after your mother passed on. Everyone had to step up. Everyone had to take responsibility. Not just me, and not just your sister – not just

John and the other old hands. Every last one of us, from top to bottom, did what we could to make sure this Company survived.' He looked his son directly in the eyes, for what felt like the first time in years. 'So the decision has to be theirs as well.'

He marched past Cal, opened the door and bellowed out, 'Hugo, call all hands. Back to the stage in fifteen.' Ed slammed the door again. 'You can make your case, Cal, and we'll put it to a vote. It's them you let down, and it's them who'll give you your second chance.' His eyes roamed up and down Cal for the final time. 'Tidy yourself up, son. You'll want to put on a good show.'

Lying with Max always stilled her heart. She thought that was why she was so drawn to him: some sense of inner peace, which radiated outwards and numbed her every stress. It was only afterwards, tangled in the bedsheets with him, that Evie started caring about Lily and the others, listening through the walls. She kept her voice low as she whispered, 'My father won't stand for it, not after everything we've been through. He's of the older generation. He was half our age, just about, when he went off to war. Choices have consequences. Cal has to see that too.'

'And anyway,' said Max. '*Bill Martin*. Your father's hardly going to jettison Mr Martin, so that Cal could take to the stage … Martin wouldn't stand for it. Men like Martin don't get turned down. It would never happen.'

Evie sensed that unusual ire again, and was about to ask why when knuckles rapped at the door. With a sudden sense of panic, she pulled the bedsheet around her and called out, 'Yes?'

'It's me, Miss Forsyth,' came Lily's sweet sing-song voice. 'Can I come in?'

Too late, the door was already opening up. Evie leapt up, as if she might catch it, but instead just ended up standing there, half-dressed, with the bedsheet wrapped around her, Max scrabbling behind.

Lily's eyes darted in every direction, as if she knew not where to look – though, of course, she'd known it all along. In the end, with one hand cupping her eyes, she said, 'Mr Forsyth's called another all-hands. We're to go back to the theatre. Ten minutes' time.'

'Another?' Max asked. 'But—'

'I don't know, Max,' said Lily, with a snort. 'But I think you better put some trousers on first!'

Then she scuttled away, saving her laughter until she'd burst through the hallway door.

Evie looked at Max, throwing him the bundle of clothes that had been piled up by the side of the bed with more force than she'd meant to. '*Cal*,' she muttered, and sharply shut the door.

Fifteen minutes had given Ed enough time to venture back across the waterlogged car park to the double-decker, and slide inside his office again. The travelling trunk was under lock and key, but Ed kept the key on a chain around his neck – and had done ever since his father passed it ceremonially onto him, as if handing over the keys to the Company itself. Down on his knees, he opened it up. Inside were all the trinkets and icons of the Forsyth Varieties' long life. His grandfather's wedding certificate was here. So too the last flier printed in the season the Forsyths abandoned their Manchester beginnings and set out on the road. The glass eye that had once sat snugly in the skull of Abel Wright, the mesmerist who'd taught John Lauder all he knew, nestled in cotton wool in a little jewellery box designed specifically for this purpose. The golden wedding ring Ed had commissioned for Bella was here, kept safely until the day it might be passed on. Bella had meant for it to go to Cal and whoever he married, of course, but Ed hadn't thought of that for years. Now, he sat for a time with it warming in the palm of his hand, then carefully tidied it away and pulled out the album of photographs he'd come for.

Him and Bella, on the day they were married.

Him and Bella, with their twin children in their arms. Cal had come first, of course, as he'd have to across all the years to come, but Evie had come easier, sliding out with barely a cramp or a cry.

There they were, growing up together.

All four of them, the family that was meant to be.

When he felt the tears in his eyes, Ed had to put the photographs away. He didn't regret looking, but it would make the hour to come more excruciating yet.

The last picture he looked at was the one hanging on the wall: Bella, on the eve of their marriage. What would she have wanted? he wondered. And of course the question was pointless, for Bella hadn't been there to see the arguments, the spectacle, the ruin left in Cal's wake – and nor had she walked the lonely road back with the rest of them.

But of course he *knew*. He *knew* what she would have told him, right now, in this moment.

'But mine's only one vote,' he told her, and repaired to the theatre, where the Company was waiting.

Most of the Company had already assembled when he strode along the central aisle between the stalls. As for Cal himself, he was waiting in the shadows on the wings, just where Ed had told him to be. John nodded to him stoutly as he picked his way to the stage itself and lifted himself over the orchestra pit to stand in the place where the spotlight should have been. There would be no spotlight tonight. No ostentations. Just the dusty gloom of a theatre out of hours, for what might be the most significant decision in the history of the Forsyth Varieties since the end of the war.

Once he was on stage, Ed gazed out on his companions. A deep, heartfelt weariness had overcome him.

'My friends,' Ed began, and, just in time, saw Evie appearing at the back of the hall. By the look on her face, she *knew* what they were here for. That dancer Max was standing beside her, altogether too closely. If there was romance there, Ed would not have been surprised, but now was not the moment to speculate, nor even let his thoughts wander. He was standing here with a much graver purpose in mind. 'First, let me apologise for calling you back from your rest. But the unexpected has been presented to us, as it so often is, and we are faced with a decision – a decision that I should like us to take together, for we are as one in this Company. You are not just my players. You are all my friends, and I value the wisdom of your hearts and minds.' He stopped, took a step to the side, and called into the wings of the stage, 'Cal, perhaps now you might step into the light.'

This Cal did. He had tidied himself up a little since his first appearance, but to Ed's eyes he still looked bedraggled. As Ed remembered, he even used to cultivate this look: the wild hair, the sullen slouch, the sad but sparkling eyes.

'My son and I have been speaking, in frank and honest terms, since he appeared in this theatre some hours ago. Five years have passed since he walked out on the Forsyth Varieties, and, in five years, a lot has changed, for us as well as Cal. Now he asks that we welcome him home.' Ed paused. 'Friends, my heart and mind are in turmoil. Cal is my son, and as he is my son I felt his absence – and the manner of his departure – like a bitter body blow. I know many of you, those who were with us in those times, feel the same. So I seek your counsel now. This is a decision the Company must take together, or not at all. In a few moments time, I am going to ask you to raise your hand in support of Cal's return to the Company – or to take a seat if you believe there is no road back to what we once were. But first…' Ed took a breath. 'It would be unfair of me not to allow Cal to state his case, to speak with you directly. Please listen to him openly and then let us do what we must. Cal,' he whispered. 'Over to you.'

Ed retreated to the side of the stage, while Cal – seemingly steeling himself for some blow – ventured to its very edge.

'Friends,' he began. Ed could hear was nervousness in his voice, such as there had never been back when he'd played with the Forsyths. 'Friends, five years is a long time in a life. I was twenty-four and grieving when I left the Company. I should not have left how I did. I will always be sorry for that. For undermining everything we worked so hard to create. For the blow it did to my father, to you all – to the memory of my mother.' He paused. 'I have not come back here looking for glory. I haven't come back with any feeling other than a deep, almost desperate need to be among you again. I remember a wise old man once said to me,' Cal looked at John Lauder, 'you spend half your youth trying to escape and blaze a new path, then the rest of your life trying to get back home. That's how I feel now. That's just it. All I'm asking for is a second chance. Let me show you I mean it. Give me six months. If I've let you down, I'll leave – without argument, without fight, without bitterness or recrimination. Just let me try.'

One of the musicians called out. 'The Royal Variety's on the twenty-ninth of October. Doesn't that sound fishy to you, Cal?'

Cal shifted uncomfortably. 'You have Bill Martin. You hardly need me. What are my songs, compared to his?'

'This stinks,' somebody else chipped in. There came the sound of footsteps, as somebody flounced off. 'Cal, you hung us out to dry. Then you went searching for your fortune. Now that you're not as big as Elvis, you want to slink back home.'

'He didn't just hang us out to dry,' Valentino, who led the orchestra, called out. 'Cal, you were a wrecking ball even before you left. The number of times you walked out on stage with a skinful in your belly. That business in Antibes, with the town-crier's sister. That glut of hecklers in Cannes – Cal, they wanted to string you up after the fight in that bar, and do you know what? You would have *deserved* it. Those days were hard enough, but we seemed to spend half our time putting out fires that *you started*.'

Somebody else said, 'He made a mistake. We're not giving him anything we can't take back. What difference does six months make?'

'Aye, and we've got to think of the Company. Cal's a talent. A man like that turns up, you don't turn him away.'

'Yes, but what's to stop him doing it to us all over again? It's hard enough out there, keeping the Company going. Keeping it alive ...'

'Enough,' declared Ed. Now that there had come a lull in the arguments, he retook the centre stage from Cal, who retreated upstage once again. 'Let us have our vote. Speak what's in your heart. We all bear the responsibility for this.'

Ed looked back to see Cal standing nervously there. Nerves were so unbecoming of him, but perhaps that was right tonight.

Somewhere, out in Seaford, church bells had started tolling the midnight hour.

In the theatre, a flurry of hands were raised, but, if they sparked any joy in Cal's heart, it would have been quickly doused, for just as many took their seats. The musicians – who Ed knew had more cause than many to distrust Cal, for they'd been so closely entwined with his act – sat down as one, but when John Lauder stood and raised his hand, so did the stagehands, the acrobats and Davith Harvard, whose dogs immediately imitated him.

Ed was diligently counting hands, but not every vote was cast. At the back of the stalls, Evie and her fellow Max still stood, but neither had lifted their fingers into the air.

'I've eighteen to stay, and eighteen to go,' Ed declared. It seemed, then, that the drama was not yet done for the night. 'I'll need all votes. I'm sorry, darling, but this decision belongs to us all.'

Evie remained unmoved. So did Max. Every eye in the theatre turned upon them now.

'Evie,' Cal ventured, lurching forward. 'I know what I did, but I know what I can do. I know I can make it up to—'

But Evie folded her arms across her chest, her face a rictus of loathing, and, just when it seemed she might cast her vote by sitting down, she turned on her heel and marched out of the room.

'An abstention,' John Lauder pronounced. 'So there's a casting vote to make.'

Now, the theatre returned its full attention to Max. The poor boy looked stranded.

At last, buckling under the pressure, Max said, 'I'm sorry… I'm sorry, I can't.' And, in perfect imitation of Evie, he followed her out of the doors.

There was sudden consternation in the stalls. Valentino barked out, 'A straight tie's a vote for the status quo. That's how it is in Parliament. That's how it should be here as well.'

'Well, hang on,' John intervened, in the booming voice he ordinarily reserved for his appearances on stage. 'We aren't done yet. There's still one vote.' And he returned his gaze to Ed. 'I'm sorry, old man. I know you wanted this responsibility shared.

You ought to have raised your hand at the outset, and left the casting decision to somebody else, but it's here for you now. Eddie, it's time.'

Ed sighed. Speak with your gut, he'd told his players. Reveal, without shame, the workings of your heart.

There was no way this would end without consternation. Stay or go, Cal's return had already stirred such complex emotions.

But there was a stillness inside him now, and he knew why it was there: it was that picture of Bella he'd been gazing at; it was the thought of love unconditional, and what she would have done if she was standing where he was, right now.

So Ed lifted his hand.

'Welcome back, Cal,' he said – and, in the room, a strange mingling of cheer and imprecation began to rise up.

3

The Ghost and the King

The house lights went down. The music struck up. Cal always liked this moment the best. He'd known the anticipation that came with those few chords since before he could walk, before he'd had language, before he'd understood what the theatre even was. Now, in the wings of this little provincial theatre, he clung to his mother's hand and could hardly keep from shaking.

He gazed up. Somewhere in the opposite wing, sheltered in the shadows behind the plush velvet curtains, his sister Evie was with their father. He tried to catch her eye across the empty stage, but already the stagehands had started working the crank to open the curtains. He felt his mother's hand tighten around his. She crouched, to look him in the eye one last time.

Everyone said he looked like her. That was what the members of the Company, especially old John Lauder, always remarked. Cal liked it when she stroked the curls out of his eyes. He was eight years old, and about to be a star.

'Your first time on the stage is always a special moment, little one. The first time you hear the roar of the crowd. The first time you startle and surprise an audience. The first time the limelight finds you. Are you nervous yet, Cal?'

'No!' he exclaimed. 'Never. Never.'

She laughed, for what greater joy was there than seeing your own child's delight? 'Well, that's good. Let me be nervous for you. I think your sister may be having some jitters.'

The curtain was yet to fully rise. Cal gazed across the barren stage, and caught sight of his father consoling Evie. Then his father looked up, dazzled them with a smile, and everything seemed right.

'Just do as we rehearsed, little man,' his mother went on. The curtains were parting, now, and the roar of applause flooded through, almost silencing the orchestra. 'You're a good singer, Cal. You're a good little dancer. Stick to the beats, don't let the audience put you off – and, above all, keep smiling. *The joy you have out there is reflected in them. They'll go away happy tonight, if they've seen us happy. There'll be times in life you'll have to fake that joy. It happens to us all. But not tonight, Cal. Tonight,* you're *the star . . .'*

The curtains were open.

The dancers rushed out.

Cal's mother hoisted him onto her shoulders and prepared to canter out among them.

'I'll always remember this moment, Cal. From now until the day I—'

Cal woke up with a start.

If the Company's arrival at the Seagate Theatre hadn't been delayed by storms over the Channel, it would have proven easy to find Cal a room among the hostelries overlooking the pier, but it had been after midnight by the time the die was cast and neither Ed nor any of his compatriots had wanted to drag one of the various landladies from their own beds to arrange another room. Consequently, for the first time in five long years, Cal was in the partitioned sleeping area at the top of the Forsyths' double-decker bus.

He'd slept more soundly in the past, but at least the dreams had not been as tormenting last night. He fancied he could still feel his mother's hand in his own. The scent of her perfume seemed, somehow, to be in the air. Cal had never believed in ghosts – no matter what John Lauder used to tell him – but there were times when that steadfast belief could be shaken. He tried to rid himself of it by standing, stretching, pacing around, but none of it worked. Perhaps, being back here, there were going to be ghosts all around.

But at least he was back. That was all he wanted. Whatever happened next, he would have to face it as it came.

He remembered that Vivienne, the old dancer who'd been in charge of provisions on the road, had always cooked up the greatest breakfasts for the Company. He hadn't seen her in the theatre last night; perhaps that meant she'd left the Forsyths, like so many seemed to have done in the years since he'd been away. Or perhaps, he wondered now, she'd followed his mother into that great variety theatre in the sky. He supposed he would find out soon enough, but, somehow or other, he was going to have to find something to eat.

He parted the blackout curtains, then looked down upon the theatre. Cal had no way of telling the time, for he'd sold his watch some days before, but it could not have been too late. The rains had left Seaford, coursing further inland by the look of the heavy skies in the north, and pale sunshine spilled over a column of dancers and musicians as they flocked from their lodgings to the theatre. There, among them, was Evie. As she approached the theatre, she stopped – and it seemed to Cal that she was about to look back, up at the windows of the double-decker through which he was gazing. Then, resisting the temptation, she marched on, disappearing through the theatre doors. She'd known he was watching. Yes, it was the 'twins' feeling of old. John used to say that twins had a mystical connection, that – since they'd been tangled with each other since conception, comforted by the beating of each other's hearts – they would always be bound, by invisible string, one to the other. He'd been wrong, of course, when he'd said that one twin might always know what the other was thinking and feeling; that was just more stagecraft and hokum. But Cal was certain Evie knew she was being watched this morning. She'd had to fight the temptation to gaze back.

He could hardly blame her for abstaining from the vote last night. The love between twins was meant to be unconditional, but even unconditional love got beaten and battered by the world.

Cal was about to retreat from the window when he saw the young, blonde, sun-burnished dancer hurrying towards the theatre. He'd been the one who abstained immediately after Evie last night. Cal had no idea who he was. He supposed he'd have to find out. There was some loyalty there – some *love?* – that he ought to know about. Unknown variables always upended a carefully orchestrated plan. He didn't need – couldn't have – any upsets now. This needed to go smoothly, unremarkably, undramatically, if it was going to work.

If he was going to be *safe*.

He had just let the curtains fall closed when he heard somebody knocking on the door of the double-decker. It wasn't locked, for his father hadn't felt comfortable handing Cal the keys to the bus. Personally, Cal thought this a strange error of judgement: it was more likely that some local ne'er-do-well crept aboard at night to ransack the bus than it was Cal might take flight in something as ostentatious and recognisable as the Forsyths' chariot. He limped to the top of the stairs, called down that whoever it was should come on up, and retreated to the bed again, to put on his boots.

He was expecting his father, perhaps John, or one of the old hands come to escort him to breakfast with the rest of the

53

Company regulars, but, instead, one of the dancers scurried up the stairs, to meet him at the top. He recognised this girl, though five years had changed her considerably. She'd grown up, grown into her elfin features, but her hair was the same vibrant red it had been on the night Cal fled. He started fishing for her name, hoping he could dredge it up from the back of his mind. Everything was easier if you remembered a name: it made the other person feel special, unique, valued in memory. That was a trick his mother had taught him. 'Every time the Forsyths return to one of our regular spots, I try and learn a few more names. It keeps the audience joyful. It makes them keep coming back. To feel special like that. To feel... honoured.'

Lily, thought Cal. Yes, that was her name. She'd been with the Company only a few months before Cal fled. Back then, she'd still been a girl. Now, to look at her, she was a woman. Slender of build and perhaps the shortest among Evie's dancers, she nevertheless looked supple and strong – and the way she took in Cal, as the curtains parted and he hung in their frame, it seemed she was expecting to be recognised, as if this was a meeting of old friends.

'You stirred up something last night, Cal. A cat among the pigeons, that's what you are.'

'Well, you know me, Lily,' he said – and though, of course, she didn't, it gave her just the kind of thrill Cal intended. 'I stir things up. That's just who I am. I'm just sorry for the timing of it. I must have lost my sense of rhythm, out on the road. I wish it hadn't been on the eve of you starting prep for the Royal Command. It's given you all the wrong idea. I'm done with fame and glory, Lily. What I want is home.'

Lily rolled her eyes, as if to say 'a likely story', but it did not diminish the smile on her face.

'Cal, I wanted you to know... It's just that...' Lily started floundering for words. Her smile disintegrated; she was, it seemed, embarrassed with herself. 'I got your record, you know. The year after you left. "Hold Me Now."' And she started humming the familiar refrain Cal had come up with, back when he was with the Forsyths. A mournful melody in A minor gave way to a triumphant burst of song. 'She's the one, one day she'll see. Time waits for no-one, but she'll wait for me . . .'

This time, it was Cal's turn to look embarrassed. 'I think they only cut two hundred copies. You must have hunted it out.'

There was a lengthy pause, until at last, Lily said, 'That's exactly what I did. It was in a little record store, off the seafront in Brighton. I even went to see you play, when we were out at Southend. You were in one of the clubs. We were at the Cliffs Pavilion. They'd have roasted me, if they'd known.'

'My name was black as mud, right?'

'I reckon worse than that,' said Lily, with sadness. 'After a time, your name hardly got mentioned at all.'

Cal hadn't expected it to sting him as much. He was still, silent, absorbing it as best as he could. 'You can't cut off your flesh and blood,' he said, at last. 'A twin's a twin. Evie will see that, in the end. Love's love.' Then he looked at her. 'Why did you come here, Lily?'

Now, Lily started floundering again. 'It was only that . . . Well, I thought you should know, it's not all of us forgot you. There's plenty here who've missed having you around. If your sister doesn't see it, well, that's her cross. It isn't for all of us. It isn't for *me*.' She lingered on the word, then added, 'I just thought you ought to know.'

And Cal leant down, to plant the softest of kisses on her cheek.

'I appreciate that,' he said, and would, perhaps, have said more, if only, at that moment, a loud gong hadn't started sounding, just inside the theatre doors.

Cal remembered that sound. It was his father, summoning the Company to work, like the bells of a temple brought the faithful out to prayer.

'We'd better get going,' said Lily. She was backing away, towards the top of the stairs, when Cal, nodding, reached into a black leather holdall he'd crammed under the bed. He'd retrieved it last night, from the place it had been hidden for five long years, in the luggage compartment underneath the microbus outside. Crumpled shirts, five years old; a pair of his old slacks, well-worn brogues and the fedora he used to wear on stage. Somehow, it had seemed a sign, that it had still been there, after all these years. His family might have pushed him out of their thoughts, but they hadn't scratched him out of every photograph, nor shredded every memory. That meant there was still hope.

Hope he could complete what he'd come here to achieve.

Lily stood there as Cal stripped out of his shirt and proceeded to choose another one from the holdall. She knew she ought to avert her eyes, but the truth was, there was something magnetic about Cal. She looked sheepishly down, but she could not fight the compulsion for long. When she looked back, Cal was still half-naked. Every muscle was defined. He was wiry and strong, like all the best dancers.

His ribs were covered in bruises, livid yellows, purples and reds.

On his midriff, a bandage was fixed in place by surgical tape, the heart of it discoloured in black and crimson.

She looked away, uncertain how to process what she had seen. Then, when she looked back, it was to find Cal fully dressed.

'Come on, Lil,' he said breezily. 'You can escort me down. I don't know if they'll want me singing for them today, but I'd better show my face. Make myself useful, if there's any way I can. Maybe then I can win my sister's trust again, piece by tiny piece...'

Ed had been up before dawn, brooding over the day to come. Long before the tide came in and the sun began to rise, he stood with his flask of hot tea out on the pier, feeling the salt spray against him, listening to the shriek of seabirds as they stirred from their roosts. Then, sometime after the first pale fingers of dawn had touched the seascape, he turned to discover he'd not been alone after all: there was John, standing behind him.

'You did a good thing last night, Ed,' John said, joining him on the edge of the pier.

'What else was there?' said Ed ruefully. The thorniness of this problem had kept him awake all night. He sighed, and drank the last of his bitter, long-brewed tea. It was just the way he liked it. 'So why do I get the feeling I made a bad choice?'

'Because there was no good choice, Ed. Banish him, and lose him forever. Lose the faith of half the Company as well. Keep him, and...'

'*Evie,*' Ed whispered. 'I wanted to speak to her last night, but it was too raw.'

'You forget, Ed. She didn't vote to banish him either.'

Ed ruminated on this. 'She couldn't wield a knife, but she hoped somebody else might. The betrayal was bitterer for her. Her mother was dead. John, I was half dead too. She carried us alone. The Company might have come apart, and it didn't – because of Evie. Now she feels the heart's being torn out of it again. Like we're willingly walking into a storm.'

'Sometimes you have to. You made it back to England through a storm. Why not this time?'

There was something suspect about the way John was speaking. 'You're the one who prophesied disaster, old friend. Why the sudden volte-face?'

John put an arm around Ed, and prepared to guide him from the pier. 'I saw it on the horizon. Some tragedy, coming to the Forsyths. But I was wrong when I thought it was in Monaco. The feeling was vivid, but I didn't know its meaning. And perhaps we still don't. Who's to say Cal's return is the disaster I foresaw?'

Ed had to grin, but at least that dispelled the sour mood of the morning. 'Do you really mean to say, John, that there might be something much *worse* coming for us?'

They began to walk.

'John?'

'I don't know, old friend. It's all so unclear. But there's the Royal Command show. Bill Martin is coming. If a disaster's coming, it might be ... spectacular.'

And Ed, who was of course in the business of creating spectacle, could only steel himself and march.

At the Seagate, some of the Company were already assembling. It was always a strange phase when the Forsyths found themselves between performances. Every time a run ended, and the joy of performance faded into memory – if only for a short time – a strange emptiness settled over the players, as they turned their attention to the road. Ed had long ago discovered that you needed these periods of emptiness to revive the spirit, to make you long for the stage, to remind you that, without performance, life was a few shades greyer than it had always been. That was vital, for it kept the hunger burning and ensured the next shows were just as fabulous as before.

But at some point you needed to relight the fire. To breathe out the magic once more.

That moment, no matter what the tribulations of last night, would have to be now.

So he struck the gong to bring them together, and readied himself by the stage.

Once more, dear Ed, for the Forsyths...

Those were the words Bella had always said to him, squeezing his hand. He missed that voice in his ear. He carried it with him.

'The Royal Variety,' he began, parading up and down the front of the stage as the Company gathered. Here came Evie now, the dancer Max trailing behind like a faithful hound. No sign of Cal yet, but perhaps that was as it should be. He'd always been late, in the old days. He'd stay up, long after each performance ended, hunkered over his piano, seeking out some new melody that could light up a club. Then, later, in that year before he left, it was off into town – chasing love (or just lust) in the bars and hotel rooms, gambling with the locals, coming back with cuts and scrapes and a burgeoning bad reputation. 'It fills you with pride, does it not, to know that, before the month is out, we will – every last one of us – be performing for the Queen? My friends, I have carried the memory of it through my life. It has sustained me in my darkest hours – and so it will for you. You will recall these moments for the rest of your lives. And the first thing I must say to you all, for I hold it as inviolably true in my heart: we have been invited to play for the Queen, because our reputation goes before us. Because the good King George filled his granddaughter's head with the story of the last time he saw the Forsyth Varieties. My friends, what I mean to say is: we deserve our place on that stage. Now let's make it *spectacular*.'

The doors at the back of the stalls opened up. In walked Cal, with one of Evie's younger dancing girls at his side. Ed furrowed his brow; he hoped, beyond hope, that Cal wasn't already stirring up new passions in the Company. He'd been among them but one night.

'My friends, this is why we have come to Seaford. It is here, in this little theatre, that we must decide on the nature of our new show and hone it to perfection. When Mr Martin comes to join us, let's show him what we've got. It's been a long time since Mr Martin worked in the varieties. Let us show him what he has missed out on by chasing the Californian dream.' He clapped his hands, and leapt onto the stage. It was strange – for Ed increasingly relied on his cane – but, sometimes, the performer in him just flourished; then, no matter how advancing his years, he felt reborn. Now that he was on stage, he proceeded to outline how their first morning would take shape. 'Our Monaco show was among our greatest. But let us go further. If this is to be the crowning moment of my time with the Forsyth Varieties, let us give them a show that will never be bettered. Let us make sure that, when the news-sheets rhapsodise this performance, it isn't just the sudden appearance of Bill Martin that they write about. Let them write about how the arts of dance and the trapeze have been so beautifully entwined. Let them talk about how music and illusion came together in a feast for the senses. Let them talk about how we took them to the very greatest pinnacles of delight.' He drew out his pocket watch, the gift he had received upon his performance in 1912. He gazed at it momentarily, then declared, 'Any and all ideas will be welcome. Let's see what we've got, my friends. Let's see how good we are.'

It was a hive of activity in the theatre that morning. Ed, who had compèred the Forsyths' shows ever since his father had retired, had little to prepare himself, so he took a seat in the stalls, instead, and watched as the various acts came and went, occupying the stage. Davith and his dogs were preparing some new tumbling act backstage, so it was Evie and her dancers who dominated. The Seagate had not seen a live show since summer's end, so the rigging was not set up for Evie herself to dangle from ropes, or soar on a turning trapeze, but the way the dancers built pyramids of each other, forming and reforming like synchronized swimmers seen from above, was remarkable. It had silenced the crowd in Monaco. Ed only wondered if it was fit for a queen.

Soon, his notebook was filling up, the pages charting every observation he'd made. The old-fashioned Varieties simply introduced one act after another, the compère leading the audience from one to the next like a horse being led. But this, he decided, would be different. Each act would explode into the next. The question was: how? There was a story to tell, he was sure. The story of the Forsyths themselves. The story of a sixteen-year-old, who'd sung for a king, and now returned to the royal fold.

There was an engraving on the back of the timepiece.

To Edward, In Celebration...

He traced it with his finger. It was strange but, the older you got, the more easily a memory seemed to wrench you back in time. And now he wasn't a sixty-six-year-old widower, preparing for his final performance. Suddenly, he was sixteen years old once more. Backstage at the Palace Theatre, he took the knee before the good King George, and when, at last, he was instructed to stand again, a velveteen box was being pressed into his hands by a valet. It was the King himself who said, 'In thanks for your service, young man.'

Ed cherished those words in the years to come – not just when he stepped out on stage, but when he was in the depths of the trenches outside Verdun, when he was in the field hospital at Arras, when he was walking through a devastated moonscape of ash and cindered trees. 'I sang for the King. I'll be damned if I don't fight for him too.' Those were the words he had said, returning to the front after the first time he'd been put in hospital. He'd never sung as well again after the war – the gas tormented a young man's lungs, just like cancers did the old – but he'd found a new role at the varieties. Charm and swagger, carefully-crafted farce and repartee – these were the talents around which shows could be built.

It was going to be different this time. He would no longer lift his voice in song for the monarch. This time, he would tell her a joke.

But how to begin …?

He was scrawling down ideas, trying to block out the hubbub around him – this was another talent you had to develop if you were ever to last long at the varieties – when he felt a shadow fall across him. When he looked up, there was Cal, swaggering into view.

'Sit down, son.'

So Cal did.

'There's something troubling you. Go on, boy. Spit it out.'

'Well, I'm here, Father,' said Cal, and put his feet up on the top of the seat in front of him. 'And I know there's a long road back to being trusted again. I understand that. I do.'

'You ever have a son, Cal, and you'll understand.'

Ed was not sure why a strange look ghosted across Cal's face in that specific moment. The silence lingered fractionally too long, as if it was deliberate, or as if Cal was scrambling to cover up some secret thought. Some secret animosity, perhaps? Inwardly, Ed swore. Why was it that, of all the people in his life, the one person whose thoughts and feelings he couldn't immediately read was his wayward son?

'I dreamt about her last night. We were backstage, the first night Evie and I performed. She was telling me that nerves were natural. Well, I never felt nervous, Dad. Never got the butterflies before going out on stage.' He paused. 'But I've got them now.'

Ed nodded stoutly, but the truth was, he wasn't sure whether Cal was being genuine or whether he was being manipulated.

'You need something to do,' Ed concluded, at last.

'It's exactly that,' said Cal. 'I'm here, aren't I? I'm trying. I'm not expecting you to put me centre stage. By the gods, you've got Bill Martin! What use could you have for Cal Forsyth?' There was some bitterness there, thought Ed – and, of course, there would be, for Cal had been playing in the clubs for years now, cutting his records with minor labels, searching for his break, while Bill Martin, himself born from the varieties, stood on the peaks of Mount Olympus, home of the gods. 'But something, Dad. Something so that I'm not just … just a ghost at the feast.'

Of course, it made sense. The vote taken last night could not be left in isolation. To take Cal back to the Company was not done in a moment; it was something that would have to be done, time and time again, across the next weeks and months.

But where to begin? In the five years since – and especially in Monaco – the Forsyth Varieties had found their rhythm. They might have been on the verge of collapse once, but now they were a well-oiled machine. Every part had perfect symbiosis with the others. And to throw Cal into any one group would only end with resentment, division, upset – and, quite possibly, much worse.

Whatever part Cal played, it had to be something that brought the Company together, not that drove it apart.

At last, Ed had an idea. These were the greatest moments in his working life, when the perfect notion presented itself, fully-formed. He turned a leaf in his notebook, took to it frenziedly with the tip of his pencil, tore it out and handed it to Cal.

Ed saw the writhing realisation, then the distaste, on Cal's face as he read through the shopping list. Then, just when he thought that Cal was about to erupt, he folded the paper neatly, slid it into his pocket and stood to do his duty.

'You can take one of the taxicabs,' Ed said, and tossed him a set of keys. 'You won't carry that lot in your arms.'

The Cal of old would never have acquiesced so easily. But there was nothing to bring a company together like a good feed – and they were damn near out of provisions. It wouldn't be forever, but Cal had always enjoyed helping Vivienne with their banquets on the road. Vivienne was long gone, of course – for a year now, Evie had had a team of her dancers mucking in with the musicians to provide fodder wherever it was needed – so Ed was sure the new appointment would be appreciated.

Cal was seething as he left the Seagate Theatre. He was seething as he marched across the car park, seething as he fumbled with the keys to open up the first black cab. Sausages and butter. Bacon and eggs. He knew what his father was up to, but hearts were not won over by buttery toast and a few salty rashers.

Little steps, he told himself. Win their trust back, bit by bit, then show them what you can do.

It took three turns of the key before the car engine rumbled to life.

'Bacon and eggs,' he spluttered.

But what, he wondered, if there was another way?

By mid-morning, Evie's dancers were ready to take to the stage.

The music struck up. Valentino's orchestra, even dressed down, were a revelation. In the moment the music began, everything felt different. Music was the clarion call. Music was transformative. Music stirred feelings long ago forgotten. Evie led the dancers out, cartwheeling into centre stage. As she stood there, resplendent, the other dancers flocked to her and joined her arms. Moments later, out came the second sally, Lily among them as they took the hands of the dancers already in place and, with immeasurable grace, leapt onto their shoulders. It took mere moments for the pyramid to form. Then, when the music reached its natural peak, they came apart, rolling away from one another, cantering in circles, and reforming. So it was that, in expressions of dance and acrobatic ability, pyramids and stars were formed and destroyed. Houses were built, then demolished. Great crashing waves, made out of arms and legs and arched backs, surged towards the audience, then rolled away with the tide.

'Stop,' said Evie, cutting the music short. It took some time for the dancers to hear her instruction. So too, it seemed, had the others among the Company who, either taking a break from their own rehearsals or seeking inspiration, were watching from the stalls.

'What is it, Evie?' asked Lily, who had been about to take her place at the top of a particularly challenging pyramid. 'Does it not feel right?'

Evie prowled up and down, chasing the feeling. Sometimes, it was easier to express yourself with dance than it was with words; dance conveyed something for which language could never quite account. But, right now, she needed to pin it down. 'This worked in Monaco,' she said, acutely aware that Max was watching her from the dancing crowd. The other two male dancers stood on his shoulders, as dark as he was fair. 'It felt bigger, somehow. It felt like it fit.'

'It's the stage,' Lily said. 'You can't capture the same thing in a dusty old regional, as you can in the open air at the Fort Antoine.'

That was part of it, thought Evie, but it wasn't the whole.

And, of course, the stage at the London Palladium would be as different again. When you took an act on the road, you could never quite account for the vagaries of the establishments in which you might play. You had to make tweaks, especially at the edges of the stage – where the building might smother or hem in a certain part of your act – but that was only the ordinary order of things. This niggling doubt she'd felt, that was something else.

Then it struck her.

'This is a summer show,' she said. 'It's for blue skies and balmy evenings. It doesn't matter a jot how technically impressive it is, not when the *feeling* isn't right. We're dancing for London, with winter on the march.'

'So what do we do?' Lily piped up.

'Well,' Evie declared. 'We'll simply have to think again.' She turned to the musicians. 'I'm sorry, Valentino. I'm sorry, boys. We might be some time. But ... well, it's probably time for some early lunch, isn't it?'

At that moment, as if on cue, the door at the back of the stalls flew open. It was Cal, strutting in here as if he owned the place. That set her nerves on edge again.

He came, marching up the central aisle – and the most sickening thing of all was that everyone was watching him. He hadn't said a word, hadn't so much as whispered, and yet every eye was drawn his way. The stage presence of the star, thought Evie.

'Grub's up,' Cal said at last. 'But I'm going to need some help ferrying it in.' He paused. Not a soul had moved. The only thing that flickered at all, in the room, were the eyes that darted between Evie and Cal, as if uncertain who they should gaze at.

'Come on!' Cal called at last. 'Evie,' he said. 'Evie, tell them?'

They were the first words he'd said to his sister. She looked shell-shocked. All was still in the Seagate. For a time, it seemed that not even a solitary breath was going to be taken.

Then, one of the musicians – Lennie, Evie noted, one of the stagehands who'd voted for Cal last night – inched a step towards him.

That was all it would take, Evie thought. Just the drop of a feather, to upend something as carefully balanced as the Company.

And yet the dancers were hers. Even those few who'd voted for Cal were gathered around, silently imploring her as to what they should do. This feeling was so familiar: she felt as if she was up on the tightrope (she'd walked it so magnificently in Monaco, like she was floating on air), when along came an unexpected breeze. Any moment, she might plunge to the left; or, if she over-compensated and moved her body's weight a touch too far, she might plunge to the right.

An old lesson came back to her. 'It's better to fall by the hand of the wind, Evie, than take the wrong step.' Even in this moment, she smiled at the recollection. Her mother's words of wisdom always reached out, from beyond the grave.

'Grub's up,' she told the dancers, and, though they still seemed reluctant, the movement had begun. The stalls began to empty, the musicians and dancers, and everyone spectating from the seats, traipsing after Cal.

It couldn't be much of a lunch, thought Evie. Almost certainly there were just loaves of bread and jars of jam lined up somewhere. Sliced ham from the butchers, some pickled onions and eggs. Hardly the banquet on which the Royal Variety should be built, but Evie had to grudgingly admit that she would like that. She'd been eating the foods of the Mediterranean all summer long; sometimes what you wanted was good old-fashioned British grub.

Yet, when she walked out of the theatre doors – the last of the auditorium to venture into the crisp October day – she found that a travelling burger van had taken pride of place in the middle of the car park, that hot dogs and beef burgers were sizzling on a griddle, and that the smell of onions sozzled in butter was filling the air.

'Cal, what on Earth—'

'Don't worry, Evie. It's all free. I haven't spent a penny.'

Evie tried to take it all in. The first of the burgers was just being served. 'What do you mean?'

'See, I met this girl in the town last night. I was waiting for you up at the Tanner Hop and – well, it's how I heard about it. I reckon – something hot, to get the day going? And, like I said, I didn't have to spend a penny because it turns out the owner, well, his wife's brother, manages the bar at a hotel in town, and if I play a few songs tonight then …'

'Oh, for God's sake, Cal!'

The words had just exploded out of Evie. She marched three strides away, stopped, then marched another two. Only then did she look back. 'Bread and milk, Cal. Bread and milk. Dad wanted you to do something simple and honest, just to show you cared.'

'Oh, but, Evie, this is – this is *better*. Look at them.' Cal opened his arms. 'A bit of a thrill, to get everyone stoked up. They deserve it, don't they? After Monaco and—'

'Yes, Cal,' she snapped. 'I was *there*.' She marched back towards him. It was his insouciant tone that aggravated her most of all. There was no solemnity in Cal. There never had been. But he was a good actor, so why in hell didn't he just pretend? No, because that wouldn't be Cal. There he stood, as carefree as if five years hadn't happened. 'What are you even doing here, Cal? Why here? Why now? Because I'll tell you something: Dad might not be able to see through it, but I can. *You* left us. You left us at our lowest ebb. You left us when we needed you most. Off to do your own thing, chase your own glory while we just put one foot in front of another, just trying to survive.'

She had burnt herself out, but at least something was chastened in Cal. The rest of the Company were trying not to watch. A brother and sister at war – it was against the natural order. They'd been asked to take sides once already. Not a soul outside the Seagate wanted to be asked the question again.

After some time, Cal said, more quietly, 'I saw you. I was playing at the Cavern in Liverpool, heading down for the sound checks... and there you were, staring at the hoardings. I wanted to talk to you, but I didn't have the guts. Sounds so stupid, doesn't it? But I just waited until you'd gone. I felt like a fool, after that. The manager at the bar said I'd fluffed my set, and he was right. I just couldn't stop thinking about... well, about everything. I was angry with you, angry you hadn't even tried to see me. So I went down to that theatre on the Wirral, where you were playing. I thought I'd sneak in, watch you all for old times' sake. But, as soon as I got there, I didn't have the courage...'

Evie groaned. 'Cal,' she said. 'You really are the most self-centred person I ever knew. I wasn't pining when I was looking at those hoardings. I wasn't itching to go in and see you, but losing my courage along the way. I was flat out *furious*. I'd not thought about you in months – and suddenly, there you were, and I was right back where I started. Our mother dead. Our father, lost in his own madness and grief. All on my own, last Forsyth standing.' She turned to stalk off, but stood rigid again. 'I know why you're here, Cal. Don't think that I don't. The Royal Variety? Dad, bookending his career? Well, you can't just walk back into the Company and expect him to hand it to you. The prodigal son, with everything served up on a silver platter, just because – just because you look like our mother! I'm the one who held it together. I'm the one our father trusts.'

Cal reached for her. 'Evie, you've got it all wrong. I just wanted to come—'

'Home,' Evie snapped, and no longer could she hold her tears in. She folded her arms and refused to dab her eyes as they welled. Then the first tear cut a track down her cheek, glistening in the pale winter light. 'The problem is, Cal, the home you used to know isn't here any more. This is my home now – and I don't care what the Company thinks. I don't care how many votes get cast. Cal, you're just not welcome.'

4

Love Me, Do

Night was coming on, the cold October darkness drawing in. The theatre had been a bustle of activity during the day, but John Lauder had managed to avoid all of it, variously watching from the window of his room in a lodging house behind the Seagate back doors, or pottering up and down the pier, trying to get lost in his thoughts. That was easier said than done. As the years went by, it wasn't just the body that slowed down; the mind had its own way of slowing. Nowadays, it was harder to pull off the miraculous than it had been when he was young. Part of that was to do with the fact that audiences were savvier than they'd been in John's heyday. When John had enlisted with the Forsyth Varieties, to shadow and serve old Abel Wright, folks had been in genuine awe of the most rudimentary tricks. Saw a woman in half, make a statue disappear, pull some stunt with pulleys and mirrors to make it seem like a man could levitate – the audience had been eating from old Abe's hand. But Abe hadn't had to deal with television. He hadn't had to deal with the past fifty years of exposure and a generation increasingly less willing to embrace the magic of an act, instead of trying to decipher precisely *how* it was done. As each season passed, John had to reach for greater and greater glories. It was, perhaps, a blessing in disguise that he'd had those unnerving portents before summer had begun – for, instead of following the Company to Monaco, he'd been able to empty his mind, step away from the stage, and spirit a startling new trick into being.

That was why he was glad that night had come along. He'd already seen half the Company embarking for Seaford town – what little there was of it, at any rate. That meant the theatre was his to do with as he pleased.

By good fortune, a couple of the lads were around to help bring his equipment out of the hold. He'd had to put much of it in storage over the summer – he'd been staying with his elderly sister up on the Norfolk coast, and she held little truck with 'magic' or 'superstition' of any kind. In fact, she considered it the devil's work, a perspective drummed into her by a Presbyterian minister she'd become quite besotted with when they were children. As a consequence, everything he'd invented this summer – everything he hoped might cause a sensation at the Palladium – had existed only in the theatre of his mind, untested by his aged hands.

Tonight was the night he put it into practice.

Up on stage, the vanishing cabinet was waiting. If it did not look like the sort of apparatus that might make a queen believe in real magic, that was simply as it should be. The greatest moments in John's career had come when he'd pulled the impossible out of the mundane. Stage magic was equal parts craft and stage presence, as you lulled an audience into believing whatever you told them to believe. If the visions John had had across the summer were right, they would think this impossible. And therein lay the beauty of this particular trick – for, when you watched the impossible unfold before your very eyes, a part of you started to question the reality around you. You could leave somebody discombobulated for days.

Tonight was for testing the rudiments of the illusion. Later on, he would have to ask Davith for the use of his dogs. He'd had a word with Ed about this already, how Davith's dog act could morph seamlessly into this piece of illusion. Davith himself seemed to be chattering about corgis – 'We'll delight the Queen, with corgis, you see, and, of course, they're a Welsh dog at heart, so it's only right it's me who brings them to stage' – but, as long as John could borrow a couple of dogs, he was certain he could make his trick work.

To evoke the right atmosphere, he had set up his projectors. Tonight, a flickering wheel of cards would make a cascade of shadows on the stage walls, but, when it came to the Palladium, John envisaged teaching Evie's troupe a 'hand dance' he'd been perfecting: twelve dancers, performing with their hands, making a shadowy kaleidoscope on the walls. Most theatres thought shadowgraphy was a dated art, and perhaps that was true – even old Abel Wright had largely left it behind – but John had an inkling that every dated art was rediscovered in time.

The music began – just a record player tonight. Once the projectors were shining and the shadow cards spinning, John began blocking out his movements on the stage. Though he spoke no words tonight – simply mouthing nonsense to an imaginary audience – he had begun to devise the 'patter' already. This was where the misdirection began. By buttering up an audience, speaking at them relentlessly and gesticulating with his hands, he would be able to direct their attention to wherever he desired. That was going to be crucial for the next part of the trick.

'John?' came a voice.

John had already turned upstage, so he did not immediately see the figure approaching through the darkened stalls. That did not matter, for he knew her voice. He'd been listening to this particular voice since his visitor first learned to talk. 'One moment, Evie,' he whispered and, without turning around, marched dramatically towards the vanishing cabinet on stage. First bowing towards it – another bit of ostentation, meant to suggest he had a deep respect for the magic he was about to perpetrate – he opened it up, put his hands together in prayer, and stepped within. As he turned on the spot to close the doors, he saw Evie for the first time, standing between the stalls with an inscrutable look on her face. He smiled at her, and closed the door.

'You want to speak to me, Evie?'

The voice came from inside the cabinet. Evie picked her way towards it. 'It can wait, John. It's just…'

'Cal?'

'Cal,' she whispered, with some regret.

'You've spoken to your father, of course?'

'Scarcely,' said Evie. 'I don't truly know what to say. It's like… am I meant to just forgive and forget? Of course,' she muttered, more darkly now, 'the rest of the Company are being won over. All it took was twenty-four hours. Even those who voted against him, I can see them melting. He's gone up to town, to play some songs at the hotel. Half the Company have followed him. And, yes, I know they need their time away from the theatre. But really, with *Cal*…' She paused. 'John? John, are you still there?'

Evie heard footsteps behind her. She turned, sharply, to see John Lauder coming slowly up the aisle between the stalls. The dissatisfied look on his face was a mirror to the startled one on Evie's. She flickered looks back and forth. Then she spirited herself up onto the stage and opened up the vanishing cabinet, only to find it bare. 'I understand how you left the cabinet,' she said, and reached in to pull the clasp that made the back door revolve. 'But how did you…?'

'There's something not quite elegant enough,' he said, and promptly stepped into the cabinet again. 'You were saying, Evie?'

'I just don't know how to stop this feeling burning. It's eating me up.'

'It's scarcely been a day.'

'All the old ill feelings just keep coming back. I just wish ... I just wish I knew what my mother would have said. John? John?'

The music stopped dead. Evie spun away from the cabinet and, peering over the edge of the stage, saw that John was sitting in the front row of the stalls, having just leaned down to lift the needle on the record player.

'John, how are you—'

He lifted his finger to his lips, inviting her to silence.

'Evie,' he said, after much rumination. 'Are you asking me what I think you're asking? Girl, it's been four years. You told me that, if ever you asked me this question again, I should tell you no. What was the last thing your mother said to you?'

Evie shifted, awkwardly, from foot to foot. 'She told me to go in peace, and let go of the past.'

'Then hadn't you better take her advice?'

'But how can I, John? How can I, when the past just swaggered in here as if it never ended?' Her voice rose to a pitch, and she beat her fists into her sides. 'I thought I didn't need it, John, but – but I do. Just one more time. I need her counsel now, more than ever. I can't go to Dad. He's too bound up in his own fears. I know him. He'll think this is some second chance, that he'll be doing my mother proud if he can bring Cal back. But it's not like that for me. I need to hear it for myself.' She paused. 'John,' she said, at last. 'I need to hear it from her.'

The Fairhaven was not the grandest hotel Lily had ever been to, but it was – by a country mile – the grandest in Seaford town. Dominating the corner where the Seaford high road met the seafront, it looked out upon the grey marina and amusement arcades crowding the end of the pier like the relic of some bygone age: a stately home, transplanted to these seaside surrounds. Tonight, the lights in its white face were dazzling.

The hotel suites had been out of reach of the Forsyths when they'd made arrangements to come to Seaford, for even in winter it commanded prices much steeper than the private landladies ever asked, but there was food and drink in the bar, a crowd of locals lured in by the promise of music, and Lily had to admit that it made a change from camping out with the Company every night. Even though those same faces were ranged around the table tonight, the hotel bar was full – and there was *atmosphere*. She hadn't known how much she'd been looking forward to a night like this.

Of course, it was Cal who had provided the opportunity. They'd followed him down, but since then they'd seen neither hide nor hair of him. Off with the bar manager, Lily thought, preparing himself to make an entrance. Her eyes kept flashing around the busy bar.

'You know he's not all he's cracked up to be, don't you?'

It took a little moment for Max's voice to cut through. He'd been bringing the drinks over on a tray – all waiters should train as dancers, thought Lily; it gave them perfect poise – and kept having to duck and weave around all the other punters. There was a raucousness in the air here that Lily liked. Lord, it could get all stuffy, living and working with the Forsyth players. Ed was a good boss – there wasn't a showman like him when he was on good form – and Evie marshalled the dancers like the big sister Lily had never had. The problem was, no matter how much they emphasised the infectious joy of performing on stage, sometimes it just wasn't *fun*. Oh, there was pride in the accomplishment, and there was beauty in what a team of dancers – especially in their more acrobatic performances – could create.

But real, honest-to-goodness *fun*? To Lily's mind, that could only be achieved by something spontaneous, something wild, something you didn't have to labour over for days and nights to create. It was the difference between the stuffy old ballroom dances of old – dances Lily was, of course, schooled in – and the raucous jiving, bopping, and rock-and-roll dancing that had first pulled her into this world.

'What's it to you, anyway?' Lily crowed, grateful for the gin and lime Max had brought her, but not for his comment. 'You weren't around before. You don't know a thing about Cal that you haven't picked up from someone. And I know what you've picked up.' She grinned at him over the top of her glass. 'Just you remember.'

Lily enjoyed the way Max's cheeks turned crimson. Most of the dancers were here tonight – save for Evie, of course, who never accompanied the troupe on soirées like this. Lily supposed it was deemed 'inappropriate' to go out drinking with your lowers in the Company – which seemed pretty stuck-up, when you thought about it. There weren't meant to be any airs and graces with a company like the Forsyths. Everyone was meant to be worth as much as everybody else – except, when your name was Forsyth, that rule hardly applied.

'Anyway,' she chirped on. 'We're only here to hear him sing. Just you listen. Then you'll know what I'm talking about. Hasn't been a star singer in the Company in all the time he's been away. They say old Ed used to sing like an angel, until the gas got him. He was always jealous of Cal's voice. It rubbed him up the wrong way, that's all.'

Max had been trying to ignore it, but Lily just kept going on and on. 'I don't think it was jealousy they fell out over. Ed's not a man to begrudge anybody else their talent – least of all his son. No, it was how Cal treated them in the months after Bella died. He wanted to transform the Company. He wanted to keep changing things, over and over and over. He just wouldn't listen.'

Lily stuck her tongue out and laughed. 'Rot! Absolute rot! Besides, maybe Cal was right – maybe things do need shaking up every now and again. There's plenty of variety companies out there who faded away, because all they had was the old standards. Maybe Cal was right... Look, here he comes now.'

Lily was right. A back door behind the bar had opened, and Cal had sauntered through, with the bar manager at his side. They appeared to be sharing some private tête-à-tête. Cal, nodding along, was led along the bar towards the place in the corner where an upright piano, a small Kemble by the look of it, was waiting.

'Five years,' said Max. 'Don't you ever wonder where he was?'

'I know where he was. He was on the road. Playing his songs. Working the clubs. Cutting those records. Doing what he does best – only he was doing it alone.'

'That was his choice.'

'Oh, *Max!*' Lily picked up a beermat and, with a deft turn of her fingers, flicked it directly into Max's face. 'Give him a bloody chance. It's only because of *you know who* that you're up in arms about it. Well, I'll tell you, nobody's a saint. Evie isn't perfect either.'

Max leant sharply across the table, fearful of the other dancers hearing – although, given the rowdiness in the bar, he'd hardly heard himself. 'You didn't tell anyone about that, did you?'

Lily snorted. 'My word's my bond.'

'That's good, then,' said Max, with visible relief. 'Only I wouldn't want—'

'Of course, everyone knows anyway,' she went on, certain in the knowledge it would alarm him. 'Oh, don't look at me like that. How long have you two been at it? Four months? Five?

You've only been with us six. Max, you can hardly be in the same room as her without swooning – and that's unfortunate, because we're all in the same room every day. Hey, Rach?'

One of the other dancers looked around at the call of her name.

'What is it you were saying about Max and Evie?'

Despite Max's consternation, Rachel ventured, 'Well, I reckon it's good for her. It's like when a rich old man's going through some troubles. He's got his whole company sniping at him, or he's losing his job – the pressure's getting too much, but he has a fancy girl he takes out for the night, p'raps gets a room in some swanky hotel. It helps him, you know? It helps him get rid of the stress.'

'Now, listen here!' Max snapped.

'Oh, we're only joking with you!' Lily hooted. 'Man likes woman, woman likes man. Where's the sin in it? It's nineteen sixty-two!'

Max was chastened. He buried himself in his bottle of stout. 'Do you think Ed knows?' he asked, at last.

But he never received an answer – for at that moment, at the head of the bar, a crash of piano chords was struck and Cal began to sing.

John lit the seventh candle.

Then they were ready to begin.

Unable to bring Evie over to his digs – where the landlady would surely be outraged by a man of John's vintage bringing a young lady back to his rooms – John had instead arranged the candles in the stage-manager's office, where the fat black cat was still refusing to budge. Now, with the electric lights turned off, those candles were the only thing to see by. Then he invited Evie to sit. Only once she had seated did he sink into the opposite chair.

'It may take some time to reach her,' he whispered. 'She won't be expecting us. Evie, you already said your goodbyes.'

'I know, John, but...'

Ed would be furious if he found them here: a cocoon of darkness in which to perform the very rite he'd outlawed, six years before. It wasn't just the scent of candlewax that hung heavy in the air; it was the sense of guilt as well.

'He doesn't need to know,' Evie had said to John, the first time she came to him. 'He might not believe – but that doesn't go for all of us. And I... I need to feel it. I need to feel *her*.'

'She's with you always, girl,' John said. 'She lives in you.'

'That's what my father says. But I need something more, John. I've seen you do it, up on stage. I've seen you speak with the dead.'

A talent out of vogue in the varieties, but – like shadowgraphy – a talent that still existed in the world. There'd been a time, back in the golden age of the music halls, when spiritualists and mediums had been in high demand. Abel Wright, who'd taught John everything he knew, had apprenticed at the side of a seance artiste when he was a lad, visiting the parlours of rich society women desperate for some consolation from lost loved ones. When John had joined the Forsyths, they'd worked a nice side-trade in rituals like this – though Ed's grandfather had, very early on, forbidden it from being part of the main act. But reputations died hard – and, when desperate folk had come, seeking some comfort, only a callous man would have turned them away. Abel had continued speaking to the Other Side on behalf of those who'd approached him. John had waited on him during those rituals, and some of the talent had rubbed off on him. He might not have advertised his services, but he was there for those in need.

He'd been there for Evie, in the year after Bella had died.

Of course, speaking to the dead was like an addiction. Ed, who had never believed in magic beyond the illusions of the stage, had lost his mind on the day Evie went to him, in his grief, and suggested that he ought, perhaps, to go visit John. 'It's a trick, Evie. A nasty, lamentable trick that we left behind last century. How dare he fill your head with it? He's meant to be my friend.' And later, when he cornered John in the hostel where they were lodging, Ed's fury was so incandescent he might have pinned John against the wall. 'You put your tricks away, John. I don't care if you think you're doing good. I don't care if you even believe it's real. We've got to heal. My children, they have to grieve. Let them do it. Leave her in her grave where she belongs.—'

'I'm not tricking anyone, Ed. You know I'm not. And Bella, she wants to speak to you too.'

As good fortune would have it, the Forsyths were not performing in the month after that particular altercation. On his return to England, John went to spend some time with his sister – while Ed, preferring alcohol to the seance, medicated his grief in an altogether more destructive way. By the time summer returned, and the Forsyths regrouped for their season at Southend, it was never mentioned again. And, although John took some persuading, he lit the candles on a good number of occasions for Evie, until – perhaps a year later – Bella herself told her daughter it was time to let go.

Now, here he was, with his eyes half closed, focusing on his breathing, entering the same trance state that Abel Wright had once shown him, reaching out with his mind for the spirits that crowded the world of the living, always hovering, always near, always just out of sight.

'Bella?' he whispered. He had reached out, across the candle between them, and now he took Evie's hand. 'Bella Forsyth, née Palmer, I am speaking to you from the other side. Bella, it has been some time – are you there? Do you hear my voice?'

Evie started shaking. There'd been comfort in this once upon a time, but that comfort seemed gone now, replaced with the same trepidation she'd felt the very first time. Her father would think she was betraying him by just sitting here – and, of course, she did not want that. But she needed some counsel.

It was like that long ago age when she'd first learned how to dance, pivoting and turning in the arms of her mother. Somebody had to lead you. By leading you, they gave you strength.

'She's here,' whispered John.

One of the candles flickered out.

And Evie knew, then, that her mother was in the air around her. Every window was closed, the draught excluder lined up against the door, the old hearth blocked up by the electric fire – and yet cold air moved across her.

'Bella,' John ventured. 'Do you hear?'

There was silence. Then John opened his eyes, piercing Evie with a look. 'She hears us, Evie.' He let go of her hand. A pencil and paper had been lined up on the table, and he lifted the pencil now. 'Speak with her, girl. Speak to your mother.'

It was only now that Evie realised she'd come here without thinking exactly what she would say. She'd been drawn here by the old feeling of it, the old need of a child – however old they've grown – to reach out for their mother. How she longed to hold her. How she longed to feel Bella's fingers combing through her hair.

'Mother, I'm sorry,' she said, into the ill-lit darkness of the room. 'I know you told me to live. The last time John reached for you, we said our goodbyes. But years have passed now, and so much has changed. Mum, I need you again.' She'd known she would feel guilty because of Ed, but she hadn't expected to feel guilty over Bella herself. The last goodbye had felt so final: two years after they'd laid Bella's body to rest, one since Cal walked out on them all. She hadn't thought she'd ever be back here, sitting in a darkened room, hovering on the fault-line between the worlds of the living and the dead. 'Mum, Cal came home.'

The candles flickered. John's fingers seemed to flinch around the pencil they were gripping.

He had started to write.

Evie inclined her head, so that she might make out the trembling letters by the faltering light.

I knew he would.

Evie nodded, cautiously at first, then growing in certainty. 'I think I knew it too. But, Mother, now he's here … all I want is for him to go again. It's like being ripped back in time. It's like all the wounds that closed up are being torn open. Dad's let him in. He's done it for you. I know he has. After all the fireworks, all the fights – he wants to know there's a future. He wants to get back to what we were: a family.' She stopped. Some fundamental piece of her did not want to say what came next. Then she saw John's hand shudder as it wrote, *Go on*, and she summoned up the strength. 'But I can't feel it. It isn't in my heart. I buried it, all that time ago. Mother, I don't know what to do.'

John's hand was moving again.

Yes, you do, my girl.

Evie laughed, wiping the single fat tear that had welled in her eye. Her mother was just as oblique in death as she had been in life. Her father had once tried to tell her that this was just the stagecraft of a seance: the mystery, the riddles, the obtuse language of the dead, all just another part of the illusion. Evie might have been convinced of it too, if only, that first time she'd gathered with John, Bella hadn't spilled the story of that first night she and Cal had performed – and the secret look they'd shared across the stage, just as the curtains went up. A private moment like that could only ever have come from Bella herself.

'Mum, I don't know if I can.'

You can.

'I know it's for the good of the Company. I've always put the good of the Company first.'

John's hand seized up. Now it was shaking, more violently than it had before. Evie saw that his eyes were still in their faraway, trance-like state, but his hand seemed to be tearing itself free, as if agitated, desperate, perhaps even distraught. This time, when it had finished its writing, Evie had to take the page, turn it upside down, and study it to make out the message her mother had sent.

It's for the good of YOU.

The moment Evie let the letter flutter back down, John's hand was scrawling again.

Blood is thicker than water.

And then, just when it seemed John's hand had seized up too rigidly to write:

I love you all.

John gasped. The pencil burst out of his grip, clattering to the ground. The moment it struck, the candles flickered out. John was reeling, like a man who'd been held under water, only to suddenly be released. This time, when he was shaking, it was for him alone. He reached out, half blind, for the page on which his hand had, quite divorced from the rest of him, been writing. One after another, he took in the missives, as if, until this moment, he'd known not one word.

'Evie,' he said at last. 'Are you OK?'

Evie was holding herself. She did not feel OK. 'Life can be so unexpected, John.'

To which, he just nodded. 'Life isn't a stage show. We don't get to rehearse it.' He took Evie's hand, though at first she resisted. 'Your mother was a good woman. She was the best of us. And when she says...'

'It's for the good of YOU,' said Evie.

John nodded. 'I think you're going to have to talk to Cal.'

Cal's hands were pounding at the piano keys, a twelve-bar blues in C major, in the bar of the Fairview Hotel, singing Elvis's 'Hound Dog'.

Some of the crowd had slipped into the music with him, helped along by Lily and the other dancing girls. The hand clapping and feet stomping quickly spread to the other tables – much to the chagrin of some of the old-timers occupying their booths against the back wall – and, in one or two places, even threatened to turn into dancing. 'Come on girls,' said Lily. 'Let's get it going!'

Lily didn't just give herself to the dance. She positively threw herself into it, with all the passion in her being. Dancing on stage was one thing but – whether their routines were rooted in the foxtrot, the quickstep or even the tango – there was a precision and craft to the performance that, somehow, kept her feeling curtailed. Dancing in a club – or even a hotel bar like this one – was quite different. Her body knew the moves, of course – her feet and hips had been trained for years, so that the building blocks of dance were finely tuned instincts – but, in a place like this, you could really give free rein to the soul. Nor did you need a partner – not most of the time, at least. With the other girls, she twirled and kicked, hopped and turned. Cal's voice was driving them to dance.

His voice wasn't exactly sweet, thought Lily. When people spoke of the way Ed used to sing, you'd think he was an angel, and maybe, if the war hadn't come along and the gas made such a ruin of his lungs, his voice would have matured into something closer to the singers she heard on those Benny Goodman and Tommy Dorsey records he was fond of listening to. Perhaps he might have ended up like one of the silky, smooth crooners who'd become so popular – Frank Sinatra, or their very own Bill Martin. Cal, meanwhile, had an altogether gravellier voice. To listen to him, you'd think he was chain-smoking cigarettes as he sang – deeper and richer than his father's, it had a rougher, darker texture, with perhaps a faint twang of the Americas about it. It helped, of course, that he was rolling through some of the great rock-and-roll records Lily had grown up with. They *all* came from America. Was he trying to impersonate Elvis as he segued from 'Hound Dog' into 'Jailhouse Rock'? When he burst into 'Great Balls of Fire', was he deliberately trying to impersonate Jerry Lee Lewis? The way he kicked back his piano stool and stood to play, bowed over the piano keys like some mad preacher, certainly made it seem so.

Cal was lost in the music. As his rendition of Bill Haley's 'Rock Around the Clock' came to its bombastic end, he barely even noticed that the bar manager – having just visited the table of some disgruntled regulars – was tapping him on the shoulder, asking him to stop.

The dancers started booing and hissing. As Cal looked up, he caught Lily's eye. Whatever the barkeep was now saying seemed to fade into insignificance; Cal rolled his eyes mockingly, so that only Lily could see, then, delighted when Lily snorted with laughter, he looked back at the bar manager. 'One more song,' he said. 'Look, I'll make it less of a riot.'

'*One* song,' the manager said. 'You've done us good, Cal, but I'm not looking for any upset.'

It would have to be a ballad, thought Cal. The Skyliners' 'Since I Don't Have You' – he'd sung that for one of the executives at Decca once, if only to prove that he could carry a big, soaring melody like that. He'd tried to write one of his own for them, something that mixed the epic romance of those great American ballads. Then he looked up. No, he thought, they wouldn't do. There was another number he wanted to play. The problem was – he'd never done it on a piano before. He'd learnt piano at his father's side, but a travelling musician could not depend on an instrument like that. That was why, in the years since he'd fled the Forsyths, it was the guitar he had been drawn to.

After a quick conversation with the barkeep, Cal slipped into a back room behind the bar, returning with an old acoustic guitar, its strap slung over his shoulder.

There was a makeshift stage behind the piano. Just a few blocks, from which a comic or a singer might hold court. Cal leapt aboard and spun on his heel to face the crowd. 'Just one more number, to send you into the night. You're going to hear a lot about the band that wrote this song. I can *feel* it. It's only been out a couple of weeks. I'm sure you've heard it on the radio.'

Cal strummed a single chord.

'I played with these lads when I was up on the Beat Ballad Show Tour. Johnny Gentle had a few support acts. This lot were one of them.' Cal beamed, as if he was the holder of a secret no other knew. 'They won't be the support act ever again, I'm telling you.'

He started to sing.

*

It took only one chorus of 'Love Me Do' before the dancing resumed. Behind the bar, the manager's face was ashen – Lily supposed he was only just realising he'd made a terrible miscalculation, letting Cal continue at all. By the time Cal reached the end of the song – then decided that, technically speaking, he was still only playing 'one song' if he looped back to the beginning and sang it all over again – half the room was back on their feet, while the other half simmered.

Now, *this* was a song, thought Lily. She and the other dancing girls turned wild circles, spinning each other around, shimmying and gliding with the strange synchronicity that only stage performers could achieve.

Cal leapt from the stage, hammering at the guitar as if trying to destroy the instrument in front of the crowd. As he threw his head back to fill the bar with the last word of the song, he wheeled his arm around to strike the final chord. Already, the audience were screaming for him to play it again. But, as Cal hit the last note, then threw his arms open wide to lap up the adulation, Lily realised that he hadn't seen the old man pottering towards the toilets, muttering to himself about the noise. His hand accidentally connected with the old rogue's cheek, sending him sprawling back towards the bar.

After that, everything happened so quickly it turned into a blur.

In an instant, the dancing stopped.

No sooner had Lily seen the man's friends catch him, the hue and cry set up. One, who had been nursing his frustration all night long, finally let it rip – and, hoisting up the empty beer bottle he was holding, let it fly towards Cal's face. The bottle missed Cal by an inch, exploding on the small stage. But that was just the starting pistol. Another man, evidently as sick as the others at the bar being turned into a concert venue tonight, tried to wrench the guitar away – but, because Cal was wearing it by its strap, the man succeeded only in hauling him forward.

Cal did not resist. He bowed, as the man ripped the guitar off over his head and tossed it aside. 'You're a bloody fool,' the man started roaring. 'Play a few songs, the man said. Bit of music on a Saturday night. What's not to like about that? *One more song*. The rest of us can't hear ourselves bloody think.'

'Our Alf's called this bar his own since he was a lad – never a more peaceful soul could you know. Did he deserve that? Well, did he?'

Cal's lips parted. Lily felt sure he was about to apologise – but he never got the chance, because out of the clot of men at the bar, another man came charging. 'I'll wipe the soppy look from your face,' he thundered. 'Long hair like that, you look like a bloody girl. Well, go on then, put them up!'

His fists were raised.

Cal's, somehow, were not.

'No!' Lily screamed out. 'Stop!' She cast herself forward, skittering around the sides of the tables, until she was almost in front of Cal. 'Stop!' she screamed again. 'It was only an accident. Only a—'

The man's shoulder connected with Lily. In seconds, she was on the ground. The man, heedless of what he'd done to her, brought back his fist and drove it directly into Cal's face.

Now there was silence.

'Love Me Do' seemed a generation ago.

'Well, go on, lad!' somebody else cried out. 'Hit him back!'

'You don't just stand there when someone's hit you, you sorry git. Lamp him!'

*

Cal looked around the room. The blow had snapped back his head. His eyes darted to Lily, still sprawled on the ground. They roamed the bar, seeing every baying face. They landed, at last, on the man who'd struck him, purple veins throbbing in his neck.

Cal lifted his open palms, backed away an inch, then an inch again. In silence, he stepped over the fallen Lily, somehow finding his way to the piano, and the place where his brown leather jacket had been left. Then, slinging it on his shoulders – and followed by gales of laughter – he started to run.

It was Max who caught up with him. He was halfway down the street when the young dancer's voice ordered him to stop. Even then, Cal ploughed on. It was only when he heard the pounding of footsteps, and Max gripped him by the shoulder, wheeling him around, that Cal ceased running.

'What in hell was that?' Max snapped. 'A fine bit of showmanship, Cal, to start a fight the second night we're even in town.'

Cal turned. 'I didn't start any fight in there, Max. You can't have been watching.'

'You were baiting him, Cal – you know you were.'

'And when have you ever been in a fight?'

Max just laughed. 'You don't know a thing about me. Matter of fact, I boxed for a time. Schoolboy stuff, but enough to see what you were doing. By God, Cal, I've heard about you – I heard all the stories they used to tell. Wild Cal Forsyth, doing as he pleases, just because he can. But we're in town until the end of the month, Cal! We have to live among these people. You bloody fool, you've forgotten what it is to be with a travelling Company.'

'Lay off of him, Max.' It was Lily's voice. Cal looked up, to discover she'd come rushing after them, out of the bar. 'Seems to me *you're* the one picking a fight now, Max – and without Evie to even see you doing it, the whole knight-in-shining-armour act rather falls short, don't you think?'

Max's golden eyes flared, swinging between Cal and Lily. 'We're meant to be promoting the Forsyths, not stirring up trouble. What would Ed say, if it was me? What if it was you, Lil? There'd be a dressing down. We'd be on a warning. We'd get pay docked. But Cal? Cal's hardly been back in town a night and he's already—'

'Look,' Cal snapped. 'I didn't mean it. I was just playing for them. It's hardly my fault if . . .' He saw the way they were look-ing at him, some level of understanding, some of disbelief. 'To hell with them anyway. They don't know good music. Just like those grey suits at Decca. They don't know what they're talking about.'

Cal turned to stalk off. This time, it was only Lily that fol-lowed. She struggled to keep pace, bouncing along in his wake. 'Just go back in there, buy the man a pint. Stand them all a few drinks. They'll forget about it soon enough.'

'No,' Cal stated, bold and simple.

'No?' Lily balked. 'No?'

'I'm not going near them, Lil. They'll start it again. There'll be trouble. Don't you see? I just don't want trouble.'

'Oh, I saw it clear enough,' said Lily. She stopped dead, feet rooted to the ground, even though Cal marched on. 'I saw it from where I was, on that bar-room floor. Didn't want to stand up for me, did you, Cal? One of the Company, brushed aside like that, and you didn't even say a word. You wouldn't have been like that once. You were strong. You cared about the Company. Cared too much, if I remember.' She shouted after him, 'Why didn't you fight for me? Cal, you've fought before – you've fought, and recently. I saw it. I saw it, Cal!'

Up ahead, Cal slowed down. He looked once over his shoulder. 'I don't get into fights, Lily. There's not one of them worth it.'

She scampered up to him. 'But tell me, Cal. There's bruises

all over your ribs. That cut in your side – it looks like it hasn't even been seen by a doctor. You weren't shy about showing it. You must want to tell someone. And…' All the anger of a few moments ago seemed to fade. She reached out, a fluttering hand to his side. There it hovered, not yet daring to touch. 'Tell me, Cal. Maybe… maybe I could make it better?'

Cal stepped towards her. He leaned down, as if he might kiss her.

And kiss her he did, as chastely as a brother, his lips barely touching her cheek as he said, 'I'm sorry for tonight, Lily. Tell the others, won't you? I didn't want to cause a ruckus. I would have stayed, but I didn't want it to get any worse.'

As Cal bowed into the darkness further along the seafront, he glanced back to see Lily standing there for a moment, before she turned and walked back to the Fairview Hotel. Then he started running. Somewhere along the seafront, the horror of what had happened in the bar washed over him. He wanted to scream, but to scream out here would only invite more attention – and attention was the last thing he needed tonight.

He was plodding his way back into town, having left the edges of Seaford far behind, when he saw the flashing blue lights and heard the siren's wail. If anything could have drummed the fear back into him tonight, it was that – so, finding a space between two shopfronts, an alley where bins were being picked over by the rats so often prevalent in seaside towns, he waited in darkness until the sirens had gone.

Then, slowly – making certain the sirens had not been for him – he sloped back towards the Seagate Theatre.

One more night in the double-decker bus that was his birth-right.

But Cal Forsyth didn't sleep one wink.

5

For Richer, For Poorer

It was the habit of Ed's lifetime to be awake before the rest of the players in his Company. This was the pattern he'd inherited from his father and grandfather before him, as a way of quietly assuring the Company that there was a leader in place. 'The lesson of kings,' his father had told him, the morning after the first Royal Command. 'Make no mistake: King George didn't need to stage the show last night. The funds we raised for the Benevolent Fund might easily have just been skimmed from the King's own coffers. The point was to be *seen*, and that's what you must be too, Ed. Yes, to lead an empire is not unlike leading a little company like ours.'

This morning, Ed was up earlier than ever, standing outside the back of the theatre with his pipe puffing grey tobacco smoke, while he persistently turned the gold band around his ring finger. Once upon a time, the wedding band had fitted him more snugly than it did now. He supposed that was the effect of the ages, or else one of the manifold aftershocks of grief. Nobody told you it could change you quite as viscerally as it did.

He was still spinning it, perhaps even a little hypnotised by it – John Lauder would have been proud – when he heard the backstage door opening, and Evie joined him in the early morning cold.

'It's a little early for you, isn't it, Evie? I thought you might, perhaps, have been ... well, warm in bed, shall we say?' He let the words linger, while he blew one last smoke ring into the air. 'With your dancing companion ... Max?'

Ed hadn't meant for Evie to pale in horror quite as much as she did. As soon as he saw it, he reached for her hand. 'I'm not a prude, Evie. I'm not a devil. But nor am I ... blind. I wasn't blind when you met that young man in Bordeaux, and I wasn't blind when you started falling for Jackson's nephew, at the costume store up in Leeds. You're twenty-nine years of age, Evie. If you hadn't fallen in love, had your heart broken, broken a couple yourself, you wouldn't be human.' With Evie still speechless, he tapped out his pipe, wrapped it in muslin cloth, and slid it into his pocket where it always remained. 'I sometimes think it's my fault.'

This was the first thing that cajoled Evie towards breaking her silence. 'Your fault, Dad?'

'The varieties isn't just a job, is it? Not for those, like you and me, who grow up with it. It's the very ordering of life. If you hadn't spent so much time on the road, you might be a mother by now. A settled life.'

'But not the life I want,' Evie said, with a deepening smile.

'If I hadn't lost myself, after your mother ... If you hadn't needed to lead this lot, while I was ... lost to myself ...' Ed faltered a little before he went on. 'I'm proud of you, Evie. That's what I'm trying to say. I know you've given years of your life to keeping us afloat. So ... I'm glad you're getting to live a little now. Just promise me you'll be careful, won't you?'

'Dad ...'

'No, Evie, I want you to promise me this. I can't tell you what to do, and, if Max is your future, I'll be as happy for you as my father was for me when I asked your mother to take my hand.'

He had started spinning his wedding band again. 'But take care, won't you? I've…' There was something he wanted to say, but some custom, some tradition, perhaps, almost persuaded him not to say it. Then he took a breath and ventured, 'I've seen plenty of babies born out of wedlock in the varieties, Evie. There's nothing like an unexpected child to change a course of a life. And…' He trailed off as she turned away, her cheeks burning crimson.

She lay her hand on his shoulder, still not looking him in the eye. 'I'll be all right, Dad. And I'm not going anywhere. This Company's my home. The truth is, I don't know what it is with Max. He's younger than I am. He's scarcely been with us six months. Who's to say, in six months' time, he isn't with a troupe dancing in Paris, or Milan, or California? He wouldn't be the first to come and go. And yet… I feel something. I don't know how to put it any simpler than that.'

Now, Ed, gazing at his feet, reached up to pat the back of her hand. 'I love you, Evie.'

'And you, Dad.'

Then, into the silence that followed, Evie said, 'I thought I'd come down here to talk about Cal, not about Max. How did you know?'

Ed just shrugged. 'This is my Company. I know everything about it. Everything… except what my son's doing here. Except what he wants.' He turned to face her. 'Evie, I know you didn't vote for him to come back – but you didn't vote for him to be sent packing, either. Does it mean there's a chance?'

'To forgive and forget?'

She had said it with at least an ounce of opprobrium, but Ed wondered if there was some hope there too. 'Not to forget, no. But to… rewrite the act.'

At that moment, Ed took his hand away from hers. 'Think about it, Evie. And – well, find him something to do, today.

95

Just until I get back. Something that isn't bacon and eggs, or that stunt he pulled with the burger van. Make him feel useful, somehow.' Ed saw the way she was looking at him, with mild disdain. 'Do it for me. Do it for the Company. He's all anyone's talking about now, but by evening all that's going to change.' He smiled, and picked his way to the corner of the theatre. From here he could see the double-decker and the canary-yellow Ford Anglia which had been scrubbed clean yesterday evening. Now it stood there gleaming. 'Wish me luck, Evie. It's going to be a night to remember.'

It wasn't often that Ed did his own driving – perhaps that was why, as he guided the Ford Anglia into the east, he felt a strange sense of freedom; the sense that he was the one in control. As he left the seafront far behind, anticipating the first grey smudges of London's surrounds, he was filled with a sudden nostalgia for the days when that had been the case every season. In 1930, anything had seemed possible. Only ten years after he was demobbed, the world had lurched into its great depression, leaving scant few families with enough leftover money to visit the variety theatre. But Ed himself had never felt more alive. With a new wife at his side, twin children about to be born – and the Company handed to him for stewardship into the future, he had felt as if the world was his to recreate as he saw it.

He got a flavour of that old feeling now, as he left motorways and petrol stations behind to join, once more, with London – the city where it had all truly begun.

London, 1962 – how vibrant it was compared to those earlier grey days when his father had brought him to sing for the King. By the time he reached the West End – where the double-deckers were thronging Oxford Circus, and the dazzling bill-boards of Piccadilly advertised Max Factor and Coca-Cola, the twin wonders of the Modern Age – he fancied himself twenty years younger. There was time to kill before his appointment – he'd set off early, but only because the anticipation wouldn't let him wait – so he idled for a while in front of the Palace Theatre, took tea in one of the eateries on St Martin's Lane, left his car in a side road and set forth for the London Palladium, if only to breathe in the dream of it all. There the Palladium sat, only a stone's throw from the hubbub of Oxford Street, quiet now, but holding within it all the anticipation that had been building in Ed his entire life.

It was, perhaps, strange that the Forsyth Varieties had not performed here before – but that would make the upcoming event so much the sweeter. The Palladium's grand white edifice was more like a palace than it was a variety theatre. Certainly, of all the hundreds Ed had played at, it would be the largest, with seats in the stalls and galleries for more than two thousand patrons – and boxes for yet more. He'd come as a boy, back when there was no Palladium on this site at all – in the days when it had been a wooden construction, housing a skating rink with real ice. His mother, whose star had risen through the ballrooms of London before she'd come to the varieties, had brought her every talent to bear, leading the young Ed Forsyth out onto the ice. In times earlier still, there'd been a menagerie here, the Corinthian Bazaar, with birds of exotic plumage, too many and too wonderful to name. A site of such luminous history was certainly fit for a king. Certainly fit for a variety performer too.

At midday, Ed headed to the Buckingham Hotel, with its ornate colonnades and its uppermost turrets tinged in copper like a crown, as if to remind both passers-by and patrons of its royal warrant.

He might have felt like an impostor, walking up the first of the hotel's sweeping marble steps, if only he hadn't felt the righteous purpose in his heart. As he reached the revolving brass doors – they'd been a fitting at the Buckingham Hotel since long before the war and were the hotel's icon, just as the Ritz had its name in flashing lights – the doorman inclined his head in greeting, then stood back to invite Ed onward, as if he truly belonged. And that was how he felt, as he went through into a vast reception hall, chequered in black and white, where concierges and porters spun past, and a striking glass obelisk, ringed in potted ferns, drew every eye.

'Sir,' Ed said, on approaching the check-in desk. 'I'm to meet an old friend, in the Candlelight Club. I understand that's on the third storey?'

'Indeed, sir,' said the desk attendant. 'Might I ask who you're to meet?'

Ed had been hoping he might ask. 'Mr Bill Martin and his entourage are expecting me.'

'Quite, sir,' said the desk attendant, as if this was the most ordinary thing in the world. And perhaps it was, to the souls who peopled this hotel. Ed had heard they'd kept foreign kings and crown princes and their governments-in-exile here during the war. A place with history like this did not, perhaps, even notice Bill Martin.

But not Ed Forsyth...

The Candlelight Club, so called because it once opened only for the evening hours, was brighter and more colourful than its name suggested. A concierge had been appointed to show Ed the way and as soon as he stepped through the doors, he was hit by the intoxicating smells of coconut and rum coming from the cocktail bar, and the warm sounds of chatter over the tables populating the open floor.

'This way, sir,' said the concierge, but, by now, Ed had spied the familiar broad shoulders of his old friend sitting at a table.

'I can take it from here, sir,' said Ed, and started sauntering forward.

'Even so, sir,' said the concierge. 'Decorum dictates.'

Decorum dictates. Ed was ever-so-slightly chastened by this, for he'd quite forgotten his opulent surrounds. Not that it mattered; the moment Ed got close to the table Bill was on his feet, turning around, and with a dazzling white smile (the teeth were certainly new, thought Ed), throwing his arms open wide.

'Teddy Boy!' he exclaimed, in an accent as far removed from the one he'd grown up with as land was from sea. 'Teddy Boy, come here, let me take a look at you!' This Bill did, first wrapping his meaty arms around Ed, and then stepping back to pinch his cheeks, like an over-enthusiastic grandmother might a child she'd not seen all summer long. Caught quite off-guard, Ed half expected Bill to declare, 'My, how you've grown!', but soon the smothering had finished, and he was shaking Bill's enormous hand energetically instead.

Bill Martin – or Will Richards, as Ed had once known him – had always been a bear of a man. In his varieties days, he'd played that to his advantage; there was nothing to give you a bit of automatic stage presence like dwarfing the rest of the players with whom you shared a stage. Since then, the years had been kind to him. Most variety performers kept in good health into their dotages – Ed himself had shrunk with the years, but he fancied himself as wiry and strong as ever – and the sunnier climes in which Billy had latterly spent his life evidently suited him. His hair was raven black (Ed suspected some dye had been applied to it, for even in his younger days Bill had been silvery), and his skin was as golden as the watch that dazzled from his wrist and the chain around his neck. The suit he was wearing, a midnight-blue affair, sparkled with yet more golden thread.

Even in the opulent surrounds of the Buckingham Hotel, Bill Martin radiated wealth.

'Come on, you old rascal, take a seat, take a seat! We've got a pitcher of iced tea right here. No, don't look at me like that, Teddy Boy, I knocked the liquor on the head eight years ago. I did it for Magdalene,' he indicated a blonde beauty at the table, who instantly lifted herself to take Ed's hand, 'but I also did it for myself. I've never felt more alive, Teddy. Sixty-eight years old, but I feel like a boy.'

There was scarcely room at the table thanks to Bill's three burly minders but Ed was happy to squeeze among them. Soon, Bill had summoned a waiter, then two, who delivered canapés as if this was some evening soirée – and, although Ed had been looking forward to a tot of his favourite bourbon (it had been Bill's drink, once upon a time), the iced tea was sweet enough to induce a little childish joy. It felt like summer, now that he was sitting with Bill Martin.

'Teddy, this is Magdalene, my wife,' Bill said.

'Charmed,' the golden-haired beauty said, in the richest Californian accent.

She was as young as Evie, Ed thought, but of course that didn't surprise him. Back when they played the varieties together, Bill had not had much luck in his romantic life. Ed had found Bella, but Bill had stumbled from one flummoxed affair to another, always wearing his heart on his sleeve but never quite capturing another's. Of course, success often changed things for a man. As Bill's star rose, so did his confidence – and it was this, Ed had always been sure, which had transformed the fortunes of his romantic life. The last time Ed and he had met, in France to entertain the troops, Billy had spoken of a Deborah, who herself was distinct from the Susannah he'd been romancing when their paths crossed in thirty-six. What had happened to Deborah,

Ed wasn't quite sure. What had happened to Susannah was less clear still. But here was Magdalene, young and – by the way she took in Bill, with fluttering eyelashes and a genuine purr every time he cracked wise – very much in love. 'It's her first time in Blighty, you know? Blighty,' Bill said, touching Magdalene's hand. 'It's what we call it. Good old Blighty. It's strange to be home, Ed. Time moves so fast, but London moves faster. It feels different, every time I'm back.'

'When were you last back?'

'Oh, there've been concerts, Teddy Boy. The Hippodrome in fifty-eight – that was a good one. We filmed *Sunset Serenade* here in fifty-six. I sang for Lord Lassiter at his estate in Suffolk that same summer. But what you've got in line, Teddy, that's the cherry on the cake. The pinnacle of a career. Mean to finish how you started? Is that it, Teddy?' Ed would have responded, but apparently a second's silence was too much for Bill Martin. 'I told you, Maggie, Ed here's the cherub of choice for the royal family. Sixteen years old, he sang for the King. Now he's bring-ing his Company back for royalty again. It's a damn good thing you've done for me, Ed, inviting me in on this. I'll make it good for you. Now, I don't mean to retire – not any time soon – but this will be the thing to kick me up again. Hollywood's a harsh mistress, Teddy – it likes to knock you down, and you have to keep reminding it you're there, so it pulls you back up. No, I reckon the studio will be chomping at the bit after this perform-ance. By this time next year...' Only now did Bill realise he hadn't allowed Ed any space to answer his question. 'Retirement, Teddy? Are you really cut out for it?'

'I think so,' Ed quietly replied. 'You and I took very different paths, old friend. There's still joy and beauty in the varieties, but there isn't much comfort, not out on the road nine months of every year. It takes its toll on the bones.'

'What you need is a company masseuse.'

At this, Magdalene gave a laugh so shrill Ed had to stop himself wincing.

'I'm serious, Ed. The studios lay it on in California. They look after their stars. You could bring a bit of that style glamour to the Forsyths. Look after your talent. You don't want to go losing them to – what was their name? The Homburgs?'

Ed nodded gravely. 'They came after a lot of our own, after Bella died.'

Bill's jaw started to wobble, almost as if the tenderness he was about to play was put on – and yet Ed had known him for so long, he knew it was real. He'd adored Bella, back when they were young.

'Oh, Teddy.'

Ed nodded. 'It's been a few years, Bill. I'm back on my feet. Back on my feet and ready to put this show together. Once more, for the Forsyths.'

'That's the spirit, Teddy, old boy. Bella was a great girl. But hang those vultures who came to pick apart the Forsyths. It's not them who're singing for the Queen this month, is it? It's not them who'll sign off their careers, giving Her Majesty the night of her life!'

Some of the more salubrious patrons of the Candlelight Club must have heard this last comment, for they turned sharply at the rising inflection of Bill's voice, as if having overheard some treachery. As for Bill, he didn't seem to mind. 'It's all about the attention.' He grinned, the great black thatches of his eyebrows wiggling up and down. 'So tell me, Ed. What have you got planned for this show to end all shows?'

This, at least, was what Ed wanted to speak about. 'It's to be a singular piece, Bill. None of the old-fashioned "one act after another" kind of thing, with me introducing each piece.

This one's going to be seamless. We'll run the dancing straight into the dog act, the dog act straight into the aerials, the aerials into the dancing again – and, in the heart of it all, John's new illusion. And there you'll be too, Bill. Evie's dancers will open up, and reveal you in the spotlight.' He stopped. He was only just warming up. 'We haven't got it pinned down yet, not in its details – but this is how it's going to be. One extravaganza, the whole Company working together, telling the story of our last fifty years: from the night of the first Royal Command, to the night we're up there, on the stage. And Bill, if you're game for it, if you really will work with the Company, we'll come up with something that won't ever be forgotten.'

'Oh, Teddy.' Bill beamed. 'You can bet your bottom dollar on it.'

'I'm going to stoke the anticipation for it, Bill. I haven't told the Company yet – but, next weekend, we're opening the Seagate. Tonight – though they don't know it yet – the troupe will be putting posters up across town. The Seagate Spectacular, that's what we're going to call it. A big one-off, to iron out the kinks – just like we'd do in the old days, before hitting the road.' He paused, for now came the question he had been trying to frame all day long, the gambit that, he felt sure, would stoke the keenest anticipation of all. 'Will you sing with us, Bill? You'd go down in legend: Hollywood come, without warning, to the end of Seagate pier.'

It had been his gambit all along, but now that he said it out loud, he wondered if he'd reached too far. The posters he'd had printed, the ones that were hidden in rolls in the office on the double-decker bus, had the legend *FEATURING A NEVER-TO-BE-FORGOTTEN MYSTERY GUEST!* emblazoned across the bottom. It had been a hope, just a vain hope – but, looking into his old friend's eyes, he knew, now, that it could be real.

Yet Bill drew back, kneading his bejewelled hands together in suspicion. 'Now, I don't know, Ed,' he drawled. 'It isn't what I signed up for. A provincial little dump like the Seagate?'

A *dump*, thought Ed. No, the Seagate wasn't a dump. But perhaps a man who'd sung at Carnegie Hall could never see it like that.

'I know, Bill, and that's why this will go down in legend. That's why your name will ring through the ages. Bill Martin, who never forgot where he came from. Bill Martin, who lives the Hollywood high life – but still loves the little local venues where he came up.' Ed paused, unable to sense if he was sailing with the wind or against it. 'I know it's not usual. But we're not in the business of the ordinary, are we? You and I never were and what would be more extraordinary than this?'

Bill still looked perturbed.

'What's the security like at this dump?' one of his henchmen interjected.

'Frankie,' Magdalene gasped. 'I'm sure it's not a dump! The Forsyth Varieties are legends this side of the water. They'd never perform in a squalid little hole ... would you?'

The Seagate might not have been the Hippodrome but it was everything Ed loved about the varieties. It had history. You could hear the echoes of past performances every time you walked through its halls.

'I'll make the security work. Not a soul will know Bill's with us – and he'll be gone the moment the house lights go up. You have my word.'

Bill beamed. 'The word of an Englishman. It's his bond!' And he reached across the table, this time not to stroke but to shake Ed's hand.

He was shaking it still when, with a widening grin, he said, 'Mystery guests, stirring up intrigue, ambushing the audience – Eddie, old man, it's almost American, that kind of showmanship! You never used to like American things. You always said it was too showy. But this? Well, it's almost like...' He stopped, for a sudden thought had occurred. 'It's like you've started taking lessons from that son of yours. Errant, wayward Cal. I remember, Ed, he was already driving you to distraction by the time he was thirteen years old. Already fancying himself a star.'

Ed looked up. This time, it was his turn to grin. He was still shaking Bill's hand, and there seemed something perfect in that: two old friends, separated by the oceans, coming back together and picking up where they'd last left off. Making a deal.

'Well, it's funny you should say that,' said Ed wryly. 'Because that storm's been blowing through the Company again.' He detached his hand and lay them flat on the table, then looked his old friend directly in the baby-blue eyes. 'Bill, about Cal...'

6

The Seaside Stars

In the stalls at the Seagate Theatre, while Evie took Lily and a few of the other girls through their paces on the stage, Max sat in shadow. No dancing shoes for him, not this morning. Just a pen and paper in his hand, and an envelope waiting to be stuffed.

Dear Nana
You will be pleased to know that I have reached English shores once again! I know how you worry for me when I travel, and that I have never been away as far or as long before. But Monaco and the Mediterranean were everything I dreamed of.

    I fear, however, it may be some weeks before I can come home. Preparations for our appearance at the Royal Variety have begun in earnest! Nana, it is the legend of the Forsyths that our Company leader, Ed, sang at the very first Royal Command show. Now, it is to be me who dances for the Queen. We have come to a little theatre on the south coast, the Seagate in Seaford town, to prepare our show. And something about this place has set me to thinking about all those summers we would spend at Aunt Mae's house in Rye. I don't know why, but it has got me feeling nostalgic. For summers on the sands. For those endless weeks, when it was only you and me – and for all the stories you would tell me about my mother, and the seasons you spent on those same sands together. It's been so long since I thought this – and, of course, I never truly knew her, so perhaps it is all a figment of the imagination – but I have been picturing my mother, watching me in Monaco, watching me, even, at the Palladium itself. I think I am right in thinking it would have brought her enormous joy to know that her son, who became a dancer just like she did, is to dance for the Queen.

Nana, there is something else. We are to combine with a Special Guest for the performance at the Palladium. Nana, I did not expect this. Never in my wildest dreams did I think I would ever cross paths with this man. I am not even certain I should tell you this, but Bill Martin is to sing with us in London . . .

'She's a fan, is she?'

Cal, who had settled in the seat behind him, watched as a startled Max almost dropped his pencil. The dancer shot up in his seat and the letter flurried up with him, eventually landing in Cal's lap. Cal passed the letter straight back, but he'd read enough already, peering over Max's shoulder.

Max, purpling with humiliation, scrambled the half-written missive into the envelope, fixed Cal with a glare. 'I'm beginning to see why they called you "the storm". Everything you touch, everywhere you go, seems to tip towards disaster.'

Cal grinned.

'I wasn't meaning to surprise,' Cal began. 'But I thought we should talk. I wanted to say, about last night—'

'It isn't me you ought to be talking to,' said Max, and together their eyes drifted to the stage, where Evie was instructing Lily in a synchronized can-can, an idea she'd had for the show's opening number, and meant to hark back to the Forsyths' music-hall beginnings in Manchester.

'Well, that's rather why I thought we should talk first. You've got my sister's ear. You've got her heart, by all accounts. And, yes, I know you've been scurrying around trying to keep it secret, but I could see it within half a day of walking back in here, so there's not a lot of point blushing about it now. I don't think you're very good at keeping secrets, Max.'

Max instinctively tightened his hold on his pencil and paper – as if that loving message to his grandmother hid something too.

'If you want to talk to her, then talk to her. She's not a monster. She's hurt – hurt by you.'

Up on stage, the can-can had stopped. One of the stagehands had started calling down from the rigging above, and soon coils of rope were unfurling, until they almost reached the stage floor. Evie dismissed Lily and the other dancers, then set to testing the ropes herself, first tugging at them for tightness, then running them through her hands as if to familiarise herself with their texture.

Cal liked watching her work. He could still remember the first day she'd swung on a trapeze (she'd called it 'the trapee' as a girl, her lisp making the word too difficult), and the first time their mother had let her walk on a tightrope more than two feet off the ground. Dancing and acrobatics went hand in hand; both arts depended on strength and balance. There was scarcely an art of the stage that didn't demand confidence too, but Evie's art certainly did: you did not let yourself unravel on a rope from the rigging to the stage, unless you were supremely confident of your landing.

Cal was still watching when he said, 'I'm afraid she won't listen.'

Max snorted. 'Well, that's your fear to conquer, Cal. I'm quite sure you're cocksure enough to—'

'No, Max,' Cal said, darting a look to his side, where Max was preparing to sit back down and return to his letter. 'I mean right *now*.'

'Cal, for goodness' sake – she's working! Have some bloody respect. That's exactly what she said you'd be like: striding back here like you've never left, expecting everyone to pay attention, expecting everyone to dance to your tune. Well, maybe she needs a little bit of time. If you grew up like I did – no father, mother in her grave by the time I was two, living hand-to-mouth with my grandmother – you'd know that, sometimes, things just take a little bit of time. And after all you've—'

'No, you *dolt*,' Cal snapped. It was the harshest word he could think of that wouldn't automatically provoke a fight but as soon he said it, he felt foolish. 'I mean I'm afraid she won't listen right *now*. That rigging she's using's the old set. Bloody fools in this theatre have just left it hanging there – but it's from the last bloody century. They had new ropes, new fixtures fitted three summers ago. I should know, because I was singing here back then. She could fall to her death from those ropes, I should think – and she's about to climb them.'

Cal was right: up on stage, Evie was preparing to scale the ropes. Chances were, she just wanted to test them first, to see how it felt to be so high above this particular stage. Later, she'd set up the harnesses, the trapeze, perhaps even the rings and silks with which she had performed so beautifully over the years. But Cal had seen accidents in a theatre before. 'Well, go and stop her, you fool! If she won't talk to me, she'll have to talk to you.'

Max had the look of a startled rabbit. He vaulted over the seats in the stalls, hit the aisle and ran to the stage.

Languorously, Cal sat down. Max had left his letter lying on the seat beside him; Cal picked it up and put it in his pocket, meaning to return it once the rehearsal was over. After that, he thought nothing of it: the further adventures of a boy and his beloved grandma were of little interest to Cal, especially if they were fawning over a star like Bill Martin. Instead, he watched as Max pulled the ropes away from Evie, explaining to her – with arms as wild and expressive as in any tempestuous dance scene – that the rigging wasn't right. Soon, Evie was peering upwards, in the unseen blackness above the stage. Max began shouting at the stagehands still up there, then vanished backstage to scale the ladders and deliver the message himself.

Now it was Evie, alone on the stage. She turned to face Cal. He saw, then, that her eyes were furrowed – as if not quite believing, or not quite wanting to believe, what Cal had done. She fixed him with a look. 'Well,' she said, 'I suppose it's time you and I talked.'

The sea was grey that day, but there was sun enough – and the wind, coming in over the waves, was gentle enough – that a walk along the seafront was not out of the question.

'I didn't come back here to stir up trouble, Evie.'

Evie tensed. It was, she decided, the worst of all possible beginnings – because, only this morning, the bar manager from the Fairview Hotel had been lurking outside the Seagate Theatre, looking to speak to 'whichever one of you runs this rabble.' 'He was apoplectic, Cal. He said his regulars were claiming they'd go drinking elsewhere. That he was changing the face of the hotel, and all because you stirred things up down there. He said that punches were thrown, Cal. *Punches.* A few days back with the Company, and there's already some fire I've got to—'

'That wasn't on me, Evie.' Cal had been ready to pour out apologies but he felt a sudden surge of righteous fire now. 'They asked me to go and play there. I was fulfilling an obligation. And it wasn't me who threw any punches. In fact—'

'I don't care who it was, Cal.' Evie had to rein herself in, because all the old anger was suddenly coursing through her as well. She had to focus on the words John had relayed last night just to see the other side of the red mist descending upon her. *Blood was thicker than water*, their mother had said. Well, sometimes she could only see the blood. 'The point is trouble loves you. You invite it in.' Frustrated, Evie ran her hands through her hair. 'You don't get it, Cal. You never did. Running the Company's about so much more than ... *performance.*'

Even as she said the words, Evie could feel some element of the old confrontations coming back. 'All the apologies in the world didn't matter to the man from the Fairview, Cal. He was looking for a few songs for an evening, not a rock-and-roll concert. Not to push away all his clientele. You've got to play to the audience you've got, Cal – not the one you *want.*'

'Sometimes a crowd doesn't know what they want until they hear it,' he ventured.

'I'll tell you what I don't want to hear,' said Evie. '*That.*'

'It's not rubbish, Evie, it's—'

'I don't care!' she yelled, giving vent to her frustration at last. 'I care about the Company. I care about our standing in the towns we visit. Rocking and rolling might work out there, Cal, but this is variety. It's for families. It's for everyone.'

Something had mellowed in Evie now. For a time, they walked on, in stretches of stilted silence.

'I thought about you a lot,' said Cal. 'I know you don't want to hear it, but I don't know if there's any point not being honest, so there it is. Every time our birthday came around, I wondered if I should come back. I always knew where the Forsyths were, of course. And ... well, Christmas Day, the day we were born, it wasn't so great being on my own. But I didn't know if there was a place for me, not after everything that got said.'

'Christmases have been empty for a few years, Cal. I can't say I've thought much about birthdays either. Just about getting from one month to the next. Making sure enough of the troupe stayed on, making sure there were enough engagements – making sure Dad didn't just walk out into the sea one morning and never come back.'

'I should have done more,' said Cal.

'You should,' said Evie.

It was easier to speak when you didn't look directly at one another.

'I don't want to make excuses,' said Cal. 'I did what I did. But maybe you can understand how it was that night? Maybe, just for a moment, you can understand *why*. It wasn't for my glory, Evie. I didn't know what else to do. What other kind of life was there to live? So I put down the piano, and I picked up a guitar. There are clubs enough to play at. There's money, if you can prove you're good enough for it. And maybe those records I cut weren't hits, but they were on the radio and I was eking it out, bit by bit. Wrote a few songs for Decca. They launched some acts with those songs I wrote. But I didn't leave the Varieties to chase my own star. I did it because – because …'

'Say it, Cal,' said Evie. She was trying not to be defensive, trying to keep in mind that message her mother had sent her from beyond the grave. 'Just say it. If there's any way to be brother and sister again, it has to start like this.'

So Cal said, 'I thought he'd end up hating me, Evie.'

Evie was still. It was not what she had been expecting.

'Mum was gone, and he was a ruin – and all I really wanted was to make the Forsyths reborn. Everything I did used to turn to gold, when Mum was alive. But after she was gone … it wasn't the Midas touch I had. Everything I touched was poison after that. The Company was in trouble, and I wanted to help it survive. I really tried, but everything I did just... well, it led to explosions.'

Nice, 1957: balmy and bright, the evenings filled with the sounds of crickets in the orange groves and the susurrations of the sea.

The anniversary of Bella's death was hoving into view, and perhaps the hardest thing about that was that it had barely been mentioned in the preceding months. Three months ago, the Forsyths had embarked for their first Continental tour since that devastating morning when Ed had woken up to find Bella scarcely breathing. 'Three months of sand and sun, and theatre in the open air,' Evie had said, trying to console their father one night, 'to make a new beginning.' But they ought to have known, by his reaction, that this summer was to be their passion, their crucible, the season from which they would emerge forever changed. It was those words, 'a new beginning', that set him off. Because Ed didn't want any new beginning. He wanted to live the last season with Bella, over and over again, without even a whisper of change.

'It can't go on,' said Cal, as that evening's performance approached. He and Evie had taken to having an early dinner together on the seafront, where sometimes the Company's fire jugglers – soon to accept an offer from the rival Homburg Varieties, and who could blame them when things were about to become so fractious and unrewarding? – performed parts of their wild, exuberant act to entice spectators into the theatre. Tonight, they were cartwheeling while their flaming brands flew in majestic arcs overhead, a hypnotic act of dance and fire. 'This show is stale, Evie. There's more excitement down there,' and he pointed at the jugglers, 'than there is on our stage. He's limping through his own routine. He's dead on his feet.'

Evie dropped her knife with a clatter. 'Unfortunate choice of words, Cal.'

But Cal didn't care. He just drank his beer, draining two thirds of the bottle in one go. This feeling had been stoking in him for months, but every time he tried to give it voice he just got shot down. Was it any wonder he'd taken to spending so much time away from the Company? Everywhere they went, every town they pulled into, he would go off and find a local bar, some hotel divorced from the rest, immerse himself with the locals – and the local girls – instead of with the Forsyths. The others might have thought it was because he considered himself better than them, but it just wasn't so. It was because, sooner or later, he was going to have to say what he actually thought – and what he actually thought was that his father was condemning them all.

The beer went straight to his head now. 'It's not working, Evie. It's just *not*. Last night, I walked out on stage and I could feel the indifference out there. Another few months like this, and the Forsyths' name is mud.'

Evie sighed. 'He needs a little more time.'

'There won't be any more time. He's wasting our time.'

'He's our father,' she said.

'Well, I'm not going to stand by and watch him do this. This is my life too.'

Now, Evie dropped her fork as well.

A round of applause, whoops and cheers, had risen up among the spectators. The fire jugglers had reached the zenith of their act, seeming to swallow and breathe out fire like the dragons of myth.

'Do you know what, Cal?' said Evie, standing up. 'I'm hurting too.'

She was already walking away when Cal, fumbling coins onto the table to pay for the meal, hurried after her. 'I know you are, Evie. I know. But this – this *rot* – isn't what Mum would have wanted. She'd want to see us embracing the new, not just withering away. And it's Dad – he won't let us help him.'

'What do you suggest?'

Cal said, 'I want to help him. We can still do this. And if you won't, well, Evie, *I* will.'

'Cal!' she called after him. 'Cal, don't be rash! Don't be—'

But Cal was already running.

There were still two hours before the show. Their father was sleeping in the double-decker, so when Cal got back to their camp he hurried to collect all the notes he'd been making across the last months and readied himself for what he had to say. Then, with scarcely an hour before the show – when the rest of the Company were already flocking to the theatre dressing rooms, steeling themselves for the night – he knocked on the door and roused his father.

'Cal,' Ed muttered, the empty bottle of whisky at his bedside still showing in the slurring of his voice, the trembling of his hand. 'Is it time?'

'Dad, we need to talk.' Cal's heart was hammering. How many times had he tried to have this conversation? Well, he had to go through with it tonight. 'The show isn't working. We're losing the audience, night after night. We survived it back home, but not out here. Dad, I've been talking to the rest of the troupe and—'

Cal's words seemed to have had an instant, sobering effect on Ed. He got to his feet, pushed past Cal.

'Haven't I already told you, son? The show goes on.'

'But that's exactly it, Dad. The show *must* go on. But it doesn't go on regardless. We can't keep serving them up the same as we were serving them last month, the month before, last Christmas. The word-of-mouth is waning. The stalls aren't full. Dad, I've got some ideas...'

'You'll do the show as we rehearsed it, Cal.'

Cal fumed. 'You may as well hire puppets!' Then he hurried after his father, who was stumbling along the theatre path. 'Dad, let me open tonight. I have a new piece. I've been rehearsing it all year. It's bombastic. It's triumphant. Mum would have loved it. Let me play it, and Evie and the others will dance. You can come in after that. It'll give you a little more time to—'

'To what, Cal?'

Cal fell behind. 'To sober up, Dad. To think. To see... There's a bad feeling in the Company. They know we're floundering. It's not like it used to be. And I know it's never going to be, but... we can be better. We can flourish.'

'We are flourishing.'

'We're not, Dad.' Ed had drifted ahead. 'We're drowning. And... and I don't want to drown.'

'It's not your Company, Cal. It's mine.'

Cal tried again the next night, and the night after that. But every time he tried, it only hardened Ed's resolve. And every time Ed pushed him away, Cal's certainty only hardened even further. 'I'm going to do it, Evie,' Cal said, one night outside the theatre. 'I'll just go out there and play. Dad will have to fall in line.'

'You can't ambush him, Cal.'

'But maybe it's the only way.'

'No,' Evie said. 'Let me talk to him. Leave it to me.'

But nor did that work, for Ed knew what his daughter was doing. 'You've let him eat away at you,' Ed said. 'Cal's been in your ear. I love him, Evie, but he's young and he's never been wise – not like you, my girl. He's headstrong and fearless. He gets that from your mother. But he doesn't see the bigger picture. He only sees himself.'

'But you're blind to it,' said Cal, bursting into the double-decker where Evie and their father had been talking. 'You're not seeing straight. I can lift the Company, Dad. I can do it for all of us. You've just got to give me the chance.'

'The *chance*?' thundered Ed, and his voice must have carried far beyond the double-decker's surrounds, for at the theatre that evening the whispers were all around. 'Every chance you ever had came from me and your mother, Cal. Or have you so easily forgotten? Well, *I* won't forget. *I* won't forget that it was she who sat with you and listened to you sing. *I* haven't forgotten how, without her, you wouldn't be able to dance or ride . . . or – or walk and talk, Cal! We go out there tonight to honour her. I won't hear any more of it.'

'Honour her?' shouted Cal. 'By grinding the Company into the ground, trying to bring her back? By God, Dad, I can't listen to it! I *won't* listen to it . . . just because you can't accept that she's gone!'

Ed barrelled towards him. It was only Evie, who slipped in between, that stopped them from coming to blows that night.

'Hit your beats, Cal!' Ed roared after him, as Cal fled. 'Sing it like we practised. The show goes on, Cal. *The show goes on!*'

The show goes on. Cal thought of those words as he hit the bar on the seafront. *The show goes on*. They resounded in his head as he drank his fifth beer and started shooting some pool with the local boys who worked the garage on the other side of the cove. *The show goes on*. With three hours to go before the curtain came up, one of the boys suggested they go for a drive to a little gambling den he knew in the mountains. *The show goes on*. With scarcely an hour to go before the curtain went up, he met a Frenchwoman a few years older than him and, accepting the offer of a cigarette from her, accompanied her on a stroll into the orange grove clinging to the mountainside.

The show goes on. The thought went clean out of his head when, kissing her there in the scented darkness, his body came alive – and all thoughts of the Forsyths were obliterated, as surely as the show would be when the curtain went up, to reveal an act without its star turn, a variety suddenly denuded of its single, most scintillating voice.

After that, the show did, indeed, go on without him – for, when he woke in the morning, it seemed clear to him, at last, that he could never go home.

And, until a few days before now, he never had.

Evie did not realise, until Cal was finished, that her eyes had started streaming. Reliving that night was like reliving a death – a second death, in the space of just a few months; the death of a world, and any chances for its resurgence. 'I didn't realise you were with a woman that night, Cal. Dead drunk somewhere, yes. Stropped off to play in some local bar, yes. But a woman, Cal? All *this*, for a woman?'

Of course, she hadn't been the first. Ed had lost himself in bitterness and drink when Bella died, Evie had lost herself in work – and Cal had lost himself in wild abandon. That cardinal rule that the Forsyths had followed for generations, that they should not fraternise with the residents of the towns they visited, that they should not invite the reputation of old carnival folk into their midst? Cal had broken it in towns all the way from Bognor to Milan.

Love was a perilous drug. One night was never enough. A man always wanted more. And, for a good-looking young man with a guitar, the 1950s was the age to come alive...

Evie turned away from him. She wasn't sure if she could look. 'A woman, Cal...'

'It's not like you think,' said Cal. 'I was drowning. Drowning, Evie. That night, it was just my raft. It was just a way to...'

'Not be where you should have been,' she snapped.

Blood was thicker than water. What on earth was her mother thinking? Maybe it was easier to forgive from beyond the grave. Maybe none of life's infinite troubles really mattered, once your heart had ceased to beat. But they mattered down here, in the world of flesh and blood. 'Cal, how could you?'

'I couldn't go on,' he said.

'You threw it all away! And I had to catch it! All the shreds you tore up, I had to piece them back together!'

They had reached the headland. Here, the road turned inland. Here, they stopped.

'I didn't stay away that night for a woman,' said Cal. 'I stayed away because... I was afraid.'

Evie glared at him. 'What have you *ever* been afraid of, Cal?'

Even now, Cal could not believe she didn't see. 'I was afraid of what would happen if I came back.'

This time, Evie's glare softened.

'That night terrified me, Evie. So I drank it away – and, yes, by the end of the night, I was whiling it away with the girl from the bar. But it was just to blot out the fear. All of it, Evie, to blot out the...' His words failed him. Sometimes, it seemed easier to put things in a song than it did to say them in simple words. 'If we went on how it was, it would all have been ruined. All of it, turned to cinders and ash.'

Evie snorted. 'It turned to ash anyway, Cal. You leaving turned it to ash.'

'Stay or go, it was ruined.'

'The difference was, you didn't stay to put it back together. I had to do that on my own.'

She turned away from Cal and began stalking back the way they had come.

'You pushed him too hard, Cal,' she called back. 'It's different now. I think he sees the future in a way he didn't back then. But Mum was dead, and all he wanted was things to stay the same. To make new acts, to change things up too much – it was like leaving her behind. He couldn't do it. And there you were, Cal, her spitting bloody image, telling him he had to wake up.' Evie wiped away a tear. 'He didn't want to wake up. He wanted to lie down with her, and curl up and go to sleep.'

Cal hurried to keep up. 'I know,' he said. 'I know.'

'And then you breeze back in here, and you start it up all over again! All over again, Cal!' She stopped dead, the fury coursing out of her. 'One night back with the Company, and trouble in town. If Dad hears about it, what do you think he's going to feel? He's going to be plunged right back there, back to Nice and Antibes and ... and every time you turned up drunk, every time some story flew round about what you were doing in the towns, raising hell, and ... and ...' The words died. 'What do you even want, Cal?'

'Want?' he whispered.

'Dad was going to announce his retirement. He'd told everyone about Bill Martin, and he was about to tell them that the Royal Variety would be his last performance with us. He was going to ...' Evie stopped short of saying 'hand me the Company' because something in her still doubted. 'You picked your moment well, that's all.'

'You've got all that wrong, Evie. I didn't come back to wrest the Company off you – or Dad. I didn't come back because of the Royal Variety or Bill Martin. I just came back because ...' He touched his side, and the bloody scar he'd been so foolish in revealing to Lily. 'I know I'm the storm. But storms peter out, don't they? They move on, and then there's sunshine.'

At that precise moment – because the Fates have a venal sense of humour – the grey clouds above opened, and fat droplets of rain fell on Evie and Cal.

'Six months, Evie. That's all I ask.'

And Evie thought back to John's wavering hand. She heard her father's voice echo as he bade the Company to make their votes – 'with your guts, my friends, the truest expression of your hearts' – and said, 'A truce, then. Six months, Cal.'

Cal's face blanched. 'Six months,' he said.

'But it isn't forgiveness,' she snapped. 'I haven't forgotten.'

Cal was silent.

'Now, let's get out of this rain. There's still a show to put together. I promised Dad we'd have something to show for ourselves by the time he gets back…'

By the time they reached the edges of Seaford, soaked through, neither could tell that the other one had been crying, their conversation turned to the Royal Variety to come, to the celebration of their father's fifty years.

'It has to be joyful,' said Evie. 'Full of wonder. That's all I can see. I keep thinking about Dad, sixteen and singing for the King – then, two years later, digging in in France to fight for him. Or all those boys who went off when we were small, to be killed in France all over again. And Dad out there cracking jokes for them, running his routines, John Lauder with his magic and Bill Martin singing – because they'd done their war, and now this was all they could do.' Evie trembled; the cold was creeping into her bones 'We didn't have war to remind us why we do this. But we do it for joy. We do it for wonder.'

'I reckon there's enough war in the world to remind us of that.' Cal looked out to sea.

'Well, that's it,' said Evie. 'That's exactly why. That's why we've got to keep going. Why we've got to make this Royal Variety the best performance we've ever given. We only get one chance, don't we? One chance on the stage. One chance at life. It isn't just for Dad. It's for us all.' She stopped as they reached the theatre, hovering in the shadow of the double-decker bus. A thought, niggling at the back of her mind until now, had just popped up. 'I didn't know you'd sung here already, Cal. I suppose you've been everywhere, played every club there is. But I'm grateful for what you knew about the rigging. Let's hope the boys have got the proper ropes down by now.'

'Oh, I wouldn't worry about that,' said Cal, striding back towards the theatre doors.

'No?'

'Well, the thing is, Evie – and while we're being *honest* with each other – there's only one set of rigging up there at all. It's sturdy as can be. Dependable as it'll be at the Palladium itself.' At least he had the decency to look sheepish about it. He shrugged. 'I needed you to speak with me, Evie. I needed your attention. Just couldn't think of any other way.'

Then he sprinted onwards, like he'd always done as a boy, desperate to be the one to reach the theatres first.

So much for full, frank honesty, thought Evie. She wasn't sure whether to rage at him or to just submit to the unruly chaos that was her brother.

Then, shaking her head ruefully, she too started to run.

It was time to dance.

Cal wanted to work with the dancers, to play the piano as they blocked out the spectacle to come, but Valentino was still sitting by the old upright and, sensing that the moment was not right to try and supplant him, even for these developmental sessions, Cal returned instead to the stalls and simply watched. His fingers longed to touch the ebony and ivory keys, but there was joy in just watching as well.

John Lauder had enlisted Davith in support of his act, and they were happily feeding Tinky and Tiny into the vanishing cupboard, then retrieving them, yapping forlornly, in odd corners of the stalls. When John was satisfied with the progress he'd made, he spent some time leading Lily, Max and the other dancers through the rudiments of the shadowgraphy he had in mind, and by the time evening fell, some semblance of an act had come together.

An extravaganza of movement and light that began with the can-can of a century ago, and then – with the shadow-dancing of two dozen hands, making a kaleidoscope on the back wall to illustrate the passage of time – marching through the decades. It was not perfect yet – there were gaps in the chronicle, a place where Ed himself might take stage, as if to recapture that moment in 1912, an elongated stretch where marching shadows might evoke those years of the Great War – but Cal saw enough to feel a frisson of envy that he was not at the centre of it.

'It should be the whole act,' he declared, when – some hours later – the rehearsal was petering out into periods of weariness and over-thought, the death knell of every creative endeavour. The troupe did not immediately hear him, for they were lost in their own musings, so he picked himself up and, vaulting through the stalls, met Evie and the others at the stage. 'It's sublime, Evie. It's *everything*.' Inwardly, he thought how the Ed Forsyth of five years ago would have excommunicated you for anything a fraction as adventurous as this – how times had changed while he'd been away.

'But... maybe you can go even further. The whole of the century, everything from Queen Victoria's reign up to Queen

Elizabeth, in one act. Well, it's what Dad's saying anyway, isn't it? Something that coheres, as a whole – all the different varieties, working as one. You've captured the first Royal Command. Then the Great War. Well, why not the Second as well? Why not the Battle of Britain? Spitfires and Junkers, tumbling over the roof of the very theatre where we'll be playing?'

'Where *we'll* be playing, Cal,' interjected Valentino, as if to remind Cal that there was no indication that he'd be joining them on stage so quickly, certainly not for the Queen.

Cal nodded, though the words were certainly more bruising than he'd thought. 'Evie, the music could change too. If you're starting with the can-can, and you're coming up through the music halls, then the ballrooms – well, it could end in rock and roll, couldn't it? It could end in...'

From somewhere behind, Lily sang the first few lines of 'Love Me Do'.

Cal could not stop beaming.

'Cal,' said Evie, guardedly. 'You're putting the cart before the horses again. It's the Royal Variety. There's got to be decorum. Something graceful, stately, regal.' But Cal could see she was turning it over in her mind. 'I'll need to speak to Dad. I'll need to think more. Maybe we can regroup in—'

'There'll be no time for that, I'm afraid.'

It was John's voice, from the pockets of darkness at the back of the stalls. Everyone turned to look at him.

'I believe this is one arrival you'll *all* want to see,' he called out. 'Even you, Cal – auspicious as your own Second Coming was, of course.'

Cal was not certain, but he thought he detected some wry amusement in John's tone as he turned to pick his way back through the theatre. Very quickly – for there was only one person this could be – the players started flocking through the stalls. Cal had to admit that the enthusiasm in the auditorium was infectious. He'd never met Bill Martin, but he'd heard of him so many times, in the stories his parents used to tell, the dances they'd share when Bill's songs came on the radio, the dazzling smile beaming out of record covers and the billboards that accompanied his every film.

'Something to tell your grandmother.' He grinned at Max as he passed, but Max only gave him a deathly stare – as if to say that, no matter what truce he and Evie had come to, it wasn't something Max could share. 'Are you coming?'

Max was hanging back, one of the last to leave.

'It's Bill Martin, Max! A finer showman you'll never have met.'

'Come on, Max,' said Evie, who was the last to leap down from the stage. 'These moments don't come very often.'

Cal, Evie and Max were the last to reach the Seagate doors. Darkness had already come and the pier was lit up in electric lights. On any other evening, those lights would have drawn the eye – but not tonight. Tonight, every eye was trained on the small convoy of vehicles that had just drawn into the car park: the yellow Ford Anglia out of which their leader, Ed, was stepping, and behind it the long burgundy limousine out of which two burly men, dressed in charcoal grey, were stepping.

The last vehicle disgorged another two men in charcoal grey. The first of these, hidden behind dark glasses, approached the back of the limousine and opened its door. The first figure to emerge was a young elfin woman, with golden-blonde hair, half hidden in a coat of pristine fur.

But it was the second figure that prompted the gasps and grins all around.

The man opened his arms wide, like a king receiving some very welcome guest, and gave the gathered throng an exaggerated salute. This man knew how to bask in adulation. This man knew how to savour a crowd.

Soon, the new arrivals were crossing the car park, Ed confidently leading the way.

Ten yards in front of them, he stopped and stepped back.

'My family, my friends,' Ed declared – and both Evie and Cal were overjoyed to see him so heartened, so proud of what they were all about to achieve. 'Might I introduce to you an honorary member of the Forsyth Varieties. Ladies and gentlemen, Mr Bill Martin!'

7

Star of the Seagate

Flitting figures of shadow were seen in Seaford that night. A midnight dog-walker, calling his greyhound as it frolicked over the moonlit sands, saw a gaggle of figures clamouring by the bus-stop on the seafront road. A lone drinker, ejected from the Tanner Hop when too few patrons remained to make a lock-in worthwhile, was not sure if he was seeing things when an elderly gentleman in a top hat and long velveteen cape bustled past with an enormous roll of paper and a tub of wallpaper paste in hand. A family of children, woken by their parents' bruising argument, peeped out of their nursery curtains to see three acrobats cartwheeling along their road, then pausing in the halo of the streetlamps to fix some poster to the polls. If anyone had been there to see, they would have seen the postboxes being plastered with smaller versions of the same advertisement that now covered the hoardings at the end of Bell Road. They would have seen every shop window and awning sporting miniature versions of the same. When the local postie ventured out on his morning rounds, and the milkman started guiding his float through the town centre, they saw it everywhere they looked: a vibrant square of forest green, with golden lettering and silver curlicues around its every edge.

THE FORSYTH VARIETIES

INVITE YOU TO . . .

THE SEAGATE SPECTACULAR!

At

THE SEAGATE THEATRE!

SATURDAY, 20th OCTOBER

7PM

FREE ENTRY, TICKETS TO BE RESERVED AT BOX OFFICE

FEATURING A NEVER-TO-BE-FORGOTTEN MYSTERY GUEST!

AND . . .

Evie Forsyth and Her Aerial Dancers!

Master Illusionist, Mr John Lauder

Davith Harvard, Tinky and Tiny

ED FORSYTH, the DEVILISH WIT

& Many More

SOON TO BE SEEN . . . BY ROYAL COMMAND!

As Seaford town woke up the following morning, it seemed that the streets where they lived had been ambushed by colour. Children on their way to school gawked. Mothers lingered at the bus stops. And if there were dissenting voices in town – for there always were – they were more than drowned out by those who awoke to discover their town had been touched by something special. 'Free entry?' somebody said as they queued at the bank that morning. 'Well, that can't be right, can it?'

'But who's this mystery guest?'

'They'll have rounded up someone you've never heard of,' chipped in the bank clerk as he opened up the doors. 'But it'll be good. I'm going to get a few tickets, second the box office opens. Just the ticket for a cold wintry weekend.'

By midday, talk of the 'mystery guest' had ricocheted from street corner to shop floor. By the time the schools were turning out, tickets were already pouring out of the Seagate box office, and the number of passers-by who had congregated to gaze upon the double-decker bus and its flotilla, still standing pride of place outside the theatre, was growing.

Among that congregation stood a tall, lean (some might say 'gawky') boy of sixteen years. Hiding behind spectacles as thick as milk bottles, he stood with his school satchel at his feet – all of its manifold books spilling onto the ground – and tried to catch sight of the comings and goings at the theatre doors.

When his schoolfriends, what few there were, jostled behind him and cried out, 'Hey, Livesey, what do you reckon? Come on, brainbox! You can figure it out!', he only smiled and shrugged, hoping they would leave him alone. Because Jim Livesey, son and heir to Seaford's finest family undertakers, was not remotely interested in who the Forsyths' mystery guest might be. No, Jim Livesey's heart and soul were drawn to an altogether grander form of mystery: the mystery of magic.

And right there, up on every poster across town, the words: *Master Illusionist, Mr John Lauder.*

*

'Stardom,' said Bill Martin, strutting across the stage inside the Seagate Theatre, 'is a power all of its own. We reach for it, just as we reach for the stars – and always it feels out of reach. But then, one day, we find that the voices of the crowd are bearing us aloft. The sparkle in the eyes of our audience, the moments they call our name, the shudder we feel when we approach the arena and they're waiting for us outside – there's such magic in it that it gives us flight.'

There was a hush in the Seagate Theatre, almost every single member of the Company sitting in the stalls and gazing upon Bill Martin. The only one who wasn't there was Hugo, who was somewhere above, operating the spotlight that followed Bill across the stage. Now it followed him to the microphone stand in its very centre. Bill tapped on the mic. It echoed around the stalls. 'Of course, the singers of old didn't need microphones to make themselves heard. But we live in different times.'

From the back row, where he was watching, Cal saw Lily bouncing in her seat – quite the opposite of Max, whose excitement seemed to have turned him rigid in the seat alongside her. Bill's reception last night had not lasted long – just long enough for hands to be shaken, for introductions to be rushed through, while his security minders ran a patrol of the theatre, making an inventory of its entrances and exits, which they insisted on calling 'points of attack'. But his return to the theatre this morning, under cover of darkness, had heralded perhaps the most memorable day in the careers of everyone present. Ed had arranged for Bill to spend the days he was with them at a manor house some thirty miles distant – far enough away, and with discreet enough staff, that his presence in Seaford might go unnoticed – but, for the next few days, he would be here in the theatre, ready and willing to share every trick he'd acquired across his long career.

'We inhabit *characters* when we are on these stages. Sometimes, I am the spurned lover, lamenting the tragedy of romance. Sometimes, I am the tender-hearted thief, stealing into my audience's dreams. Sometimes,' he grinned, 'I am even the villain. I can draw on little pieces of me for each of these roles...'

Cal heard Lily whisper to Max, 'Max, can you believe it?'

'What, that Bill Martin could ever be a villain?'

Lily spluttered with laughter; then, realising she'd caught the attention of the star up on stage, flapped her hands in apology and sank into her seat.

'What I mean to say,' Bill went on, 'is that, on the road to stardom, while we wait for stardom to come and whisk us away, we can still inhabit the role of a true, bona-fide *star*. If every one of us walks out onto the stage at the Royal Varieties like we belong to the constellations themselves, our audience will believe it. Stardom is a spell that gets woven. If we believe it, ladies and gentlemen, so will they.' He lifted the microphone from the stand. 'Hit it, Valentine,' he said, and, in the orchestra below, Valentino (ignoring, for the moment, that Bill Martin had mispronounced his name) cracked his knuckles as he reached for the piano keys. 'Bear in mind, my friends, that we have all been summoned by royalty. We are anointed by the hand of the Queen. We have long been destined for this...'

'I don't believe the Queen even knows, does she?' Cal heard Max whisper to Lily. 'That Mr Martin is going to sing with us?'

'Shush up, Max, he's going to sing!'

'This is one of my newer renditions, ladies and gents. Let no man say that Bill Martin doesn't keep up with the times.'

And he began to sing 'Can't Help Falling in Love'. The version he sang was scarcely a year old (though the melody harked back centuries, '*Plaisir d'amour*' one of the first classical pieces

Cal had learned to play), the signature song from the Elvis movie of last year.

The Forsyth Varieties were rapt, and had every right to be so. Bill Martin's voice was a rich tenor, buttery and lush. He started soft, but soon his voice was filling the auditorium. Even Davith Harvard's two dogs stopped chasing each other's tails to listen as Bill's voice soared, syrupy and magnificent in equal measure.

After he finished his rendition, Bill reached further back in time – to Nat King Cole and his 'Unforgettable', and finally Jo Stafford's aching monument to romance, 'You Belong to Me'. Then, when he at last came up for air – and the applause in the theatre, passionate enough to rival a full house, faded away – he flung open his arms. 'There we have it. What beauty and magic we human beings can weave. So let us begin. We've got – how long is it, Ed?'

'Six days to the Spectacular.' Ed stood up in the stalls, leaving Evie to rally the dancers, and made his way to the stage to stand alongside Bill. From there, he gazed out on his Company. He had, he thought, never seen them as unified as they were today – or, if he had, it could only have happened in the long-gone days of Bella, when everything was good. But now, though the Company was different, reforged across so many difficult years, he could *feel* the common purpose in the air.

Last night, Evie had told him she'd walked with Cal, down by the sea, that they'd aired some of the grievances between them, that they'd agreed they would *try*. That had filled his heart, no matter what his own grievances might have been with his son. He looked for him in the audience now. And, of course, there he was, at the back of the hall, half hidden by shadows.

Who was it he was speaking to? thought Ed.

Magdalene, he saw. Bill's wife.

Something in Ed twisted. Some memory surged up in him, like a knife. The pain of it was acute – because, of course, there'd been trouble with girls before. Cal knew he was a good-looking boy. He always had. That was his mother's fault, Ed used to say – back when Bella was alive, back when it was all just a jest, Cal enjoying the fawning looks from the audience, and the occasional wink from some passer-by in whatever town they had come to play. But that year, after Bella had died... Ed shuddered to think about it now. Cal had torn his way through love lives, then, barely caring to hide any of it – anything from the machinist's daughter in Glasgow, to that dancing girl who'd left to join the Homburgs, claiming Cal had broken her heart. Ed knew a little about the rush of an addiction. He'd let the drink conquer him, once. But being addicted to the frisson of romance, the electrifying feeling of a first touch – a first kiss, or even more – could be every bit as destructive. Lives were ruined in the fallout.

Looking at him now, Ed supposed that his son had not lost that wild part of him in his five years in the wilderness. He wondered, now, if Cal and Evie had spoken of it, out on the sands. Whatever the terms of their truce, it did not seem to include keeping Cal from charming women he shouldn't.

Ed cast a sidelong look at Bill, but his old friend seemed to have been too busy lapping up the adulation of the Company to have noticed. Ed made a mental note to speak with Cal later. Bill had been a jealous man in his life and Ed was determined that nothing, no matter how minor, would disrupt the week they had planned.

'My friends, last night was a triumph,' Ed announced. 'I'll have a better idea this evening, when I speak to the Seagate's front of house, but I've a feeling tickets are flowing. And that means, the time when we all need to apply pressure has arrived.

My friends, in only six days we must devise and finalise a show that we will be trialling right here on this stage before revealing it to a queen. It is the show by which we will all be known for years to come. The show with which I intend to ...' He stalled. *Hang it*, he thought, *I'll say it out loud, say it in front of every one of them – and deal with the consequences later.* 'The show with which I intend to announce my retirement from the Company.'

'I say it not to put fear into you all,' said Ed, seeing the shocked faces and wondering if, perhaps, he had made one of the rare missteps of his career. 'And nor do I mean to hang up my hat the moment we take our bows.' He said this, though, of course, it was exactly what he'd been envisaging: one last curtain call, for a queen. 'I say it only to impress upon you how magnificent I want this moment to be. We all reach the twilights of our careers. Mine is on the approach, and each of you already knows it. But let us not let Her Majesty down. Let us not let ourselves down either. Evie, perhaps you can come to the stage?'

Evie left Lily, Max and the other dancers behind, and joined her father on the stage.

'Evie has already composed the great shape of this show, and I am in full accordance with what she has in mind. But that show is full of blanks. We must fill them in, and quickly, then fine-tune their cadences until we all work as one. My friends, we have the benefit of Bill Martin. The years of wisdom to draw and depend upon. I'll be watching from the stalls. Bill, Evie – let's get this show underway.'

'So, are you going to sing for me, or are you just going to stare?'

Up on stage, Evie seemed both exhilarated and shell-shocked by their father's words. Cal kept trying to catch her eye above the milling heads but, the one time he thought he had, she seemed to look straight through him, as if he wasn't there. Perhaps that was just the way of it, he thought, but it certainly lent some new resonance to Evie's fears about his reappearance. If only there was a way to convince her, he thought. A way to make her see that, of all the reasons Cal had returned to the Company, wresting its ownership away from her wasn't one of them.

It was better not to think about it. Better not to think about anything at all. There was only one way Cal would be able to truly convince her he hadn't come here with some shadowy, second motive – and that was to tell her the truth.

He wasn't ready for that.

None of them were.

He was straying too far into those tangled thoughts when he heard Magdalene say, in her honeyed Californian accent, 'Well, Cal, if what you're saying's true, and they're really not making room for you in this show, we may as well have a little fun, mightn't we? I'm bored, Cal.'

Bored? he thought. It beggared belief, to Cal, that she might be bored, when the theatre was coming alive with invention – and her husband, the man she loved above all others, was in his element, holding court, Evie's dancers fanning out around him as they worked out how to incorporate him into the show, how to reveal him to the Queen.

Magdalene must have read his thoughts, for soon she was saying, 'Darling, you can't imagine the number of these shindigs I trot along to. Not concerts, you understand – just empty auditoriums, meetings, pow-wows. Lord, there's never a thing to do – and you're an entertainer, aren't you?'

Cal stared.

'Then entertain me.'

There was a studio backstage, a little rehearsal room with a baby grand piano – at least fifty years old, and salvaged from woodworm twice in its life, by the looks of it – and a small space meant for choreography and dancing. A pile of stage blocks in one corner were evidently meant for dragging out every time they were needed.

Cal had never felt self-conscious in front of an audience before, but the irony was that, the smaller the crowd, the more unusual it could feel. In front of a crowd of hundreds, you often felt less watched than in front of a single pair of eyes. The feeling of sitting at the piano, in front of Magdalene, was not so different from all those times he'd walked into the offices of record producers on Denmark Street in London, then been invited to sit down, show them what he had – and knew that, in the next few minutes, his craft would be criticised, judged, and his fate decided upon. He'd sold a few songs like that, along the way. Most producers had an act or five they were trying to launch, and they always needed new material to do it. But, no matter how many he'd sold, he'd always lost out on three times as many.

He tried not to let that spirit of weariness and artistic deject-edness colour him now. He tried, too, to forget that this was Bill Martin's wife he was singing for. A woman who'd fallen in love with a man because of song. A woman who heard a superstar like Martin singing so often she found it boring.

Could that really be correct?

His fingers found the melody. The hairs on the back of his arms had stood on end the first time he'd heard 'Can't Help Falling in Love' in *Blue Hawaii* starring Elvis Presley; only a short time ago, it had filled the auditorium of the Seagate Theatre, in the buttery tenor of Bill Martin. Well, Cal's rendi-tion would not be like either of those. His voice was throaty and raw and he fancied that it cast him as a more plaintive, desperate, yearning kind of lover. There might even have been an element of fear in the way he sang. What Bill Martin had said about impersonating a character on stage was certainly so, but sometimes the best way to connect with an audience was not to impersonate an audience at all. It was simply to be yourself.

He lifted his eyes. There stood golden-haired Magdalene. She must have heard this song a hundred times, he thought, but she was transfixed.

As the song finally tailed off, she said, 'I've never heard it sung like that before. You sounded almost... broken, Cal.'

Cal shrugged. His fingers itched to find some new melody. He thought back to the Fairview Hotel. They'd been dancing there. There'd been emotion running high. That was the power of music. It could make you weep, or it could make you fight. And, at its very best, it made you feel it all at the very same time: possibility, hope, despair and devastation. Music made you soar, then brought you crashing back down.

'What do you like to listen to, Magdalene?'

'You can call me Maddie,' she said. She had started walking a circuit around the room, as if she couldn't sit still.

'Well, Maddie? Was it Bill's voice? Is that what made you fall in love?'

'Oh, Bill has a lot of attributes,' she said. 'Millions of them, in fact. But his voice? Well, I'd be telling a lie if I said it wasn't his *presence* that bowled me over.' She smiled, almost demurely, though Cal wondered if there was something a little more knowing in that smile as well. 'Love might cross the generations, but musical taste often doesn't. I love Bill's voice. I just wish he'd shake it up a little, sometimes. Loosen himself. Now, Fats Domino – there's a musician. Do you know Fats Domino, in England?'

Cal beamed. He fell at the piano and played the first bouncing chords of 'Blueberry Hill.'

'Yes!' Magdalene exclaimed. 'Yes, that's it. That's the one. Now, Bill mightn't be the Fat Man – he has a different feel about him, you know? He's *Bill Martin*. But times change. Stars fade. And I have a feeling his star might shine just a little bit longer, if only he'd … well, *embrace* a change.'

This was the feeling he'd been trying to convince his father of five years ago. It was the feeling that, if there was any way he could contribute to the Forsyth Varieties now he was back here, he had to convince him of now. Tastes changed.

As if on cue, the door to the rehearsal studio opened and there stood his father.

'Dad, you're just the man I need to speak to.'

'I was looking for you out there, Cal.' His eyes, threaded with some hint of suspicion, lifted up to take in Magdalene too. 'Maddie, Bill's looking for you. They're out there, taking a break.'

'Duty calls,' Magdalene said, with the slyest of smiles. Then she skedaddled, past Ed and out into the stalls.

'Cal, what are you doing back here?'

'Just playing,' Cal said, seemingly oblivious to whatever intimation Ed was making.

'Cal, they're married.'

Now, at least, Cal understood. 'For Heaven's sake, Dad, it's just a song.'

'It was never *just a song* with you, Cal.'

Cal kicked back on the piano stool. 'She wanted to hear a song. I played it for her. Where's the damage in that?'

'Where's the damage in whispering words with a married woman? I need this to go smoothly, Cal. Whether you've got anything in mind with Magdalene or not, I want you to stay away from her. Do you understand?'

Cal just stared – until, remembering the confessions of the seafront, the anguished look in Evie's eyes, he finally said, 'I get it, Dad. And I promise. I'm not here to cause trouble. I'm here to …' *Keep my head down*, he thought. *Just get through it.*

'Dad, you know they won't *remember* it, don't you? What Bill's doing out there, all those old standards? 'Unforgettable' and 'You Belong To Me'... Dad, he might as well be singing 'The White Cliffs of Dover'!'

By the ghostly look on Ed's face, Cal's words might have been a treachery in themselves. 'Well, what's wrong with that? Vera Lynn? Don't you know what that song means to people? Don't you know how she got us through? Come on, Cal, you were hardly a little boy for the war. A little older and you'd have ended up in uniform yourself. You're old enough to remember it. That's music that moves people, that is.'

'Dad, I thought you wanted this to be memorable? I thought you wanted it to echo through the years. A Royal Variety never to be forgotten – that's what you said.'

'And it will be.' Ed came forward, to lean on the baby grand. 'He's Bill Martin. He's the man who started out on the bill at the City Varieties in Leeds and ended up...'

'I know the legend, Dad. But – but legends are old. Bill Martin can sing, Dad. But he's a... fossil.'

Ed shook his head but didn't reply.

'Dad, just listen to me – just two minutes. Please? Two years ago, I took a meeting with a chap on Denmark Street. I'd been in and out of their offices for a time, flogging whatever tunes I could write. It was enough to pay some rent, for a while, but not much more. But then this chap offered me a wage: six months, to crank out some songs, to help launch a dozen acts. Well, those acts might not have gone anywhere – not yet, at any rate. But it taught me a thing or two about stardom too. It showed me what gets remembered. And you can do one of two things for this Royal Variety, Dad – you can pay homage to the past, in songs like Bill's singing, or you can have a moment. You can have your moment. Because the things that stick in the memory,

Dad, they're not the stately, grand performances of songs of old. The moments we remember are when something changes. And that, with the right songs, could be what this Royal Variety's all about. The year everything changed – with us, the Forsyth Varieties, at its vanguard.'

Ed just stared, his brow furrowed into deep crags, until finally he said, 'Right songs, Cal, or right singer?'

Cal had been about to return to the piano – there was a bombastic introduction he was eager to play – but his father's words forestalled him. He felt like a fool.

'I'm just trying to help, Dad. I didn't mean to—'

Was there really another argument brewing, or was it just the storm of an old memory blowing through? Both men fell silent, while both asked themselves the same question.

At last, without playing a single note, Cal stood and moved past his father, marching towards the door.

'Cal,' Ed called out.

Cal turned.

'I just need to get through this, OK? I just need this to be perfect – so that, whatever happens next, we did Her Majesty proud. I know what you're saying, son. The century moves on. Fifty years ago, I sang for a king. Now it's his granddaughter sitting on the throne. And, pretty soon, it will be somebody else sitting on the throne of the Forsyth Varieties as well.' He sighed. 'I'll find a place for you, Cal. I don't know how yet. I don't know where. I can't ask one of our stalwarts to step aside for you.'

'Dad,' Cal interrupted, trying to control his exasperation. 'I didn't ask for that. It's not what I want. You don't believe me? Well, I'm telling you, here and now: I don't want to play at the Palladium. I don't want to play for the Queen. I just wanted...' He felt a sudden stitch in his side, a shot of pain, and his hand fell to the place in his midriff where the bandage still clung.

It needed changing; he'd seen it discoloured yet further in the morning. He would have to attend to that soon. 'I just wanted to come home, whether you believe it or not.'

Then he marched away, through the stalls where the Company was still rehearsing, and off towards the Seagate doors. As he passed, he looked for Magdalene in the crowd. There she was, by the side of the stage, fawning over Bill as she mopped at his brow. It would not pay to linger over her for long; Cal knew what his father was insinuating – that he was back to his old ways. Not for the first time, he wondered if it really was possible to ever come home.

Cal wondered if he should find a bar somewhere in town, some-where just to sit and think – and to stay out of trouble. But the wound in his midriff was still burning, and perhaps now was the moment to right that. If only he'd sorted out some lodgings, this would have been easier – he'd have to talk to Evie about that – but, for now, the microbus would be enough. There was a water tank in the back, meant for making camp, and enough privacy that he could clean himself up without being interrupted.

He was just crossing the line Bill Martin's security men had established when he saw a young man remonstrating with them. The suit he was wearing was certainly three sizes too big, and the boy even knew it; he'd rolled up the sleeves, and the trouser cuffs were upturned too. There was pomade in his hair (too much, by far), and the overall effect, thought Cal, was that he looked like a ventriloquist's dummy brought to life.

'Everything all right here?' Cal asked, as he sauntered by.

'Everything's under control, sir,' said one of the security men flatly. 'I'm afraid we've got ourselves a Bill Martin fanatic here, but we've been firm. He can't come in.'

'Bill Martin?' The young man balked, as if he hardly even knew the name.

The security men were holding him at bay with outstretched arms, as if forming a human fence, but the boy had obviously not tried to breach their barrier; he stood two yards distant, barely raising his voice.

'He reckons he's come to see John Lauder,' said the security man. 'But we got the kid's number. We've seen it all, Jack and me. Look at him, sir. He's got the look of a Bill Martin fanatic, through and through.'

Cal gave the young man a cursory look. To Cal's eye, he looked more like a 'warm Ovaltine for bedtime' kind of fanatic more than a Bill Martin fan. For a start, he was half a century younger than the average Bill Martin listener. If the boy had heard of him, it was only in the off-hand way children knew things about their parents' generation.

'John Lauder, you say?'

The boy switched his attention promptly to Cal. 'My name's Jim,' he said, uncertain of himself, doing his damnedest to feign confidence. 'Jim Livesey, the... the... Master of the Forgotten Arts!' He gave a great flourish with his arms, and out of one sleeve erupted a crumpled, beheaded rose stem, its petals fluttering to the ground. 'I believe... I believe Mr Lauder's expecting me.'

'A likely story!' The security man laughed. 'Why don't you just sling your—'

'Hold on,' said Cal. He stepped past the security men, picked up the rose stem, and returned it to Jim Livesey's trembling hand. 'You really want to meet John Lauder, kid?'

Cal thought. Lauder hadn't been in the theatre so perhaps that meant he had returned to his lodgings or was resting aboard the double-decker bus.

'He – he's expecting me.'

This part was not true; Cal was certain. The boy's eye started twitching, which was the biggest 'tell' Cal had ever seen. Cal used to play cards with the Company, back when he was growing up; it was easy to spot a liar, when you knew how.

When you were one yourself.

Cal looked back at the theatre. Something still irked him about the way his father had spoken to him. All that talk of honouring the old ways, that way he had of dismissing the new. Well, the world needed to move on.

He looked back at the boy.

'I – I've come to audition,' said Jim. 'I'm a m-m-magician.'

'The stuttering sorcerer!' The security men laughed.

'I'll take it from here, chaps,' said Cal, and reached past the security men to usher Jim forward. 'Jim's with me. We've been waiting for him.'

'You have?' gasped Jim, his eyes wide. 'I knew it! I just – just knew it! Mr Lauder's got the second sight. I knew he'd have foreseen my coming.'

At this, Cal had to stifle some laughter of his own – and this he did, because he did not mean to join in with the security men now looking at him with befuddled expressions.

'Come with me, Jim,' he said, and steered the nervous boy past. 'Welcome to the Forsyth Varieties.'

8

The Sorcerer's Apprentice

Last night, when Jim Livesey had gone to sleep, he'd certainly not expected to spend the following evening in the company of a master illusionist. He supposed that if he, Jim Livesey, had been born with the same second sight that he'd read about in John Lauder's feted biography, *Through the Illusionist's Lens*, he would have been able to foresee it. But no prophetic dreams had coloured his sleep last night.

But, in this moment, that hardly mattered – because now he was following the man who'd introduced himself as Cal across the front of the Seagate; now he was waiting at the doors of the double-decker bus as Cal snooped about inside; now he was traipsing after him, to the row of lodging houses on the theatre's seaward side, waiting patiently as Cal (apparently uncertain which lodging John had taken) knocked on doors until one of the wizened old landladies told him he'd come to the right place.

'Wait here, kid,' said Cal. 'I won't be long.'

Then he slipped inside, leaving Jim alone on the step – with only the hammering of his heart, and the incessant whispering of his nerves, to keep him company.

Cal had to knock three times on the bedroom before the shuffling of footsteps on the other side told him John was awake.

It was the silliest thing: the moment he heard those footsteps, it was as if all of the nerves the boy downstairs was trying to smother had suddenly been transferred into him. Nervousness – it was so unbecoming of Cal Forsyth, so alien an emotion; and yet it had plagued him ever since he'd set foot in Seaford town. If he'd been feeling any calmer after his seaside walk with Evie all of those uncertainties came back the moment John's jowly, amphibious face appeared in the door.

John Lauder: his was one of the oldest faces Cal could remember, a fixture in life since before he was born. Ten years older than Cal's father, John had been the Company's grandfatherly figure since he was scarcely middle-aged; there had always been something about his demeanour – or so it had seemed to the youthful Cal – that suggested the wisdom of the ages, as if he had inherited not just the tricks of the trade from Abe Wright but the sagacity of all the magicians who'd come before him. As a boy, Cal had been fond of telling Evie that John was watching them, no matter where they were, no matter what they were doing.

'He's asleep at the hostel, Cal!' Evie would say.

'No,' Cal would correct her. 'He's watching us through the eyes of the birds.'

Such things did not seem so fanciful when you were a child. The problem was that it didn't seem fanciful even now, standing in the doorway under John's withering eye.

'Cal,' John said, in that old dulcet tone. 'I'd been wondering when you might come and see me. How long is it now? Two days? Three? You've been rabble-rousing with the troupe, but you haven't been to see Uncle John. How do you suppose that makes an old man feel?'

The shame of it was already prickling Cal. Not for the first time, he felt that rush of familial guilt

'I've been meaning to come, John. I wanted to. I've been … well, my head isn't in the right place, you know?' He looked into John's pale eyes, greying in age just the same as his curls. 'I reckon you never thought to see me again. That's right, isn't it?'

'Cal, you've forgotten who I am,' intoned John, with a twinkle in those ethereal eyes. 'I've known you were coming back from the moment you left.' He stepped back, as if inviting Cal into his room – a spartan little thing, with a simple bedstead, a chest of drawers, and a gilt-edged mirror, which, for some reason, had been turned to the wall. Cal thought nothing of this – John had always had his peculiar ways.

'You didn't think I'd make it on my own, John?'

Cal was testing him, but John had never risen to Cal's bait back when he was a boy, and clearly he wasn't about to start now. 'On the contrary, child. If you'd have *made it*, as you so eloquently put it – leaving aside all the things I tried to teach you about *making it*, what a nonsense those two words really are – I believe your return to us might have been hastened. Stardom would have simply been the accelerant to your homesickness. Like paraffin, poured into a fire.'

Cal shifted awkwardly. He touched his side. If John truly had second sight, he thought, then he'd know homesickness was only a part of it. The paraffin poured onto the fire? No, that was something else.

'The good or the bad,' John said. 'It's all life's rich tapestry. I'm an old man, Cal. I long ago figured out that it serves us best not to be too indebted to either the good things or the bad things in our lives. Just try and see it all, for what it is.' John paused. 'There's something else I'm seeing right now. I'm seeing… this isn't why you're here. Not to catch up with an old man, at any rate.'

Cal grinned. He had always enjoyed being worked out by John; it had always made him wonder where talent ended and showmanship began. In song and dance, the two were intermingled, but stage magic was a carefully orchestrated fraud, and some element of its wonder came from trying to pick apart its seams.

'There's a boy here, says he's come to see you. Says he's even expected.' Cal gave a winsome grin. 'He *said* he's come to audition, and that you'd know about it. He's been down there for some time, talking the ear off those guards Bill Martin has stationed out there.' Cal thought it was interesting that, at the mention of Bill Martin and his security team, John's eyes rolled. 'There's some spirit in him, John. Some pluck. Fancies himself a magician, by the looks of him. He seems to know all about you.'

'What do you think, John? Have you got a little time for an ardent fan?'

John looked Cal up and down. 'Your father gave an express order: not a single soul to come near the theatre until show night. There's a secret to be kept in there. If I didn't know you any better, Cal, I might think you were stirring things up ...'

'Me, John?' Cal laughed. '*Me?*'

John shook his head. A rush of old memories were tumbling back over him – every time Cal had shook up a show, every time he'd been riotously, unstoppably *him* on the road. The Cal he was looking at now was not the same as the one he used to know. He was older, yes, but there was something else about him; something subdued, perhaps; something suppressed.

But the old Cal was certainly in there, thought John. You could see a man's soul when you looked into his eyes.

'Show the boy up, Cal. Let's see what this is all about.'

To Jim Livesey – left on the doorstep with only his strings of handkerchiefs, carefully arranged deck of cards and the loops of knotted rope that formed the centre of his proudest trick – it seemed that an aeon had passed. What was it John Lauder had said in those memoirs of his? *Time, like an ever-rolling stream, bears all its sons away*... No, that wasn't it; that was something else – Jim loved to read (if only his family would stop haranguing him about it). John's words had been more mystical somehow. He said them out loud.

'"Time is the great deceiver. It makes promises it will not fulfil, then holds us to those promises itself."' It was part of a passage where John was trying to put into words the heart of an illusionist's work: the way a stage magician bought time with his patter, while some deft sleight of hand was creating the illusion of a sorcery come true. '"A magician may need but a second, but to gain that second he might spend a minute buying his audience's trust. So have I bartered time with kings."'

'If you say so, kid.'

Jim looked up. There was Cal looking at him with a droll expression.

'I – I was – I was just thinking,' stammered Jim. 'Of – of Mr Lauder. It's from Mr L-Lauder's book. He's talking about stagecraft. The audience don't know it but you're m-manipulating them, s-stalling for time. And...'

'I'm teasing you, kid. John's up there. He'll see you when you're ready. Top of the stairs, first door on your right. If the landlady sticks her head round the door, just tell her you're not staying long. They can be dragons, these landladies.'

Cal stepped past Jim, taking to the street. If he heard Jim's whispered 'Th-thanks,' he did not show it. He only looked back when Jim called out, 'I – I don't suppose you ever had to do this, did you? G-go up for an audition with a man as talented as John Lauder?'

'Not at the varieties, Jim,' said Cal, with an air of what Jim could only think was sadness, before he drifted on.

Jim's legs were hardly his own as he plodded up the lodging-house stairs. 'Come through, young man.' Strange, but he hadn't expected John Lauder to sound like that: so rich, so composed, a beautiful baritone voice that spoke of the plush theatres of London's West End, Shakespeare and Marlowe and all those grand Elizabethan dramas that his English master tried to drum into him – while, all the time, he was daydreaming about David Berglas and Harry Houdini, Howard Thurston and John Nevil Maskelyne, the great stage magicians of the past.

Not to mentionthe man who now appeared in the doorway, wearing a burgundy waistcoat and his shirtsleeves rolled up.

'Mr Livesey, I presume?'

Jim stuttered, 'Y– yes, sir,' and almost fell over his own feet as he entered the room.

Jim had seen several magicians perform live – in fact, he'd seen a perfectly good one, Neil Klaasen, at the Seagate itself. But it had been the dream of his young life to see John Lauder. He'd always imagined it might be in a theatre, or a cabaret club like the ones in London. He'd never anticipated it being this close. This real.

Jim found he was tongue-tied, almost silenced by his sudden nerves.

'So, what will it be?' asked John, stepping back into the room to invite Jim in further. Perhaps you might allow me to show you a couple of tricks, if I—'

'No!' Jim blurted out, spreading his arms in the lavish gesture he'd been rehearsing. The exclamation took even Jim by surprise; it had burst out quite without him realising. 'It is *I* who will show *you* some tricks!'

In the next second, the air was filled with confetti. John Lauder stood there, in a deluge of spiralling scraps of red, blue and white paper, the colours of the Union Jack turning a mini-ature hurricane around him.

Then, before John could give Jim a moment's applause, the younger man started convulsing. To an outsider, it might have looked as if he had been punched directly in the stomach. He doubled over, he groaned in agony, he clutched his belly with one hand and put the other to his gagging mouth – and then, with one last retch, a fountain of coloured handkerchiefs started erupting from his mouth. Jim, sensing he might yet be saved from this debilitating attack, started pulling at them, only to discover they were knotted in a chain. First there were five, then there were ten, fifteen, twenty – until, finally, fifty coloured handkerchiefs coiled in a pool around his feet, and Jim Livesey was saved.

He took a bow.

There was silence in John Lauder's lodging. Then the old man, with the most marvellous magnanimity, gave Jim the loudest (and indeed the only) ovation of his life.

'Young man, you have talents beyond your years.'

Jim – who did not, in the moment, care whether he was being indulged or simply praised – bowed again.

'Jim, there's one thing I'm more impressed by – more, even, than this display you've pulled out of the air.' John smiled. 'When I was your age, boy, I'm not sure I would have had the courage to do what you've just done – to sashay into a magician's room and start performing my own feats of sorcery. So, bravo, boy, you've got nerves of steel.'

Jim, who was about to start stammering again, had never believed it – not until this very moment. But John's words were like magic itself. It instilled some new confidence in him, confidence enough that he could say, 'Mr Lauder, you don't know what this means. I've been reading about you since I was a boy.'

He stopped, looked at himself, and added, 'Well, a *younger* boy, if you take my meaning. I had your Memory Cards when I was eight. It's from you that I learnt my very first tricks. Ones with coins, and cups, and little lengths of string. I begged and begged my father to take us to the Forsyth Varieties when you were in Brighton last summer – I'm not much one for song and dance, Mr Lauder, but I'd have given anything to see you. W-when I saw your name up on the poster, I knew I had to come. And – and I suppose I *should* have waited for the show. Everyone's getting tickets. There's two teachers bunked off from my school to go to the box office this afternoon! But, well…' It was only now that Jim's voice faded. 'Here I am,' he said. Then, with a final flourish, 'Would you consider signing my copy of your book?'

John had written that memoir twenty years ago, when he considered himself at the peak of his powers. Some elements of it shamed him now; reading old work could be like reading an old diary, or looking at old portraits of yourself – it revealed aspects of you you would rather remained lost, to the sands of time. Even so, he was touched enough to say, 'Of course you might, Jim.'

'It's over there, sir.'

John's eyes narrowed.

'On your pillow, sir, with a pencil for signing.'

John turned around. There, quite unbeknownst to him, a copy of *Through the Illusionist's Lens* lay open on his pillow, the pencil marking an inside page, the start of *Chapter IX: Sketches of a Seance.*

John wandered over. Jim was delighted to see the slightest perplexity in his eyes. In that perplexity, thought Jim, there was genuine admiration.

'Chapter One, sir. "A magician's best talent is not the deftness of his fingers, but the slipperiness of his tongue."'

John's frog-like face burst open in a great guffaw. This pleased Jim even more than the perplexity in his eyes. 'You have your own style of patter, Jim. You pulled the wool right over my eyes – and I'm seventy years a magician by Christmas.' He shook his head ruefully, still full of strange admiration, and invited Jim to sit at the desk in the window. This Jim did. 'An illusionist's patter is ordinary an offensive of charm,' said John. 'You flatter and ingratiate yourself with the mark, seeking to befuddle and divert the attention. Well, you had the second part to perfection, Jim – only, instead of flattery and charm, you used awkwardness and guile. Yes, yes! I like it very much, Jim. Very much indeed.'

Jim did not know what to say.

John wrote his name in ornate flourishes across the frontispiece of Jim's book, then slid it across the table. When Jim lifted it adoringly upward, it was only to discover that three coins had mysteriously appeared underneath. 'Show me what else you can do, young man.'

The truth was, Jim had been anticipating something of this sort. He had been practising coin tricks for years – and, on one particularly memorable occasion, had managed to make an entire pocketful of coins vanish from his mother's purse. She'd been furious with him after that.

Soon, Jim had vanished two coins into the ether, then revealed the first propping up the leg of the table at which he sat, and the second underneath John's mattress. John, of course, knew that these were just sleights of hand – coins tucked up sleeves and revealed at the most opportune moment, but at least he seemed to admire the craft. 'Of course, Jim, these tricks are all well and good. But to make an audience sit up and pay attention, in today's day and age? When they've got television and rock and roll – and, dare I say it, teenage romance, to distract them? Well, that's a tougher challenge. Sleight of hand is one thing,' said John, and, with the merest click of his fingers, the curtains in the room drew closed of their own accord, 'but spectacle is something else.'

'I know, I do know,' said Jim, nodding fervently. The spot on the end of his nose was itching fiercely, but he refused to touch it, for fear of spilling the third coin from his sleeve. He was determined to make it reappear in the nest of John's hair, if only such a thing were possible. 'I've read about spectacle in your book. "Spectacle is what separates magic from the mundane. Spectacle is achieved at the tipping point between belief and disbelief, when an audience who have hitherto been enjoying a set of splendid tricks suddenly begins to believe in real magic. To w—"'

'Yes,' said John, not unkindly. 'But it is more and more difficult to achieve as the generations pass. Families see wonders up on the silver screen these days. How do we make them shiver at a magic show? How could you or I possibly hope to achieve the spine-tingling sensation that Percy Selbit did when he first sawed his assistant in half up on stage? A date that lives in wonder, young Jim – the Finsbury Park Empire, the winter of twenty-one. Or the feeling Richard Potter's audience had one hundred and fifty years ago, when he plunged his hand into molten lead...?'

Jim was silent.

'It is not so easy, is it, young man? True spectacle might be achieved for but a few moments of a lifetime...'

Jim had a sudden thought. 'C-can you really read a mind?'

John did not answer the question directly. A good magician never did. 'Can *you*, Jim?'

He nodded eagerly. Then he dropped his gaze, performed his best imitation of a trance and said, 'Your name is John Evelyn Lauder. For seventy-six years have you roamed this Earth. I'm seeing... your first moment on stage! Apprenticed to Mr Abel Wright, latterly of the Forsyth Varieties. For three years, you sat in his audiences as a stooge, waiting to be chosen, waiting to participate in a trick...'

John had started laughing. Jim opened his eyes.

'What is it?' he said. 'Am I wrong?'

'No, young man, but you're holding on to a copy of the memoir I myself wrote, chronicling my own life story. You'll have to do better than that, Jim.'

'Then how do you do it, Mr Lauder? Reading minds – is that spectacle?'

'Sometimes,' said John. 'Bow your head, young man.'

Jim did as he was told. In the next moment, his idol had laid his hand, wrinkled like old leather, on his brow and begun to take deep, long-lasting breaths. 'Young man, I can see your beginning – but I cannot see your end. Two paths diverge before me. Two possibilities for your future.'

'Young man, down one of these paths you have a steady, comfortable, safe life. You inherit the undertakers' from your father – and, using your exceptional talents, it flourishes under your leadership. Your father, Mr Reginald Livesey, is enormously proud of you.'

Jim stuttered, 'But h-how... how did you know?' He hadn't said a word about the family business. And nor had he mentioned his father's name!

'Down the other path...' John stopped, some element of worry, some fear, creeping into his voice. 'This path is less clear. The mists are too heavy. But I do believe I see... No, I mustn't say.'

Jim's eyes opened again. 'Oh, but you must!'

'Jim,' said John, and retreated into his chair. 'I think I see spectacle.'

It was all Jim needed. He jumped up out of his seat. There was, he decided, no way other than genuine second sight for John Lauder to have known these things about him. Never had he wanted what he'd come here to petition for more.

'I don't want to work for my father, Mr Lauder. I don't want to spend my life working with the dead, then just die myself. It would be a life wasted! Just … gone!' John was smiling. 'You say it yourself, in your memoir, Mr Lauder – magicians can't go on forever. Abel Wright couldn't. Your hands slow down, your patter wanes, imagination falters … Well, maybe I can help!'

'Now, Jim, do you really think you're ready for this?'

'I know I am. I know it, Mr Lauder.' In the silence that followed, Jim was certain he had lost Mr Lauder's attention. More softly now, fearing the worst, fearing he was about to be dismissed, he said, 'We're not all born to performing families, Mr Lauder. Some of us are born undertakers. But it doesn't mean we don't have the gift, does it? It doesn't mean we can't dream.'

John smiled, sadly. 'It doesn't, young man, but, Jim, though there's magic in you, I'm just not certain this is the time for you.'

Here it was: Jim Livesey's biggest test. He knew he had to pass this one, if there was ever to be any hope for the future.

So he picked himself up, held his head high and said, with as much dignity as he could muster, 'I don't know how you read my mind, Mr Lauder, but one day I'll find out – and, some day soon, I'll come back and show you. That I have the talent too. That I really am worthy.'

And, when John Lauder smiled, Jim felt certain he had, at least, passed this test.

'Until that day, young man,' said John, and shook Jim by the hand.

*

As he turned to leave, John saw, dangling from the collar of Jim's oversized suit, the label that read *REGINALD LIVESEY, LIVESEY & SONS UNDERTAKERS, FOUNDED 1882* and inwardly smiled. Yes, this boy had talent – and, more than that, he had *hunger* – but he didn't have the simple, lateral thinking that the best magicians needed. But perhaps all that would come. Perhaps that dream he'd had, three months ago, really was right. Big change was coming – not only to the Forsyth Varieties, but to the world. The generations were shifting. One guard was retreating, while another took full flight. Cal Forsyth's return was, perhaps, not the only sign of that. And, of course, John had always known he couldn't last forever. The truth was, he didn't know if he could last another season on the road. Perhaps the time really was coming when he would hang up his hat, just like his old friend Ed Forsyth. Perhaps the Varieties really did need new blood, a new master magician to steer them onward, to the century's end.

And perhaps, today, fate had shown him the way.

But the boy would have to buck his ideas up first.

A label in his father's suit indeed! It had all been too easy.

Jim's eyes were blurring as he returned to the street.

He was just picking through the small crowd still standing curiously at the car park's edge when he shoved his hands in his pocket to ward off the coming winte

He lifted it out, just a scrap of notepaper, and angled it to the light of one of the streetlamps above.

Come back and see me when you UNDERSTAND, read the words. *Yours, John Lauder.*

In that moment, all the tears that had been threatening to spill from his eyes dried up.

His heart soared.

'The test isn't over!' he cried, to the absolute consternation of two of his classmates who just happened to be walking by on the other side of the street. 'It's still happening. It's happening right now!'

Lauder hadn't given up on him. He'd set him a challenge. Sent him off into the world to pick it apart. A *quest*. That was what this was. A bona-fide quest.

And he would see it to its end, if it was the last thing he did.

9

Runaway Lovers

The dancers had formed an arch in the middle of the stage, the lights picking out them alone, leaving the centre of the arch in perfect blackness. One after another, the dancers came apart. The archway opened and closed, a network of interlocking bodies, each braced against each other, according to Evie's design.

The opening chords of 'Unforgettable' struck up.

And, through the dancers – soon to be lit up in silver lights – appeared Bill Martin.

'Now, *that's* star quality,' said Ed quietly, sitting in the stalls.

Evie saw it too. She herself was in the wings of the stage, the better angle to see exactly what her dancers were doing. It had taken her some strength of will not to step out among them for this part of the act, but she had rarely choreographed something so specific and, ultimately, decided it was better for the piece if she was an outsider, consistently looking in. She'd already drilled them a dozen times in the motions, stopping to correct them whenever one of the dancers wasn't holding the right posture, or to rearrange them according to their size. Lily was a full foot shorter than Max, and that always presented some challenges in choreographing a group dance like this – especially where dance was only one component of the spectacle, where bodies had to clamber upon each other to make an illusion in which the audience could invest.

'Mathematics,' her mother had once said, upon realising what Evie was trying to do – for, before Evie, dance and acrobatics had been kept quite separate among the Forsyths, each taking their turn upon the stage. 'It's a problem of geometry. That's what it is. How one body fits into another.'

The problem, right now, was that she was certain the geometry was right. It was something else that was wrong. As Bill Martin came to his song's epic conclusion, she peeped out of the curtains and saw her father on his feet, hands raised above his head as he applauded. It was the highest form of applause Ed Forsyth ever gave – but it was for Bill, not for the Company at large; it was the flattery – and, yes, the adulation – he employed to keep his star guest sweet. Evie had learned a lot from Ed about that – that, in running a company, you had to pander to the needs and wants of your stars as much as you paid attention to the performance itself.

But tonight that was Ed's luxury. Evie *knew* something wasn't right. Something in the feeling of the piece they'd put together. It was too functional, somehow. Too mechanical.

And she thought she knew exactly what it was.

It was Max.

She found him after the rehearsal came to its end. Bill's security men, who'd been pacing the perimeter of the theatre all day long, were now sweeping through the Seagate, readying Bill for his departure. Magdalene, who seemed to have spent the day luxuriating backstage, was itching to leave, but, first, Bill had to make his rounds of the performers, grasping hands, sharing words of encouragement and advice. It was all part of another kind of performance, thought Evie – the performance of being a *star* – but the performers seemed to love it. Lily, especially, was thrilled when Bill took her hand and planted a kiss on its back.

Max had already returned to the dressing rooms behind the stage. There, he was kicking off his dancing shoes. He looked up when Evie approached.

'I know what you're going to say, Evie. I know it. It's … I'm struggling today, that's all.'

She sat beside him. 'Is it the piece? Does it feel wrong?'

'No, it's – it's nothing like that.' He kicked off his last shoe and threw himself back in the chair, running his hand through his hair. 'Don't you ever have these days? Days when you wonder what you're doing it for?'

Everyone did, thought Evie. A performer wouldn't be human if, every now and again, they didn't have days when they thought about throwing in the towel, running off to some quieter, more manageable existence. Emotion was so important in what they did.

'The Palladium's coming, Max. The dream of a lifetime.'

'I know, I know, but—'

'It was the high of your life, Max, when my father revealed it to us.'

Now was the first time Max had smiled. 'No,' he said, softly, and reached for her hand. 'That was later that night.'

Five months ago, the start of an English summer. The Forsyth Varieties had been on a two-week hiatus between their spring shows in Oxford and the summer tour to the South of France, a tour that was to culminate in the shows at Monaco and the Fort Antoine – and it was in that hiatus that Max, answering an advert Ed had placed in the *Dancing Times*, had been hired to the Forsyth Varieties. Now, as the Company rallied for a run of three shows at the Hippodrome in Bristol – a warm-up, they privately said, for their summer odyssey on the Continent – Ed summoned the Company for an all-hands dinner at a steak restaurant in town. The restaurant, balking at first at the number of guests they would have to accommodate, had done a fine job with the food – but it was the atmosphere, convivial and unified, that Ed had been seeking. There he sat, at the head of the table, and whenever Evie's eyes flashed in his direction, her heart felt swollen – for, through those dark years, she had often wondered if her father would ever seem as light, strong and capable as he seemed right now.

She'd been drawn to Max from the beginning. At first, it was his talent – for there was nothing more attractive to a dancer than to see talent shining in somebody else. If she had recognised it as a romantic attraction, she had not dared articulate it to herself. It was only when her father stood and made his announcement that she'd felt the bolt of electricity that told her Max was more than just another dancer coming through the Company's ranks. As her father spoke the words, 'The chance of a lifetime, my friends. A dream come true, for this old man – and, I can only hope, a dream for each and every one of you. My friends, we have been invited to perform for the Queen. The Royal Variety Performance will take place, this year, on the twenty-ninth of October – and, for the first time in fifty years, the Forsyth Varieties will take to that stage.'

Evie remembered the shock, the awe, the jubilation that carried them through the dinner, and off into the balmy Bristolian night. The wonder of it was like a wave that bore all the performers up and ever upwards – and, just when it seemed that it had reached its peak and was about to crash down, it carried them ever upwards again. She would have remembered that night for the rest of her life, even if – in those heady moments after her father had made his revelation – she hadn't felt Max's eyes on her, and hers hadn't been drawn to him. She would have remembered it even if, following the rest of the troupe out into the night – where they fanned into the various bars and nightspots that proliferated around the Hippodrome – Max hadn't suggested they get a drink together. Yes, that night would have been one of the stars that shone the brightest in the constellation of her life, even if Max hadn't told her all about his life: his father absent, his mother long buried, all the things that had driven him to be a dancer. How his mother had performed in the varieties, in those difficult years of the Great Depression; how he had grown up, with his grandmother, poring through the various postcards and posters she'd saved of all the shows she'd been in; how he still had her old letters, all the ones she'd received from the many magnificent performers she'd danced with along the way.

'But she took her own life,' Max had said, 'when I was but two years old. I'll never know what made her do it. I suppose – the *years*. It's hard to make a living as a dancer, when you've a child to raise – and no man to put a roof above your head.'

'Oh, Max,' she said. It was the first time she took his hand.

'I don't remember her very well now. But I remember the feeling of her. And ... when I dance, that's when I feel like she's near me, like she's still my guiding hand.'

Evie had to stop herself telling him to go and see John Lauder. *You could speak with her*, she wanted to say. *Hear everything she wants to say.* The truth was, she was never quite certain whether she believed in John or not; it was the *need* to believe that drove her to him when she was at her lowest, and for her that need was enough. It might not be the same for Max. And it would not be right to stir up such feelings, not when she hardly knew the man.

Soon she was telling Max about Bella's last days, and the ruin that was her father, how hard she'd worked to keep the

Company together while, everywhere she turned, things were fracturing apart. How she was certain she'd lost some talent as a dancer, for she'd had her head in management and politics and people for so very long...

'If you've lost any talent at all,' said Max, 'you must have been the very, very best – and you must have lost just the tiniest fraction of it. I've seen you dance, Evie. I've seen you.'

It was then that they kissed. Never before, in Evie's life, had a first kiss turned into a first night together; nor a first night so instantly, seamlessly, into a second or a third. She wondered if her mother – who, she was certain, had waited patiently for their marriage night before being with her father – would have approved. Evie would surely have sought her approval, if Bella was still among them. But she wasn't, and Evie didn't care. The year was 1962. Things were changing. The headlines, still filled with gloom – all the defiant posturing of the Soviet Union and the Americas, with Europe sandwiched between them, trying to make itself heard. In a world like that, why not take every chance for happiness that came your way?

So that was what they did, Evie and Max. They'd been together ever since.

Back in the Seagate dressing room, Evie shuffled her seat closer to Max and stroked the hair from his brow. 'You're tired,' she said. 'There'll be time, before the Palladium. We're to go to London. We'll have a day before rehearsing begins in earnest— we can take an afternoon. Just you and me.'

'Maybe just one night,' said Max. 'To go dancing – at the ballroom at the Savoy, or ... the Buckingham Grand?'

'It's a swell place, kid.'

Startled, Evie turned around. Max was already releasing her hand and getting to his feet. How Bill Martin had sauntered into the room without his security men announcing his presence, neither one of them knew.

'We're out of here,' Bill said. 'But I couldn't leave without saying,' he took Evie's hand, to plant a kiss on its back like a knight to a lady, 'it's been a pleasure to work with you today, Miss Forsyth. Your dancers – I don't think I ever knew the like, back when I was in variety myself. Yes, things have certainly changed.' He paused. 'You know, you'd have a great career as a showgirl, Evie. You and all of your dancers.' His eyes lifted to Max. 'Present company excepted, of course. I'm sorry, young man, but there isn't much of a place for showboys Stateside.'

Max's eyes flared. 'Evie wouldn't leave the Forsyths. It's her family name.'

Bill beamed his dazzling white smile. 'You've got a bucking bronco there,' he said to Evie, completely disregarding Max. 'No, I can see – the Forsyths are your home, and that's as it should be.' He bowed his head, softened his voice. 'And I should thank you for it. When I heard about Bella, and what her passing did to your dear father – well, my heart bled, and that's God's honest truth. If I hadn't been contracted in so tightly at the studio, I'd have been here in an instant. Now I know I had no need to be – because he had *you*, Evie, and you were everything to him.' He kissed the back of her hand again, and there his lips lingered. 'I don't know how to thank you for that, young lady – except to say that, these retirement plans of his? I'll put in a good word.'

The moment Bill was gone, Evie whirled around to face Max. 'A good *word*?' she said. 'A good *word*? I carried this Company all that time – and it's going to take a good *word* in my father's ear for him to ...'

Max, who seemed to be nursing some resentment of his own – 'no place for show boys!' – swallowed it down and said, 'I think he was trying to be kind, Evie. But men like him ...'

Evie just stared.

'Well, they don't remember what it was like,' Max said, as if catching a second thought, 'when they were starting out. All they see is the glamour. They don't remember the hard work.' He shrugged. 'That's how it seems to me. And it is hard work, isn't it, Evie? I don't just mean for the body. Your body gets used to the hard work. It loves it, in the end. But... for the mind.' He slumped. 'God, I don't know what's got into me. It's *Bill Martin*! He's the very symbol of where the varieties can take you. If I end up with a fraction of what he's got, I'll count myself lucky. But my mother...'

'I just can't help feeling resentful,' said Evie. 'A good *word*? Like an accomplishment isn't enough – not for a woman. Like, now that Cal's back, there's a bloody competition. Well, is there? Is there?'

Max steeled himself before he said, 'There's something off about your brother, Evie. I didn't want to say it. But that night at the Fairview...' Max just shrugged. 'It was like he was drawing all the eyes in the room. Trouble was just rippling out of him. I've known men like it. They have a knack for trouble. A talent for chaos.' With one final breath, he added, 'You can't let him anywhere near the Company. He'll draw trouble to it.'

'I called a truce with him,' said Evie. 'But there's something he's hiding. I can feel it in him. He told the truth about the night he left, but...'

'But not what came after,' Max said darkly. 'Evie, I want you to be careful.'

Evie had only rarely heard him speak so sternly. Something was bristling inside him. She decided it was how he was protecting her, but the way his eyes darted, the way he'd been coiled all day long – the way his body hadn't moved right, when they were out rehearsing on stage – troubled her now.

'Half devil, half angel,' said Evie.

'Wasn't your brother always like that?'

Evie could not keep herself from recalling the confessions of the seafront. Quietly, she said, 'I suppose that he was.'

'A rogue's always a rogue.' Max paused. 'Evie, I'm on your side. I have been, ever since that first night. Before that, if truth be told. The second I laid eyes on you. And what Cal did? Well, it might be forgiven one day – but it won't be forgotten. Whatever your father has planned for the Company, it's you he's thinking of. It isn't Cal. It couldn't be.'

While he had been speaking, Max had disrobed. Now, as he pulled on his slacks, he said, 'I'm not sure I can stand being out in Seaford tonight. Evie, can it just be you and me? Just off somewhere, away from the rest?'

It was then that Evie blurted out, 'My father knows.'

Max's face paled.

'They all know, Max. I was a fool to think we could keep a secret, in a company like this. But Max... I think he wishes us well. I think he sees me in him, and...'

'Your mother in me?' grinned Max. The colour was returning to his cheeks, now that he knew Ed wasn't incandescent with fury. And yet – how could he look him in the eye at rehearsals tomorrow? How could he shake his hand, without blurting out the words, 'It isn't a fleeting thing, Mr Forsyth. Sir, I'm in love with your daughter'?

Evie nodded. 'So maybe we should go into town, with the rest of them. Off to the hotel, or the restaurant, or wherever it is they're all getting a feed in tonight. Just walk in there, like it's the most ordinary thing in the world – and it *is*, Max, it is. Just two people in love.'

Max was silent. In truth, he liked the idea of leading Evie in there on his arm. There would be sniggers about Evie being older than him; about how it was she leading him, and not the other way around. There might even be the odd insistence that it was only because of love that Max was dancing with the Forsyths at all. But he knew he could weather all that, for the feeling it would give him to be with her and not have to worry about prying eyes.

And yet...

'I think I'd like just one more night,' said Max. 'One more night when it's just us alone.'

Evie smiled. 'Then we'll face the world tomorrow.'

In the empty theatre, Cal stood alone.

Here he was, resplendent in his second chance. Evie would tolerate him, for another few months at least. One by one, the Company would come round. He'd have to work on Valentino and the orchestra. Their eyes still seemed most scathing of all. But surely there was a way. If he just kept his head down, kept out of trouble – if he could just forget about the burning itch he'd started feeling to perform among them again – he might yet get through this unscathed.

But there stood Valentino's piano. It had been arranged in the heart of the stage itself, where – come show-night – it would be revealed by the parting dancers, with Valentino already hunkered over it, ready to weave his magic spell. Ready for Bill to sing.

But those songs...

He had to remind himself that they were classics. And, of course, they were. People would be singing 'Unforgettable' when Cal himself was in his dotage – *if*, he reminded himself, touching his side, he made it that far. And yet...

His hands reached for a chord.

He started to sing. 'Runaway lovers... running for cover... I wish this was over... one way or another...'

His fingers faltered at the next chord. How aching this song had felt when he'd first composed it. How confident he'd been, that afternoon he'd marched down to the offices on Denmark Street and, promising them he had something special – a stone-cold classic for the age in which they lived – had started to play.

How bewildered, devastated, confused he'd been when, having been ejected from the first office, he'd gone to the second, the third, the fourth and fifth, only to hear variations of the same words coming from a dozen different mouths. 'It doesn't have what we're looking for, Cal. It's big, yes, and it has a tune – but *what* is it? What are you trying to write? Who are you trying to be? I'll tell you what it's like: it's like Irving Gordon tried to write a song for Elvis Presley. It's not a golden oldie, but it's hardly for the kids now, is it? You need to know who you're playing to, Cal. This song – it's not *for* anyone.'

It's for anyone who has a heart, Cal tried to tell them. It's for anyone who had to leave the person they loved. It's for *anyone* ...

In the Seagate, his voice rose again. 'The reason that they're singing ... is the same from Penrith to Berlin ... If it's not on account of her ... then it's on account of him ...'

Cal let the last note ring out, a declaration of pure, untroubled, unbridled love.

He still didn't care what they'd said. Roy Orbison would have made 'Runaway Lover' soar. Anyone who had made a hit of 'Only the Lonely' would have known how to sell Cal's song. 'Running Scared' and 'Crying', that was the feeling he was reaching for – something lovelorn, something epic, something that married the balladry of old to the rock and roll he'd seen coming up through the clubs.

He struck the first chord again, his hands running into a riot of music.

It was his very best song.

*

Lily had spent half an hour dragging two of the other dancing girls from one door to another in Seaford when, at last, she decided that there wasn't a place in town to 'get the juices flowing' tonight. 'We'll just have to accept it, girls. There isn't going to be any high life until we reach London.'

Until then, the Tanner Hop would have to do. 'A pub?' Verity ventured. She'd been with the Company just as long as Lily, and, though she was as flamboyant as any on stage, she didn't carry that showiness into her everyday life as Lily did. Lily joked it was because she was raised better. 'Come on, Lil, we can't go in a pub. It's old men. It's darts. It's ...'

'It's the nineteen sixties,' Lily cried, with a roll of her eyes.

'Even so, Lil ...'

'No, I'll hear nothing of it. We deserve a drink, don't we? And, besides, look who's already settled down for the night ...'

The girls looked through the window. There, with his dogs curled at his lap, was Davith.

'I suppose if Davith's there, it might just about be allowed,' said Betty, who'd been with the Forsyths three years longer than Lily

There were plenty of errant looks at the thought of three working girls walking into a public house. Even the landlord – who, as well as his ales and stouts, was embracing modernity with a place for Babycham and Cherry B behind his bar – gave them a sharp look.

Lily, either oblivious or totally defiant of the looks, marched across the pub to where Davith was sitting.

'Mind if we join?' Lily asked, hardly waiting for a response before she took her seat.

'Oh, girls,' Davith said, quite distracted. 'I'm afraid I can't stay too long. There's a chap I'm due to telephone. He's got a few dancing corgis, would you credit it? Those would be a fine thing, to prance for the Queen, don't you think?'

'Oh, Davith.' Lily laughed. 'This isn't a work night, not for us. We're off the clock. We just want to have a good time. I'm sorry, Davith, old chap. We might have to ask you to get the drinks in for us. You'd be a gent, wouldn't you?'

Davith had been perfectly happy spending the evening with his dogs, his newspaper, and the pickled egg and pork scratchings that comprised his dinner. Now, his eyes flickered in surprise. It wasn't often in life that you suddenly got the company of three lovely young ladies. 'I say, girls, are you sure ...?'

'It's just a drink, Davith,' said Lily.

So Davith got to his feet. 'I'll bring you ladies some pickled eggs as well. It's just the thing to line the stomach.'

Davith was exactly the kind of chaperone Lily had wanted. There wasn't a soul in the Forsyth Varieties who didn't have a soft spot for the old Welshman: he never had a cross word to say, patient, wise – and almost completely disinterested in the human species. Evie said it was what made him a great performer: he was willing to let the dogs upstage him at almost every opportunity.

Now that he was off at the bar, collecting their drinks – Lily had ordered half a pint of mild, a provocation (or so the others thought) to the disgruntled men propped at the bar – Lily finally felt relaxed. 'It's just a drink, girls.'

'They'll think you're pick-ups,' said Davith, coming back with the first drinks. He'd only been able to carry two, and the pickled eggs had been left at the bar too (a fact of which Lily was momentarily appreciative). 'Coming into the pub like that. The landlord can refuse you, you know.'

'He should be so lucky!' Lily cackled, accepting her drink.

'I'm serious,' Davith said. 'Back in Wales, this would have

been sacrilege, this. Like all that *skulduggery* John peddles. It's against the natural order.'

Lily, who had seen Davith's dogs dressed in nun's habits, howling along in tune to Bing Crosby, thought that there were many more things against the natural order in this world. 'We're performers, Davith. We're meant to buck the rules.'

'A young woman in a pub in Wales, without even a young man on her arm to stand for her honour? These lads,' and Davith made eyes around the room, 'would think you were ...'

'Yes, yes, Davith,' said Lily. 'I'm quite sure we know what they'd think. But we're not in the valleys now.'

'No, girls, but you're not in London either. Look, I can see one young man's got the devil in his eyes for you already.'

Lily looked around. Davith was right. One of the younger men at the bar, a broad-shouldered man with hair almost as red as Lily's, his face an atlas of freckles, was looking at her out of the side of his eye, lingering over her every time his great hand brought his tankard to his lips.

Later as Lily returned from the pub's water closet, she head the man say with a gruff northern accent: 'You're with them Forsyths, ain't you?' Lily, pretended not to hear. 'I'm talking to you', he said putting his hand on her shoulder

Lily had heard that tone before. It was the tone a man, three beers in his belly, took when a good-looking girl ignored him in the street. You learned to ignore those voices, just like you learned to ignore the heckles of less well-natured audience members, but his hand on her shoulder was harder to shake off. She turned towards him and, with her sweetest smile, said, 'That's right. We just got into town. Are you coming to the Spectacular, then?'

She needn't have been worried. The man might have seemed aggressive, but now he started smiling. 'I don't know about that.

I'm not one for the theatre, not normally. I just don't have it in me. But then I saw them posters of yours. Your *mystery* guest. That got the mind whirling, I don't mind telling you.'

Lily's eyes darted quickly at Betty and Verity at their table fearful they'd all been gossiping too loudly about the rehearsal that day – that, perhaps, they'd given away Ed's closely guarded secret. Yet they only seemed to be gazing at her, as if she was still on stage – as if she and this burly man were some show they were eager to see to its conclusion.

'Well, you'll have to come and see for yourself if you want to know about that,' Lily replied. Ed would have been proud.

'I'll bet it's a ruse.' The man laughed. 'Just to get bottoms on seats. I know what you theatrical types are like. A little white lie never hurt, did it? Not if it sells some tickets.'

Lily almost wanted to tell him now, but something told her she was being led on. 'Well, you'll be the one missing out!' She laughed. Suddenly he said, 'It wouldn't be Cal Forsyth, would it? This mystery guest of yours?'

Lily froze. A single image scythed into her mind: Cal, pulling on his shirt in the double-decker bus, all of those bruises colouring his ribs, the ugly stain in the bandage on his side.

'Cal... C-Cal?' she stuttered. 'Well, it would hardly be a mystery, would it? Cal Forsyth? The Company's got his name!'

'Well, see, I've heard of this Cal Forsyth,' the man went on, leaning back from Lily, appraising her with his eyes. 'Quite a songsmith, by all accounts. Went off to be his own star for a while. I've got one of his records, somewhere or other. Decent little tune, if a bit forgettable. Yes,' he said, nodding more confidently now. 'That must be it. Cal Forsyth, the mystery guest. The prodigal's return.'

'You're barking up the wrong tree,' Lily snapped, suddenly defensive. 'If you think Ed would do something as silly as make his *own son* a mystery guest, you've got another think coming. No, he's got something much bigger in store than that.'

'Who?' said the man, simply and bluntly, placing one hand on his hip.

'Well, I can't say, can I?'

The man guffawed. 'You're full of it! You dancing girls have got a way about you, I'll grant you that.'

'What's it to you, anyway?' asked Lily. Then a sudden thought struck her. 'You're from one of the local rags, aren't you? You're looking for a story. Well, here's a story for you: dancing girl knows how to keep her lips zipped!' And she clamped her lips between forefinger and thumb.

'I've got a message for Cal,' said the man.

Lily's blood ran cold.

'Yes, that's right,' said the man. 'Tell him he's wanted. Tell him we've got to talk. Tell him this thing needs sorting out, and fast, before it gets bigger than us all. You tell him – tell him I'm staying at the Fairview Hotel, where I'm told they're still raging about that high-wire act of his.' The man paused. 'Just tell him that Sam wants to see him, and soon.'

Cal's voice reached the final chorus, for the final time. 'Runaway lovers … running for cover …' he sang – and, just as in his most powerful performances, his voice broke, the desperation of those few words fading into the song's final plea. 'I wish it was over … one way or another …'

How many times had he sung it? Somehow, it never got old. It wasn't like churning out the standards in a club, all the oldies delivered in time so that he could get his drink and get the next bus home. This song inhabited him. He lived in it, and it in him. It could have – it should have – made him a star.

He heard the clatter of footsteps. So long had he been lost

in the song that he hadn't noticed how quickly an hour had passed. He realised his eyes had become bleary; Cal Forsyth hadn't wept, but there was emotion enough in the song that tears still prickled his eyes.

Standing in the stalls, her face turned up to him with and eyes filled with wonder, was Lily.

'That – that was beautiful, Cal,' she said, coming forward in faltering footsteps. 'Was that … was that one of yours? I've never heard it before.'

'Just one of the forgotten songs, Lil,' he said, and left Valentino's piano behind as he jumped from the stage. 'I thought you were in town tonight. Headed out there with all of the rest. I'll bet they're frothing about the show, are they? You're getting those looks everywhere you go?' Cal remembered that feeling: the first night of a new tour, the anticipation heavy in the air; new town, new people, new promise. 'What is it, Lily?' he said. 'You look like you've seen a ghost.'

'There's a man in town,' she said, and Cal detected some hesitation in her voice. 'Cal, he's asking after you.'

Cal froze.

'Said his name was Sam.'

Cal's lips parted, as if he truly didn't understand. 'Sam?' he asked.

'A big man. Red hair. Face covered in freckles. He's staying at the Fairview Hotel. He said he needed to see you. That there's business you need to sort out, and … and …' She couldn't keep it back any longer. 'Cal, are you in some sort of trouble? You are, aren't you? Don't lie to me this time.' She moved closer to him. 'It's the reason you came back. It isn't home – or, at least, that's not all of it. But you didn't run back to the Forsyths, Cal. You're running away from something – and this was the place you came.'

Cal pushed past her. 'You've got it wrong, Lil.'

He was halfway across the stalls, heading for the box office and the Seagate doors beyond. Lily cantered after him, calling out his name. 'Cal, this is serious. You came here, bloodied and beaten up. You told them all you missed them, that all you wanted was another chance. But, Cal, you *lied*.'

In the same moment that she reached for him, Cal spun around, near knocking her off balance. Now, realising what he had done, Cal reached for her, took her hand, set her right on her feet. 'Lily, listen to me now. You have to leave this alone. It's a mix-up, that's all it is. He's an old friend. I still have friends, you know.'

Lily said, 'You've got *me*, Cal.'

'Who else knows this? Who were you with?'

'Just two of the girls,' said Lily. 'But they just think he was trying to pick me up. I didn't tell them anything he'd asked after you by name. I didn't tell them there was a message.' She paused. 'Davith was there too, but he was more interested in corgis. He's going to meet a man about a dog.'

Cal grimaced. 'Davith's no problem. The old soul doesn't think beyond his dogs. But … corgis, is it? Corgis, for the Queen?'

'Cal, what can I do?'

'If you really are a friend to me,' he whispered, 'you'll keep this to yourself. A lot of life happens in five years. A lot of good, and a whole lot of bad. But it isn't anything that needs to dog me now. It doesn't have to follow me here. It's a misunderstanding, Lily, and I'm going to put it to bed.'

There was a long, lingering silence. Then, just when Cal was certain it had gone on too long, that he had asked too much of her, she lifted herself onto her tiptoes and planted a single kiss on his cheek.

'Cal,' she murmured. 'You have my word.'

10

A Secret Betrayed

The London Palladium: what an institution this was, what history lived in its hallowed halls. But tonight it was empty. The galleries were lit up in gold and bronze. Row upon row of empty burgundy seats reached from the lowest stalls into the very gods themselves. But all was silent.

John let his hands trail across the seats, and by doing so heard the ghosts of times long gone.

Then he heard the screaming.

It had come, he knew, from somewhere backstage: a single, anguished howl, which tapered off into a breathless, guttering protest. His eyes sought out its direction, and immediately he took off, loping towards the stage as fast as his aged legs would carry him.

Only now did he understand this was a dream – for, no matter how urgently he walked to the stage, it only seemed to retreat away from him.

'I'm coming!' he called out. 'I'm coming!'

It had been this way in the deeps of Flanders, once upon a time. On the outskirts of Ypres, where a much younger John had been barracked, pouring over the top into a world of razor wire, ruptured earth and blackened trees. The terror of those old days coursed through him now. The next depression in the earth, the next foxhole where he might find some temporary reprieve, had always retreated into the distance as well. He grappled out to reach it.

It's only a dream, he told himself. *It's but a dream.*

But what did it mean?

Somehow, he made the stage; somehow, he heaved his aged body up onto the boards, across which he staggered like a man already driven senseless by the bombs raining down. This stage had been a source of such joy, but treading it only filled John with horror and despair. Eager to leave it behind, through the back passages he hurried. The scream was already dead – so too the guttering breath – but, by the strange logic of dreams, he knew which way he was going.

He staggered to the final dressing room on the right. The door was ajar, light spilling from within.

The name on the door read: *CAL FORSYTH*.

It was then that he noticed that light was not the only thing spilling through the door.

He'd seen blood before, of course. He'd held his companions as they'd died, lacerated by enemy fire.

But that had been years ago.

That had been war.

And this?

This was the London Palladium.

Finding some last reserve of courage – for so much of it had been squandered in those days of blood and fire – John pushed through the dressing-room door.

The body was lying, spread-eagled in a chair in front of the mirror.

The blade was buried, up to its handle, deep in his breast.

John woke up in a cold sweat. His heart was hammering far too wildly for a gentleman of his vintage, his sheets were tangled around him – and, by the moonlight streaming in through the curtains onto the pocket-watch on his dresser, it was scarcely one o'clock in the morning, which meant there was a whole night-time of dreaming yet to come.

He lay back and shivered.

The dreams he'd had before had spoken of disaster, but not quite like this.

Now, when he closed his eyes, all he could picture was the London Palladium, and the floor of Cal's dressing room, dripping with blood.

John Lauder was not the only one to experience a sleepless night in Seaford. In the partitioned section of the double-decker, Cal tossed and turned, Lily's few enigmatic words – 'There's a man in town … he's asking for you … said his name is Sam …' – repeating over and over in his mind.

In a lodging house not far away, Evie lay awake with Max sleeping fitfully by her side – simultaneously worried about what was unnerving him, and what it might have meant that her father, having announced his impending retirement, had yet to announce his plans for the succession.

In a little bedroom on the other side of town, just above the sign that said *LIVESEY & SONS UNDERTAKERS, FOUNDED 1882*, Jim Livesey sat brooding long past the midnight hour, forever turning that slip of paper John Lauder had left for him in his hands.

Come back and see me when you UNDERSTAND.

It was the capitalisation of that last word that vexed Jim the most. He kept saying the word, over and over, giving it a slightly different emphasis every time – but nothing was revealing itself to him. Getting this note into his pocket had been a simple piece of sleight of hand. But the rest of it was a mystery to Jim. How could Mr Lauder ever have known such things about Jim? Was it possible that he had truly read the boy's mind?

Somewhere around 2 a.m., Jim began rereading *Through the Illusionist's Lens* for the seventh time. John Lauder never broke the stage magician's cardinal rule – he never revealed the workings behind his most wonderful tricks – but there were plenty who plied that trade, breaking down magic piece by piece, and Jim had a trunk full of those books and magazines as well. The problem was that, nowhere in all of that writing, was there any suggestion that mind-reading could possibly be real.

So how had Mr Lauder done it? How had he tantalised Jim so?

He was still brooding on it when he finally fell asleep, sometime past four. He must have dreamt of it, too, for when his mother started hammering on his door at a quarter past seven, it was from a dark dream – of a blood-drenched theatre and John Lauder telling him that, when you read a mind, you never quite knew what you might find – that he was hauled. 'I'm coming, Mum!' he called out, then blearily stumbled down the stairs to join the rest of his family for breakfast.

His father was already dressed in funereal black – Reginald Livesey was reputed to go to bed in the same – and his little sister Amy was burying her face in a bowl of porridge, while their mother clucked around, pouring tea, scraping pans, and grazing on whatever she could find while she looked after her brood.

'Put that book down, boy,' Jim's father snapped, showering toast and jam across the kitchen table. 'You've got enough of books coming at that school o' yours today. Get your head up, look smart, and start eating some of this grub your mother's cooked up for you. I've never seen such a skinny rake. When I was your age I was …'

About to go off to war, thought Jim, though he'd grown wise enough not to say it.

'And where were you yesterday evening anyway?' his father asked, considering him with those dark, implacable eyes. 'I could have used a hand in the workshop. You've got responsibilities now, James. You're not a child any more.'

'Yes,' said Amy in her sing-song voice. 'So enough of that magic!'

Jim's little sister was only eight years old, but there was nothing she enjoyed more than taking their parents' side against her brother. The thing was, Jim could have understood their disapproval if he'd been out chasing girls, risking unwed pregnancies and generally giving the firm a bad reputation around town. People needed to respect their undertakers. It was one of the last truly noble professions.

'Mum,' he said, quite ignoring his father's frowning eyes. 'Did you get tickets for the Seagate Spectacular? They're talking about it all over town.'

'So *that's* what it is,' said his father, reaching out to pluck the book from Jim's hand. 'This occultist's there, is he?'

'He's not an occultist, Dad,' Jim objected, trying in vain to take the book back. 'He's an illusionist. See?' And he prodded the book's cover. '*Through the Illusionist's Lens*. It says it right there.'

'He'll be a crackpot. They all are. Talking to the dead, indeed. It makes a mockery of your profession, young man. James, it's a Livesey's job to put folks six feet under the sod – not to go around pretending you can have a natter with them after they're gone. You ought to have grown out of this by now. I need you to focus.'

'Mother, did you get them?' he asked again. 'It isn't just Mr Lauder. There are so many different acts at the Forsyth Varieties.'

'As well we know,' Jim's father said darkly. 'The way they bombarded our town with those posters. My lads had to scrape three of them down yesterday. The damn things are abominations. We've reported it to the council.'

'It's just a bit of light, Dad. It's just a bit of fun. They've got dancers and a dog act, and Mr Lauder does shadow theatre – and there are acrobats too, Dad. That's not to even mention Ed Forsyth – he's compère, of course, but I'll bet he's funnier than any of those on *Sunday Night at the Palladium*.'

'Do they have a strongman?' Jim's father asked.

Jim stuttered, 'I – I don't think they do . . .'

'Then we're not interested, are we, Gertie?'

Jim's mother stopped wringing her hands on a dishcloth. 'I just don't think we've got the time, James. I'm sorry.'

'Oh, but—'

'No *buts*, young man!'

'It's a once in a lifetime chance!' Jim cried out. 'They're taking this act to the Royal Variety. Please, we *have* to see it. Don't you . . . don't you want to see Bill Martin himself?'

At this, Jim's mother – who had been returning her attention to a sink full of washing up – froze. 'What did you say?'

'It's this mystery guest of theirs, Mum. I heard them talking outside the theatre last night. That's why they've got those security guards posted out there.'

'Oh, codswallop!' Jim's father exploded. 'Bill Martin? Star of *With Love, Hattie*? Hollywood's finest? In . . . Seaford?'

'I know it sounds strange, Dad, but it's true. I heard it with my own ears.'

Reginald Livesey shook his head and returned his attention

to the morning newspaper. 'Gertie,' he proclaimed. 'Our boy has quite lost his marbles.'

But, at the sink, Gertie Livesey had suddenly got a dreamy, faraway look in her eyes. 'Bill Martin, Jim? Bill Martin, you say?'

It wasn't long before his early recording of 'To the Moon and Back' was playing on the record player in the Livesey household.

It wasn't long after that that the first rumours began.

Evie and her dancers were ready when the burgundy limousine and its security vehicles returned to the Seagate Theatre that morning. By the time Bill and his coterie of guards – trailing Magdalene behind them, in a fug of cigarette smoke and Chanel – appeared backstage, they had already blocked out the opening number, and near-perfected the choreography that would unfurl to reveal Bill Martin to the Seagate stage.

'I don't know about how it looks,' said Bill, as he emerged from the wing. 'But it *sounds* magnificent. Come on, guys and dolls, let me see it as it's meant to be seen. Then we'll get these songs really *flying*. I'll need the orchestra ready for the first number in fifteen. No need for vocal exercises this morning – this old voice of mine was singing plenty in the shower this morning!'

The gales of rapturous laughter that met Bill's comment as he sauntered across the stage – taking the hand of each dancer, before taking up his position in the stalls alongside Ed – were certainly not deserved. Yet there was, Evie decided, something so infectious about his presence that it sprinkled some magic dust on everything he said. She supposed he would call this the quality of 'stardom', and to Evie it was as if his entire life was a performance, that there was an audience wherever he went – whether he was on stage or back, or even out in the world, at the hotels, casinos, golf courses and fancy restaurants a man like him frequented. In all likelihood it was an exhausting way to live, but Bill made it seem easy.

'Well, then,' she said to her assembled troupe. 'Shall we show Mr Martin where we're at?' She had a sparkling smile of her own, one she could summon even when energy reserves were low; the dancers responded to conviction like that. Once they saw someone full of pep and vigour, they started to feel it themselves, even if they were flat-out exhausted. 'We'll break after this. But once more, dear friends...' Lily and the rest fanned out, but she noticed that Max still looked drawn. 'You're unwell,' she whispered to him, as the dancers prepared. 'You need to rest. Maybe tonight... your own lodging?' The landlady knew, of course, just like the rest of the troupe. But most good landladies could pretend they saw an imaginary wedding band when they needed – and especially off-season, when guests were few and far between.

'Never,' whispered Max, and the simple exchange seemed to restore some of his vigour. He hurried to take his place among the dancers, and then they began.

In the stalls, Ed could not have felt prouder. He could still count the time they'd been in Seaford in hours, and yet this show was already nearing completion. Later this afternoon, he would watch Davith's dogs vanish and reappear through John's cabinet – invoking more mystery than ever, for how could a dog work the latch on a secret panel, or be expected to contort itself through an unseen door? – and know that the twin pillars of the piece were complete.

All that was left to worry him now were his own lines. He was sure he could rely on regular patter, old lines for the Seagate Spectacular, but when it came to the Palladium, things would have to change. He'd seen Norman Vaughan in the flesh only once, but he'd caught him on the television innumerable times over the years; to be compèring his own act, while Vaughan held together the entire show, presented peculiar challenges.

'You know what it is,' he whispered to Bill, as the dancers performed. 'It shouldn't feel like a competition, so I have to get the tone just right. I mustn't try and upstage him. It's a battle I'd lose. So the tone has to be different. It has to stand out. It's just—'

'Eddie, my boy, you're every bit as consummate a showman as ol' Norman Vaughan. He's just a Liverpudlian lad who made it good. If you were twenty years younger, it might have been you taking over on *Sunday Nights at the Palladium*. It might have been you and this young scamp, Cliff, touring variety.' Here, Bill leaned in conspiratorially. 'I don't know what the youngsters see in him, this Cliff Richard, but he must have something about him. He's up on the bill too, ain't he? Him and those Shadows of his?'

'Where Norman Vaughan goes, so do Cliff and the Shadows. I wouldn't know much about them, Bill. You'd have to ask Cal. I suppose he'd know. They probably played in the same clubs.'

'You see, that's Cal's problem,' said Bill, lowering his voice even further. 'Now, the boy has talent. You always knew that. But – well, ain't he just a bit too *old*?'

This young Cliff, do you think he'd have got a look-in in our day? The boy can't be twenty years old, and he's *everywhere*.' Bill paused. 'Cal has the looks. He has the talent. But he hasn't had the luck, and … well, he's thirty, not eighteen, you know what I mean?'

'Bill, you're awfully cynical.'

'It's all just timing, that's what it is. You might have been hosting the television. Cal might have been a rock-and-roll star. The stars need to align.'

'That's how it was for you, then?'

'Well,' said Bill, with a new air of pride, 'the stars align more easily for some than they do others. What can I say?' He paused. 'Ed, you ever think about what you're actually going to do when you give this all up?'

On stage, Evie's dancers fanned apart, revealing the portal along which Bill would emerge. It was nearing the end of their number.

'Me and Bella used to talk about the countryside. Suffolk, where she took the twins when we were out in France.' Ed gave a bittersweet smile. 'Norman Vaughan was out there too. I can only just remember him, just a slip of a lad. In uniform, of course – not like us. He struck up with that lot who ended up on the radio. Milligan and Secombe. Now, Secombe – there's a variety performer; *there's* a voice.'

'But, Ed... what would you do out there?'

'Well, I'd do what Bella and I always talked about. I'd keep house. I'd work the garden. There might be a little theatre, in the next village along, where I'd help some youngsters along.'

'Oh, but, Ed,' said Bill, a little more softly now, a little less starry. 'Alone? Is that what she would have wanted?'

Ed grinned. 'There'll be grandkids, one day,' Ed said. 'Evie and her young man over there...'

'The blond Adonis?' Bill laughed. 'Hercules? You know what they call that in the States, Ed? They call it a... toyboy.'

'I rather think that's a British idiom, Bill. We Brits invented the language, and don't forget it. Don't forget *you're* one of us too.' After they had laughed together, Ed went on. 'I think it's the real deal. I don't know why, but I get a sense of things. Unconventional couples do take flight in the varieties.'

'And what about Cal? Always had a wandering eye, didn't he?' Bill paused. 'Hey, where is he?'

There wasn't any need to look far – for there was Cal, head bowed in conversation with Magdalene at the back of the stalls.

Ed's heart sank. He'd tried to tell the boy. No, he had told him – spelled it out in no uncertain terms.

There was a moment in which Bill looked furious. Then, he took a deep breath and seemed to calm down.

'I'll tell him to let her just watch,' said Ed, getting up out of his seat while trying to disguise his inner ire. 'It's just Cal, Bill. Cal, with nothing to do.'

'Well,' said Bill – and it was clear, from the set of his jaw, that he hadn't really let go of his irritation, that he was just corralling and harbouring it instead. 'Maybe you ought to find him something to do in this show of ours. Something to occupy his hands, so the Devil doesn't find a use for them. Put him in the orchestra, at least.'

'I can't do that, Bill. Valentino didn't vote for him to stay. They were close to him, back in the day. He just walked out. Bridges were burned. But, listen, I'll find him an errand. God, I'll send him up to London for logistics. Davith's looking to get some corgis for the Palladium. Cal can—'

But, as Ed looked again, it seemed he had no reason to spirit up something for Cal to do – for, at the back of the Seagate, he was already leaving Magdalene's side, already leaping over the seats and sauntering, hands shoved in the pockets of his brown leather jacket, towards the box-office doors.

'Where's he going?' Ed whispered.

But, up on stage, his voice was drowned out.

'Well, Mr Martin!' Evie exclaimed. 'Are you ready to join the act?'

And Bill leapt out of his chair, as sprightly as a much younger man, and declared, 'You bet your bottom dollar I am!'

Ed turned to watch them. Whatever Cal was doing could wait. *This* was why he was a performer. To take part in the creation of a show like this, it was what every man dreamed.

Rumours are like viruses; they have lives of their own.

'Bill Martin?' the town said, in varying degrees of excitement, disbelief and confusion. 'Bill Martin, in Seaford?'

Most who heard it dismissed it as stuff-and-nonsense, of course.

But if only one in ten raindrops reach the ground in a storm, it can still be a deluge.

And the capacity at the Seagate Theatre was only five hundred and twelve.

Lily was certain Cal had been there the moment they started the dance, but she was equally certain he was not there when Bill Martin had finished his soaring rendition of 'You Belong To Me'. Somehow, this portion of the show would have to morph seamlessly – covered by only a moment's patter from Ed – into the illusion John Lauder had been plotting all summer. She could see John slipping like a shadow into the stalls to meet Davith and his dogs already waiting there. But of Cal there was no sign.

She flashed a look at Evie, wondering if she ought to say, wondering if – even in spite of the promise she'd made Cal last night – she ought to betray his trust. Because there was only one place Cal could be, if not here at the Seagate. Not nursing his wounds in the double-decker bus. Not backstage, hunched over the piano while lovelorn balladry cascaded from his fingers. She looked at the clock on the wall. Yes, midday was approaching – and that meant the opening of the bar at the Fairview Hotel. He'd only come to the theatre at all this morning to kill time while he waited. Now, he was gone – to face whoever it was who was searching for him.

Lily pirouetted on her heel. Some of the other girls were following Max from the stage, off to their well-earned rest – and no doubt whatever luncheon the lodgings had agreed to provide. As for Evie herself, she was lost in conversation with Bill Martin; the older man held her hand and was fawning over her as if it was Evie who was the star.

'Evie, might I...'

She needed permission, of course.

But Evie was enraptured – or, if not enraptured, a captive audience to Bill Martin alone. And, when she thought about it, it didn't have to take long. They were all due a little rest. Time away from the stage was almost more important than time on it; the body needed to relax, and so too did the mind.

So, for a little time at least, she would not be missed.

And if she was?

Well, Lily decided, it might be the most important rule she'd ever broken.

It would have to be the Fairview Hotel, Cal thought. No doubt there were a few folk in there who'd seen him sing the other night, then watched him flee from the ruckus – as if he was a coward, or as if he simply didn't care.

He opened the door and strode into the bar.

Cal was finding it hard to be courageous now. He'd written a song once, which he'd called 'Orpheus', a three-minute rock-and-roll number about going into hell for someone you loved. The suits at Decca had called it overly pompous, but what did they know? It had gone down a storm when Cal had played it in the Blackpool clubs, or on his tour between Glasgow and Aberdeen. But in an industry built on such arbitrary opinions, and such pig-headed self-importance, there was only so much you could do.

Cal tried to hide his nervousness as he sauntered to the bar.

At the bar, while Cal waited for the landlord to catch his eye, he lifted his wallet from his pocket. Inside, its edges frayed and worn, was a photograph taken on a distant seafront, some months before. By the look of the thing, you might have thought it was years old – but Cal had carried it with him ever since, taking it out to gaze upon in every private moment, and it was starting to wear.

He looked at it now. In its centre stood Cal himself. Beside him, a woman with flame-red hair. Even depicted in black and white, that voluminous hair was striking, cascading in waves around her. Crowding their shoulders were others: an elderly couple, and a younger one too. It was the man of this younger couple that Cal dwelt over. In the picture, he was smiling, but Cal knew it to be a lie. That man's smile hid a thousand sins. If only they'd seen it sooner.

Cal was still brooding over the picture when the landlord appeared, looming over him with two glass tankards in his meaty hand. There was no escaping his gaze; he knew who Cal was, all right. 'Back to cause trouble, are you?' he asked, the coldness in his voice every bit as bitter as the wind coming in from the sea.

'About the other night...'

The barkeep just stared. Then, when the silence had already gone on too long, he said, '*Out.*'

Moments later, he was lifting the hatch, striding out of the bar, casting his dishcloth aside so that both his fists were free.

'Listen,' Cal said, opening his palms. 'It wasn't on me. You *know* that. You invited me here to sing. You didn't tell me the bar would be full of...' Cal's eyes darkened as he realised he'd been about to cast aspersions on all the regulars who frequented the Fairview Hotel. 'Look, I didn't fight back, did I? They came after me, and I didn't so much as …'

'Aye, well, I've unhappy punters, boy – and unhappy punters means less in the till. This isn't a charity. I invited you here to entertain these people, not to put the frighteners up them. Not to get them all riled. *Dancing* and cavorting around! …'

'I didn't *do* anything.'

The barkeep was almost on top of Cal now. 'I can't serve you in here, boy. Not unless I serve you a bloody hiding. So sling your hook, and the quicker we forget the other night, the better.'

Still, Cal did not move. He had come here for a purpose. He had to at least try to see it through.

'It's not a drink I'm looking for,' he said, so close to the barman now that he could feel the dewy warmth of his breath. 'At least, not yet. It's …' And he turned the photograph around, indicating the smiling man who stood at the left of the image. 'He's staying here, isn't he? I'm told he asked for me by name?'

The barkeep screwed up his eyes. 'Can't say I've seen the bugger,' he said. 'And I know everyone who's through here. So if that's all you're after, now you can …'

Cal furrowed his eyes. 'Are you certain? I got word that—'

'Look, son,' the barkeep said, and bunched his fist around Cal's collar. 'I've been a publican all my life. I grew up in pubs. I've owned two and worked in more. If there's a memory for faces you can trust, it's a landlord's. And I'm *telling* you, that man ain't been in here.'

'No,' came a familiar voice. 'But I have.'

That voice, it was like a bucket of ice-cold water being thrown over Cal's face. It was like a punch to his jaw. Like a knife in his side. It shocked him so much that he whirled around, freeing himself of the barman's grasp, ready to face whatever came – and there stood a broad-shouldered man with tight red curls, his face coloured by thousands of freckles, his jaw revealing that he'd been on the road for some time, for it was already covered with a dark auburn fuzz.

'You,' Cal gasped. 'I didn't know it would be—'

Lily barrelled through the doors of the Fairview Hotel. The wind flurried behind her. One of the patrons barked out for her to hurry up and close it quick, but neither Cal nor the bearded man standing in front of her turned to look. Instead, they just stared at each other. It was as if, Lily decided, they were a tableaux, the frozen piece of a performance, a position held by a dancer while her choreographer inspected it for elegance and poise.

She wanted to call out, but, for some reason, suddenly she felt frozen too. The words choked in her throat.

The man's hand came back. His face, a solemn mask, started to pale.

Then his hand darted forward.

It snatched Cal's own.

'Cal, you devil,' he said, with a sudden, broad smile. 'You shook off that beating swiftly enough, didn't you?'

'You frightened me out of my skin, Jack.' Cal seemed breathless too. For the first time, Lily realised how tightly he'd been wound, and how quickly the fear was leaving him. 'I came here thinking it would be *him*. Why didn't you just announce yourself? Why didn't you send for me by name?'

'I did that in Grimsby, Cal. And I did that in Bexhill. I've been following you round this country, trying to get your ear.'

The adrenaline was leaching out of Lily too. She'd meant to leap in here and defend Cal but, instead, some element of confusion was sweeping over her. Why had the man who'd introduced himself as 'Sam' been embraced by Cal as 'Jack'? What had he to do with the bruises that marked Cal's breast, the knife wound in his side, if he wasn't the one who'd inflicted them, if he wasn't the one hunting Cal?

'Two pints of stout, old man,' the man named Jack said to the landlord. Then, after a pregnant pause – still loaded with irritation – Jack went on, 'Look, I'll vouch for him. There's going to be no trouble here. And I'm a guest, aren't I? I'm a guest, and he's my guest. So just make it two pints, would you? I've come a long way.'

Their landlord's next words were mumbled, but Lily soon noticed that two pints of stout were indeed being poured, and that the two men were repairing, like long lost friends, to one of the booths by the window.

As they went, they stopped by the jukebox in the corner. There they lingered – like two young boys, scouring a record shop for the latest Bill Haley – until a record had been selected. As they wended their way to their table, Elvis Presley's 'Return to Sender' started ringing out. Lily liked this song. Those opening bars – they always made her want to dance. And yet, dancing in the Fairview Hotel had already led to such disaster, so, resisting the ridiculous temptation, she slid after Cal and his new companion, lingering by the jukebox as they took their seats.

She had to concentrate to listen. Elvis's voice filled her ears, so that at times it was near impossible to hear what they were saying. She studiously avoided the irritated looks of the barkeeper as well; no doubt he thought she was some wanton woman who dared to venture into a drinking establishment on her own. That was, of course, if he hadn't recognised her as the rabble rouser from the other night. The best thing to do was to keep ignoring him, keep feeding coins into the jukebox so that neither Cal nor this 'Jack' came back over, and just try to understand.

'Sam's desperate to see you,' Jack was saying.

'I don't know what I'm meant to do here, Jack. So Sam wants to see me. What am I meant to say?'

'Well, that's why I'm here, you dumb brute. You singers never did have much upstairs. Would I come all this way, when you didn't even leave a clue as to where you might be going, if I hadn't sorted this out?'

Lily saw Cal's brow furrow in disbelief. 'Sorted it out, Jack? *Sorted it out*? But what about ...' He dropped his voice so that Lily could hear nothing but Elvis caterwauling in her ear. Not that it mattered, because she could make out the word sure enough by the movements of his lips. 'The police?' he had mouthed, and inside, Lily felt her stomach start to tie itself in knots.

'There isn't any police. They were never involved, Cal. Bruce has bothered the police enough in his time. He was never going to go running to them when things turned against him. He's done his time. He doesn't trust an officer of the law.' Jack paused. 'But that doesn't mean he's not looking for retribution, Cal.'

Cal's fists tightened. 'I know all about his retribution, re-member.' And he touched his side, the exact place where Lily had seen that bandage soaked in dark effluent. 'But I took that beating so that *they* didn't have to. And now he wants more?'

'That wasn't his retribution, Cal.' Jack laughed sourly. 'That was just his anger.'

'So what is it? What does he want?'

'Five hundred.'

'Five hundred pounds?'

Jack nodded. 'You can thank me later, old boy. He started at two thousand. It's me who went to broker the deal with him and his brothers. It's me who put himself on the line for you. I could have ended up in the gutter, just like ...'

Cal nodded, started opening his hands as if in apology. 'I'm

193

sorry,' he said. Then, rushing the words, he said it again. 'I'm grateful, Jack. I really am. And if five hundred's the blood money he wants to make this go away, to make *them* safe again – well, that's the price. But, by God, Jack, where am I meant to find five hundred pounds? I was scarcely on nine hundred a year when I was pumping out songs for Decca. Do you know how much I made off "Hold Me Now"?' Cal paused, as if to make a point, and Lily felt a sudden flush of warmth for him. She had always loved that song. 'Twenty pounds, I should think, and most of that gone touring the bloody thing. A few pennies to sing in a club, Jack. Bruce and that lot think I'm lounging in a bed full of crisp pound notes, but it isn't true.' He hung his head. 'Five hundred!'

'This needs putting to bed, and fast, Cal.' Jack paused before saying the next words. 'You have until the end of the month.'

Cal blanched. 'It's not even two weeks.' His fists pounded the table. Lily had the sudden, stark image of Cal – her Cal, her poet, her hero – pounding those fists into somebody's face instead. Because – wasn't that what had happened? Wasn't that what Cal and Jack were talking about right now? 'My father's taking the troupe to the Royal Variety before the end of the month, Jack. I can't visit this on them. I came here to hide. I didn't mean to—'

'Look, Cal.' Jack's voice had become stern for the first time. 'Everything's on the line here. My sister's on the line. Sam is on the line. If you don't settle it this month, the deal's off. I can't promise it will come again. And then where will you be? Sam's safe now, Cal, but not if you don't—'

'I can't spirit something out of nothing!' Cal roared. 'There's a magician back at the theatre. Old John Lauder – he used to pull shillings out of my ear. I can hardly ask him to pull out ten thousand of the damn things!'

Jack drained his pint. Lily watched as he stood. 'I've got to go,' he said sadly. 'If I don't get back north soon, and tell them I've delivered their message, I'll get dragged into this even further. I've done my bit for you, Cal. Now do your bit – if not for you, then do it for Sam. And do it for my sister.'

Jack marched away. He was almost level with the jukebox, Lily sinking back in a panic so as not to be seen, when Cal called after him. 'And Meredith? Did *she* send me a message?'

Jack sighed deeply. He turned back round, narrowly missing seeing Lily as she shrank back further still. 'I haven't seen her. She's still in Northumberland, where we sent her. But I've spoken to her, Cal. She's struggling, you know? She knows what you did was right, but it doesn't change the fact it's stuffed everything up. There were better ways. You might have been killed.' He paused, and fixed Cal with his fiercest glare. 'You might yet, if you don't find a way.'

Jack turned again, then made for the door. Too late, Lily saw that Cal was on his feet and aiming to follow. 'Jack,' he called out. 'Jack, you've got to get me some more time. Jack!'

But this time, Jack didn't look back. He simply marched away, his piece already said.

'God damn it!' Cal uttered, throwing his head back in barely-concealed fury. 'God – damn – *it*!'

Some of the other patrons must have heard, for Lily saw dirty looks being cast in Cal's direction. Behind the bar, the landlord was getting ready to march out again. But Cal didn't seem to notice. Still muttering unintelligible curses to himself, he spun around to march back to his seat...

...and came face to face with Lily.

Lily reeled back. 'Cal,' she blurted out. 'It isn't what you think. I didn't—'

'You followed me!' he snarled. Then, brushing past her, he

snatched his brown leather jacket from the booth where he'd been sitting and hurried for the door. 'Lily, I've a good mind to ...' He let the thought die, then kicked open the door with such force it bucked on its hinges, before plunging into the spray of the seafront.

Lily hurried after him. 'Cal, I had to. Don't you see that? You're hiding something – something serious! You have been from the moment you came.'

'You promised me, Lil. You gave me your absolute word, and now look at you!'

'I gave you my word I wouldn't tattle,' Lily declared, finding her gumption at last. 'And I haven't told a soul. But you listen to me, Cal Forsyth. I didn't give my word I wouldn't ask more questions.' She stopped. Cal still wouldn't turn around, so after a moment's hesitation she picked up the pace and started running. Only when she was in front of him did she stop, throwing herself into his path so that he had no option but to stop and stare. 'Believe it or not, Cal, I *care*. And, if you don't believe I care about you, then believe, at least, that I care about the Company. The Forsyth Varieties is my life. And if thugs extorting money out of you are putting the Forsyths in danger somehow, you have a duty to tell us. You have a responsibility, Cal.' She stifled a sob. Anger wasn't getting through to him, but perhaps raw emotion would. 'What am I supposed to do, Cal?'

'Nothing, Lil,' Cal snapped. 'Nothing, unless you have a spare five hundred pounds!'

'You have to tell them,' Lily declared.

'Tell them?'

'Your father. Evie. Mr Lauder. They might be able to help.'

'Oh, Lily!' Cal crowed. 'Help me? Help me, after I walked out on them? Help me, after I abandoned them? Help me, when they all think I've come back here for my own glory? To sing for the Queen, or ... or to take over the Company after my father's gone? To do Evie out of what's rightfully hers? No, Lil. Why would they want to help me?'

'You're family, Cal!'

'Just get out of my way, Lily. I've got to—'

'If you won't do it for the Forsyths, Cal, then – then ...' Her mind wheeled back, there was so much in there that didn't make sense. But one thing did: that name 'Sam', at the centre of every-thing. Sam, who was desperate to see Cal. Sam, to whom Cal was clearly devoted. If Sam hadn't been the man who'd come for him, then who was it? Samantha, she thought. Yes, that made sense. A lover? A friend? 'If you won't do it for the Forsyths, Cal, then do it for Sam!'

Cal had been about to push past her, but now he froze. 'What did you say?'

'I heard everything,' Lily said, her voice more broken now. 'You obviously care for her. She's desperate to see you – that's what Jack said. And ... and you can't go back, can you? Because of whoever this Bruce is? Because of whatever you did that got you bloodied and beaten up. Oh, Cal! You're not thinking straight. This can't go on.'

'You don't know what you're talking about,' he snarled. 'I told you, Lily. I told you to keep out of this.'

'But I can't. I can't. Don't you see?' She tried to take a step towards him, something, *anything* that might make him under-stand. 'I want to help,' she whispered. 'Who is she, Cal? Who is this Sam?'

Cal put his head back and roared:

'He's my son, Lily! Sam's my bloody son!'

II

A Star Brought to Earth

Ed Forsyth could hardly believe his eyes. In the stalls at the Seagate Theatre, he had just watched two dogs disappear into the ether.

Davith Harvard was an excellent dog-wrangler, but – after all these years – it turned out that he was an excellent comic and mime as well. It was strange what hidden talents people you'd known for years and years could suddenly reveal. Now, as Ed watched, Davith tumbled around the stage, miming his horror and panic at the apparent kidnapping of his dogs. All the while, John Lauder stood solemnly by his cabinet, nodding his head.

Then, somewhere behind Ed, a theatrical flash went off, and, when he and the few dancers and musicians making up the audience turned around, Tinky and Tiny trotted happily out of a wreath of smoke, apparently as bewildered as Davith was up on stage.

Ed got to his feet, raised his hands to applaud, and gave a single, overjoyed cheer. 'It's a triumph, John. An absolute triumph.'

'There's something still niggling me about it,' said John, a few moments later as he reclined in the stalls with his old friend. 'I just don't think it's noisy enough. Wonder's the thing in stage magic. You want the audience gasping, wondering how on earth it was done. But when the piece is to nestle inside everything Evie's got planned? When it's to come second to Bill Martin?' John shook his head ruefully. 'This would be a triumph on any other night, but it needs something extra.'

'What do you mean?'

'We need the corgis.'

Ed wasn't sure if John was jesting or not. He'd known John all of his life. Ed could remember him as a very young man, dutifully following Abel on stage while Ed was still too young to play a part. He could remember John on the night of the first Royal Command performance. Backstage, the twenty-six-year-old John had recited a little incantation he'd insisted would take away all of the flutters in Ed's belly. Whether by magic or mind trick, it had worked as well. But, across all those decades, he had never been able to work out the nuances of John's tone.

'Corgis?' asked Ed.

'The apparatus could generate more dogs,' he said, musing on an idea. 'Tinky goes into the cabinet, and countless dogs start appearing. A self-perpetuating dog machine. Suddenly, there are corgis popping up all over the Palladium.' John smiled. 'It was Davith who got me thinking. He's got a fellow, back in Wales, who has a few corgis he trains. Just imagine it, Ed. The contraption goes awry – and suddenly, a corgi here, a corgi there… How might Her Majesty love that?'

Ed brooded on it, for only a moment, before he said, 'She's been enamoured of corgis since she was a girl.' Scarcely seven years old she'd been, when her father – himself not yet sitting upon the throne – had presented her with Dookie, the first of her beloved Pembroke Welsh corgis. Yes, he could quite imagine the delight it might stir up, if suddenly corgis were popping up all over the auditorium. And yet, he said, 'I'm not sure the

Palladium can accommodate a hundred corgis, John. And where on earth would we source them?'

'Well, therein lies the beauty.' John smiled. 'Because they wouldn't be real, Ed. I'd only need a few – these few Davith's going after. Give me a few corgis, Ed, and I'll spirit up the rest out of the ether. Mirrors, Ed. I'd do it with mirrors...'

Ed had started laughing. 'Who knows, it might end up being Welsh corgis they remember through the ages...' Ed flashed a look around the place. 'But where's Bill?'

'He's catching forty winks backstage,' Evie called out. She'd been sitting with Max by the edge of the stage, enjoying John's spectacle. 'We're going to run again in a little while.'

John turned to Ed. 'Is this really it, old friend? A swansong, for the ages?'

Ed was still. He looked at Evie, holding court with her girls. 'We all leave the stage one day, John. Abel Wright was decades younger than you when he set sail.'

'Aye, and dropped dead six months later. It was the stage keeping his heart alive, Ed.'

'It won't be the same, not for me...' He paused. 'She's ready, though, isn't she? She's no second fiddle, John. She's the real thing.'

John nodded. 'But you're forgetting Cal.'

Silence reigned between them, until finally Ed said, 'Cal does present a problem.'

'Cal always presented problems.' John grinned. 'It's what makes him so magnetic.'

After a time, Ed said, 'Don't you ever think about it? About what happens next? Oh, I'm not talking about the grave. I'm not talking about ghosts and voices from beyond – the way you still seem to talk your tricks through with Abe Wright every so often. No, I'm talking about for us. When we're not on the stage.

When the world's moved on? I have a vision, John. I'm there in Suffolk, and the Forsyths come back to that lovely old theatre in Bury. I keep hearing rumours they're going to reopen it. That all those glories of the past will be revived. And, in my dream, I go to watch the Forsyths for the first time – the first time as a member of the audience! How wild that would be! And there's Evie and ... and it's marvellous.' He stopped, a strange sadness sweeping over him. 'And then: Cal ... John, he looks so much like his mother. I can see her in him. I thought I'd given up on him, but no – not now. When I die, I want to go to Bella and tell her that everything's OK. The Forsyths go on. Cal and Evie, they go on ...'

It was then that John, first steeling himself with a deep breath, declared, 'I've been thinking about retirement too, Ed. Oh, it hadn't crossed my mind, not until you all came back. But this *change* – it's in the air, isn't it? The young folk, they're listening to new music now. They're dancing to different rhythms. We got old – *I* got ancient! – and it happened so quickly.' He paused. 'I've been thinking about a little shopfront, somewhere in London – magical confections, and a little seance parlour out back where people might come. There's a boy who came to see me. Just some slip of a lad, from the undertakers' in town. He's been practising magic. For a boy who's never been before an audience, who's never been apprenticed, he had a few tricks. Well, there's thousands that do. But ... I liked him, Ed.'

'John Lauder,' said Ed with some modicum of surprise. 'Are you thinking about taking on an ...'

There came the sudden sounds of furious barking, emanating from the box-office doors. Ed shot a look that way, only to discover Davith rushing back through into the stalls. Evidently he'd led Tinky and Tiny away from some recuperation of their own – and perhaps a little release in the theatre car park – but now he was staggering back through, as if engaged in another elaborate mime. 'Mr Forsyth,' he called out. He had called Ed 'Mr Forsyth' ever since he'd joined the Company, and no amount of familiarity would make him call his employer by his first name. For Davith Harvard, it just wasn't the way things were done. 'Mr Forsyth, I say! There's a little matter that might need some attending.'

Ed was on his feet in a second. He reached for his cane. 'Mr Harvard?' He liked to return the gentlemanly feeling when he could. 'Whatever is it?'

'It's Tinky,' Davith gasped out. 'The poor dear was so traumatised by this teleportation trick that he got in quite a kerfuffle. Quite a kerfuffle indeed! I thought: a spot of fresh air. Yes, that's the ticket. A biscuit and a little potter outside. But... but it's only upset the little mite further! There's just too many of them, you see.'

'Too many *what*, Davith?' asked Ed.

'You'd better go for yourself,' said Davith. 'Through the box office and to the theatre doors. I'm afraid I shan't let my beloveds be confronted like that again!'

Some moments later, Ed and John stood in the open doorway of the Seagate Theatre and gazed out across the car park. Beyond the line of vehicles, where Bill Martin's two harassed security guards stood resolute, a crowd vaster than the curious spectators of yesterday had gathered. Four rows deep and many more abreast, it was growing bigger still. Ed could see three more people emerging from a car parked up on the verge beyond the theatre's periphery. Drawn to the Seagate like moths to a flame.

'What do you think then, Ed?'

'I'm thinking the Forsyth Varieties has never been *quite* as popular as this. John, I don't think we need your fabled second sight to see what's going on here.'

John nodded gravely. 'Secrets are slippery things, Ed.'

'Indeed.'

'They always come out in the end. The big question is … who's going to tell Bill?'

'Your son?' Lily breathed, her face etched in disbelief. 'Cal, your *son*?'

Cal's entire body was tensed, every muscle knotted, every joint held fixed and rigid.

'Lily,' he groaned. 'You had to poke your nose in, didn't you? You just couldn't let it be.'

'Cal, you have a son?'

'Walk with me, Lily. I need to work this out. He's counting on me. I haven't seen him in months. Do you know how long that is, in the life of a baby? He might not even recognise me – that is, if I ever get to see him again …'

'But, Cal!' Lily cried out. He had started to walk again, inching around her to take off up the street. 'Cal, you're going to have to explain!'

So, as they walked, that was exactly what Cal did.

'I'd been writing for Decca a year when I met her. I must have written two dozen songs for them, and all for other acts. One or two of them got cut as records, got up on the radio. But it was just a job. Just an office clerk with a piano. That wasn't what I wanted to be. So I went back to what I knew. I'd started saving the best of my songs, the ones that came from the heart, the ones that sounded best in my *own* voice. And, well, Mr Todd – he's one of the money-men over at Decca – gave me a shot. It took months to win him round, but he agreed to give me a chance of my own. I'd write *and* sing my own songs, just like I'd always dreamed about.'

He paused. 'And that's about the time Meredith started

working there. Lily, I'd never met a girl like her. There was just *something* in the way she moved. She'd come down from County Durham, miner's daughter, just upped and left home rather than get bogged down with some lad from the pits. She had a dream too. I think that was what drew us together. She just wanted to *live* – and London, at the start of a new decade? Lily, that was where it was at. That was where life *happened.*'

'You fell in love,' whispered Lily, and she was grateful that the wind rolling in from the sea smothered most of the words – for she hadn't expected to feel so forlorn; she hadn't known, until precisely this moment, how much she'd been yearning for Cal.

'My records didn't sell, Lily. I worked those clubs, but the radio play didn't come. Oh, I could sing for my supper, but I couldn't break through. I might have hit rock bottom. But, yes, I was in love. There she was. Meredith – *my* Meredith – and she loved me too. It was Meredith who convinced me that it wasn't over. Meredith who convinced me I didn't need some old city boy patronising me at Decca – that all I had to do was get out there and find the people who loved my music. It was nineteen sixty, Lily. It felt like the start of something. I'm sure my father would think it frightful, but we pretended we were man and wife and rented a little bedsit together, in Lambeth just south of the river. Meredith was a secretary at Decca by day, but by night she was writing to the clubs, sending them pamphlets, inviting them to whatever pub I'd scored a stage in that night. She was going to be my *manager*, Lily, and we were going to fly to the stars together.' He paused. They were almost at the Seagate now. 'But then ...'

'She got pregnant,' said Lily.

Cal nodded. 'And then everything changed.'

*

'No,' said Ed. 'It has to be me.'

He was standing on the stage at the Seagate Theatre, readying himself to go to Bill's dressing room, when Evie hailed him. 'Let me,' she implored, following him to the stage. Most of the Company had gone to watch the crowd descend from the box-office doors. 'If he takes it well, then everything's good. But if he takes it badly? Well, it's better that he's furious with me than furious with you, Dad. Just let me handle it.'

'Handle what?' came a Californian voice, dripping with honey.

Ed and Evie turned, as one, to discover Magdalene wandering up from the backstage door, picking her way onto the stage.

'Magdalene,' Ed said, forcing himself to meet her eyes. It was an old performer's trick; whenever the nervousness came, you had to meet it head on. 'I'm afraid we have something of a problem.'

'Problem?' she ventured, bewildered. 'Eddie, what could possibly be wrong?'

Ed puffed out his chest. The feeling of it was like telling a joke that was bound to fall flat. You simply had to go through with it, then deal with your punishment. 'Magdalene, the secret's out. There's a crowd out there. They know Bill's here.'

Cal strode along the road. The Seagate Theatre was almost in sight now – and yet, on the edges of the car park, just as he rounded the corner, he could see people congregating, a crowd forming as if the show was already about to begin. He stopped momentarily, juddering forward only when Lily crashed into his behind.

'We had to leave London behind,' Cal said. 'Maybe we could have made it. I asked her to marry me, there and then, in a little Vauxhall pub. But something in her just wanted the comforts of home. And there are clubs aplenty up north. London feels like the world, but it isn't, not really. I could still sing. I could still build things. But I could do it as a father, as a married man, with Meredith's family all around.

'We had to do the service quickly. She didn't want to tell her parents what she'd done, but of course they knew. It didn't matter. They knew, and I think they loved her regardless – they just needed to pretend that everything was right, that it had all been done in order. So we found a home. I could see the cathedral in Durham from the nursery window – and by this summer, Sam came into the world. I was a father. A father, Lil.' Cal's face had broken into a wild smile, even as his eyes creased in confusion, for the crowd outside the Seagate was deepening by the minute, and neither he nor Lily had any idea why they might have been there.

'But it wasn't rosy, was it, Cal? Something happened, or you'd be up there still …'

'I wanted to send word back home. I kept track of where you were all performing I'd run off, left Evie and my father to fend for themselves. The shame had been gnawing at me. And I thought: I'll tell them there's a baby coming; I'll tell my father he's to have a grandchild for the very first time. Babies are new beginnings. They heal old wounds. Maybe they'll want to rebuild the bridges I burned. But one week turned into the next. Meredith got big, and I was just swept up in it. I didn't want to face my fears. And, by the time Sam came along, you were all in Monaco and the Med, on one of those great odysseys – the kind I walked out on. Never matter, I thought, I'll find you when you're back. I'll introduce you to Meredith and Sam.'

'The best-laid plans, Cal – they come to nothing. But what happened? Who's Jack? Who's Bruce?'

'Jack's Meredith's brother. I think he always thought I was

bad news. Travelling singer, penniless songwriter – what kind of future is that, for his little sister?'

'And Bruce...'

'Well,' said Cal. 'God sent his Son to Earth to parlay with mankind, and so did the Devil. That's Bruce, Lily. He's the devil himself.'

It was Ed who knocked at the dressing room door, though Evie insisted on being at his side. Magdalene was there too. She'd already marched – quite an accomplishment in her scarlet high heels – to the box office and looked out of the doors. Those security guards Bill employed were up to the task so far, and they'd been bolstered by various members of the Company including Max who'd gone out to charm and assuage the congregation.

Inside, Billy had been relaxing. His head was draped in a towel, and he was inhaling the steam pouring from a bowl of hot water, honey and lemons. 'It's his secret trick,' Magdalene confided as the three of them came into the room. 'To take care of the voice. Bing Crosby showed it to us. He's been doing it ever since.'

'What's up, folks?' Bill asked, from under his towelling shroud.

Evie opened her mouth to explain, when Ed clasped her hand. Only then did she realise her father was serious. 'It's my duty,' he whispered. 'I'm the one who made him the promise.' He straightened himself. 'Bill, we might have a little bit of a problem. Now, I'm working on a solution – and I don't want this to upset the day, but...'

After it was done, there was a long, lengthy silence.

Slowly, Bill peeled back the towel from his head and looked up.

Was it just the steam that had bunched his features? Just the steam that made his lips so puckered, and his flesh so incandescently red?

Could it really have been the steam that made the vein beneath his left temple swell and throb with such fury?

'Ed, what was the *one* provision I had, if I was going to perform for you at this little provincial dump of a theatre? What was the *one* promise I asked for, so that I could honour our friendship and bring a little bit of Hollywood pizzazz to this rotten little backwater?'

Ed knew he had to ignore the invective being thrown at the Seagate, one of Blighty's finest seaside theatres, but that didn't make it easy. At last, he said, 'Bill, I don't know how this happened, but I'm going to find out.'

'You must understand,' said Magdalene, shrill voice rising in panic as she loped to Bill's side and draped herself around him. 'It's ever since Las Vegas. The summer residency in fifty-eight. Bill was playing to sell-out crowds at the Desert Inn – four weeks of shows...'

'Just like Noel Coward did a few years before, only I got paid more!' Bill interjected.

'And there was a time the crowds got so, so passionate. They just overwhelmed him. Security had to beat them off. Bill had to be escorted away. He'd have gone straight to the jet if they'd let him – but thank God they didn't, because then there was that terrible accident and...'

'Two jets just collided, right there over the Valley! I'd have been like Buddy Holly, Ed. KABOOM!'

'It's been a fear, ever since.'

Bill reared up. 'You don't know what these people can be like, Ed. They think they own you, and just because you serenaded them from the stage. It's their hands – their creeping, scuttling hands! Now, look, I said I'd do this as a favour. I had *conditions*.

And now – and now... Damn you, Ed, how's a man supposed to trust anyone if he can't trust an old friend? Once they know I'm here for the Spectacular, do you think you can keep this theatre at capacity? You've blown it, old boy. It's ruined.' Bill stopped dead. 'I gotta see it for myself.'

'Now, Bill.' Magdalene fawned over him. 'Is that really such a good idea?'

'I gotta look this thing in the eye, doll. I've got to see it for myself. Face my damnation. That's the thing to do.' He gripped Ed's hand. 'Lead on then, old friend. Let's see exactly what kind of mess you've got us into.'

Out in the car park, Max held the line.

It was surprising how insistent a conglomeration of middle-aged Seaforders could be. By Max's reckoning, it was the middle-aged housewives of the town who'd grown the most vocal. One of them reached for his hand now, with the air of a doting grandmother begging a favour of her favourite grandson. 'Go on, love, you can let us through, can't you? I'd love a quick look through that window. Just to see him rehearse.'

'I can't do that, madam,' Max said, as sternly as he was able.

'But it's him in there, is it? It's not just stuff and nonsense? The Forsyth Varieties, featuring Bill Martin?'

Max supposed he wasn't meant to out-and-out lie, but he'd blurted it out before he had time to give it a second thought. 'I'm afraid not, madam. It's just us real variety performers in there. I'm sure Bill Martin is far too *grand* for the likes of us.'

'Then why all the kerfuffle?' came a separate voice.

'If you didn't have Bill Martin in there, you could let us have a gander!' somebody else called out.

The logic in this last statement seemed to inflame the on-lookers who had suddenly started crowding around Max. For the first time, one of them tried to simply stride past. Max, mindful of the way Bill's security guards were currently being flummoxed by some fans further down the yard, put his arm out to stop them.

'Steady on, lad!' one of the men at his side called out. 'We're only having a look. What did you put all those posters up around town for, if we weren't allowed to have a look?'

The jostling started again. This time, one of the old dears really did stumble past. Quite without thinking, Max reached out and took hold of her wrist.

'That's my wife, that is!' a man from the crowd cried out.

Immediately, Max released the woman. At least she darted back into the crowd, and for a moment the line held in place. 'Listen to me,' Max announced – and, judging by one or two of the dark looks in the crowd, he was suddenly very grateful that he'd spent some of his youth in the boxing ring, as well as the dance halls. Boxing and dancing were, he had sometimes reflected, common bedfellows – no matter how much professionals from either side might like to think otherwise. Both demanded neat footwork; both demanded poise; both demanded unbridled passion, to be pent up and then released. He had to tell himself to take a breath, to stay calm, to make no move he didn't need to. This situation did not need inflaming any further.

And it was all down to Bill Martin…

'My friends,' he called out, imitating the way he'd so often heard Ed speak to the crowd. 'It's wonderful to see so many passionate fans of variety theatre here today. But the Spectacular is still some days away. And,' he raised his voice, for so many in the crowd didn't seem to be listening, only considering how they might best bustle their way past, 'unless we're given the time to rehearse, in the privacy of the theatre, the show we'll put on for you will miss that vital element of magic I know you've come to see. So please…' He had closed his fists, but now he compelled himself to open them again. 'Please,' he went on. 'Let's not spoil this. Let's not turn this into more trouble than it needs to be…'

As Cal and Lily reached the edge of the throng, they finally understood what was drawing the residents of Seaford down to the theatre.

'Secret's out,' whispered Cal. 'By God, my dad knows how to pull in a crowd. But this can't be…'

'Bruce!' Lily called after him, taking him by the hand to stop being lost in the crowd. 'What happened, Cal? What did you do?'

Cal clasped her hand and drew her on. 'Meredith had an old friend, Faye. They'd gone to school together, got their first jobs together, done everything together – at least, until Meredith took the train to London, to a new life down there.'

He drew her on. In the corner of his eye, he was quite certain he could see Jim Livesey standing next to a woman he was equally certain, by their identical features, was his mother. And there was Max, remonstrating with some particularly ambitious intruder.

'Well,' he went on. 'It turned out Meredith and Faye did everything together, even when they were hundreds of miles apart. They fell in love. Meredith found me, and Faye found…'

'Bruce,' Lily said.

'There was something wrong about it, the moment we met them. Bruce was full of charm, but Meredith hardly recognised Faye any more. She said it was like the light had gone out of her eyes. Like something had just changed inside her. Faye used to be bright and fizzing – that's what Meredith said – but that wasn't the girl I'd met. The girl I'd met was quiet and withdrawn. I'd have thought she was just shy… until, one day, she had a bruise blooming across the side of her face. A ripe, black eye. She told us she'd fallen into a door handle, but of course that wasn't the case. Maybe you haven't met men like Bruce, Lily, but there's plenty of them about. Plenty of them in that home town where Faye and Meredith grew up. No wonder Meredith wanted to leave. You see, Bruce wasn't just Faye's lover. He was her keeper. He was her captor. He was older than Faye. Older, and bigger as well. And when we realised what he was doing to her...'

'Cal, what did you do?' Lily stopped dead, her feet frozen to the floor. 'Cal?'

She hadn't let go of his hand. Now, she heaved him to a stop as well. Images slashed through her mind: how somebody as valiant as Cal, somebody with actual decency, might decide to stand up to such a man.

But Bruce was still alive, wasn't he? She knew that, from what Jack had said.

She softened slightly at that realisation, but still she stood firm.

'I saw him one day,' said Cal. 'Just berating her, there in the corner shop. His finger in her face, like it must have been every night of her life. Lily, I just snapped. I'm so slight compared to Bruce, so I suppose it was my fury that carried me. Before I knew what I was doing, I had him on the floor. I'd grabbed a glass bottle from one of the shelves. I smashed it into his face. Then I got Faye out of there, as fast as I could.' Cal sighed. He'd spent the next three days in hiding, certain the police would come looking for him.

But, of course, it wasn't the police who caught up with him in the end. It was Bruce's friends, the ones he drank with down in the Butcher's Hook. They were the ones who set about him with fists. They were the ones who'd carved that notch in his side, with the pen-knife one of them carried for prying stones out of a horse's shoe.

And now they were the ones demanding five hundred pounds, before they hunted him further.

'But you can put an end to it, Cal. You know how now!'

'You make it sound easy, Lily.' They had almost fought their way to the front of the crowd, where the security men were still vehemently denying they had ever heard – let alone let slip – the name Bill Martin. 'Five hundred pounds. They know I can't get hold of it, not by month's end. That's why they've done it. They know I can't, but they can't say they haven't given me a chance.' Cal pushed through the last of the crowd. 'Meredith and Sam had to go into hiding, just in case they got caught up in all this. I wouldn't put it past Bruce and his gang to go after them when they can't get a hold of me – so they're off with Meredith's grandmother, up in the hills, until I figure this out. And now... Five hundred pounds! I'm a dead man, Lily. A dead man walking.'

'Cal's out there,' said Evie, peering through the blinds in the box-office window. 'And...' She sighed. *Lily*. She hadn't even known she'd slipped out of the theatre. Quite where they'd been, she didn't know, but the idea that they'd been up on that double-decker bus, or back in Lily's lodgings, engaged in some kind of a liaison was not far from her mind.

Out there, Cal was remonstrating with the security men – who seemed insistent he was just another Bill Martin fanatic, oblivious to the fact he'd been in and out of the theatre all week long. Some of the other Forsyths, who were out there trying to charm the crowd, looked on in disbelief.

She found Max in the throng. He seemed to have taken charge of the situation now, supplanting even Bill Martin's

security detail. No, she told herself – trying to remain mag-
nanimous – if Cal and Lily had been engaged in some romantic
tryst somewhere, that was their business. It was what she and
Max had done, and look where that was leading. It was what
their parents had done, once upon a time. People found each
other. It was one of life's mysteries, but one of the things that
made life worth living as well.

'Ed, you dog!' Bill Martin's voice echoed through the theatre.
Never before, thought Evie, had a man with such a mellifluous
tone seemed so demonic. She could hear Magdalene too, shrill
as she tried to assuage her husband's fear. 'Ed, this is beyond the
pale. I know what you did, you scoundrel. The oldest showman's
trick in the book! You let it slip, so you could pull in the crowds.
You're stoking anticipation for the Royal Command, and you're
using *me* to do it!'

'Now, Bill,' came Ed's voice. 'That isn't true at all. You know
me better than that. Showmen can have integrity, Bill. Just because they might have forgotten that in Los Angeles, doesn't
mean we've let it go in the Varieties…'

'You need to get rid of them, Ed! There must be a back way
out. A back door?'

Evie abandoned the box-office window and rushed to meet
her father. 'There's the stage door, Dad. We could bring the
limousine round. He'd be out of here in moments.'

'That's exactly what they did at the Desert Inn, isn't it, Bill?'
cried Magdalene. 'Now, I wasn't there, of course – not yet being
betrothed and all – but that's how it goes, isn't it Bill? They tried
to hustle you into the limousine, but the crowd just crashed
around you.'

'It was like drowning,' Billy whispered. By now, he had taken
off up the hallway – unable, at the last moment, to peer through
the window at all – and stumbled to the edge of the stage. There

214

he clung to its lip, panting. 'Ed, you made this mess. You solve it. Do you hear me?' And his voice lifted from its despair to the height of fury again.

Soon, Magdalene was rushing to his side, but not even her exclamations seemed to douse Bill's temper. Evie, in turn, rushed to her father. 'She's right, of course. The moment we move that limousine, the crowd will just follow.' She paused. 'How on earth did it get out? Who let it slip?'

'It wasn't me, that's for sure,' said Ed. He put an arm around Evie and hustled her back along the stalls, out of the earshot of the raging Bill Martin. 'I don't pull stunts – nothing more dramatic than a few posters going up overnight, of course. This is more like the sort of thing Cal would have done.' He stopped, hanging his head. 'He wouldn't have been so foolish, would he? He wouldn't have risked everything? He wouldn't have just blown back through here and detonated another one of his bombs... would he?'

Evie wanted to say no, but the word would not come. 'We need a distraction, Dad.'

Ed took a breath. 'Evie, I'm going to go out and speak to them myself.'

The doors of the theatre opened up and the baying in the crowd turned, temporarily, to silence – for an old, esteemed gentleman had appeared and was striding towards them. It took some moments for the crowd to realise this was not Bill Martin approaching.

. As soon as Ed reached the burgundy limousine, and the line the security guards had formed with members of his Company, the chatter began again. Ed had to use his most authoritative, stagey voice to reclaim the silence. 'My friends,' he declared. 'If I'm right, there has been a little misunderstanding. But all shall be revealed in three nights' time. The night of your Seagate Spectacular, which is being prepared in the theatre this very moment.'

'Where's Bill?' somebody cried out.

Ed summoned another attempt. 'I can promise you delights incomparable to any other – but only on the stage, and only on the night of our performance. Friends, it is my pleasure to see you here today. It is the honour of a performing life to inspire such anticipation. But a little mystery is always required, and were I to tell you, today, the identity of our mystery guest, it would dispel so much of the magic we have been—'

'It's Bill Martin!' somebody cried out.

Inwardly, Ed groaned. He looked around himself, scouring the faces of the Company who'd come out to hold the line. Worse things happen at war, he told himself grimly – but there was something all too familiar about facing a horde like this. He caught Evie's eye, and this gave him some confidence. He caught Cal's, and felt only disquiet.

'It's a bloody siege,' Ed muttered.

'I told you, Dad. Words won't work.' Evie shuffled near. 'We need a distraction. Something to draw the eye…'

Among the crowd of Forsyths surrounding the limousine, Cal's eyes flashed upwards. 'Dad,' he called out. 'This one's for me…'

'Leave it alone, son. I'm handling this.'

'Mr Forsyth, he's right,' said Lily. 'He can stir them up – I know he can!' Not waiting for Ed's response, she evaded the scrabbling hands of Bill Martin's security detail and soon slipped through the doors of the Seagate, where Verity and Betty were waiting to sweep her within.

Some of the members of the crowd spotted Lily's flight and decided this was their turn too. It took all of Ed's restraint not to scream at them, and every ounce of charm he'd ever oozed to convince them to remain where they were, just a little longer. While he was engaging them, Lily reappeared with one of the orchestra's guitars in hand.

'My friends...' Ed went on, for the first time breaking into a sweat, floundering over his words.

'*My* friends!' Cal announced.

When Ed looked around, he could see Cal was suddenly standing on the bonnet of the burgundy limousine, quite oblivious to the consternation of Bill Martin's guards. Too afraid of taking their eyes off the crowd to deal with Cal, they tried to ignore him as he spread his legs, took up his stance, and strummed a single majestic chord.

Cal had won over rowdy audiences before. He'd stood on the stage in tiny little basement clubs and started singing while nobody cared. Sometimes it had taken him two, three, four songs to win their attention. Those were the nights where you felt you'd really played, where you knew that you'd grafted hard to have any audience at all – and, if they started dancing, it was the best feeling of them all.

'Evie,' Cal hissed, while the crowd continued chattering on. 'Once I have them, I'll start shifting around. Take the limousine round the back, OK?'

Evie said, 'Cal, I'm hardly your—'

'Just do it!' Cal glared at her. 'Dad's getting flustered. It's coming crashing down. I don't want it to happen like that. Not after everything he's been through.'

Evie stiffened. 'I rather think I know what he's been through a little more than—'

But she never got to finish that sentence, for in that moment, Cal started singing.

Few of the congregation cared when he started singing 'Rave On'. Even fewer paid attention when he segued into 'Peggy Sue'. They need something older. They'd come here for Bill Martin. Yes, he thought, so Bill Martin was what he would give them.

He strummed another opening chord.

His fingers darted in search of the melody.

Not Elvis, this time. Not Jerry Lee Lewis or Bill Haley. None of the records he loved, and which lived in him.

'You Belong to Me', Jo Stafford's timeless classic, billowed out of him and filled the air above the congregation, followed by 'Unforgettable'.

It was somewhere in the heart of the Nat King Cole classic that he knew he had them. Did it sound as majestic as it did when it came out of Bill Martin's mouth? Perhaps not, but what did that matter? 'Now,' he whispered from the side of his mouth, between verses, as he leapt from the bonnet of the limousine to the bonnet of one of the neighbouring black cabs. 'Evie, go!'

In the end, it was Max who heaved on Evie's arm. 'I hate to say it, Evie, but he's right. Now's the moment. Come on!'

By now, even the security detail had worked out Cal's ruse. As the audience fixed on him, one of men slipped behind the wheel of the limousine. The engine might have drawn the eyes of some among the crowd, but by now Cal was daring to up the tempo of his set and he kept their attention with a sublime rendition of 'Since I Don't Have You.' The feeling of this was perfect, he thought. They might not have been his songs, but the attention was absolute.

He barely noticed as the limousine pulled away. Nor did many of the crowd. Where the car had once been, Max, Lily and the rest of the Forsyths closed ranks and barricaded the path to the theatre doors – but they needn't have bothered. The crowd were too rapt to care.

*

To Lily's delight, she heard a strangely familiar sequence of chords start chiming, and Cal's voice rose in splendour.

'The reason that they're singing ... is the same from Penrith to Berlin ...'

'What's this one?' Max asked, in the barricade beside her.

'It's ... "Runaway Lovers"!' Lily beamed. 'It's Cal's song.' And she thought of his story: of Meredith, and Sam, and everything they meant. He could not possibly have written it with them in mind, for the timing did not work, but, in this moment, it seemed to be about them and them alone. 'He's singing them his song, Max, and they're loving it!'

At the back of the theatre, the limousine screeched to a halt. Ed, who'd tumbled into the back seat, was promptly helped out by Evie, who'd hurried alongside. Both hustled to the backstage door, where Tinky and Tiny let out a hailstorm of barks in welcome. There, Davith was shuffling from foot to foot in one of his frets. John, holding court, said, 'We saw you from the window. Your son's got some gumption, Ed.'

'Well, we always knew that,' said Ed, sardonically. 'Bill!' he called out. 'Bill, it's time!'

Bill appeared from one of the dressing rooms, Magdalene clinging to his hand, his face as pale as a ghost. 'How many of them are there?' he uttered. 'How many do we have to fight through?'

'Not one,' said Ed. 'Not one if we hurry!'

Bill needed tempting to the doorway, but, as soon as he saw the limousine standing free from fanatics, he found some fresh vigour and leapt for the open door. Moments later, the engine was roaring and, in a plume of black exhaust, Bill Martin was being ferried from the Seagate Theatre – perhaps, Ed thought, forever.

By the time he and Evie returned to the theatre frontage, Cal's song was reaching its height.

'Runaway lovers ... running for cover ...'

The crowd seemed even bigger now than it had when, moments ago, they'd fled. Arm in arm, they picked their way to the place where the Forsyths were standing. And there was Cal, standing with his legs apart on top of one of the old taxicabs, his head thrown back and his voice howling out like a wolf.

'What is it?' Ed asked.

This time, both Lily and Max replied. 'It's one of his own,' said Max.

'It's "Runaway Lovers"!' Lily beamed. 'I heard him at the piano. It's his song, Mr Forsyth. It's Cal's big song ...'

Some songs were big, thought Ed. 'Saturday Night is the Loneliest Night' was a big song, especially when rendered in Frank Sinatra's golden voice. But there was something *different* about this song. It was a soaring ballad, like the singers of old used to sing – but something in its rhythm, its driving beat, spoke of the more modern songs Cal had always pushed to include in the Forsyth Varieties, back in the days when he still performed among them.

Songs could be a lot of things. They could be joyful or dark, carefree or filled with regrets. They could be paeans to sorrow or odes about love. Some songs – and 'Runaway Lovers' was certainly one of them – could touch on each of these emotions, and draw them out of you in turn. The best songs played tricks, somehow, on the soul. Ed's father had told him that song was mankind's first and purest art. 'We've been singing for centuries, boy. We've been singing since before we could talk.'

*

Here, Evie knew by some strange, unarticulated instinct, was one of the finest songs she could remember. She'd heard only a fraction of the whole, but somehow a solitary chorus and the tail of a verse had filled her with such yearning, such regret – and yet such splendour – that she felt moved to her soul. She felt as if she was on fire.

'Dad,' she said, and reached again for her father's hand. 'Dad, do you hear it too?'

Ed simply stared, confounded, in disbelief. 'He was always a good little songwriter.'

'But this, Dad. This?' How was it, she wondered, that he hadn't cut it as a record when he was out on the road? How had this song gone unrecorded, unheralded? 'Dad, you said you wanted something for the ages, at the Royal Variety, didn't you?'

'Something so that we'll always be remembered,' Ed said, 'for my final show.'

'Well, Dad, imagine this song… with the voice, the face, the fame of Bill Martin?' Evie paused. She could speak no longer, for the song had reached its sublime final notes. All across the car park at the Seagate Theatre the identity of the fabled 'mystery guest' was forgotten. All that mattered, in these few minutes, was the burst of emotion at the end of this song. 'A song that straddles the old and the new. A torch handed over. Dad, they'd remember this. This moment, right now, we'll remember. But up on the stage at the Palladium, with the Queen gazing down?'

She was right.

He could see that now.

And, as Cal raised his head for one last, victorious note, he pictured how it would be: Bill Martin, sending this song into the stratosphere as the great, the garlanded and the good gazed down.

He hadn't known there'd been a piece missing from his act, but now that he had found it, it seemed to be something he'd been looking for all his life.

His errant son had just brought the feeling back home.

12

Slightly Magic

The offices of Livesey & Sons, Seaford's finest undertakers, were solemn this morning. Solemnity, of course, was a prerequisite of the trade, and Jim Livesey had been trained in it since, at the age of eleven years old, he'd first been invited (or 'instructed', as Jim thought of it) to join his first funeral procession through town. Now, as he waited for his father to emerge from the inner office – where he was dutifully leading a bereaved family through the preparations for that afternoon's sombre affair – Jim felt it like a heavy stone around his neck.

All good and proper, thought Jim as he sat there with his hands folded in his lap, but there were other places he'd rather be on a Saturday afternoon, other things he wanted to be doing. Like poring over John Lauder's memoirs, trying to glean some insight into the man who'd plumbed the depths of his mind. Like trying to work out the meaning of that message he'd found slipped into his pocket. Like finessing the tricks he knew, perhaps even inventing some new ones – so that one day, he too might stride across the stage like his hero.

The door to the inner office opened up, and out of it two middle-aged women appeared, wearing identical dresses of charcoal grey. Jim's father came behind them, his face etched with the practised lines of undertakers the world over – lines like scars, to tell the bereaved that their agony is shared. 'My son, James,' Reginald intoned darkly. 'He'll be responsible for setting up this afternoon. He's a fine, upstanding young man. He'll do dear Lionel proud, won't you, James?'

'I'm s-so sorry for your l-loss,' stammered Jim, just as he'd been instructed.

The first woman looked at him oddly. 'Well,' she said. 'It's to be hoped your boy's got his head screwed on today, Mr Livesey – after all that scurrilous nonsense about Bill Martin down at the theatre.'

Jim turned white as a ghost. He opened his lips to reply, but his father's glare only made him swallow down the explanation he'd been about to blurt out.

'An honest mistake, Mrs Chamberlain,' said his father, shepherding the ladies on their way to the door.

'A quite scurrilous one, I should think – to have the whole town hopping crazy like that.' The woman, Mrs Chamberlain, shook her head stoutly as she reached the door. 'My Lionel had a soft spot for Bill Martin. He liked all the old crooners. I'm only thankful he wasn't here to listen to any of that nonsense. It would have killed his old heart, to have his hopes dashed like that.'

'Yes,' said the other woman, as they left. 'Quite shameful, what the young will do today for a bit of attention. Bill Martin indeed. And that so many of us fell for it!'

'I have to say, Mae, I didn't believe it for one second. Not *really*. Not *truly*.'

And their voices faded away, leaving Jim standing bereft in their wake, with only his father's cold stare to accompany him.

'Dad, *you* know I wasn't lying.'

'Now, James,' Reginald said. 'We've been through all this. Get your head screwed on, my boy. We have a duty to fulfil.'

'I'm not a liar,' Jim whispered.

'What was that?'

It would have been so easy to walk away from it, to forget it had ever happened, to accept he'd been a fool and prompted the madness in Seaford town. The problem was that Jim really *wasn't* a liar. He'd heard the name, as clear as day. 'You'll all find out tonight,' he ventured, wary of what his father might say next. 'When we're at the Seagate, and out walks Bill Martin – then you'll see.'

Jim's father had been about to return to the inner office, and whatever crucial ledgerbooks awaited him there, but instead he turned on his heel, marched towards his son and inclined his head so that their eyes were but inches apart. 'You won't be attending this Spectacular with an attitude like that, my boy. It's time you saw sense. I don't care whether Bill Martin, Frank Sinatra, or Elvis stinkin' Presley is on the stage at the Seagate tonight – there's a life been ended, and it's down to you and me to shepherd him into the ever-after. So not a word more, James. It's time you worked out what was truly important in this life. It's time you *grew up*.'

With that, Reginald Livesey withdrew his face from his son's (Jim was thankful – he didn't like coffee at the best of times, and even less so when it was on his father's breath) and turned on his heel.

It was as he strode back into his office that Jim saw the label sticking up out of the back of his father's jacket.

The realisation hit him with the force of revelation.

It might have felt like magic, but it wasn't *sorcery* after all!

'I'm sorry, Ed,' said Magdalene, her voice pregnant with all the fears and tensions of the past days. 'He's not going to be moved. I think he made up his mind right there, by the box-office window. He's ordered up the suite at the Buckingham Hotel. We're to return to London by noon.'

Ed had made the drive to Bowlderby Manor five times now, but this was the first occasion at which he hadn't even been granted an audience with his old friend. He'd been understanding – at first. He'd grovelled in his apologies to Magdalene, sworn oaths that Bill's privacy could be protected, remonstrated fiercely against the accusation that it was all some sort of deliberate ploy to pull in a crowd. 'I'm a craftsman. I don't *need* to pull stunts to get a crowd!'

'Magdalene, let me speak to him. Bill's a reasonable man. He knows there hasn't been malice here. I would never betray a trust.'

'It isn't about malice, Ed. Not any more. Bill's been very clear with me. There isn't any way around this. The secret's out. They'll mob the Seagate at the Spectacular tonight, and there'll be no way out. Bill doesn't want to be in the middle of a siege.'

A siege, thought Ed, trying not to betray how his dispiritedness was turning to anger. Bill Martin might have been beset by ardent fans and lovers in Las Vegas, but he didn't truly know what it was to be besieged. As for Ed himself, he still remembered Passchendaele.

'Magdalene, be reasonable.'

They were standing in the grand sweeping driveway of the manor, beneath a bleached winter sky, and now Ed looked back at the canary-yellow Ford Anglia he'd driven up from Seaford. There, standing by its bonnet, was Evie. She'd insisted on coming for moral support, and Ed – after resisting for some time – had finally relented. By the look on her face, she already knew the news Magdalene had come out to pass on. And it occurred to Ed, now, that that was why Evie had come, because she'd known from the start what Bill was going to do – and she wanted to be there, for her father, to prop him up when the devastating blow came.

'I *have* been reasonable, Ed.' It was Bill's voice. Ed looked sharply upwards. There stood Bill, on the terrace that comprised the drawing-room roof. He stood among the evergreen shrubbery kept in carefully tended pots up there, wearing only his dressing gown, precariously open. Perhaps, Ed thought, this was a perfectly ordinary sight on Sunset Boulevard – but at Bowlderby Manor, with November only nights away, it was pure madness. So was the cocktail glass in Bill's hand, frothing with some unknown mixture.

'I was reasonable when I said I'd indulge your little show, Ed. More than reasonable. Do you know what they would say to me back home, if they'd known I was playing in a destitute little flophouse like the Seagate? They'd say I'd lost my marbles. They'd tell me it would reduce my stock. Any one of my managers, Ed – and there've been plenty – would have told me to forget this enterprise. But I did it for *you*. For old friendships and old times' sake. And look, Ed, *look* how you repay me.'

Bill had come to rest on the balustrade surrounding the terrace now. He threw back his cocktail, whatever the devilish mixture was, in one clean gulp.

'Now the secret's out, I'M OUT!' Bill bawled.

Ed craned his neck upwards. 'If not the Spectacular, Bill, then... the Royal Command. Please, Bill. It's the story of my life. It's the end,' and he flashed a look backwards, at the brooding Evie, 'of my career.'

Silence stretched out between them, until finally, Bill said, 'After this unholy mess, you think I'll sing for you? You really think I'll trot around after you, like I'm your show pony? You just wanted to stir something up, attract some attention for yourself. Well, I'm not your stooge, Forsyth. I never was. You can crack wise for the Queen without me. I'm Bill Martin. I don't need to be a bit-part player on the bill of your Varieties. I'm going back to Hollywood, where they know how to treat royalty.'

Then Ed watched as, the tail of his dressing gown flying behind him, Bill disappeared.

He was almost shaking as he said to Magdalene, 'Magdalene, this isn't right. I've created a show around him. The crowning moment of...' The tears were about to come. It was the words 'crowning moment' that had done it. He'd built it up so much in his mind. He kept imagining how proud Bella would have been. It was the real, deep-seated need to perform, one last time, for himself – and to do it on the grandest stage of all.

Magdalene seemed full of emotion too. Ed would never be certain if it was only his own agony infecting her, or if she was feeling something else altogether. 'I don't know what I can do for you, Ed. You heard him. Now you know. Now you know what he's like when...'

'It's our show, Magdalene. It's for Her Majesty the Queen. How can he just walk away from that?'

'He's frightened, Ed.'

Ed took three great strides away. 'Frightened?' he called back. He managed not to say it, but the truth was he seemed more vindictive than he did frightened. 'The best security in the world will be swarming all over that place, Magdalene. Queen Elizabeth the Second's security detail – not good enough for Bill Martin? By God, he's lost his mind if...'

Ed glanced up. There was Bill, still framed by the window, his cocktail glass still in hand.

The pause was enough to let Ed regain his composure. 'I've got a show to put together,' he said to Magdalene, through gritted teeth.

As soon as he slid back into the driving seat of the Ford

Anglia, Ed smashed his brow against the steering wheel. For the first time his despair transformed into real rage. He brought the engine to life and, growling just like the car, swung it around to leave Bowlderby Manor diminishing behind them. 'Do you know, Evie, I'm glad I never reached fame – not real, world-spanning fame like Bill.' He shook his head. 'To think he's too garlanded and great for a place like the Seagate – the real, beating hearts of performance in this country? To finally, finally think not even the London Palladium's secure enough for him? No, I'd rather be who I am, any day. There isn't a treasure in the world I'd swap for it.' He stopped. 'But we still have to work out the show. There's a gaping hole in the heart of it.'

'Dad,' Evie ventured. 'We already know. You already know.'

They drove on in silence.

'Dad, you're looking it straight in the eye. You *saw* him. You *heard* him.'

'I did,' Ed said. 'But don't tell me you're so sure about it either. I love him, and he's my son. But...'

'The Company haven't forgiven him yet.'

'But if it was for the good of the Company, mightn't they think differently?' Evie didn't know if she was making sense, or even if she believed in it herself. 'If there wasn't any enmity in it, we'd have Cal in a second. Dad, we don't have another singer, not one nearly as good. Now, we could refashion the show, or...'

'Or take a chance,' said Ed. 'But it's one hell of a chance. Cal might have won some hearts in Seaford after the other day, but it's still only days since he caused a ruckus in town. Yes, I've heard about that. You can't keep a thing hidden in a company like ours. He changes with the wind, Evie. He always has.'

'What other choice is there? And, Dad, that song...'

Ed nodded. There was no denying the majesty of that song.

He'd dreamt about it since. In his sleeping mind, he'd heard exactly how resonant and memorable it could sound in the voice of Bill Martin. A statement for the ages, he'd thought. A testament to the power of song.

But without Bill, it was just a song – one of the hundreds of thousands sent out into the world to capture hearts and souls.

Wasn't it?

'It's Cal's song. I know it isn't what we intended, but he'd do it for us.'

'Cal wasn't meant to sing at the Spectacular, Evie. He's my son, but what does it say to the rest of the Company? That he could just forsake us, then waltz back in like it never happened – and, within days, be singing in the place we reserved for a star? What kind of message would that send?'

'What kind of message does it send to have him brooding around in the wings, like some … like some king in exile?'

Ed slowed the car, if only so that he could look sidelong at Evie, narrowing his eyes. 'Why the change of heart? Your brother could never charm you, Evie. You were about the only one he couldn't.'

How could she tell him that she'd gone to John Lauder? How to tell him that she'd listened to the counsel of her mother, speaking to her from the other side?

She couldn't, so instead she spoke the words her mother had sent her, the ones that had made her understand.

'Blood's thicker than water, Dad,' she said, with just an ounce of hope, 'and he really could help us out of a jam and we might just solve the biggest riddle of them all.'

'What's that?' asked Ed, as he returned his eyes to the road.

'What to do with a man like Cal Forsyth.'

*

One of the problems with being old, John had often reflected, was one's propensity to nod off, quite without meaning to, in the middle of the day.

And one of the problems with *that* was the opportunity dreams had to corrupt your inner eye...

Now, though some inner piece of him knew he was only dreaming, he stood in the London Palladium, stumbling between the stalls. How he knew this was the London Palladium, he did not know – for the blackness in which he staggered was absolute. It was just a feeling he had.

The feeling of catastrophe, coming down.

And here it was, that catastrophe, churning all around him. His first realisation: he could hardly walk, for the theatre was suddenly flooded, and a dark current moving against him. His second: he was staggering not only because of the water, but because some quake was suddenly moving through the deluged auditorium. He lost his footing – and, by the strange logic of dreams, found himself falling upward, past the first circle, past the second, where at last he found the gallery on fire. Now, by the strobing light of those flames, he could finally see. A hole had been torn in the Palladium roof. The stars above London cascaded by. He watched as they winked out, one by one.

Then, from behind the sounds of surging water and crackling flame, he heard another sound.

Somebody was singing.

The words seemed so far away, and yet so clear:

'Runaway lovers... running for cover...'

It was those words that drove John up, through all the terrible layers of sleep, and into the waking world. There he opened his eyes, in the stalls of a very different theatre – the Seagate, so much more diminutive, so much more benign than the Palladium on fire – and tried to make sense of his surroundings.

Ed, it seemed, had just returned to the theatre, a solemn-looking Evie at his side. Now the Company was gathering by the stage, all of the musicians, dancers, acrobats and stagehands drawing near. By the look on their faces, every soul in the Seagate knew that Ed was not bringing good news. Even Davith's dogs had adopted poses of sombre reflection. Valentino's face was set with a deep scowl. Only Cal, separate from the rest by several yards, looked impassive, but, then, that had been Cal's way, ever since his return.

All at once, John was reminded of the last dream he'd had. The screaming in the Palladium. The way he'd reeled through the backstage warren to find the dressing-room door. The blade buried in the poor man's breast, and the name on the door: *CAL FORSYTH*.

John picked himself up and inched nearer, the better to hear Ed's voice.

Ed breathed a deep sigh. 'My friends, everything has changed.'

The mutters and groans around the Seagate stalls betrayed all the hopes the Company had been clinging to. Ever since the posters had gone up, the rumours unleashed, and the crowd descended upon the box office, the dream had seemed dashed – but hope was a funny thing; it was not stamped out as easily as that, and few among the Forsyth Varieties had truly given up on the idea that Bill would be with them tonight.

But here they all stood, their hopes ground into the dust.

Evie took his hand and stepped in. 'We have to rally, people. The show is happening in a little more than six hours. And listen to me – it's a damn fine show. It's our best. And Mr Martin might have been its centrepiece, but, friends, this is our spectacular.'

It was the way Evie had used the word 'friends' at the end that made John lift his eyes, and finally start shedding the after-effects of that dream. She was, he thought, imitating the way her father spoke, those age-old inflections that instilled such confidence and grandeur. He tried to catch Ed's eye, as if to tell him that *yes, Evie will make a fine leader once you're gone*, but the thought of Ed vanishing into retirement only returned him to that dream.

He reached back in time, to the days when he'd been learning everything Abel Wright could teach, and one day in particular sprang out at him. 'Dreams have meanings beyond their literality,' Abel had said, in that gravelly voice. 'To dream of death can mean rebirth. To dream of a world in flames might not mean the world in which we stand. It might mean one of the smaller worlds we make for ourselves. Perhaps a marriage is to end. Or perhaps it prophesies a death...'

'A death, Abel?' the younger John said.

'I dreamt of my father dying, once. In my dream, I was a boy again – and the horse chestnut that once dominated our garden was being felled. In the moment it crashed to the ground, I saw my father's passing. He left us, two weeks later.'

John hadn't thought of that memory in such a long time, but it chilled him. He closed his eyes and found the burning gallery of the London Palladium seared into his vision. He felt himself listing.

He'd had one dream of a death at the Palladium already.

But did this point to the same thing?

He opened his eyes and searched out Cal.

It was then that he heard Evie say, 'And that's why, with so little time to go and such little time to prepare, my father and I have decided that the solution is staring us directly in the face. Cal,' she said. 'I know we struck a deal when you came back to the Company. I know we both said that you wouldn't perform with us, not now...'

'It's not why I came back,' said Cal, sternly, for suddenly every eye in the Forsyth Varieties was upon him. 'I needed you to know that. I didn't come back for the glory of it. I didn't come back to hog the limelight at the Royal Command. I came back because—'

John was not mistaken, though nobody else seemed to say the same thing, that at this point, Cal's eyes darted to the young dancing girl Lily, who suddenly cast her eyes to the ground, as if she was harbouring some secret on behalf of the young man.

'It might not be what you came here for, but it's what the Company needs.'

Valentino cried out, 'Ed, Evie, steady on for a second! Cal's to take Bill Martin's place? This really, truly takes the biscuit – as you fine upstanding Englishmen always say. Here stands a man,' and he indicated Cal, 'who bailed on us all, who left us standing naked in hell, and now – a few days back on the job – he's being trotted out to sing for the Queen. Put on a pedestal we built for Hollywood royalty? Ed, I've been loyal. By God, I've been courteous since Cal slunk back in among us. But surely you can see why we might be … bristling, at this?'

It was Cal who spoke next. 'I don't want it,' he declared. 'I didn't come back for this.'

'Came back for something though, didn't you?' one of the other musicians barked out, before Valentino took over once again.

'The second you came back, you were causing a stir. If it wasn't that punch-up in the Fairview, it's … gallivanting around the car park, centre stage again!'

'I didn't start any fight!' Cal protested, seemingly unwilling to put up with the attack. 'And I didn't ask for the car park, either. Hey – I did you a favour! I got rid of that crowd so that Bill got away. If I hadn't …'

'If you hadn't,' Valentino returned, 'then what? Bill might have ditched us? Well, look at us, Cal – because that's what he's done anyway!' In fury, he wheeled around, marched halfway across the theatre, then stopped and looked back. 'You singers are all the bloody same. In it for your own personal glory, every one of you! Well, listen – you'd be nothing, nothing, if it wasn't for the music.'

'Friends!' Ed declared.

Every eye in the theatre, which had moments ago been focused on Valentino and Cal, returned to Ed now.

'Friends, I know there are mixed feelings in this hall, regarding my son's reappearance among us. Life is not a simple business. It can be complicated and fraught. But here he is, and we are in need of a singer.' He fixed his glare on Cal, cautious of everything Valentino had said. 'Cal, all I'm asking is that you stick to the beats we've rehearsed. To sing the songs we had planned with Bill. To play his part. Nothing more, but nothing less. We don't need any heroics. We don't want any stunts. Just something solid, dependable ...'

'Cal should sing "Runaway Lover"!' Lily piped up.

The mutterings of discontent only increased at this. John could see the musicians stiffening, faces like storm clouds. Valentino threw his hands in the air. 'And now he's rewriting the set-list! This is incredible! Unbelievable! We're meant to be a company, not the Cal Forsyth show. We haven't been sitting around pining for him for five years. We've been getting on with it. We've been pulling in the crowds. We've been the best we've ever been!'

Alone among the Company, it was Cal who was silent. He looked, thought John, as if he'd seen a ghost. Around him, voices sniped back and forth, some arguing in Cal's favour, others casting him down.

In the end, it was Max who cried out, 'See what you do, Cal?

Everywhere you go, you just leave trouble – trouble everybody else has to clean up.'

'You're out of your mind,' Cal finally snapped. 'This is Bill's mess, not mine.'

'We stick to the songs we rehearsed,' Ed declared – and this, at least, seemed to mollify some of the dark looks among Valentino and his orchestra. 'Valentino, I hear you. I understand your fire. But there are only hours until these curtains open. I need you – as my bandleader, and my friend – to help me now.'

Ed reeled around at the Company – and, this time, nobody in the theatre could ignore the muttered imprecations in the room. 'It doesn't matter, today, how any of us feel. There's a show with a bloody great hole in the middle of it, and here's a talent that can fill it.' Ed had cowed them all. It wasn't often that he spoke so forcefully – tact and diplomacy had always come so easily to Ed – so perhaps that was what had quietened the whispers. Or perhaps it was simply that common logic had finally won out, for what other choice was there, but to forsake the Spectacular altogether, to abandon the show?

And yet, still, Cal was silent.

'Well, Cal? What do you say?'

John could see his skin paling under the lights. This wasn't like Cal, he thought – not the Cal of old, not the Cal who embraced the stage. It was almost as if – and he fancied he was having some other prophetic thought, sliding inside the younger man's mind to find it a chaos of confused thoughts – Cal didn't *want* the attention.

'He still thinks he's better than us,' one of Valentino's musicians muttered darkly. 'Too good to sing the golden oldies. Isn't that it, Cal? Couldn't bear to sing a song by someone as *old* and *lame* as Nat King Cole. No, it's "Runaway Lover" or bust for our Cal.'

Cal frowned. 'I didn't say the name of the song. I wasn't thinking it. Wasn't thinking about any of those songs, as it happens.
And—'

Evie stepped forward, seeming to sense the bitter argument
to come. 'Cal, it's your decision. But the Forsyths are in need. I
thought you might *want* to help.'

And as Cal said, 'I'll do it, Evie. I'll sing your songs,' John
detected just a hint of the defiance of old in Cal.

The orchestra might have been disgruntled at the prospect,
Valentino's face might have been purpling in fury as he bottled
up his rage, but what did that matter? By the time the curtains
rose tonight, Cal Forsyth would be back where he belonged.

The twin dreams, and the feeling of something coming to an
end, were playing on John as the Company went through the
process of integrating Cal into their act. It was fortunate that
Cal was a seasoned professional, for it took only a little rehearsal
time to embed him in the choreography Evie had devised – and
the orchestra, though half-peopled by different musicians since
Cal last worked among them, soon adjusted to the different
cadences and rhythms of Cal's performance. Being able to set
emotion aside to get on with the job at hand was part of being
a professional performer – but, all afternoon long, Valentino
refused to look Cal in the eye.

It helped that Cal seemed content not to reinvent the songs.
As Valentino remembered it, that was what Cal always wanted
to do. 'It needs a bigger beat,' he'd insist, trying to enliven a song
like 'You'll Never Walk Alone', an anthem that existed in pure
emotion and needed absolutely no 'modernising' whatsoever.
Today, however, Cal seemed to be doing a passable Bill Martin
impersonation. If it discombobulated the Company, it filled
them with fresh confidence as well. Cal being unremarkable

was about the most remarkable thing that had happened that day. The show could survive like this. It might not have the extra magic that Bill would bring, but for the people of Seaford it would be sublime.

The problem was those dreams, and the chain of thoughts they'd set off. John would have sat down and talked with Ed about it, if he could – he'd have made a point, too, of telling him how wonderfully Evie had handled that moment in the stalls. But Ed had enough on his mind today, without John deluging him with thoughts of change and death.

So John had done the only thing he could think of doing, the thing he had refrained from doing for many long years.

He invoked the spirit of Abel Wright.

The last time he'd done it had been in the aftermath of Bella's passing. The time before that, the days after the Normandy landings – when the voices of the dead had been so many that John had hardly been able to find Abel in the great beyond. That was the time Abel had told him it was time: that John was a man long grown up, already growing old himself, and that every ounce of wisdom Abel had passed on was already a part of him. He'd broken his promise only once before, seeking guidance on how to help shepherd the Forsyths through their most difficult moment.

He felt he needed to break the promise again now.

And Abel's words, when he'd reached into the ever-after and felt the strange tugging beginning on the pencil in his hand – his old master's words flowing out through the trembling motion – had made so much sense. Well, they always did. *You're seeing your own end, John. Oh, John, the century catches up with you in the end.*

'You mean my ... death?' John whispered. He was not afraid of dying, though he would admit to some nerves regarding how the moment might come.

Perhaps. Or perhaps an end in some other way. Ed retires, does he not? He plans his succession. Well, John, how about you?

The thought dominated him now, as the afternoon paled and evening approached. Succession. Yes, he'd been a fool to have put it off for so long. There'd been apprentices before, of course. It was a variety performer's duty to invest in the next generation, to make sure that the shows went on, even after you were six feet under the sod. Most of them had moved on to other companies, sensing in John an illusionist who would still be performing long into his dotage

But Abel's words rang with the same truth John had always found in them. He ought to have seen it himself. If Ed's days with the Forsyths were numbered, than John's were already running out. The Company ought to be left with an illusionist. Plenty of variety arts had died out but stage magic was eternal. There ought always to be an illusionist at the heart of a show.

That was why, by 4 p.m. – and with only hours to go before the curtain rose – John stood outside the offices of Livesey & Sons, watching as an empty hearse returned to the yard.

Reginald Livesey was not, it seemed, in the mood for visitors; an undertaker's office was always welcome, but at the end of a service he expected quiet and contemplation. It was only because, upon seeing John, he was expecting a commission – for a man of John's vintage surely had loved ones to pay for, if indeed he wasn't preparing for his own funeral rites – that he entertained a visitor at all.

'It's about my … end,' John ventured, and this seemed to pique Reginald's interest.

'Well, Mr Lauder, in that case you've come to the right man. Livesey and Sons has been administering to the *end* for eighty years, and I'm proud to say it's been my life's endeavour. Tell me, what is it you're thinking? Is it a burial, or perhaps, a cremation?

John accepted some shortbread and dunked it in the tea that had been kindly provided. 'You misunderstand me, Mr Livesey. I am, of course, of a certain vintage – but it is not death that I speak of. Not yet, anyway.' He flashed Reginald the strangest smile. 'Mr Livesey, I'll be frank. I am the illusionist travelling with the Forsyths. We perform at the Seagate Theatre tonight. Perhaps you are coming?'

Reginald Livesey's eyes narrowed. 'I believe tickets have been sought – but, after all this unnecessary business with Bill Martin, well...' He suddenly stopped short. 'I know why you're here. It's because of my son. He's the scoundrel who started that rumour—'

'Mr Livesey, I am in need of an apprentice.'

There was silence in the inner office.

Silence in the outer office too.

Silence, it seemed, across the entirety of Seaford.

'An apprentice?' Reginald Livesey seethed.

'Your son, Jim, presented himself for my inspection just the other day. I wonder if you knew: he has some talent...'

Jim hadn't been able to believe his eyes when he saw the stout figure of John Lauder tramp ceremonially into his father's office. Now, he couldn't believe his ears as, standing secretly by the door, he heard those words. 'He has some talent,' John Lauder had said, and it felt as if Jim had suddenly taken flight. All day he'd spent putting on a practised dour expression, passing on condolences, standing in reverential silence, all of the tricks his father had taught him. It was, of course, every bit as much a performance as stage illusion was – but how much more enliven-ing, awe-inspiring. was illusion?

He'd been so swept up in those words that he didn't, at first, register what came next. It wasn't until the sparkle of that moment was leaving him (a moment in which he'd tumbled across the outer office, found a scrap of paper and begun scrawling upon it a special message), that he came back to his senses and listened on. Evidently, while his head had been in the clouds, he hadn't registered what his father had said in reply – but it didn't take long to discern its general message. 'The boy's already an apprentice,' his father was saying, with no small amount of horror. 'He's apprenticed to me, as he's been since the day he was born. A proper trade, my good man! An *honest* trade! None of this prancing about on stage, as if any of it mattered. None of this messing about with make-up and lights.'

'Mr Livesey, I'm trying to tell you that your son—'

'You're trying to tell *me* about my son?'

'To present him with a chance. The boy has a dream. He's been schooling himself. I could—'

'You could *what*, sir?'

There was a pregnant pause before John Lauder declared, 'I could school him.'

Jim shut his ears to what his father said next. The only thing he really knew was that his father had got to his feet. Jim – who knew what was good for him and knew just as well that his father hated eavesdropping – was reeling back from the door when it flew open.

By good fortune, Mr Lauder came first; that was the thing that gave Jim the chance to skitter backwards into the darkness settling over the yard. By the time Mr Lauder followed, his father's voice barracking him from behind, Jim was hidden by the bank of hearses, his heart hammering out a wild rhythm in his breast.

'You're welcome here, sir, if – and only if – you require a casket!' came his father's furious voice.

Jim watched as Mr Lauder, first appraising the premises oddly

– as if trying to pick apart a rival magician's best trick – turned to tramp away. Some moments ago, Jim had been elated beyond measure; then he was destroyed, robbed, belittled, and more. Now, he wasn't sure whether he was meant to be proud that Mr Lauder even remembered him, or furious with his father for denying him this chance.

Then he remembered: he owed Mr Lauder an explanation. He'd been set his task, and he'd fulfilled it. Picked apart the trick, as it were.

If his dream really was going to be dashed tonight, at least he could look Mr Lauder in the eye and tell him: *I know how it was done.*

A teenage boy can ordinarily catch up a septuagenarian with very little trouble – but Jim was no ordinary boy, and the strange mixture of exuberance and devastation he was feeling made him trip over his own feet as he hurried after John. He cried out, 'Mr Lauder! Mr Lauder, please!' but a lifetime of working with orchestras and crowds had dulled John's hearing, and he didn't stop to look back until Jim had cried the seventh time. By that point, Jim was quite out of breath. He was still wheezing as he said, 'It was – the – jacket! The … jacket … I borrowed from … my father!' He drew his deepest breath. 'You saw it dangling there. You weren't ferreting around in my mind at all. It was all just a trick.'

John Lauder's frog-like face broke open in a glorious smile. 'That's not to say I can't read your mind, of course, young man. It is only to suggest that, on this occasion, a little observation was more efficient.'

Jim was still panting. Through his breaths, he said, 'Mr Lauder, you – you said I had talent. You – you said you could school me.'

John was silent. 'How old are you, young man?'

'I'm sixteen, sir. I'll leave school this year.'

John thought back to that long-gone age when he'd been sixteen. Old enough, once upon a time, to go and fight for King and country. Only two years ago, Jim would have been plucked from his apprenticeship at his father's firm to fulfil his National Service obligation. Old enough to take a leap...

'The trick I devised for tonight's performance is lacking a certain something, Jim. I had it in mind that your performing career might begin this very night. That I might look for a volunteer in the stalls, and find you there.' John paused. 'That you might vanish into my cabinet, and be held ransom until the illusion's end.'

Jim's face was brimming with delight. 'But Mr Lauder, I should love to—'

'Jim, we travelling performers are a funny breed. It is a strange life. I would not have had it any other way, but...'

'Nor would I, sir!'

John liked how zealous he was. One day, he would have to learn that to perform with the Forsyth Varieties was not all magic and wonder; there was hard graft in it, long days, aching muscles, tortured hearts. A life like this was replete with magnificent highs, but so too did it have its share of hardships and trials.

But for now, he thought, the wonder was just right. If you couldn't feel wonder at the very beginning, then why embark on a life like this at all?

'You'd need to come with me now. I would need to show you how my illusion is to work.'

Jim darted a look backwards. 'My mother is doing dinner, but... an hour? I could come for an hour? And then...'

'They'll be fuming with you, of course,' said John, 'when I pick you, out of all the hundreds, and bring you to the stage. Your father will think I have been conniving – and, in a sense, that's precisely what I've done. But you have your own life, Jim. My old master used to say the same: we all have a choice; do we want to spend our lives in secure mundanity, or do we want to risk it all for the chance of *enchantment*?'

Jim didn't need to think. 'I'll risk it, Mr Lauder. Even if it's just one night. Even if, after this, you decide you don't need me after all. I just want to feel it. I just want to be a part of it. I just want to know how it... tastes.'

John smiled. 'Taste' was a good word. The feeling of an illusion successfully pulled off tasted divine.

'Then let us hurry,' he said. 'Jim, you've a lot to learn. But your tuition's already begun.'

13

The Spectacular

Ed Forsyth had always taught his Company not to sneak a peek at the audience as they filed into their shows. To this, Ed always added his belief that an audience should never catch sight of a performer before the lights went up. 'It ruins the magic,' he would tell his players. 'It breaks the spell.' Cal had grown up in that belief and adhered to it like religion, until his years in the wilderness had come – and, travelling from club to club with only his guitar in hand, he'd come to see things differently. 'It feels so raw when you can see the whites of their eyes,' he'd said to a fellow performer, drinking together after they'd filled the Cock of the North, beneath the railway arches in Leeds, with the sounds of rock and roll. 'It's like you can see the effect your music has on them.'

But Cal did not want to go out and see the 'whites of their eyes' tonight. Darkness had descended on Seaford town, the stage of the Seagate Theatre had been stripped bare and shrouded by curtains – and, as the stalls and galleries filled up, he stood in one of the few quiet corners backstage, seemingly unable to settle into the rhythms that the Forsyths normally went through before the curtains came up.

An hour before the show began, with Evie steeling the dancers and the musicians enjoying the single bourbon that was their tradition before a performance began, Cal drifted into the rehearsal suite behind the stage. By rights, he ought not to have sat down at the piano and exercised his fingers but he needed something to settle his nerves.

Yes, he thought, as he reached for a major chord, *nerves*. That was what this was. But not the nerves that beset an inexperienced performer before he stepped onto the stage.

These were a different kind of nerves.

He hardly dared give them any voice.

'Runaway lovers ... running for cover ...'

He had allowed his hands to roll into the first refrain when he sense a presence behind him. Immediately, his voice died. He looked up – it was Lily.

'They should let you play it,' she said, with a firmness that did not ordinarily belong to her tone. 'Cal, why don't you fight for it?'

Cal's fingers fell, making some discordant sound – the effect Valentino might give to one of Davith's pratfalls in one of his earlier acts. 'You know it better than anyone else in this Company, Lily. I don't need any more attention. I don't want any more conflict. I just need to ... come through. Do you see?'

Lily went to his side. 'Sing it for me.'

Cal shook his head. 'The show's about to begin. What do you think they'll all say, if I start playing this now? Valentino will think I'm goading him ...'

'It's *better*, Cal. They all know it too. We all heard it, out in the car park. It's *glorious*. It would set the show on fire.'

'It's better that I do as I'm told, Lily.'

'You don't have to pay penance, Cal. You left because it wasn't working. You didn't do wrong. And ... you're still a Forsyth, aren't you? This is still your Company. It's still your heart. Your blood.'

Cal furrowed his brow. He let the silence stretch out between them. 'You don't know the half of it.' Then he added, 'What does it matter to you, Lil?'

Lily could only shrug. The fact was, she just wasn't sure. She'd thought it was love, or at least its first beginnings. She'd thought it was just how Cal drew her to him, like a moth to the flame. That was how it had been in the first months after Lily had joined the Company, but, until Cal's return, she'd cast it off: just a silly, teenager's infatuation. But now she knew that Cal was married, now she knew he had a son? Well, she just wasn't the kind of girl to let herself fall for someone so unobtainable. So that just left her concern for him, pure and simple. Her conviction that Cal wasn't a bad man, no matter what some other folk in the Company might think; that he was, in fact, the best of men – and that all he needed was a little help, before the grand ambitions of his life could be made real.

'Five hundred pounds, Lily.' Cal sighed. It was as if he'd been able to divine her thoughts. He hung his head over the piano keys, then looked her in the eye. 'I forget about it when I sleep, but every time I wake up, it's hanging in front of me – like my father's strung it up in lights.'

'You can do it, Cal.'

'I'm going to ask my father. It's all I can think of. Throw myself on his mercy. Just come clean, tell him the whole thing. Tell him he's a grandfather. That I want to go back to my son.' He gritted his teeth. 'They'll think I'm a snake, of course. They'll think I had this in mind, ever since I waltzed back in. It won't matter a second that it isn't so, because that's how the story will go: Cal Forsyth forsook his family, then came back to rob them.'

'It isn't robbery, Cal!' Lily snapped, quite taken aback by her own passion. 'The Company's *yours*. If you'd have stayed, who knows what would have happened? How bad it would have got? It doesn't stop you being a Forsyth. People grow up and leave home. It's what happens. You're allowed to find your own place. My goodness, if that wasn't so, I'd be back in Mansfield, stitching garments just like my mother.' Lily took a breath. 'Just sing tonight, Cal. Sing your song. You don't need the orchestra for it. I've seen you play it on guitar just as well. In fact, I preferred it.'

Cal's look said: *don't be silly, Lily; it's a piano ballad; it's an oldie, for the modern age. It's everything I thought music could be* ...

'Five hundred pounds,' he said. 'Maybe, if tonight goes well, they can count it an advance on future earnings. I'll sing for the Company for bed and board alone, for the next two years ...'

'And what about Meredith? What about Sam?'

Cal's face instantly darkened, that she'd even dared to breathe those names, and yet still Lily went on, 'They need you too. They'll need support. No, Cal, there's another way. I know it. You just have to hang on.'

'I can't hang on! Didn't you listen to a word I said? It's like sand, Lily – sand rushing through my fingers!'

The door to the rehearsal space opened, and in walked Max. 'There you are, Cal.' There was a modicum of frustration in his voice. Cal hadn't forgotten how eagerly Max had wanted to defend Evie, and the same indignation was in his voice now. 'Everyone's looking for you. It's curtain in ten. You're wanted backstage.'

Cal lifted himself from the piano. 'It'll be all right, Lil,' he said, beneath his breath.

'It will be more than that, Cal. It will be *glorious*.'

But as Cal followed Max into the wings – where his father Ed was waiting to receive him, resplendent in his pinstripe suit, bowler hat and forest-green bow tie – he knew that it was going to have to be more than glorious.

It was going to take a miracle.

The Livesey family were among the last to reach the Seagate tonight. Indeed, it was only how much Jim's mother was frothing with excitement – she'd laid out her finest dress, the one she'd worn on the first night of their honeymoon down in Margate – that convinced Jim his father couldn't lock them all up for the night. Even so, his sourness delayed them so much that, on approaching the theatre, Jim was certain they were going to be late – and that, by being late, he would miss the single greatest opportunity of his young life. He felt like a dog straining on its leash as he led them to the box office, then through the theatre doors.

The air was heavy with the smells of velvet, cigarette smoke, and the beeswax the theatre attendants used to polish the fittings. Jim had to wait impatiently as his father collected tickets, then as some usher directed them across the hall and through one of the auditorium doors.

Jim knew that people spoke with reverence about the big London venues – the Royal Albert Hall, the Hippodrome, the Palladium where the Forsyths would soon be playing – but, right now, the Seagate was the most inspiring place in the world. He'd seen it, of course, only scant hours ago: the stalls empty, the stage hosting John Lauder's vanishing cabinet alone. But how much more inspiring was it to see it filled with spectators?

'What are you looking so smug about?' Jim's father asked him, as they settled into their seats in the very middle of the stalls.

'Nothing,' said Jim, though his father's frown told him he didn't believe him.

'Leave the boy alone, Reg,' whispered Jim's mother, her

attention divided between his father and Amy, who couldn't see a thing over the big, bald-headed brute sitting in front of her. 'They're just excited. It isn't every week something like this gets sprung on you.'

And inwardly Jim thought: *no, and it isn't every week that your life – your* real *life – decides to begin…*

Backstage, Cal lingered at the back of the group as the Forsyth Varieties gathered in rank and file, like a troop about to do battle. Ed's hand, extended to clasp Valentino's, shook up and down three times, in quick, metronomic succession. 'You've always done us proud, sir,' Ed said, with a wink. 'All of you,' he said, to take in the rest of Valentino's orchestra. 'We might not have Hollywood singing for us tonight, but when did that ever stop us from putting on a show?'

Some moments later, once the orchestra had filed out and assumed their positions – and all the waves of applause that had greeted them were ebbing away – their first bombastic notes resounded across the theatre. 'The Forsyth Theme' was a piece of Valentino's creation, a triumphant blend of pianos, trumpets and guitar that could make the most unwilling member of an audience expect staggering things to come.

Ed reached for Evie's hand. Cal hadn't seen that before; it was, he decided, some new tic, a new ritual developed in the years he'd been away. He supposed he ought to be feeling the same elated anticipation that Lily, Max and the rest were feeling. Even old Davith Harvard seemed to be energised, down on his haunches with his arms around his dogs. Cal just hoped that, when he stepped onto the stage, the excitement was there for real. An audience could smell insincerity from a mile away.

But how was he supposed to buzz with excitement when

he couldn't stop picturing Bruce's leering face, demanding five hundred pounds?

'I meant what I said to our esteemed orchestra. We have never needed Hollywood before. We don't need Hollywood now. My friends, there is enough magic, wonder and delight in what we have been working for, all of our lives, than there has ever been on the silver screen.' Ed took a breath. 'Six hundred people wait out there, asking to be entertained. It is the business of our lives.' He detached his hand from Evie's, then marched from the wing and into the centre of the stage. 'The Forsyth Theme' was coming to its extravagant end. The curtains were about to go up. 'Well, then,' he declared, upon looking back. 'Let's entertain them.'

The strident march of the music had brought silence to the Seagate stalls. In the second it ended, and the applause went up, the curtains parted. Jim watched as a single halo of light picked out the debonair figure of Ed Forsyth standing on stage, pristine in his pinstripes and forest-green bow tie.

'*There* you are!' he declared, with a face as flummoxed as a tourist in Leicester Square. '*There* you are. All this time I've spent back and forth – and here you've been, all along, just waiting.' He shuffled, by virtue of his cane, to the front of the stage, harried by the spotlight. 'Let me tell you: there isn't a place on God's green planet that I'd rather be tonight. And that's not just because the purveyors of this fine theatre have put a bottle of Bollinger backstage.' Here he leaned in towards the front row, conspiratorially, and added, 'Don't tell the other performers about that, of course. It's on a "need to know" basis; careless talk costs lives, and all.'

'No,' Ed Forsyth went on. 'There isn't a place I'd rather be because I've seen what you're about to see. I've watched this fine Company rehearsing this show as if their lives were at stake.

I've watched men vanish into thin air, then reappear out of the ether. I've heard the soaring music play, while dancers conjure landscapes of the mind, and their shadows dance the polka on the theatre walls. I've seen multiplying dogs. I've heard—' Jim thought he detected some hesitation before Ed went on, '—the voice of our mystery guest, a euphoric return to the stage. And I'm on fire tonight, because not only do I get to experience it again – I get to reveal it to *you*...'

The lights went out.

The Seagate was plunged into blackness.

In the auditorium, six hundred souls held their breaths.

And, when the lights returned – but an instant later – the stage was alive with dance.

Jim looked to his right, where his mother and Amy were clenching each other's hands, entranced by the sudden trans-formation. Then he looked to his left. His father still held his prim and proper pose, but it was not lost on Jim that his fist had uncurled and that his palms were joining the applause that moved, like a wave, across the stalls.

Nor was it lost on him that his father's dour, pursed-lips expression was slowly transforming into a smile.

Lily, Betty and Verity had led the first sally out onto the stage. The can-can they launched into, symbolic of variety's begin-nings in the music halls of old, was performed in concert with a troupe of shadow dancers, projections plastered across the stage's scenery at John Lauder's hand. The old magician was hidden among the orchestra, working his contraption, cowled in black so that even the most eagle-eyed in the audience could not see him.

Not that a soul in the Seagate was searching for the way this magic was done. Too fixated on the dancing girls, too swept into the music, they hardly realised that half the troupe were simple creations of light and shade.

Backstage, Evie dispatched the next dancers into the fray. Out on stage, the century was growing old; the music halls of old were changing and variety theatre was being born. It was strange to see the dance from this angle – it allowed Evie to see the joints and seams in the show, hidden from the audience's eyes – but it gave her a thrill as well. Watching the troupe at their best was like peering through a child's kaleidoscope and all its myriad pieces coming together, then spinning free again.

It was almost time for Evie to cast herself into the whirlwind. One after another, the others streamed into the storm – until, at last, only she and Max remained. She was about to dispatch him when suddenly she saw Cal, brooding in the shadows at the rear of the wing, prowling up and down between two great crates, overflowing with props. 'My brother's nervous,' she whispered, as on stage the animal dances of the early twentieth century began.

As a girl, Evie had loved it when her parents had illustrated this craze – American in origin, of course, as some of the strangest fashions were. 'Oh,' Bella would tell them during those long summer days when the world was at war and none was certain if the Forsyth Varieties would ever reform, 'in those days we'd dance like almost any animal we could think of. There was an old showman, came out of Chicago and – don't ask me how – he ended up plying his trade with the Forsyths when your father was small. A song-and-dance man – though he had a strongman act as well. By the time I joined the Company, he'd sailed off – men like him never stay long – but he'd left all these dances behind…' The grizzly bear had a great, stomping beat. The chicken flip, the kangaroo dip, the camel walk and bunny hug had simple, but idiosyncratic, flourishes that each marked them out. 'But nothing was more scandalous than the turkey trot,' Bella had told them – and proceeded to display it for them, with its bobbing head and flapping arms. 'The president of the United States himself banned it! If you dared to dance the turkey trot at a formal dance, he could put you in chains...'

Well, they were dancing it now. It was, perhaps, a more refined – and certainly more synchronized – version than the one that had caused such scandal in the cities of America, where the police had locked dance halls down if anyone dared to dance it within, but it still had the sideways hops, the one-legged strut, the flicks of the feet and abrupt about-turns. Just to look at it brought a ridiculous, sublime kind joy, thought Evie. Another decade chronicled. A simpler time, perhaps. Before war had blighted the Continent. Before the violent century had begun.

She vividly remembered Cal dancing the turkey trot, once. Now, there he stood, looking as if he'd rather be anywhere else but here, waiting to perform. 'It's not like him,' she told Max. 'Something's not right.'

'Evie, I've been doing some thinking. When we get to London...'

There was a sudden serious timbre to Max's voice. It was the only thing that could have ripped Evie's attention from the unfolding dance. She looked at him, with panicked eyes.

'Yes, Max?'

'I'd like you to come and meet my grandmother.'

If it wasn't serious in the way she'd thought, it still felt significant. Max's grandmother: the woman who'd raised him since he was small. He spoke of her often: how it had pained him to leave her behind as she went into her advancing years, but how he wrote to her every week, how there was no soul in the world he respected more. 'After my mother, she might have given up. She didn't run away or hide. She was there for me, when I needed it the most. She kept my mother's spirit alive – showed me the world she used to be a part of. The world of dancers and lights...'

She was the one who'd encouraged Max to take up boxing as well, for – having lost one child – she needed to know that the next could stand up for himself, no matter what the circumstances.

Now, backstage at the Seagate – with only seconds to go before they rushed out to join the fray – Evie saw Max's invitation as so much more than just afternoon tea. It was, she thought, the door being thrown open to the most precious part of his world.

'I'd love to,' she said.

But then the musical cue was upon them, then Evie and Max were gliding out to join the rest of the dancers – and neither of them got to see the tortured look on Cal's face, as if Cal Forsyth, the consummate performer, a man who lived his life for the stage, didn't really want to sing at all.

One after another, the dancers were gone. Now, only their shadows remained – dancing independently, by the magic of John Lauder's projector and the silhouettes turning before it.

Then, in a sudden flash of light and an upsurge of smoke, a single cabinet appeared on stage. Jim – who knew how it was done, and had just about spotted the figures dressed head-to-toe in black who ferried the cabinet on through the smoke – could not stop himself from shaking. He kept having to tell himself to calm down, that serenity was the most significant part of every stage performance – those were words he'd got from *Through the Illusionist's Lens* – but those were sentiments easier to rehearse in the privacy of your boyhood bedroom than they were here, in the stalls of the theatre, when, in but moments, John Lauder was going to pick him out.

'Ladies and gentlemen,' John Lauder intoned. He was such a

different presence on stage than he was off it. All his warmth and avuncularity was gone; on stage, he seemed somehow unreal – a manifestation, perhaps, of the magic he was about to perform. 'The days of my life are numbered, but I am on the cusp of a great discovery – a discovery that might see me, yet, perform for your children and your children's children, in the years to come. My friends, who among us has not dreamed of ... *immortality?*'

The reverential hush turned to a disquieting one, as John Lauder went on to declare that he had found the secret of bodily transformation – and that the cabinet now dominating the centre of the stage, the cabinet with the ornate bronze fittings and indecipherable etchings, was the pinnacle of a lifetime spent delving into sorcery's infinite depths.

'Enter this cabinet, and the magic I have wrought will transform you. One day, it will transform me into a much younger man – such that I might live my life over, and perform my illusions for centuries to come.' John paused; there was such heaviness in this silence, laden with meaning. 'And yet, my friends, my quest is not complete. I am on the cusp of entering the Wardrobe of Infinity myself – but, before I commit my own body to the Infinite Mystery, I require a volunteer.'

The lights changed. In an instant, a spotlight was roaming the auditorium – picking out first a frightened face on the second circle, then pockets of consternation among the stalls.

'Who among you,' John Lauder intoned, 'is brave enough to Go Beyond?'

In the stalls, Jim had almost reached the edge of his seat. He looked left, to where his mother was holding his sister tightly – evidently the dark, atmospheric tone the show had taken was not to Amy's liking. He looked to his right, where his father sat stony-faced – perhaps fearing the spotlight might land on him. Then he looked upwards.

It was just like John Lauder had described: the light would come for him, and beckon him towards magic.

'Put your trust in me, folks. I will ask you to enter this cabinet, and you may emerge from it unutterably changed – but I assure you, you will be returned to us.' He stopped. 'Well, your body will return. Who knows what changes might have been wrought in the depths of your mind?'

The light had been roaming the stalls, but now – with a sudden jerk – it landed on the Livesey family.

Amy screamed, comforted only by her mother.

Reginald Livesey cringed away, sliding out of the light.

But Jim was on his feet.

'Sit down, James,' Reginald hissed. 'You bally fool, you're making a scene of yourself. *Sit down.*'

'Young man,' John cried out. 'Do you accept the invitation of the Infinite?'

'I do!' Jim barked out.

'You bloody don't!' Reginald snapped – but he was too late in snatching Jim's sleeve, for Jim was already clambering over their neighbours in the stalls, staggering into the aisle and making his way to the stage – almost as if he had rehearsed it ...

Backstage, Cal watched. At least the childhood wonder of watching John Lauder perform his illusion was filling his heart now. The boy John had invited onto the stage was the very same Cal had brought to the lodging-house door, and it made him smile to know that some connection had been made between the two of them. John didn't often like using plants and stooges in the audience; that was a peculiarity he'd inherited from Abel Wright too, who thought that every stooge was a chance for a spell to be broken, for a secret to be unleashed. That could only mean John was drawn to this boy somehow.

It could only mean…

Cal flashed a look between Evie and his father.

Did it mean John was looking for a successor as well?

Out on stage, John opened the cabinet. Cal could sense six hundred souls with their hearts in their mouths as Jim stepped inside it and turned around to wave the audience goodbye as the doors closed on him.

Focus on the trick, thought Cal. *Try and see if you can tell how it's done. That's what you used to do, when you were small. That's how you used to plague old John Lauder.*

That might take your mind away from five hundred pounds…

In the cabinet, all was black. Jim could feel his heart racing. He could feel the sweat beading his palms.

'You'll need to do so little, Jim,' John had told him, 'so have no fear. You'll be guided all of the way.'

But, of course, there was something he needed to do first. The latch he needed to unfasten was somewhere in this blackness. He'd done it before. Blindfolded and turned around to mimic the disorientation of this moment, he'd still been able to find it.

But the seconds were counting down.

And there were too few of them already.

At last, he felt the latch under his fingers. This was no normal latch, just a knot in the wood near invisible to the eye – and, when he found it, the panel in the wardrobe's posterior opened up and the grasping hands of two of the Forsyths hustled him through. 'You know what's next, kid?' one of them asked.

'I do,' Jim said, panting. 'I do.' His voice was drowned out by the creeping, dread-filled music rising up from the orchestra pit.

'Then on your way!' one of the assistants mouthed. 'This trick's got a long way to go…'

*

'Ladies and gentlemen, behold!'

Cal watched, from the wing, as the cabinet opened. Instead of Jim Livesey, there stood two perplexed-looking dogs.

The gasps in the audience quickly turned to guffaws as Tinky and Tiny trotted out, looking about themselves with the same wide-eyed wonder that a pantomime Dick Whittington did upon first visiting London.

'Well,' John said, rubbing his chin in confusion. 'This wasn't what I had in mind.' He looked up. 'Can the boy's parents please make themselves known?'

Cal craned to see. In the stalls, a young girl seemed torn between tears and laughter. Her mother was standing. A sour-faced man sat next to her with his arms folded, as if he'd really rather not be here at all.

'Sir, may I have your name?' John began.

'You know bloody well what my—'

The man had real vitriol in his voice, but his wife quickly interjected, 'We're the Liveseys. I'm Gertie. This is Reg.'

'Reginald,' muttered Mr Livesey, loud enough to raise smirks and titters from those he was sitting alongside.

'Well, Gertie, *Reginald* – and little *Amy*, is it?'

The girl was astounded, Cal saw – for how on earth could the stage magician possibly have known her name?

'I'll have your son back in one moment. But first – we have an expert dog handler among the Company. Ladies and gentlemen, might I present to you, the one and only, the legendary Davith Harvard?'

Cal felt movement behind him, Davith – fretful as ever – shuffling past to tumble, disconcertedly, onto the stage.

'Davith, we have a problem,' John began. 'A boy has become twin dogs, and must be restored.'

Though Cal didn't see it, the over-the-top, perplexed look on

Davith's face had cut through the tension in the auditorium; a gale of laughter followed.

'We must return the dogs to the cabinet, Mr Harvard. Avast!'

It was a perfect piece of farce – though, quite how the magical element of it was being performed, Cal didn't know. The dogs, playing the part to perfection, would not be rounded up together. One escaped into the cabinet and emerged again as two collared doves. The doves returned to the cabinet, only to turn into Betty, from the dance troupe. Betty returned, and behind the closed cabinet door became one mannequin, then two, then three – and, all the while, the fugitive dog was charging about the stage, running rings around Davith as he tried to catch it in his net.

'Cal?'

It was Lily's voice. He turned to see her. 'I'm nervous, Lil. I'm nervous as hell. I'm going to go out there and I'm going to sing … and, well …'

'You're going to be amazing. It's your rightful place.'

'That's not my point. I don't care about the performance. I care about—'

'Cal, that's not you. You're not thinking straight.' Lily paused. 'Look!'

Out on stage, the trick was transforming. At last, the first dog had been reconstituted, and the pair were back in the cabinet. By rights, Jim ought to have reappeared – but, instead, there was nothing. Then, all at once: barking from the gods; barking on the dress circle; barking at the back of the stalls.

Heads turned.

Tinky and Tiny were cantering through the audience, scrambling around the orchestra and leaping back onto the stage.

'It's meant to be *transformation*, not *teleportation*,' John sighed.

And on it went: in went the dogs, only to reappear in different corners of the theatre. On stage, Davith lost his marbles – petrified for the safety of his beloved dogs. John, feigning terror, set about investigating his cabinet for flaws in the design.

And it wasn't until a cry went up in the middle of the stalls, and the spotlight abandoned the chaos on stage to pick out, instead, the agonised faces of the Livesey family, that anyone noticed Jim Livesey had reappeared exactly where he was first found: sitting among his family, in the middle of the stalls, his eyes wide open in wonder.

At least the applause dulled the thoughts tumbling through Cal. At least it blotted out Lily telling him he was courageous, telling him he was as much of a star as Bill Martin, telling him that Sam would be proud of him tonight, for what he was doing. She was only trying to encourage him. Only trying to make him see that this – right here among the Forsyths – was where he belonged.

But not even she understood what he was risking tonight.

It was too late to back out now. '"Runaway Lovers,"' Lily kept saying. 'Just sing it, Cal – sing it for all of us.'

But no, he thought. *That isn't the commission. It wouldn't help. I already sang it for them once. I oughtn't to have done that. Not when…*

Five hundred pounds.

The lights had gone up, John and his contraptions faded into the background. Now, into the spotlight, Cal's father sauntered.

'Magic,' Ed began. 'Well, folks, we've seen it done. Staggering sights, indeed. Which reminds me of the greatest illusionist I ever saw. A Spanish sorcerer, renowned the world over for his feats – and in particular for the vanishing act he performed each night. *Uno*, he would count. *Dos*! And then he'd disappear without a *tres*!'

Backstage, the dancers were ready. Cal felt them milling.

Evie's eyes were all over him. He ought to have gone to her, ought to have told her it was going to be OK – that he'd turn it on, the moment he got on the stage – but something kept him from saying a word. He simply nodded at her.

Then the music struck up.

Out they fountained: Evie, Max, Lily and the rest. At least, now that the moment was coming, Cal found that those darker thoughts no longer distracted him. He had to march out to face his audience. So he waited, as the dancers formed their pyramids and startling shapes, as they moved in three dimensions, constantly building and blowing apart the constructions they made. Then, as the music shifted gear – and so too did the atmosphere in the theatre reach some new pitch, the mystery of John's performance forgotten in this upsurge of vigour and verve – Cal saw the dancers forming the archway through which Bill Martin ought to have been revealed.

Mystery guest, he thought. Well, the whole of Seaford was either expecting Bill Martin – or else just daring the rumour to be true. He'd show them mystery. He only hoped he wasn't going to let them down.

He stepped, unseen, onto the stage.

For a time, he stood in the eye of the dancers' storm. Evie winked at him, so much like their father, as she scythed past. The archway was pulsating, forming and reforming, pushing Cal closer towards the edge of the stage with each iteration.

Time passes strangely on stage. A single moment might last forever, or it might pass in the space between seconds. One moment, Cal thought he had an entire song's length before his number began; the next, he was on the precipice, and beneath him Valentino was playing the familiar opening refrain that would forever be identified with Nat King Cole.

The dancers fanned apart.

The lights of the stage washed over Cal.

The audience held their breath, then screwed their eyes – for, of course, it was not Bill Martin that they saw. Eyes were certainly rolled – and, in the heart of the stalls, Reginald Livesey (still smarting at his son's magical disobedience), looked at Jim sidelong and said, 'Bill Martin indeed!'

But none of it mattered to Cal.

He was already starting to sing.

'Unforgettable' – he'd never sung it on stage, because he'd never thought it suited his voice. A golden classic, so laden with emotion, a paean to the simplicity of real love – and yet, to Cal's ear, it somehow felt like a hymn, something from a much earlier time.

Soon the audience were quite forgetting that they'd been promised Bill Martin. If the 'mystery' they'd been sold was that they would be tantalised by Hollywood, then delivered end-of-the-pier, suddenly it didn't matter at all. For these fleeting moments, Cal Forsyth owned the theatre.

'You Belong To Me' suited Cal's voice better. Valentino had arranged a faster version than Jo Stafford's original – and, if it didn't have the urgency of the rock and roll Cal had once fallen in love with, he could inject more passion into it, driving the song along with emotion he summoned from deep within. Suddenly, he was thinking of Meredith and Sam, of the moment she first placed his newborn son in his arms. 'You Belong To Me': it was the anthem of a life.

The song chronicled an aeon in only three minutes of wonder. By the time 'Can't Help Falling In Love With You' began, Cal was weaving a spell, and binding the audience to him.

As if it had been planned all along, six hundred voices joined together for the final five words of the song.

Then the roaring began.

Cal had received applause before, but it had been some time since he'd performed for a crowd this size. The ovation, he decided, was for the entire evening's entertainment, not for him alone, but the very fact that they were cheering for him – when, only three songs ago, they had been anticipating Hollywood stardom, made him feel like he could fly.

His mind was empty of everything but song.

No longer did he think about the five hundred pounds.

No longer, the wound in his side; Bruce's leering face as his fist connected with Cal's jaw.

Only the music and the joy it could bring.

'One more!' They were cheering from the gods, through the circles, to the stalls below. 'Encore! Encore!'

Valentino looked up, and, though he was not smiling, at least his eyes connected with Cal's. For a moment, they burned, and Cal's eyes burned in return. Then, whatever elements of discontent remained, simply burned out. Cal shrugged, as if to say, 'Your call, Maestro', and Valentino implicitly understood. In moments, he was rallying the orchestra to go again.

Cal's eyes flashed around. He saw his father. He saw his sister. He saw Lily, and of course her eyes were pleading with him. "Runaway Lovers"!' she was saying, though she needed no words to make her meaning known.

Cal crouched down. Lily, and the rest of the Company, saw him whispering to Valentino in the orchestra pit. At least Valentino's face was no longer set with a sneer. That had to mean something. Just another truce, perhaps, like the one he'd made with Evie – but truces were where peace really began.

This was it, Lily thought. Cal would surely sing his own song. Even if he defied his father, now, nobody would mind: the audience were with him, just as she'd known they would be; they would fall in love with 'Runaway Lovers', just as she had.

The music began.

Cal opened his mouth to sing and Lily's heart sank, even as his rendition of 'Love Me Do' got the crowd in the theatre to their feet. There wasn't often dancing in the aisles of the Seagate Theatre, but they danced tonight.

But they did not dance for 'Runaway Lovers', and for the life of her she could not understand why.

In one great, warbling note, the song came to its end, and Cal flung open his arms.

'You might not know that group yet,' he cried out. 'But, by all the gods of music, you're going to *love* them.'

After the curtain calls and bows, after the adrenaline and excitement had faded away, after the encores and the autographs the Company gathered backstage.

'My friends, I think we can call that a triumph.'

'Cal, I haven't always held truck with these songs of yours. I've worried, across the years, that you don't honour the traditions of variety as we must, if we're to keep this Company alive. We forget our heritage at our cost.' Ed paused. His smile would not be diminished. He loosened his bow tie, crossed the room, and took his son in his arms. 'Cal, love me do, indeed. We've all had our differences in this room – but, if tonight proves anything, it's that you cannot keep a good company down.' He laughed. 'That's nothing, for a company like ours. We promised them Spectacular – and that's exactly what we gave them!'

A sudden knock startled the Company from their celebration. Drowned out at first by spirited conversation, it wasn't until it came a second time that Lily rushed to answer it. Then, she turned and called, 'Mr Forsyth, they're asking for you.'

Ed picked his way over, his cheeks still ruddy, his smile unconquerable. Standing at the dressing-room door was one of the theatre ushers, and at his side a doughy man in braces, greying hair and a great black slug of a moustache bristling on his lip.

'Mr Forsyth, this is—'

'Graham Carpenter, sir,' the doughy man said, and thrust out a hand, with fingers fat as sausages, for Ed to shake. This Ed did, for he already knew what this man represented: he had dealt with a thousand local pressmen in the past, and they always had the same air. '*Seaford Gazette*. We're syndicated across the county. I have to say, sir, when you threw up those posters on every square inch across Seaford, I did think it might have been overkill. I've seen plenty of variety before – all of it passable, very little of it spectacular. But yours, sir? Yours takes the crown. I wonder if I might take a few quotes – from you and your star turn over there.'

He had gestured into the room, where Cal was surrounded by the rest of the troupe. There was no doubting who he had meant when he said 'star turn'. A few scant hours ago, there might have been mutterings at that. Now, eyes sparkled. Faces glowed. Indeed, the only one among them who didn't seem to want the sobriquet was Cal himself – who only half smiled, and slunk further back among the Company.

'What is it, Cal?' Lily, gravitating to his side, whispered.

'Well, I'll be pleased to give you a few words,' Ed said to the reporter at the door. 'Son, come with me. Let's give the public what they want.'

Cal was silent. After a moment's rumination, he said, 'I'm just a stand-in, Dad. It's you they should write about. Your penultimate performance – your preparation for the Palladium.'

The reporter's eyes lit up. 'Well, here's an angle,' he said. 'You're to retire then, Mr Forsyth? One last night at the London Palladium, and Seaford's where you chose to warm up?' Gears seemed to be turning inside his head. 'Yes, I can see it now – I can see where that rumour of Bill Martin came from. Because he's on the bill, isn't he? For the Royal Command?'

Ed bristled. The less he said about Bill Martin tonight, the better. He might still have publically been on the bill for the Royal Variety Performance, but the last time he'd seen him he'd been decrying them all – and it seemed very much as if the Queen would have to be let down.

There was time for regret and recrimination later. Right now, the Company was jubilant – and so they deserved to be.

Ed stepped into the doorway. 'Come on, Cal. A few words here, and we can celebrate long into the night.'

Cal wanted to vanish. He wanted to remain rooted to the spot. Perhaps the dancers would close ranks around him, or the musicians put up some protest at the black-sheep boy coming back to steal all their thunder – exactly the thing he had sworn an oath not to do. But none of that happened. By their glistening eyes and encouraging words, they seemed eager for him to follow his father through the doors.

He sought out Lily's eyes. Surely she understood? Cal's brother-in-law had already tracked him down. What more would it take for Bruce and his fellow thugs to come after Cal? A report in a newspaper ought to do it: runaway Cal Forsyth, returned to the stage, the 'mystery guest' starring in the Seaford show?

He'd come here to keep his head down, to stay out of trouble – at least until this situation was over.

And instead he'd exposed himself to the world.

Yet, now, there was nothing to stop this. He felt himself sailing on a tide, through the doors, after his father, and onto the front page of the syndicated *Seaford Gazette*.

The clock was counting down to the end of the month.

He might have been able to forget about the five hundred pounds for those fleeting moments on stage – but now it was all that he thought about.

John Lauder envied the young. Their ability to ride the applause and adulation long past the curtains were closed was not one he had ever had – he had always preferred the quiet contemplation and study of his craft than the raucous party atmosphere that now proliferated backstage. That was why, while Ed and Cal were being interviewed by the local reporter – and Evie led the rest of the Company in their shenanigans backstage – he was content to plod out into the nocturnal air across Seaford.

And there, standing exactly where John had expected – for his second sight never grew weary – stood Jim Livesey.

'Sir, it was incredible. It's been more than I dreamed. Did I do a good job? Did it feel right?'

'Jim,' John said, radiating warmth. 'You were perfect. But then – I knew you would be. I could never have risked the act.'

'My father's furious. He thinks we had it planned.'

'Well, we did.'

'But he doesn't know that.'

'Well,' said John. 'It hardly takes second sight.'

Jim muttered, 'I suppose not. But now I'll be cleaning out coffins all month.' He looked up. 'It was worth it, sir. I'd do it again in a heartbeat.'

John didn't doubt it. Indeed, that was why he said, 'I may yet have need of your services. Jim, you remember where our next commission takes us?'

Jim faltered, scarcely believing before he said, 'Mr Lauder, you go to the London Palladium. You go to perform for the Queen.'

'And I shall be in sore need of an assistant. Somebody to sit among the great and the good, and volunteer to enter the cabinet once more.' He paused, cogitating the problem. 'We should need to dress you up as some lord's boy, of course. It would, perhaps, be too visible a trick if you were to come as you came today. And I shall need to speak to the ushers at the Palladium, that you might sit there – among the great and the good. But ... there are ways and means, and certainly your father could not object if his son were summoned to perform for Queen and country.'

John could see the look of astonishment colouring every one of Jim's features. To the young boy, it must have felt like the hand of God, reaching down from the clouds to anoint him from on high. 'I make no promises, Jim. My efforts in the organisation of this may come to nought. And only a few days separate us from the Palladium's curtains opening wide. There is not even, I should think, time for the Royal Mail to deliver you an invitation.' He paused. 'So you must look for a canary-yellow Ford Anglia outside Livesey and Sons on the morning of October twenty-ninth. Do you understand? Magic is calling to you, Jim – and, when it does, you must answer the summons.'

14

The Royal Summons

The sky was grey over the hilltops and steeples of Durham. Black clouds amassed in the north, casting the grand cathedral spire into permanent shadow. The deluge was happening somewhere in the hills and valleys beyond, but soon it would be cascading over the city streets, filling the market square, turning the River Wear into a torrent and the gardens of ancient Crook Hall to a mire.

But for now, the storm was just a threat – like the threat that hung over the errant Cal Forsyth, promising swift retribution and violence to come – and, in the redbrick miners' welfare hall in the ragged little village of Bearpark, two men sat with fists curled around their pints of beer, a haze of pipe smoke around their heads.

'Here, lads, you ought to see this,' said a third man, as he strode into the smoke and took his place at the table.

The miners' welfare hall was not busy this afternoon. Consequently, few heard these men as the first took the rolled-up newspaper from the newcomer's hand, spread it out on the table and gave a sharp, dry laugh.

THE GREAT AND GOOD GATHER AT
HER MAJESTY'S COMMAND

Two days before the commencement of this year's Royalty Variety Performance, the finest entertainers from the Commonwealth and beyond are arriving in London, determined to put on the most memorable show the London Palladium has ever seen. Even for these seasoned performers, tensions are high, and so are expectations. This is to be the third year when the nation will be able to join in the celebrations from home, with the performance to be televised by the BBC for an audience that is expected to reach twelve million and more.

And what can these millions expect to see? Well, the bill is a starry one indeed, with rising star Norman Vaughan compéring a roster of global stars like Bob Hope, Eartha Kitt and Bill Martin, young stars of the future in Cliff Richard and the Shadows, and home-grown talent like the legendary Forsyth Varieties.

The Forsyth Varieties are of particular note this year. Led by the renowned impresario Ed Forsyth, the Forsyth Varieties were on the bill of the very first Royal Command Performance in 1912 – an evening when Ed Forsyth himself, then just sixteen years old, serenaded King George V. For this, their second royal summons, they are to work in concert with one-time star of variety theatre, Bill Martin – who has since forged a stellar career on stage and screen, and now resides permanently in Los Angeles, California. In a recent warm-up performance, hailed by the local press as a triumph – 'a piece of the Palladium brought to sleepy Seaford town' – the Company was joined by one-time member Cal Forsyth, who brought some verve and youth to proceedings with what locals called a 'glorious, feet-stomping, fantastic' rendition of 'Love Me Do'...

The burliest man at the table drained his glass and wiped his whiskers across the back of his sleeve. 'Making a show of himself, as usual, then,' he grunted.

'*This* is what he thinks of as "laying low"?'

'Like he could stay out of sight, running back to his daddy and getting on a stage?'

The third man snorted, summoning the bar girl with a sudden jerk of the head. 'Well, he knows the terms now. And how long has he got? Five days? Six?'

'Seems to me,' the first man said, 'that he's not making any attempt at settling this debt, if he's prancing about on stage again, singing his songs. I told him already: knuckle down, get a real job, *be a man*. And yet...' The man screwed up the newspaper, his eyes like fire. 'A few more days. He's got a few more days. We're men of honour, here. That matters, in this town. But listen to me, boys – I reckon it's time we got ourselves to London, in time for this bloody performance. Because if there's one thing Cal Forsyth's proven, it's that he's a slippery bastard. He'll do a runner, and leave his wife and kid behind, rather than face what's coming. So it's up to us now. To not let him slip away again. To make sure he faces up to what he's done. To make sure he pays for what he did to Bruce.' He paused. 'And, well, at least we know where he's going to be now: at the London Palladium, night of the twenty-ninth – ready to either take a beating, or to make us very rich men.'

London: city of colour, city of lights, city rising resplendent from the ashes that went before.

The Forsyth Varieties had not often played in London, where a hundred different companies campaigned to stage shows in music halls and theatres from the East to West End. Ed remembered a summer spent at Wilton's Music Hall between

Whitechapel and Wapping; John recalled a particularly magical set of shows staged at the Empire in Hackney. Evie and Cal had performed, along with countless others, at Alexandra Palace in the north. There was always something special about London. It was, Ed said, the beating heart of the world – and it was to the London Palladium, sitting on the corner of the bustling Oxford Circus, that the world would soon be turning its eyes.

The flotilla of vehicles could not make it to the Palladium doors – and, of course, the sight of a glistening red double-decker hardly inspired the same wonder in London as it did in the parishes beyond – so it was by railway that the majority of the Company made their way into the city.

While Hugo and John Lauder – who allowed no other soul to take charge of his vanishing cabinet, his guillotine, all the various mirrors, false-bottomed trunks and retractable swords of his trade – oversaw the delivery of the Company's cargo to the Palladium's stage door, Evie marshalled the troupe to their digs in Soho. Only two nights separated them from the moment they would stride out under royalty's gaze. Not enough time, perhaps, to explore what Soho had to offer, but there was life enough in these streets to make Lily, Betty and the rest feel as if they were already on the stage.

Not for Cal, however – and not for Ed either. For, even as Evie showed Max to the dancers' digs and left him with a lingering look, telling him she would find him soon, Ed and Cal Forsyth were crossing the hectic thoroughfare of Regent Street, then wending their way through the grandiose townhouses until they reached Berkeley Square, a corner of London where – thanks to its dedicated gardeners – it felt like summer, even as winter approached.

Cal had never seen the Buckingham Hotel before, though apparently his father was familiar with it. 'Kings and queens

273

from across the globe have stayed here, over the years. Half the world lived in the Buckingham Hotel, during the war. These clubs and suites have seen history unfold, Cal. So let's just hope we're about to make a little piece of history ourselves.'

Ed had been to war, and seen second-hand the ravages of another, so he did not like comparing any other feeling in life to the perils of the battlefield – yet even he would admit to a certain trepidation as he followed one of the concierges into the grand environs of the Queen Mary restaurant, which dominated the eastern wing of the Buckingham's ground floor. Ed had eaten in the finest restaurants of Europe – as well as the grottiest hot-dog stands at the end of every pier – and had always prided himself on being able to happily exist in either world. Yet the opulence of the Queen Mary restaurant was something he had rarely encountered. In his years he'd dined in the Dorchester, played a turn at the Ritz, danced in the ballroom of the Savoy – but the Queen Mary, replete with its golden chandeliers over each table, the shimmer of crystal at every table, the waiters in their silver brocade pirouetting from guest to guest like ballroom dancers of old, was grander than any.

Bill Martin was waiting in his favourite booth, overlooking the splendour of Berkeley Square. Nor was he alone. Magdalene, wearing a simple dress of grey satin, was draped in pearls. She would not, Ed thought, have looked out of place among the elements of high society who peopled this hotel during the war – and, judging by the guests at the other tables, still did. Bill's security detail, Ed saw, were sitting at a table alongside Bill's own; evidently one of the perks of looking after a man of Bill's stature was a little fine dining.

Ed's heart started to pound as he and Cal crossed the lounge. By the look of him, Bill seemed to be in finer fettle than when Ed had last seen him, parading the grounds at Bowlderby Manor as if he was a thunderstorm personified, but Ed had seen how quickly a stormfront could change. Still, the fact that he'd agreed to take this meeting at all had to mean *something*; whether it suggested his heart might yet be won over, Ed did not know.

As he and Cal reached the table, Bill seemed to be doggedly refusing to look up. Indeed, he only lifted his eyes from Magdalene when Ed and Cal were formally introduced.

'Well, here you are!' he declared, with more jubilation than Ed had anticipated – though, of course, as the consummate showman that he was, there was every possibility it was all feigned. 'Sit down, sit down! I took a liberty, Ed. I ordered us some steaks.'

By the look of things, Bill had already finished his, while Magdalene made her way daintily through the shrimp on her plate. There was something wrong about the way she greeted them, thought Ed – but, then again, Americans were not English, no matter what language they spoke; perhaps it was totally ordinary, in Los Angeles, to wear sunglasses for lunch in the first breath of winter.

'Yours will be along shortly, Ed. They're sharp here. I like that. They don't keep you waiting, and—' he leant in, as if to take Ed into his confidence, '—they don't broadcast that I'm staying here.'

It was the first sign Ed had had that the bitterness of Seaford had not been forgotten. Indeed, by the way Bill glowered, it seemed clear to Ed that it had been nursed since then, that the bitterness not only persisted, but had grown richer still. Like the fine wines Bill had no doubt been enjoying since he'd repaired to the Buckingham Hotel, bitterness could *mature*.

Ed said, 'Bill, I wanted to say: I understand. What happened in Seaford was unforgivable. I've conducted a thorough investigation in the Company, and I'm afraid I'm no closer to finding out how our secret leaked. But I want to assure you of two things: firstly, that whoever let our secret slip out will be dealt with accordingly, and, secondly, that this was not an act of planning, and certainly not one on my part. I didn't need to shore up the Seagate sales, Bill. Seaford was simply a prelude to the Palladium.' Ed paused. In truth, he was quite certain – having spoken to Cal, and from certain things John had said about the local boy Jim Livesey – that the secret had slipped out because of the security men enjoying their midday repast at the neighbouring table, but there was no advantage to be gained in telling Bill that. 'So that's it, Bill: my apologies, pure and simple, from one old friend to another.'

Bill Martin's storm-stricken face looked momentarily becalmed. 'You let me down, old man.'

At Ed's side, Cal tightened. It took a sidelong look from Ed before Cal softened once more.

'But I have to admit,' Bill went on, 'I shoulder some of the blame myself. You see, I was a damn fool to accept that invitation. I trust too much. Misplaced faith – it's the curse of every good man. Isn't that right, darling?'

Cal watched as Magdalene looked up. Evidently, she'd been so focused on her shrimp that she'd hardly registered the unfolding conversation. But now Cal saw his face reflected in her sunglasses. He tried to see through them, but all that he saw was a blank stare – a contrast so complete to how she'd been in the Seagate, charming him backstage with her Californian purr, that a little piece of him wondered if it was really the same woman behind the shades. Well, Bill Martin was known as a man who frequently swapped one lover for another.

'Oh yes,' Magdalene said, in her familiar tone. 'You're the very best, darling.' But she was gripping her fork so tightly that Cal could see her knuckles whitening.

'Bill, nobody regrets the kerfuffle in Seaford more than I.'

Bill was about to raise a monumental objection to the word 'kerfuffle' – which seemingly minimised the trauma he'd been through – but Ed, sensing the distraction, quickly ploughed on. 'But you should know that the show was a triumph. The press reports have been more than I could have hoped for – they've gone so much more widely than any other show at the Seagate might have done. That's on account of the Royal Command coming up, of course – and our place on the stage. Expectations are running high. I don't want to let the other performers down, Bill. That's why...'

Could it be that Ed Forsyth's words were failing him? Suddenly, Cal felt distinctly uncomfortable. He wanted to weigh in, but he'd made a promise to his father to let him take the reins – and, after all the false starts and misplaced promises of the past, this was a promise he meant to keep.

'Bill, you agreed to see us today. I believe there's a reason for that. I believe you're a showman at heart, and that you wouldn't want to let the other stars down.'

Now Cal saw the act his father was playing. Words hadn't failed him at all; it was all part of an act, manoeuvring Bill towards the end he desired. His father's opening gambit had been pitched perfectly: just enough acquiescence to make sure Bill knew he was still respected, but not so much that Bill thought Ed had come here to grovel. There had already been grovelling enough.

It was his next line, however, that was the best scripted. A line Ed had devised for one purpose alone.

'I don't want to let Her Majesty down, Bill. Do you understand?'

Bill Martin paused.

'It's why I'm glad you didn't get on the first plane back to LA, Bill. The Queen is waiting. We're pulling out all the stops to make this special for her. Bill, we're in this together. It's both of us up on the roster. We've *both* been summoned by Royal Command.'

It was a faultless performance, and Cal could see its magic being reflected in Bill's eyes right now.

'Ed, you let me down,' Bill declared. 'But I don't have any intention of letting Her Maj down. The very idea you'd think it of me, that gets my blood boiling.' *Her Maj* – he said it as if he hadn't been born one of her citizens, as if he hadn't once spoken with the accent of his native Accrington, not his current Californian twang. 'But, Ed, if I'm to do this for you, things have got to change. I'm not just talking about my fee – though there's that to take into account as well. I'm not just talking about security. I'll put my people in touch with Security at the Palladium. They'll give me guarantees. They shot Lincoln in a theatre, you know. It can be dangerous to expose yourself by going up on stage.'

That struck a chord with Cal, sure enough. He'd known, too well, what would happen when he'd followed his father out of the dressing room to pow-wow with Graham Carpenter, the roving reporter. 'A precursor to something very special,' Carpenter had called it, narrating at length the turn Cal had put on, and rhapsodizing John Lauder's illusion, Evie and her dancers' acrobatic prowess, the shadow-play that underpinned it all. Cal would have felt elated, if only it hadn't included his name. He would, perhaps, have gloried in it, if only it hadn't travelled so far.

'I'm sure the Palladium is secure, Bill – Abraham Lincoln, or not.'

'History is made on the stage, Ed. Don't go poo-pooing my concerns again. That, my old friend,' and Bill skewered his final piece of steak on the tip of his fork and jabbed it directly at Ed, 'is how you got me into this mess in the first place. No, Ed, I'm going to need some more *stage time* if I'm to do this for you. What you've got going on with the Company is all well and good, but it's hardly stuff to stop the world turning on its axis. Now, I've a few ideas. We can jettison the magic act, for a start. It's old hat; they've seen it all before. So here's what we'll do: we'll open up the middle of the act, throw some more music at them. I'm thinking "White Cliffs of Dover", sung in a good ol' American style.'

Ed had to focus deeply on his breathing to keep his face from turning crimson with horror. 'Now, Bill, you know I can't sideline the rest. This is our moment too. But...'

'Ed,' Bill declared, with a sudden flurry of fury. 'You don't seem to know which side your bread's buttered. You've got *Hollywood*, playing with the *varieties*. Unless you give me a bigger piece of this pie, then...'

Now was the moment. Ed looked at Cal. Cal nodded, as if somehow it was Cal giving his father permission to go ahead.

'Well, Bill, that's why I'm here. Bill, we're a team. Together, we could define this year's Royal Command. We came here today to show you how we'll last for all the ages, Bill. How you'll bring the house down, with us at your side. Bill,' he declared, and dared for the first time to smile, to hope, to truly believe again. 'We have a song.'

The Berwick Street market was thriving, and the rest of the dancers too consumed with ducking in and out of its vibrant shops, its bawdy cafes and public houses – where, even on a blustery October afternoon, the Soho drinkers were in song – to notice as Max and Evie slipped away.

If Max was not as adept a Londoner as the hordes hustling up and down the Regent Street arcades, he was wiser to it than Evie – so it was Max who took them to the bus stop, then pointed out the sights as they sailed through Piccadilly, all of its enormous billboards lit up in vibrant colours, and on into Trafalgar Square, where an ocean of crowds lapped around Nelson's Column. Soon, having sailed along the Horse Guards Parade and past the Palace of Westminster, they were crossing the river – and coming, at last, to streets that Max knew well. The warren that was Lambeth, with all of its narrow causeways and dead-ends, the overgrown gardens of the Lambeth Palace – and, at last, Number 30 Lambeth Yard.

It was a narrow terraced building, with barely enough breadth for a single room on each storey. 'Most of this got bombed out during the Blitz,' said Max as they approached the gate. 'But we were lucky enough. I can just about remember the street how it used to be. What would I be? Three years old? Maybe four? Christmas had just been and gone. I do remember that. And then … well,' Max shrugged, 'it wasn't Christmas any more. Do you know, we barely stayed away a day after that? Well, we had no other place to go. No family to take us in in the country, so here we stayed.'

Evie felt momentary guilt – for, of course, her own war had been spent in that same countryside of which Max spoke. A gilded war, in so many ways. She hadn't felt the fear every evening, nor listened to the sirens sing. Sometimes, she thought of those years – just she and Cal, with their mother to look after them – as a golden age. It was only at moments like these, standing on the sites of former ruin, that she appreciated how fortunate she'd been.

'She doesn't know you're coming,' said Max. 'As a matter of fact, she—'

Max hadn't even knocked, and yet there was movement behind the frosted glass in the door. Now, as Evie watched, a frail hand rattled with the latch and the door opened up.

Max's grandmother was a diminutive woman. She stood at less than five feet tall, and her stoop made her seem smaller still. Her hair, which must once have been as blonde as Max's, was a shock of white, her skin wrinkled and mottled by age – but when she saw Max, her eyes sparkled with the same vivacity as a newborn just taking in the world.

'Max?' she stammered. 'B-but... Max?'

'Nana, you remember I said we were in town to play the Palladium?' Max was beaming, his face so radiant that Evie remembered, suddenly, precisely the feeling she'd had when she first fell in love. 'Well, here we are.'

'This I can see!' Max's grandmother crowed. Then her shrunken eyes appraised Evie slowly, roaming up and down the length of her body. 'But who's this?'

Evie's instinct was to introduce herself. Perhaps it wouldn't have been, once upon a time – but those days running the Forsyths, while her father was lost in his grief and Cal gone to the wilderness, had given her an assertiveness she had not hitherto had.

She stepped forward, until at last she stood by Max's side. 'My name's Evie Forsyth,' she ventured. 'I'm the principal dancer and choreographer with the Forsyth Varieties. I'm Max's—'

She was about to say 'boss', but suddenly it was Max who was speaking.

'Girl,' Max said, concluding Evie's sentence with a smile. 'Nana, Evie's my girl.'

The Buckingham Hotel's most feted attribute was its Grand Ballroom. For more than thirty years, this vaulted chamber – with its resplendent stage and sprung dance-floor, its three sprawling chandeliers and the balustrade of gleaming ebony – had been the centrepiece of London Society. As Cal walked through the plaster archway, decorated in perfect cherubim, and entered its opulent surrounds, he could quite see why.

As the history washed over him, Cal felt suddenly small; it was a dizzying, unsettling feeling.

As he followed Ed and Bill down onto the dance floor, Magdalene lingering at his side, some new doubt gnawed at him. Was the song he was about to play enough?

'Have you been well?' he said to Magdalene, walking at his side.

She pinched the bridge of her nose and shifted her sunglasses. 'These are difficult times, Cal. But they say you rocked the room when you took Bill's place. I should have liked to have seen it. But instead …' She paused. 'Well, London has so much to offer. You should explore it while you're here.'

Evidently, she did not want to talk – and nor was there any time for it, because Bill and Ed were already stepping through the balustrade and crossing the lacquered chequers of the dance floor. As Cal followed, he could not help but remember his mother – and how vividly she had danced, once upon a time, in ballrooms much like these.

The stage at the far end of the dance floor was dominated by a gleaming white grand piano. Cal felt tinier still as he stepped onto the stage and took his seat on the stool. He looked down, upon his audience of three. Then, out of the corner of his eye, he saw a fourth figure appear: a man bedecked in midnight blue, walking by virtue of an expertly crafted walking cane, the bulb at its head a depiction of dancing shoes, their laces intertwined. This, Cal understood, was none other than the Buckingham's director, who had gifted one of his most prized guests the ballroom for but an hour. Ed said he had once been a garlanded dancer, a man their mother admired very much – a champion of the Continent, the darling of dance, the King of the Grand. Yet the war had taken dance from him, for now he walked with only one leg. And so he had swapped the ballroom for the boardroom – and now, the Buckingham Hotel was his fiefdom, just as the Grand once had been.

He just stood there and watched. Evidently, he still held love for music in his heart.

'Bill, this is a composition barely played in public. As such, it runs quite counter to the other songs we've rehearsed.' Ed paused. 'But there's magic in it. Such passion and yearning. I don't know how else to describe it. You know how I respect the standards. But this song, Bill. I believe it will be remembered. And, after all, isn't that what we all want? To linger long in the memory, even after we're gone?'

'Steady on, old boy,' said Bill. 'I'm not the one retiring.' Bill had started to pace up and down, his hands folded in the small of his back. 'All right then, young man. I'm game to listen. But remember – you could have written the greatest song in history, but if it ain't right for this voice, it's got nothing. A song needs to live, if it's to be sung. I need to know this song is for me, Cal, not you. That's what the best songwriters do. They hand over their precious babies, so that some singer – some singer with a voice like mine – can take it to places they never imagined.'

At the piano, Cal tried not to grimace. Bill was a star, but stars rarely knew what it meant to write a song – how you poured your heart into it, how the melody came from the soul, how a lyric could distil a feeling so particular to you that few others ever knew exactly what you meant. That, Cal had always supposed, was why the countless songs he'd churned out for those fat cats on Denmark Street had never set the musical world on fire: they were workmanlike studies, forced compositions, not pieces of wonder teased out of his soul.

Not for the first time, he wondered why he had agreed to this at all. And, not for the first time, he reminded himself that it wasn't just to please his father. Perhaps the rest of the Company thought it was Cal's gift to them, part of his penance for leaving them as he had. But only Lily knew the truth – that this was the only shot Cal had. If the song succeeded as it could, if it filled the Palladium with such emotion that it drew the eye of the world, perhaps some record producer would come along and snap up the rights to it.

And, if that happened, perhaps he could go back to Meredith. Perhaps he could be a father to Sam.

'Hit it then, boy,' Bill declared. 'Let's hear why everyone's raving about this tune of yours.'

It would never be the same, thought Cal, coming out of the mouth of Bill Martin. It would never be as honest.

But there was something noble in the sacrifice he was about to make. He would gift away his greatest song, sell a little piece of his soul – and, by doing so, draw his family back together.

It would, Cal decided, be the most valuable song in the world.

So he started to sing. His hands rolled up and down the piano keys, conjuring a coming storm. One set of chords cascaded into the next. His foot beat out an urgent rhythm.

And then, at last, those opening words:

'Runaway lovers ... just running for cover ...'

After that, even Bill Martin stopped his pacing and paid attention.

Max's grandmother was still shuffling around in the kitchen, making the tea, as Max showed Evie into the sitting room. This was the palace of a lifetime, thought Evie – for, on every wall, and across every surface, sat portraits taken from earlier times. 'It's my mother,' said Max. 'Nana always kept such a close watch on her career. Just like she's doing mine.'

And what a career Max's mother seemed to have had. By the pictures on the walls, Evie took her for a consummate ballroom dancer. Here was a rosette awarded to her in a competition of 1926, when she was still a girl. Here was the programme from a show at Wilton's that she'd performed just a couple of years later. Snippets from the *Dancing Times* had been cut out and stitched together by Max's grandmother's loving hand. Through them, Evie fancied she could see the whole chronicle of Jane Everly's life – from the girl who'd dreamed of dancing, and taken lessons in the local hall, to the girl who'd auditioned for a place as a demonstration dancer with the Buckingham Hotel, who'd once trodden the boards at the Hackney Empire, who'd collected ticket stubs from all the music halls she'd been to in her quest to make this dancing world her life.

'I see you're looking at pictures of my Janey,' came Max's grandmother's voice.

Evie had been so rapt by these mementoes of a life cut brutally short that she had not realised Max's grandmother had come back into the room. In her hands was a tray covered in a cross-stitch cloth – and, on top of that cloth, a silver teapot, three cups and a little bowl of sugar cubes. Max rushed to clear a space for it to be set down – the little table in front of the hearth was an avalanche of newspapers and magazines – and gently took the tray from her. 'Biscuits, Nana,' he said, in such a gently chiding way that Evie instantly knew the kind of relationship and rapport they'd had while Max was growing up. 'I'll fetch the tin, Nana. You two can get yourself acquainted.'

Evie did not want to be seen watching him go, but the discomfort of the moment was acute. How could it be that the eyes of such an aged woman pierced her so?

'Max's girl, then.' She pottered about, pouring the tea, but seemed never to take her eyes off Evie. 'Max's girl. He must think a lot of you, dear, to want to bring you back home. Now, I'll trust my Max – he's a grown man, and he deserves that trust – but, just so you know, there isn't a thing I wouldn't do for that boy. I've been protecting him and looking after him ever since that good-for-nothing father of his drove his mother to ruin, and I'll keep on doing it until the day I die. Do you see?'

The tea was poured. Max's grandmother added just a dash of milk, then offered it up to Evie with the sweetest smile.

'I saw you once,' Max's grandmother said.

'Excuse me?'

'Up on stage. Yes, I did. You were performing at the playhouse in Eastbourne. Year of nineteen thirty-seven. My husband, my daughter and I had taken a trip to the sea. This was before all the nastiness, of course. Before she met that man, and everything went to rack and ruin. She was quite a dancer, my Jane. She was in competitions by the time she was twelve. I daresay she'd have been crowned on the world's own stage if things had been different. But we thought, well, let's try something a little different. The ballroom world can be awfully stuffy, can't it? There are rules for everything. There's beauty enough, of course, and, my goodness, how you swoon to see those elegant dancers fly. But the music hall? The varieties? Well, there's *fun* in that. There's real joy. When I was a girl, I used to like the mimes they had at the Canterbury, right here in Lambeth. I liked the couples, doing their funny walks and singing nonsense rhymes. You won't know who Marie Lloyd is—'

Evie nodded. 'Oh, but I do! Everyone in variety knows who Marie Lloyd was.'

'She'd sing these songs – I thought they sounded silly when I was a mite, but when I got a bit older, I knew what she were singing about, if you take my meaning. She'd twirl her parasol and wink for the gents in the front row. Oh, it was joyous.'

'It can't have been me in thirty-seven,' Evie said. 'I'd have been just a girl, only four years old.'

'Oh, I know it was you, girl. There you were, at the curtain calls, up on your mama's shoulders, looking proud as can be. And that brother of yours, I reckon, up on your daddy's shoulders too. Waving for the crowd. Looking like this was the *life*.'

Yes, Evie remembered it now – there had been times, even before they were invited to perform on stage, that she and Cal had run out to meet their parents as the last bows came. Golden moments, captured in time – back when the family was as one.

'Of course, it was me who suggested Jane try out in the music halls. Well, the ballroom's an old-fashioned place now. Isn't that so? What's good for High Society isn't always good for us plebs. But the music hall? Now, that was for everyone. And variety theatre's just the same.' She shook her head, ruefully. 'But *he* was a song-and-dance man. *He* was a star on the stage. I daresay she wasn't the first to fall under his spell. But once a young woman's been bewitched like that, it's her that comes to ruin. The man can just get on the train and move on, like it never even happened.'

'She was a beautiful woman,' said Evie, returning her gaze to the pictures on the wall. 'She looks like Max very much.'

'Yes, indeed,' Max's grandmother said with pride. 'I happen to think Max doesn't carry an ounce of his father inside him. He's Jane's son, through and through. I've brought him up to honour her. And I've brought him up to be everything a good man should be: strong and proud, and resilient too. It isn't just dancing I had Max doing, you know. Before he went in for his National Service, I had him trained with a pair of boxing gloves, down at the local club. Dancing helped him in that. He became quite a star in his regiment. Might not have come home with medals from the King, but there were medals enough for his boxing. And now, no doubt, there'll be medals for his dancing too! With you as a teacher, of course.'

It was at this point that Max returned, the biscuit tin in hand, and, finding his grandmother and Evie locked in intense conversation, decided to lighten the mood by handing around melting moments. 'Nana makes the best biscuits,' he said. 'I was raised on them. Half the street were.' He paused. These biscuits, which ought to have been snaffled up, were not being accepted as eagerly as they might. 'You're talking about *him*, aren't you? You're talking about my father? Nana, I thought we agreed?'

'What that man did—'

'I know, Nana,' said Max, more consolingly now. Taking her by the arm, he led her to one of the armchairs, and urged Evie with his eyes to take the one beside it. 'I know exactly what he did. But what am I supposed to do? I've got to live my life.'

Evie wasn't certain she understood, except to say that the decisions this man had taken still echoed through the years. One act of malice or disregard could colour a multitude of lives. And the more she thought about that, the more she harked back to the 'fun' and 'joy' Max's grandmother had been speaking of, only minutes before. Life threw so much darkness at a soul; it was the duty of performing folk to make sure it conjured light as well. 'Shall we have some music?' she asked, as if to change the atmosphere in the room. Max's grandmother was evidently an admirer of good music, for a rack by the chimneybreast was overflowing with records, with the player on a little cabinet just alongside. Evie started browsing the sleeves, looking for something to lighten the mood. All of the greats were here: the Tommy Dorsey Orchestra; Nat King Cole; Bing Crosby singing ballads for Christmastime. There was no Bill Martin here – Max's grandmother seemed to be more of a Sinatra kind of girl – but all of the big swing bands featured. Evie chose a Benny Goodman and listened as the band struck up.

She had thought it would end the conversation, but Max's grandmother only bit into her biscuit and carried on. It was, Evie supposed, the story of her life, the one by which she'd come to define herself, and it was not easily let go. 'All the neighbours thought I should be ashamed, of course. But shame's just a crop that them who think they know better use to whip you with. They told me I should be ashamed when my Janey came home, in floods of tears, to tell me she was pregnant – and that the rat she'd fallen for had run off, leaving her in the lurch. They told me I should be ashamed when life drove her into such deep sadness that, one night, she took sleeping pills enough that she never had to wake up again. But I've never been ashamed of my Janey. Never.'

'It isn't quite true,' Max said, some moments later, while his grandmother tided away the tea paraphernalia. 'When my mother came back here, she was already starting to show. In those days, my grandfather was still with us. He knew shame, all right. His daughter defiled. *How could she be so foolish?* he kept asking. Foolish,' Max said, and Evie could sense the real bitterness growing in him now, 'to fall in love. So my grandfather shut the door on my mother. Kicked his own daughter out into the world, with a baby to raise and without even the love of her parents to see her through it. I doubt, very much, that my nana could have taken me in, if my grandfather was still alive. It's my good fortune the hateful old sod was dead by then, or I'd have been in some orphanage somewhere – and then what might have happened?'

Evie had never heard bitterness in Max before. He'd spoken of his mother's passing only with love and regret – the sadness a man might feel for a world that no longer exists, all the possibilities and the might-have-beens – but not with the broiling anger she saw in him now. It did not suit his angelic features; it was not right that such hatred was colouring those beautiful eyes.

'Max, it's a new world now. It's you and me—'

'That's the thing that's been on my mind, Evie.' He glanced up, to see if his grandmother was returning. Only when he was satisfied she was not, did he say, 'What happened to my mother won't happen to me, or to anyone I love. She made a mistake and she paid for it. One moment, and it dictated the rest of her life. It dictated her death. Well, I want to do things properly. I want to do things like they ought to be done.' He took a breath. 'I want to marry you, Evie.' His perfect face had flushed bright red. His fist dived into a pocket, and out came a small, worn box, covered in velvet rubbed bare. Deftly, he flicked it open. The wedding band sitting within was not ostentatious, just a simple silver ring. 'It's all I could afford. I don't have an heirloom to pass on, Evie. I've just got me. But, if you'll have me, I should like to become your husband. I should like it if you were to be my wife.'

There were very few times in Evie's life when she had been speechless, but this was one of them. Her eyes flashed between Max and the ring. How long had she known him? Six months, and perhaps a few days? How long since that night they first fell together? Three months? Four? Was a hundred days really enough to make the decision of a lifetime?

How did you *know*? There was no rule book in love. Max's mother had found that out to her deepest cost. But Evie's parents had taken the same bold step – and their love had only been shattered by a death.

Could it be as easy as a feeling? So much of dance and performance was in the feeling of it, but even then you had your craft to rely on, the countless hours you put into rehearsing before you reached the stage. No, in dance feeling was important – but so too was preparation.

Evie didn't feel prepared for this.

But then she looked into his eyes and she thought: *this isn't a performance; I'm not on the stage. This is real life, and in real life there are no rehearsals. There's only feeling. Nothing else but what's in your heart.*

'Max,' she said, and realised that her life was irrevocably changing, from one moment to the next. 'I'd love to. Yes,' she said. 'Yes, I'll marry you.'

The ring was not yet on her finger, but Max took her in his arms. There they were, holding each other – each imagining how the future might look, and all the years they'd be holding each other, all the manifold stages of a life – when Max's grandmother returned.

With her hands planted squarely on her hips, she looked at them both and asked, 'Is there something you young lovers want to share with me?'

So that was exactly what they did.

'And Nana,' said Max at last. 'There is one more thing, before we have to go.'

A terrible look flickered over Max's grandmother's face, for immediately she remembered the moment her Jane had come home with a confession of her own. But, 'No, Nana,' Max said with a grin. 'It's nothing to be afraid of. Quite the opposite, in fact.'

At this moment, Evie started beaming as well. 'We've got you a ticket,' she said. 'As rare as gold.' And she pulled a small ivory envelope from her coat pocket, then pressed it into her hands. 'To watch the varieties live, in the heart of the London Palladium. To watch Max and I dance, by royal command.'

*

The early winter dark was growing bitter, but, by the time they reached the Palladium steps, none of that seemed to matter. The theatre was closed this evening, so Evie and Max came hand in hand to the stage door, where a taciturn fellow in a bow tie and braces checked their names against a roster, then permitted them within.

There were some venues you entered and felt a warm glow. Others, you sashayed through and could picture, immediately, the atmosphere of a show night. Some theatres had a cosy, warm, intimate air; others suggested raucousness and disorder. All venues had characters of their own – but it was reverence, pure and simple, that the London Palladium inspired. Approaching the stage was like entering a church, for the London Palladium was nothing more than a temple, devoted to song and dance; a shrine to entertainment.

'I've only seen it on the screen,' said Evie, as they came via the backstage halls, following the sound of voices, and emerged together on the plush, carpeted aisle between the stalls. 'Sammy Davis Jr, basking in the glow of all those faces. That was his year. Perhaps this is ours.' Ahead of them, the stage was a hive of activity. Men were in the rigging. Voices hailed them from some box above, as spotlights were swung into place and calibrated. And there, up on the stage, stood John Lauder and Hugo, the Forsyths' driver, heaving the vanishing cabinet into place, marking out paths on the boards with different coloured chalks, judging lines of sight and angles of deviance – all of the miniscule technicalities that went into making a seamless show.

'Evie, you're here,' John called.

He was beckoning them over, but, before they set off, Evie turned to Max and whispered, 'We'll tell them after the show. Now's not the moment – not when there's so much to do. The Company comes first. Do you agree?'

Max nodded. 'Nothing to upset the balance of the show, Evie. What difference does a few days make? We have a lifetime after.'

Some of the other Forsyths were making their appearances now. Before Evie reached the stage, Lily cantered over. 'You won't believe it,' she said. 'They're saying Eartha Kitt's here tonight, to make her soundchecks, to block her positions for the lights.'

'Norman Vaughan's already here. He's backstage right now,' Betty chimed in.

'Tomorrow afternoon it's the Shadows.'

That was Verity. Together they gathered by the edge of the stage and looked up. The galleries stretched into the vaulted darkness above. The boxes where, forty-eight hours from now, Her Majesty and companions would be sitting, gazing down upon them.

A voice hailed them from the back of the stalls. Evie turned. There was her father and Cal, walking down the aisle.

Though the activity went on around them, every member of the Forsyth Varieties stopped dead, their attention focused on father and son.

'We come with news,' Ed declared.

'What news?' Lily blurted out.

Ed and Cal reached the edge of the stage. Here, the Forsyths gathered.

'The show's going on, exactly as we planned it.' Ed and Cal parted, to reveal the third figure advancing along the aisle behind them. 'No last minute panics, no dramatic volte-faces – our show, exactly as we'd planned it for the Seagate, with just one little difference.'

Bill Martin appeared between them, his arms thrown open wide, his pearly white teeth open in a dazzling smile.

'We've got ourselves a hit song,' Bill declared, 'and *I'm* going to sing it!'

15

The Real Bill Martin

'Runaway lovers ... running for cover ...'

'Yes,' said Cal. 'Yes, that's almost it. But you've got to slide into the proper feeling of it. They're just young and in love. They think the world's against them. Maybe their families have forbidden it. Maybe they're from different sides of the tracks. They shouldn't be together, but that's part of the fun. So, you see, it's like they're being ... hunted, I suppose. And it's tearing them apart. They just need a little respite, a little break from it all, a little sanctuary, to get themselves together, to enjoy one another – until the world catches up with them.'

'Hey,' said Bill, leaning in over the grand piano Cal was playing. 'You leave the *selling* of it to me. I know how to sell a song, kid. How do you think I got where I am?'

'Let's take it from the top,' Bill said. Then he looked down at Cal, who until now had been playing the piano. 'Cal, old son, maybe it's time to let Valentino take over. The clock's ticking now. Less than two days to bring this thing together.'

Cal looked up. 'One more time, Bill. I want to see how it feels.'

'Time's running short.' Bill tapped the gold watch on his wrist and shook his head. 'I need to know this song's gonna fly, if I'm going to sing it by Monday night. I'm sorry, Cal. You've done good, but let Valentino take over now. He's got to get the song under his skin as well. He's got to get the music running under those fingers.'

It was the weight of expectation that drove Cal up from the piano stool. In acquiescence, he threw his hands in the air. This was just like being on Denmark Street again. You sat before people who didn't know a thing about writing a song and ... Cal took a breath. He had to remind himself: Bill Martin had conquered the world. He did know music. He did know the craft of a song.

But where was the respect? Where was the admiration? Singers poured their hearts into their performances, that much was true – but a songwriter crystallised a piece of his soul, then sent it out into the world to be judged. When the curtains came down, the singer was finished, but the songwriter went on.

He was almost at the door when Bill called back, 'Hey, Cal?'

Perhaps he'd thought again; perhaps he was going to venture forth with just a few words of gratitude, encouragement, thanks. 'Yeah?' Cal said.

'I'm gonna need that lyric writing down. Just until I've got it in my head, all right? All these runaway lovers, running for cover ... la la another ... Well, it ain't as snappy as I'm used to, you see?' Bill patted his pocket. 'Magdalene's waiting out there, Cal. She'll get you a paper.'

Every word Cal tried to utter somehow caught in his throat, so instead he just nodded. Then he strode out of the door.

Magdalene was waiting at the end of the hall, past the dressing rooms where some attendant was currently placing little bronze plaques etched with names on each door. Cal had walked past *Rudy Cardenas*, the Mexican juggler who used his shoulders, his neck, his chest – as well as his hands and feet – in his astonishing displays, and *Sophie Tucker* – they called her the

'Last of the Red Hot Mommas', and her act comprised a series of riotous, risqué songs

Magdalene barely looked up when Cal approached. She was sitting outside the door marked *Bill Martin*, like one of the hair stylists or make-up artists often left to linger on a step until the talent inside was ready.

'Magdalene,' he said. 'Wouldn't you be more comfortable inside?'

She was wearing those sunglasses again, Cal saw – hiding away, as if she didn't want to be here at all. How was it that the Seagate seemed to thrill her, but something so grand old world as the Palladium needed to be blocked away?

'The cleaning crew are coming along,' said Magdalene, her voice a soporific drawl. He'd only heard one other person speak like that, apart from those who'd had too much to drink – and Magdalene certainly didn't have the scent of gin or wine about her. In the minutes after she'd given birth, Meredith had been much the same, all the nitrous oxides she'd been given still coursing through her and having their effect.

'He wants my lyrics, written down. He said you could help.' Cal reached for the dressing-room door. 'There must be a pencil and paper—'

In the same moment he opened it up, Magdalene leapt to her feet and grabbed his arm. 'Let me,' she drawled – but it was already too late; Cal had already seen the wreckage within.

The room, palatial in size, was anything but palatial in cleanliness and order. Glasses had been shattered across the dressing table. Chairs had been upended. A crystal decanter, turned on its head, had spilt its finest bourbon across a Persian rug, itself marked in patches of blackness where the chewed-up stubs of cigars had been carelessly tossed around. The mirror was smeared with what at first appeared to be blood, but Cal quickly took for the same lurid shade of lipstick he'd seen Magdalene wearing when they first met.

Cal stepped across the threshold, Magdalene still pulling on his arm. 'What happened here?' he breathed.

'It's—' By her tone, she was about to say 'nothing', but for some reason the will left her. In a single juddering motion – which only made Cal more convinced she'd taken some tranquiliser – she let go of his arm and, reaching up, took off her sunglasses.

The flesh around her left eye socket was purple, turning to black. A gruesome corona around the bruise was feathered in green, like oil on water.

Cal reached up. 'Oh,' he said, and flashed a sudden look over his shoulder. 'Oh, Magdalene.'

'It looks worse than it feels,' she said. 'He didn't mean it. It's the pressure of this trip. It's been getting to him. He's a courageous man, but sometimes the tap runs dry, you know? The pressure cooker just blows.' She gestured at the destruction in the room. 'It's better when we're at home. You might not think it to look at him, but he's a creature of comforts. Being on the road just pushes his buttons, you know?'

Cal dared to touch the edge of the bruise around her eye. It did not pulsate with warmth, and that could only mean that it wasn't fresh – certainly not as fresh as the destruction in this room, because Cal had seen Magdalene wearing her sunglasses, the better to cover up her bruising, at the Buckingham Hotel earlier that same day. 'He did this to you?' he whispered, and – to avoid being heard – brushed the door shut behind them. 'Bill?'

'Don't close the door, Cal. If he comes and sees…' She rushed to open it again, then slid the sunglasses back on her nose. 'He thinks you were cruising around me back in Seaford. You were trying to pick me up.'

'Is that why he—'

Magdalene snorted, wearied with the world. 'Oh, don't flatter yourself. This was because the bourbon wasn't right.' She indicated the destruction in the room. 'And this,' she lifted the sunglasses, just for a moment, 'was just because. Look, it's just Bill, all right? It's just ... stars. I know plenty of wives back home who get worse. The studios dismiss them, or there's some bad press – or some hack's out with his camera, waiting in the bushes, waiting to catch him taking out the garbage, or taking a pee in the rose bushes. It's what they do. But it isn't them who get it in the neck for it. It's the nearest and dearest.' Magdalene shrugged. 'It's a pact,' she went on, though nothing she said seemed to have very much conviction any more. 'We all make them. I just never thought—' At once, Magdalene started to cry, but, when Cal went to console her, she only brushed him away. 'I told you. If he walks through that door...'

Something had changed in Magdalene's demeanour. From some hidden depth, Cal knew not where, she found new strength. She marched across the room, snatched a pen from a pot on the dresser, and pressed it into Cal's hand. An envelope – one that had come with the flowers now strewn across the room – was the only paper to hand. This she handed to Cal, too. Then, with her arms folded, she said, 'Don't breathe a word of it, Cal. I'm going to handle this on my own.'

'Handle it?' said Cal – and suddenly he thought of Meredith's friend Faye, Bruce's hands around her neck, the rings of black around her eyes. All the fire of that moment was back in him. He'd quite forgotten how it had felt. The animal need he'd had to deal unto Bruce what he was dealing to others. By God, he'd been on fire. To look back on it now, it hadn't felt like him at all. Something else had taken over, and the songsmith Cal had just sat back and watched. '*How* are you going to handle it, Magdalene? How on earth do you intend to handle this?'

Magdalene shook. 'I don't know, Cal.'

Not for the first time, Cal wondered what Hollywood did to a soul. How many months had it been since the newspapers were plastered with the story of the sad, tragic end of Marilyn Monroe? Norma Jean, plucked from obscurity, given a new name, sent to sing for presidents and kings … and then, suddenly, just gone. Fame, success, adulation – it either killed a soul, like it had done with Bill, or it killed outright.

Magdalene forced Cal backwards, over the threshold and out into the hall.

Cal headed back to the rehearsal room, pressed the paper against the wall and took his time writing down each lyric, determined that – if the arrangement were not to be his, if the voice and feeling were not his own – he would, at least, make sure Bill sang the story as it went.

Then he slipped in, where Valentino's musicians were gathered around Bill, like devotees praying at their icon. Bill's voice trembled fabulously:

'And when I … look at you every day … That's when I know … you're my runaway …'

The moment Cal entered, brandishing the lyric sheet, the music died and every eye turned upon him. '*I'm* your runaway,' Cal said. 'You're saying you belong to her, not that she belongs to you. It matters, Bill. It makes a difference.' He wasn't sure why that was the most important thing, right now – because, suddenly, his song seemed but a footnote. The black rings around Magdalene's eyes, the rage that had been unleashed in the dressing room – weren't those more important? How could Bill stand there, acting every inch the lord of song, when hours ago his fists had rained down?

'I like it better my way, Cal.'

Oh, but of course he did. Bill Martin, it turned out, was not a man who could ever give himself wholly to another person. By the garish shade of his young wife's face, he seemed the sort of man who needed to own, punish, control. Yes, Cal had met one of those before. He wondered why he hadn't already seen it.

'Composure, Cal!' Bill called out. Thank God one of Valentino's musicians had scurried over to collect the paper, because Cal wasn't sure what might have happened if Bill's hand had touched his own. 'That's what this song needs. A bit more refinement. Some *stature*. It's too fast. We need to slow it, just a touch, to let these verses breathe. Leave it with me, Cal. We'll do your baby proud.'

Not for the first time, Cal could summon no words. Instead, he turned on his heel and hurried through the network of passages backstage. A mixture of rage, confusion and bad feeling dogged him as he left the Palladium behind, and bowed out into the Soho night.

And, perhaps, if his thoughts hadn't been so tangled, he might have known he was not alone as he picked his way back to his Soho lodgings. He might have seen the three men who, having waited at the Palladium stage doors like the ardent fans of some singing sensation, began following him through the dark winter's night.

He might have known that his worst fears were coming true – and that, though the end of the month was still four days away, a violent rogue's word was not always his bond.

When the next day dawned, and Ed Forsyth woke up, he was sixteen years old and about to live the dream of his young life.

Fifty years separated the man from the boy, but this morning it felt like barely a breath. As the leader of the Company – and as a performer returning to the Royal Command – Ed had been offered a place in one of Piccadilly's finer hotels; not nearly as grand as the Buckingham, of course, nor as majestic as the Savoy, but a place more peaceful and restorative than the Soho lodging house he'd just woken up in. But Ed had never intended to end his career that way. No, he would end it in exactly the way he had started it: as one of the players, at the heart of the Company that bore his name. That was why he'd awoken in this particular lodging house, in this particular room, overlooking this particular little corner of Golden Square.

If memory served him correctly – and if the changing face of London, for the city was so different now to how it had been back then, had not deceived him – this was the very room in which he'd awoken on the morning of the first Royal Command in 1912. The only difference was that, back then, he'd been bunking with one of the other players, one of those lost in the fields of France, never to perform again. Now, he awoke alone, from dreams of Bella, ready to face the day.

The landlady provided breakfast and cordial conversation, though Ed did not let on what his duties of tomorrow would entail. He'd been overlooked in 1912, just another slip of a lad come to London, and somehow he preferred it that way. Alone with his eggs and bacon, he perused the morning paper, where anticipation for tomorrow's event was high.

On Monday, the Royal Variety will return to the London Palladium for the first time in five years. This year, the London Palladium will be open to every soul in the nation, with cameras entering the Palladium for the very first time. Much has been promised, and a show involving Bob Hope, Eartha Kitt, comedy from Mike and Bernie Winters – and the return, after fifty years, of the Forsyth Varieties, who for one night only have added none other than Mr Bill Martin to their ranks – looks to have something for everybody. For those of us who have grown up with the twentieth century, Miss Sophie Tucker will be an attractive prospect – but for those of us a little younger, the new singing sensation Cliff Richard and his Shadows will offer high entertainment. The BBC broadcast will . . .

Ed folded up the newspaper and tucked it beneath his arm with a smile. To sing for his King had been one thing; but to sing for his country as well, that would be the honour of a lifetime.

He meant to take a long, quiet stroll to the theatre. Today was reserved for each act's technical rehearsal, for the lighting and sound technicians to refine their plans for tomorrow's event. There was such technical trickery involved in the Forsyths' show that he wanted to be there to oversee it. Then, this evening, there would be time to see elements of it unfolding on the stage. If Ed was fortunate, too, he might find some time to pore over his material with Norman Vaughan, perhaps even to share a few words with Bob Hope, with Mike and Bernie Winters, the legion of comics who would be leading the guests through the show tomorrow night. Just to be among them, for his final night as a player – it was, he decided, the stuff of dreams. And, for perhaps the first time in the last six years, he did not stutter through a pang, wishing Bella was here to stand on stage beside him – for he knew he carried her in his heart.

But he hadn't gone ten steps before, suddenly, Evie and Max had appeared to walk alongside him.

'Dad,' Evie said. 'There's something we wanted to tell you.'

'We were going to leave it until after the show,' said Max.

'And we won't tell another soul, not until then.'

'But it felt wrong to keep it from you.

'I wanted you,' said Evie, 'to be the first to know.'

And when Ed found out, none of the plans he'd made seemed to matter. All that truly mattered was that his daughter was in love, that he was to have a second son – and that, perhaps, his retirement might be spent as a devoted grandfather, called upon to pass on the tricks of his trade after all.

By the time they reached the Palladium, they had spoken of everything: wedding plans, and children; the speech Ed would make, harking back to the speech of Bella's father as he himself had been wed. Inside, the auditorium was a hive of activity. The rest of the Forsyths were not due until afternoon, but one among them had arrived before dawn – for here was Davith Harvard, and trotting along behind him, like he was some canine Pied Piper of Hamlyn, came not just Tinky and Tiny but four proud corgis, each resplendently groomed.

Davith seemed to be taking them on parade. Up and down the aisle they came, with Davith conducting them like an orchestra, first telling one to sit here, then telling another to stay there, then summoning them all with an almost inaudible whistle, so that they came lolloping back into formation.

'Mr Forsyth!' he cried out, upon seeing Ed. 'Let me introduce you to Diamond, to Dusty, to Elton and Weasel. Aren't they just *bootiful*, Mr Forsyth?'

Beautiful, they certainly were – and, if Ed had a flash of fear that untested dogs might interrupt his show, it was quickly off-set by the thought of Her Majesty cooing over so many suddenly-appearing corgis. 'Now, Davith,' he said. 'Don't let your corgis upstage our stars.'

'Oh, Mr Forsyth, they'll *be* the stars!' And, at once, the corgis began rolling backward and forward, turning somersaults at Davith's command. 'He's trained them to perfection, Mr Forsyth. An afternoon with Mr Lauder, and we'll make magic of them yet!'

Ed could believe it, but he could also believe that the magically manifesting corgis could quickly become the most memorable part of the act. That wouldn't sit well with Bill Martin – who, right now, was wending his way to them through the stalls, up bright and early, with Magdalene nowhere to be seen.

'Might I share your news?' Ed whispered, as Bill approached. 'Just with an old friend? He'll be so pleased for you, Evie.'

Max frowned, but Evie's look quelled him.

'It's only Mr Martin,' she said. 'As long as it's not the Company, it won't stir things up.'

'Bill,' Ed declared, grasping his old friend by the hand. 'The good news keeps flowing. Bill, I'm to welcome Max to the Forsyth family.'

'Wedding bells?' Bill beamed, flashing them a look. 'Can it be so? Are we truly to lose another fine young woman to the bonds of holy matrimony?' He threw back his head to laugh. 'Put it there, son!' he cried out, and extended his hand.

Max didn't take it. He only stared.

'Go on, *son*! Put it there!'

Bill grabbed him by the hand, and shook it so energetically that Max's whole body rippled.

'You're locking up a good one here, son. A prized treasure, and don't forget it.' He lowered his voice, still grinning, to a conspiratorial whisper. 'Take it from one who's been around the block, tried out a few models before he found the right one. Treat her right, and she'll be yours forever. And never, ever forget what you've got. A good woman's hard to find – and, *son*, you found the best.'

The wind was brisk across Soho. He'd not come here in winter before. Cal's Soho days were ones of sun-kissed summer, when the girls lounged every lunchtime beneath the trees of Soho Square Gardens, and in the long evenings musicians would gravitate to every square. He'd taken his guitar to that little corner by Berwick Street so many times, just to earn a few coins to later drink away in the John Snow or Blue Posts. Those were the kinds of pubs where they didn't mind you taking your girl. Nobody had thought of Meredith as a loose woman when she went for a drink with Cal. This was Soho, at the dawn of the 1960s: a place to just *be*. Now, as he picked his way through the old winding lanes, he found that he missed how free those days had been – when the only expectations in life came from the ones he poured onto himself.

The memory of those expectations weighed heavily on him, however, as he crossed the Charing Cross road and picked his way to the corner of Denmark Street. For a street that loomed so large in his imagination – and his sense of everything he'd so far accomplished in life – it was not particularly vast. Just a little slanted row, with the churchyard at St Anne's – where he'd sometime gone to ponder, seeing in the names on the headstones the whispers of untold stories, the possibilities of songs – at one end, and the heaving station of Tottenham Court Road at the other. The shops and cafés, frequented by the musicians, poets and writers who haunted the nearby clubs, nestled between the publishers' offices where Cal used to ply his trade. In New York City, they had 'Tin Pan Alley' – but, in London, Denmark Street was where it was at.

Somehow, the dread of those days – taking the narrow staircase between the cafés, and up into the offices above – returned to Cal, the moment he set foot in the street. He had to steel himself with hot coffee in the Giaconda café – he'd come here so many times too, all the songwriters of Soho with their notebooks in hand – before he dared press the buzzer for No. 4a, then clamber up the stairs between Regent Sounds and the old metalworkers' union next door.

He did not recognise the girl who sat on the reception desk

on the first floor – but, of course, he wouldn't; the last time he'd been here, it had been Meredith sitting here, and in her eyes all the promise of his life yet to come. Consequently, when he gave the girl his name and asked to see Mr Brownlow, the girl gave him short shrift. 'I'm afraid it's appointment only, and that not easy to come by. Look, you obviously know our address. What have you got, some songs? You can notify us of where you're playing. Somebody might come out. But you'd better be piling up press clippings too, because there's hundreds come here every week and there's only so many hours in a day. Or, if it's lyrics you're writing, the postbox will do you more favours than just strolling in here and…'

Cal bristled. He'd known this type before. She'd been schooled too well by Mr Brownlow and his ilk, more of a club door-man than a champion of new music. Thinking on it now, that was exactly why Meredith had stood out so much, exactly why he'd started falling in love. When she'd sat on this desk, every songwriter who'd stepped through the door had been the chance to hear something life changing; everybody else seemed to grow dour and dismissive. It had always made Cal wonder why they'd come to London for music at all.

'Just tell him Cal Forsyth's here, if you would.'

'Is it a name he'd recognise, sir?'

'Only about seventy-three times over. That's the number of songs I wrote for him.' Cal paused. 'I'm not here to cause trouble. I have something he'll want to hear.'

The girl stared at him. Then she stared at him some more. She was still staring at him when she said, icily, 'All I can do is relay a message. Mr Brownlow's a very busy man.'

Cal sighed. 'Yeah? Well, if he's too busy to hear about Bill Martin, that's too bad.'

He had turned to saunter away when he heard the click of a

telephone receiver being picked up, and the desk girl hurriedly whispering into the mouthpiece. With a deliberately slow gait, he made his way to the office door, then to the head of the stairs – and was just about to take the first step, when suddenly he heard, 'Forsyth, you rogue.' Not the desk girl, then; this was the gravelly voice, forever tainted by cigarettes, of Mr Brownlow himself. Cal turned to see him standing there: the balding rake of a man, who treated music as if it was just another commodity, like sugar or tea, and sold it with all the grace of a market tradesman. 'You've got five minutes, Forsyth. Five minutes, and you're out on your ear.'

'I don't need five,' said Cal, shrugging. Dismissiveness was the only language a starched shirt like Brownlow knew. It had been a strange lesson to learn – when you treated a man like this with deference, he thought you were a maggot, barely worth his time, but if you acted like *he* was the maggot, then suddenly he paid attention. 'Ten seconds will do. My song, "Runaway Lovers" – you dismissed it by the time I got the second verse, but I've forgiven you for that. Everyone else dismissed it by the time I reached the chorus. That's the only reason I've come to you now. The reason I've *chosen* you. Mr Brownlow, turn on the BBC broadcast for the Royal Variety show tomorrow night. Listen out for Bill Martin. He'll be singing my song, Mr Brownlow – but it's still mine. I've loaned it to him, one night only. After that, the rights are up for sale.'

'Now listen here, Forsyth, you can't come in here and—'

'It's your choice, Mr Brownlow. I'll be in the Giaconda for breakfast, Tuesday morning. You can make me an offer then. Full buy-out, if you like. But I have my price.'

'And what's that, Mr Forsyth?' Cal had already taken a step on the stairs. He did not look back. 'What's that?'

It would not do to give him an answer. Cal had seen the way

men like Brownlow operated; they were shrewd manoeuvrers, always thinking a step ahead, always trying to get a good deal – and the thing they hated, most of all, was to be left waiting. It would do him no harm to be the one left dangling for a time. Cal was a fair man, but five hundred pounds was the steepest price.

By the time he reached the Palladium, the auditorium was bustling. The lights were in place, the projectors whirring – and a three-piece band Cal had never seen before was playing a jaunty end-of-the-pier tune while a handsome man with sculpted black hair cavorted across stage, casting balls and bell-sticks into the air, then spinning three top hats, each nestled inside the other, from his head and adding them to the ordered chaos of juggling above.

The stalls were dark, but, among them, Cal's eyes lit upon his father. Ed had seen Cal too. They came together in the aisle. 'I know I should be preparing,' Ed whispered. 'But, son, this is the best preparation – just to be inspired. Isn't he incredible?'

'Juggling, Dad? For the Queen?'

Ed grinned. 'Anything's an art if you perfect it. They called him the Little Rastelli back home. He was opening nightclubs in Mexico City by the time he was eight. Two years later, juggling his way around the casinos. Rudy's earned his place here, Cal – there's no doubt about that.' Ed paused. There was, or so it seemed, something else he was eager to say. 'And so have you, Cal. Look, come. Come with me.'

It was difficult to leave the otherworldly juggling skills of Rudy Cardenas behind, but Cal followed his father into the backstage halls. 'Evie's decided the dancers have trained enough. They're taking a break, until the run-through tonight. Bill's done singing for the day too. He's off taking lunch with Magdalene somewhere. She's a sweet girl,' said Ed.

Sweet girl? thought Cal. Could his father really have been so blind? How was it that when the world looked at Bill Martin, what they saw was confidence and grace, a talent that had conquered the globe – but nobody spoke about the devastated dressing room, the devastated lives? Cal was quite certain, by now, that Magdalene's was no isolated incident. He remembered men like Bruce too well to ever get tricked into that.

'Here,' said Ed, when at last they came to the string of dressing rooms deep behind the stage. 'See?'

Up on the door, where once the sign had read *Ed Forsyth*, now the name read *Cal*.

'But, Dad, what – what's this?'

Ed cleared his throat, his eyes darted around – and, for perhaps the first time in his life, Cal thought that his father, who'd sung for a king when he was half Cal's age, who'd spent his life in front of paying audiences, was nervous. 'It's my gift, Cal – to you, my son.'

'I don't understand.'

'Then I'll tell you. Your place is here, with us, boy. I don't pretend to understand what happened between us, after your mother died. I don't pretend I know what was going on in my own heart, let alone yours. But I do know this: you came back here, and you made a gift to us – a gift of your song. You didn't need to do it. You didn't expect anything in return. But I'm giving it.' Ed paused. 'I've spoken to Valentino. I've spoken with Bill. It took a little charm to grease the wheels, but Bill's agreed: we want you to play piano tomorrow night, Cal. To be a part of your song, in front of all the great and the good who'll be out in that hall. Cal,' he smiled, softly, 'it was the honour of my life to sing in front of the King. I carried it with me for fifty long years. It's been my shining light in my darkest hour – and, whatever happens in your life, I should like you to carry the same fire.'

'I – I don't know what to say.'

'There've been enough words, Cal. I'm just…' And here words began to fracture and come apart, to fail Ed Forsyth at last. 'I'm glad you came back. Your mother's looking down on us now, son, and she's glad too.'

'The dressing room, Dad. I don't need your—'

'Maybe not.' Ed grinned. 'But I don't need it. It's my last night, Cal. I want to be back among the troupe – back where I belong.'

When Cal had been silent too long, Ed said, 'I don't need the space – so it's yours, if you want it. Just a gesture, Cal. You always wanted your father's dressing room, back when you were small.'

Cal looked again at the door: his own name, etched in bronze and screwed into place. His father had gone to no small effort to make this happen. And the thought struck him then that it didn't matter any longer; even if he was up on the BBC screens tomorrow night, his face broadcast into homes across the nation, it would be over by break of day. He'd be sitting in the Giaconda by breakfast, and Mr Brownlow would be paying handsomely to take 'Runaway Lovers' away from him – and, in doing so, unlocking his freedom to go back to Meredith, to be a father to Sam, to forget that Bruce and his thugs had ever existed. If Bruce and his thugs saw him playing piano, by the time they caught up with him, it would be done.

Cal smiled. He pushed open the door – and there, through the frame, he saw himself and his father standing together in the mirror on the opposite wall. Side by side, as equals, for the very first time.

16

Curtains!

Dawn over Seaford. Jim Livesey had been awake since the earliest hours, sitting through the black watches of night in his bedroom window, looking down on the empty funeral yard below. His focus was not on the street cats, the post van, or the milk float rolling by. His eyes sought only a flash of yellow, the appearance of a brightly coloured Ford Anglia arriving in the yard.

But the sun came up and there was nothing, and before long his mother was calling him down to breakfast.

'Cheer up, James,' his father said. 'Monday morning comes for us all, son. It's better you just get on with it. You can't hold back time.'

'Leave the boy alone, Reg,' Jim's mother chipped in. 'Our boy's had a taste of the big time. Haven't you, Jim?' She tousled his hair, as if he was still the same age as Amy, gleefully clapping her hands in the chair alongside. 'He's been up on stage. You must be a big star at school, Jim. They'll all be asking you how you did it, are they?'

'He still hasn't told you, then?' Reginald smirked.

Jim's mother's eyes goggled. 'He's not told you!' Then, riven with doubt, she asked, 'Has he?'

'He doesn't need to. It's obvious, isn't it? You don't really think that old fraud turned him into a couple of dogs, do you? Those dogs were on the bloody poster. They're just show dogs.'

'But how do you explain them disappearing and popping up all over the place?'

'Obvious, isn't it?' said Reginald, and started buttering his toast. 'They've got a dozen of the bloody things, all painted up to look the same. It must cost a fortune in dog biscuits.'

Reginald returned his attention to the newspaper, so Jim never got a chance to retort. It was just as well; he'd taken oaths to the arts of magic that he would never reveal the complex arrangement of talent, misdirection and special equipment that allowed John Lauder to perform his magic – and the urge to prove his father wrong was overwhelming.

'Well, off to school then,' Jim's mother declared, once the breakfast was half eaten, 'and cheer up, Jim. It was a magical weekend. It's just that – well, sometimes a magical weekend can make everything seem a bit more hum-drum. The trick is, not to let it bother you too much. You can't have the highs if you don't have the lows. That's what a wise man once said. And Jim, my love, if you can accomplish that, that's *real* magic.'

It wasn't that Jim didn't appreciate his mother's attempts to make him feel better. As he stepped out of the house, he realised she'd even packed him an extra teacake for lunch. It was the expectation they had of him that hurt most of all. Yes, it was a dreary Monday morning – and, yes, the magic of the Spectacular had already faded in the days that had since flown by – but Jim could have coped with all that, if only they hadn't kept dragging him down, expecting him to be grateful for his lot in the world, demanding he be joyous at the idea he'd be spending the next fifty years tramping around after hearses.

So: school it was. They'd asked him about it already, but by now the Seagate Spectacular was rapidly fading in the memories of the younger residents of Seaford. They'd all tune into the Royal Varieties tonight, of course – and perhaps some of them would marvel that those same players had been performing in Seaford, only nights before – but, soon, it would all feel like a dream: something that had happened to other people in another time.

Jim wondered if it would feel like that for him too. Perhaps, in ten years' time, he'd be proudly arranging the services for Livesey & Sons, wondering how he'd ever dreamed of being a stage magician at all. 'Just a boyhood phase,' he'd tell the children he'd one day have. 'And you'll grow out of yours too. You've got to live in the real world. Take your head out of the clouds. An undertaker's son from Seaford can no more be a stage magician than …'

A car beeped its horn.

Jim looked up.

His whole life changed.

The canary-yellow Ford Anglia was crawling along the kerb beside him, and now its window was winding down. At the wheel sat a gargantuan man, his great hands dwarfing the wheel, his head permanently bowed beneath the car's low roof. 'It *is* you,' he said in a broad West Country accent. 'I been driving in circles looking for the undertaker's yard, and then I sees you. Truth be told, I didn't know if I'd recognise you – but, on reflection, it isn't often you see a boy transform into two little dogs, so you've stuck in my mind. You're Jim,' he declared, as if Jim didn't already know this, 'and I'm Hugh. Well, look sharp, lad. It's a decent drive back to London – and there's work to do once you get there.'

The words cascaded over Jim, but it seemed to take some time before he properly understood. In his mind, the dream had passed – and yet, here it was, a vision of bright yellow, a hand beckoning him from the side of the street.

'I thought you'd ... I didn't know ...' At last, Jim said, 'I was on my way to school.' He looked back. 'They won't know where I am.'

'Then hop in,' Hugh said. 'We'll go and tell them.'

But as soon as Jim had opened the passenger door, then slipped within, he had another idea. 'They'll only try and stop me. They'll tell me to get my head out of the clouds. But Mr Lauder wants me, doesn't he? He needs me for his act.'

'Jim, young man, the message he asked me to pass on to you is pretty clear.'

Jim just stared.

'Jim Livesey,' he announced. 'Destiny is calling.'

Then the engine roared back to life, the seafront whirled by in a rush of blues, greys and gold – and Jim thought nothing of his parents, nothing of his schooling, nothing of the chaos that was bound to greet him upon his return, because London was calling out to him, and he was going to perform in front of the Queen.

Soho was at its sleepiest at dawn on a Monday morning, but that did not mean the streets were dead. By the time the Forsyths left their lodgings the vibrant cafés of Carnaby Street heaved with city clerks on their way to their offices – and even one or two of the less salubrious drinking establishments had thrown open their doors, if only to air their insides before the day's first drinkers descended. A cleaning crew was marshalling at the stairs that led down into the basement Midnight Rooms, while only a short distance away, the doors of some private artist's residence were thrown open wide to invite the discerning customer within.

By the time John Lauder was summoned to the trades-man's door, there to meet Jim Livesey – wearing an expression like a rabbit caught in headlights – it was nearing noon, and the entirety of the theatre seemed to be holding its breath, anticipating the evening to come. As the time the afternoon started paling – and the show's manager had visited each set of performers in turn – the anticipation had reached a strange pitch. With the stage now vacant, the lights in place, the last rituals of cleaning being performed through the stalls and circles above, time ceased to mean a thing within the Palladium walls. For the Forsyths, the hours either cantered or dragged by. Time stretched and then contracted, like a concertina.

John – afforded a dressing room of his own – held court over a chorus of corgis along with Jim and Davith. Ed lost himself, for a time, in conversation with Norman Vaughan. Lily and the girls caught a fleeting glimpse of Sophie Tucker, escorted to her dressing room by ladies-in-waiting as if it was she who was royalty. Backstage, when the Shadows arrived, Max could hear the distinctive twang of guitars being tuned, and musicians jamming together, through the walls. Their singer, foppish and slight – but possessed of boyish looks Lily and the rest would die for – was being lectured to by Bill Martin, while the American contingent, who would be dominating the second half of the show, gravitated towards one another in one of the common rooms.

Cal could hear Bob Hope's assistant, Edie Adams, talking, her voice like syrup, and he wondered if Magdalene ought to go to them, at least to be among her fellow Americans, but so far she'd seemed to prefer the privacy of a devastated dressing room.

Show days did not often have such empty hours, but the theatre was locked down while security teams roamed its every cranny, itineraries were made and registers taken. Tired of his own company, Cal left the dressing room and picked his way from corner to corner – until, at last, he stood outside the door marked *Bill Martin*. Bill's voice was still booming from further down the hall, so perhaps he was not risking much by gently knocking on the door and venturing within.

There was Magdalene, the room half restored around her. Nothing could mask the shattered glass, but some order had been imposed on the chaos. She and Cal looked at one another, until gently she removed her sunglasses. Makeup had been enough to mask much of the bruising, but Cal could still see it, through all the powder and lotions she'd applied. 'You should leave him,' he said, simply. He'd said the same to Faye, too many times.

'It isn't that simple.' Faye had said that too.

'No,' said Cal, his mind whirling back to Meredith once more. 'But it could be. And it will be, if you don't do anything about it. One day, it will be as simple as a slap too hard, or a gentle push at the top of the stairs. But you've got a life to live, Magdalene. I don't care about your *pact*. You have a life.'

That was all he wanted to say, though the urge to speak with Meredith grew so much stronger with every word that left him. He turned to leave, but then Magdalene asked, 'Did you tell anyone? Cal, did you tell your father?'

He shook his head.

'You don't have to stay in a smashed-up dressing room, Magdalene,' he said. 'I don't need mine. I'm barely even a performer tonight. Go there. There's somewhere else I've got to be.'

It was not an easy task to leave the theatre, even by the tradesman's door. The security detail sent to oversee the Palladium tonight were sharper, more precise and more ruthless than those Bill Martin had brought with him to Seaford: just clowns in suits, playing the part of officers of the law. The two besuited gentlemen who barred Cal's way subjected him to a fierce interrogation, voices buzzing back and forth across their radios, before they begrudgingly permitted him to leave. 'Take this,' the first told him, and, having first asked him to stand against the wall, then affixed a Polaroid picture of his face to a small card, instructing him to return within an hour. 'The doors will close before the first guests arrive. If you're not back by then, they'll have to cope without you tonight.'

Cal shoved the pass into his pocket. One hour was more than enough for what he had in mind.

The red telephone box at the top of Carnaby Street was occupied by a beggarman, his pockets full of loose pennies, so Cal had to run further, to the passage of St Anne's. Sliding inside, he lifted the receiver and waited for the crackle to subside, then for the operator's voice to issue forth. 'County Durham,' he said, and recited a number he knew by heart.

'Connecting,' said the operator dully, and Cal began feeding what coins he had in his pocket into the slot, tapping his foot in mounting impatience as the crackling went on.

'Hullo,' came a voice.

'Jack,' Cal blurted out. 'Jack, it's me. It's Cal.'

'Cal, you bloody fool. I've been trying to reach you. What in the name of God do you think you're doing? Up on stage? Making a name for yourself, again? When you said you were going to keep a low profile, I took you at your bloody word. And then, there you are, front and centre!' At first, Jack's voice was full of vitriol, but somewhere along the way he started to laugh. '

'It doesn't matter now, Jack. It's about to be over. By midday tomorrow, I'm in the clear. But I ...' He paused. Who knew how long a call like this lasted? He fed another coin into the slot. 'I need to talk to her, Jack. I need to hear her voice.'

'You'll have to wait a day then, Cal. If it's really over, you can see her then.'

'It's just a phone call, Jack. Jack, please. It's been too long. I want to tell her myself. I want to know they're all right.'

'They're being looked after, Cal. Locked away from prying eyes, like bloody Rapunzel, but they're OK. It's you they're worried about.'

'Then let me speak to them. Let me tell them I've got this sorted. Let me tell her …'

'Sorry' seemed to be the hardest word, but the truth of it was that Cal wasn't sure if he really was 'sorry' at all. After he'd confronted Bruce, Meredith had said that he hadn't been thinking straight, that there were different ways, that he was a father now and ought to have known better – but, in his heart, he knew that, if he'd just walked away, she would have looked at him differently; something would have changed in her eyes. What kind of a man would he have been, what kind of a father, if he let Bruce's madness go unchecked? No man – save perhaps for John Lauder – could see the future, but there were times when Cal wholeheartedly believed he had saved Faye's life.

'She isn't here, Cal. You know that bloody well. They don't even have a phone up there.'

'Then fetch her for me, Jack. Please. I want to tell her myself. It's going to be OK.'

'It's a half-hour drive, there and back – and that's even if she agrees. There's snow in them hills.'

'I'll owe you.'

Cal could tell Jack was softening to the idea. 'I'll try. It's all I can offer you, Cal, but I'll do it. Read out the number where you are. I'll have her call the box. Just be waiting.'

After Jack had hung up, Cal craned a look up at the sky. Night was coming on, and in only a few hours' time, the Palladium would open its doors.

And yet – the doormen had given him an hour. There was time enough yet. Then, later tonight, when his fingers rolled into the first chords of 'Runaway Lovers', he would be thinking of her – and she would be watching him, up on the television screen.

In the cold of the Soho dark, he permitted himself, at last, to smile. He was close now. He would be able to touch her soon.

It was an agonising wait. Twice, some passer-by hammered on the telephone-box door and turfed him out so that they could make their own calls. By the time half an hour had passed, the panic that – even after all of this – he might miss her call had begun to rise, so he occupied the box and feigned making calls every time someone passed by. He was in the middle of feigning another when the telephone started ringing. Quick as a flash, he whipped it up and fumbled it to his ear. 'Meredith? M-Merry?'

'Cal?'

It felt like her voice grabbed hold of him and wrenched him through the phone. All of a sudden, he was no longer standing on a frigid Soho street corner. He was by the hearth with her. They were lying in bed. They were looking at each other, across the breakfast table, through a haze of steaming hot tea and smoke from the fire.

They were cradling their baby, in the moments after he'd been born.

'Cal, where are you? Cal, are you all right?'

'I am now,' he said, and couldn't help but laugh. 'I'm sorry, Merry. I had to hear your voice. I had to tell you myself. This deal Jack brokered – I've found a way. And it was with me all along. It's "Runaway Lovers".'

'Cal, you're breaking up. This line's just static. Are you there?'

He took a breath. 'I'm here. Meredith, I'm coming home. But turn on the BBC tonight. Turn on the Royal Variety. I don't know if the cameras will catch me, but I'll be there – down in the orchestra, playing our song. "Runaway Lovers", Merry – it's going to get me back home.'

'Cal, we've been so scared. Every car that comes into this village, I see Bruce or one of his thugs. It's like being in prison. I don't want our son to grow up in prison. He needs you.'

'And he's going to have me. The Royal Variety – tonight! Tell him I'm there. Tell him, if he looks closely enough, he might—'

The door of the telephone box opened up.

A cold hand gripped Cal's shoulder.

He started to turn, but the hand was already turning him. So fiercely did he spin, the telephone receiver fell from his hand. Now it just dangled there, with Meredith's faraway voice buzzing from the tiny speaker.

It was a good job she couldn't see the vision filling up Cal's eyes – for there stood Bruce, his face still sporting the scars of the bottle Cal had clubbed him with, and on either side his drinking pals, with fists like prize hams and smiles missing teeth. Cal's heart started racing, but a consummate performer knew how to project calm while his insides turned to jelly. He rolled his head left; he rolled his head right. There was no way to avoid them now, not sealed inside this telephone box as he was. There'd be no losing them in the Soho night. All he had were his words.

'I wondered when you'd show up,' he said, darkly.

Bruce leered. 'Just in time for show night'

'Tell your butler to unhand me, Bruce. You and I made a deal.'

The man at Bruce's side had started bristling – he tightened his hold, digging dirty nails into the flesh of Cal's shoulder. This time, Cal could not stop wincing. The only reason he didn't cry out was because he could still dimly hear Meredith's voice buzzing down the line. 'Cal, are you there? Cal, what's happening? Are you alone, Cal? Cal?'

One of Bruce's men leaned over, as if they might cut the connection, but Bruce brushed him aside. 'No.' He grinned. 'Let her hear this.' He straightened himself, filled out his chest. 'We may have made a deal, Cal, but I don't see it being fulfilled. So we've come to pay you a little reminder – just a little reminder of what's in store if you don't keep up your end of the bargain.'

A fist connected with Cal's face.

Pain blossomed across him. Lights strobed across his eyes. His head had snapped backwards, connecting with the back of the booth – but somehow he stayed upright. Once the lights had faded, his sight returned. So did his hearing. Evidently, Bruce had been speaking throughout, but Cal only heard the tail end of what he was saying: '...a taste of what's to come. Well, you didn't think you'd get away with it so easily, did you? Jump me, in my own home town? Make a fool of me, would you? Well, Cal, your songs won't save you now...'

'They will!' Cal snapped. Everything still felt so distant, but he was certain he could hear Meredith screaming – screaming for him, from three hundred miles away. 'I'm getting your money, Bruce. This time tomorrow, you can have it all. Meet me in the Coach and Horses, first fall of dusk. I just need a little more time. And... you told Jack, the end of the month. That was the deal. That was the—'

This time, it was Bruce's hands all over him. He wrenched Cal out of the telephone box, then cast him onto the cold stone of St Anne's Passage.

Cal looked up. 'Bruce, you'll get your blood money.'

'Oh, I know I will,' said Bruce, as he loomed above. 'But that wouldn't be quite as satisfying. So I'll take my blood money, Cal – but, first, I'll take a little blood...'

Bruce's steel-capped boot was only the start of it. Soon, Cal was being hoisted up; then, he was being forced back down. Soon, the fists weren't only for his face, but for his chest, his kidneys, the place where their knife had caught him last time round. Soon, he felt the sickening crunch of bone on bone; then, the ice cold of the pavement kerb. And, by the time someone shouted out, one of Soho's Good Samaritans refusing to turn the other cheek, all that he could see was stars.

'Bruce,' one of the thugs said. 'We've got to go.'

The beating stopped. Cal fell back, for the final time, to feel the brutal kiss of the ground. Then, before blackness washed over him, all he could see was Bruce's face, hoving into view like a car crash in slow motion. 'It's just a taster, Cal. Just a little hint of what's to come. And the thing is, if I don't get every penny you owe, it won't just be for you.' Bruce picked himself up, marched into the telephone box and picked up the receiver. 'It'll be for Meredith too,' he said. 'You can't hide forever, girl,' he said, into the receiver. 'She's counting on you, Cal. Don't let her down.'

17

A Prophecy Unfurled

In living rooms across the land, families settled together. Their dinners were done, their glasses were full; children had either been put to bed for the night, or settled by the fire with cups of warm milk and biscuits to raise in celebration with the wines and beers in their parents' hands. Television sets, most of which had first been bought so that families could share in the coronation of Queen Elizabeth II, were now tuned again to the BBC to see the cream of the entertainment world celebrate ten glorious years of her reign.

The picture strobed. A flickering image of the London Palladium, lit up in lights so wonderful it almost seemed as if – a miracle! – the television screens of Great Britain had lit up in colour, appeared on screen. And, in the rich baritone so familiar to viewers, the BBC's grandest continuity announcer began.

'Good evening, ladies and gentlemen, and I hope you're sitting comfortably. The BBC is proud to welcome you tonight to the London Palladium, where Her Majesty the Queen has just taken up residence in the royal box. We're promised a fine spectacle indeed...'

'Are we ready in here?'

Backstage at the London Palladium, it felt like a dream. Fifty years ago, Ed had been riven with the feeling he did not truly belong. Now, here his Company stood – and he knew, without doubt, that this was the place they were meant to be. Having gathered in the chorus dressing room, they were lost in excited chatter of their own when knuckles rapped at the door, and Norman Vaughan pushed his way through.

'He looks just like he does on TV,' Lily whispered – but evidently not quietly enough, because at once Norman dazzled her with a smile.

'In the flesh and blood, ma'am,' he said, with a sharp nod of the head. 'Are we all good in here? Getting the engines stoked? It's a special moment, isn't it? The circle's full, there's not a seat left in the stalls. The lights are about to go down. Two minutes, and the orchestra will strike up.'

The anticipation in the room was intense. Even the little pack of corgis, who gathered around Davith like peasants presenting themselves to their vagabond king, seemed to bristle with it. Tinky and Tiny looked most put out, for their master's attention to be so devoted to the new hounds. The corgis looked so regal beside the border collies, their noses pushed haughtily into the air.

'Right, so the act's in order?' Norman went on. 'All we've got to do is get you to the stage. Ed, you've got about an hour until you're brought into the wings. You're coming up after Rudy, but he's not on stage forever – so they'll come to get you when Dickie's still playing. That should give you plenty of time to get in order. Now, we know who's going where, do we?'

Ed nodded. 'We're in good order, Norm. You send for us, we'll be there.'

Norman nodded, flashing a look around the room. 'Bill's not here. We're sending for him separately, are we? Do the stage boys know?'

Ed nodded. 'We'll sweep him up on the way. Bill's a part of the Forsyths tonight – we come as one. Norm,' and Ed stepped towards him, to shake him by the hand, 'break a leg tonight, son. You can count on us. We're not going to mess this up.'

A gentle knock at the door announced one of the stage managers, who whispered in Norman's ear that the moment had come.

'Well, my friends, we're about to do battle. Break a leg, Forsyths!' Norman announced. Then, retreating back through the door, he lifted a finger and said, 'Enjoy tonight, my friends. This night will live in you forever.'

Norman Vaughan had scarcely left the dressing room when the Palladium reverberated with the waves of applause that met the first music of the evening. Somewhere in the wings, the first acts were congregating.

Ed looked, lovingly, at his Company. 'Here it begins.' He turned their gazes upon the small black-and-white television set in the corner of the dressing room. The flickering BBC image showed the curtains peeling back, the spotlight finding Norman Vaughan. 'We share a stage with luminaries tonight. Let us stand proudly among them...'

The same images that the Forsyths gathered around, in their dressing room, were being broadcast far and wide. In sleepy Seaford town, families who'd watched the Company hold the Seagate enraptured gathered again, and felt as if they were themselves part of the act. From London to Edinburgh, Morecambe Bay to far-flung Penzance, families watched as Norman Vaughan introduced first Harry Secombe, then the Australian musician Frank Ifield. Gales of laughter broke out when Edie Adams – later to accompany Bob Hope in the show's finale – caught the audience in her spell. Hearts were lifted when the young Cliff

Richard strode out with his Shadows and filled the Palladium with the sounds of his hit song, 'Living Doll'.

And on a Soho back street, where the late October night was welcoming the rain, that song penetrated the mind of an unconscious man, dragged unceremoniously from the corner where he'd been discovered to the warmth of a street-side tavern.

First there was darkness, the infinite black of a starless night.

Then, patches of light swam across his vision.

The sounds, which had seemed so distant, came into focus.

The light coalesced into shape and form. As well as the sounds of Cliff Richard, he could hear the guttering of a motorbike, the beeping of car horns. Somewhere near, a bus's bell was ringing.

'He's awake,' came a voice. 'Fetch the doctor. He's awake.'

Cal sat up and pawed at his eyes.

The pain had retreated. Now, instead of the sudden explosions of Bruce's fists and boots, a dull ache characterised his entire body. He reached up, to touch his face. By morning, he'd be sporting dark bruises – Bruce would enjoy seeing that, when the moment came – but, for now, the swelling was not too vast. He tried to pick himself up, shaking off the smothering hands of those who had evidently dragged him in off the road. Though the room was still bleary, he knew by scent and sound that he was in the back room of a public house. A whisky had been set before him – medicinal purposes, one of the people was saying – and a doctor dragged away from his friends at the bar. Cal's tongue felt too thick to tell him he wasn't needed, so instead he just got shakily to his feet.

A back door was open, revealing a narrow staircase to the publican's quarters above. Cal moved his head from side to side, and tried to shake out some of the numbness and pain. It would help if he could shake off that song as well. He always felt he'd written so many better.

The whole world listed. He had to reach out to right himself against the wall.

Then he realised: *that song*...

His eyes flashed to the staircase.

If Cliff Richard was singing, that could only mean...

'What time is it?' he slurred, at last. The taste of whisky was on his tongue; apparently, they'd been feeding it to him while he slept. 'What time?' he repeated, more urgently now.

'It's almost eight.'

Cal's eyes widened. 'How long was I out?'

Before anyone had the chance to reply, Cal lurched towards the staircase. 'Not that way,' one of his benefactors called out. 'That's private. That's the publican's...'

But Cal had got to the top of the stairs before they reached him. In a little room off the landing, the publican's wife had settled down in front of her flickering black-and-white television set. In its frame, Cliff Richard and the Shadows were coming to the end of their song. They raised their hands, and guitars, skyward, to soak in the adulation of the Palladium crowd.

The curtain had gone up an hour ago. Acts had marched out, enthralled the crowd, and returned to the wings to await their post-show audience with Her Majesty the Queen.

He turned around. The patrons of the pub who'd been nursing him in the back room were halfway up the stairs now, urging him to come back down.

But Cal needed no urging.

The Royal Command was already underway.

In only a few minutes, the Forsyths would be called to the wings.

On legs that could hardly stay upright, he started to run.

*

Ed had been anticipating the knock at the door. The moment Rosemary Clooney came to the end of that vibrant hit she'd had some years ago, 'This Ole House', and the Palladium got to its feet, he braced himself. In the same moment that Norman Vaughan welcomed Dickie Henderson to stage, the knock came. A thin, bewhiskered stage manager put his head around the door and announced, 'It's time, ladies and gentlemen. Forsyth Varieties to the wings.'

Ed gathered the Company. 'No fear,' he declared. 'No nerves tonight. This is your memory. May it carry you through fifty years, long after I'm gone, into your own dotages. This moment may never come again. Embrace it, my friends. Now,' and his tone changed, shifting from one of wonder to simple logistics and business, 'do everything as we rehearsed. Let's form our lines. Stick to our beats and we can't go wrong.' He looked around. 'We'll pick Bill up on the way.'

Ed was almost at the doors, preparing to lead his perform-ers out into the backstage hall – where the stage manager was waiting to usher them on – when Evie sidled near.

'Dad, where's Cal?'

It took a moment for Ed to register the question. 'He'll be lounging in his dressing room, no doubt. You remember your brother, Evie. He always longed for a dressing room of his own.'

Evie frowned. It didn't seem right to her, somehow.

She gave a near imperceptible shrug, cautious that none should overhear. 'You don't think… Is it possible he…'

Neither needed to voice it, for both had spoken of it so many times over the years. Yet it seemed so unreal, tonight, that Cal should abandon them again. That night in Nice had still felt so raw just days ago; now, it felt a relic of some ancient past. Cal had gifted them his song, the one he held most dear to his heart. Ed had brought him back to the fold, found a place for him, given him his dressing room. Small gestures, perhaps, but every journey began with the tiniest step.

As the door opened and the stage manager hustled the Company out into the hall, Valentino drew near. A dark, disgruntled look had scudded across his features. 'Mr Forsyth, say it isn't so.' In reply, there was only stony silence. 'Ed, you invited him back in. He can't have just ... ditched us again?'

Some of the other musicians heard the timbre of Valentino's voice. Heads turned. Eyes darted.

'Ed, I know Cal's your son. I know what he means to you. But ...' Valentino had to look away; his hands were curling, in disgust, into fists. 'You promised me he'd stand up for us this time. Look, Ed, it's not that I can't find my way through that song of his. If Cal's run again, the show goes on. That song's all about the *mood*. It isn't so intricate when you break it down. I can find the chords. We've got the rhythm. The thing we might not have is the ... feeling of it. But it's Bill's song tonight, so mayhap that doesn't matter. But, Ed ...' He paused. 'Flaking out on us again, Ed! It's like he came back just to ditch us. Just to rub salt in the ...'

'There's something going on with him,' said Evie solemnly. 'There has been, ever since he came back. He's my brother, but ...'

'Five years changes us all,' said Ed. 'But I'm sure he hasn't left us in the lurch this time. Somebody, to his dressing room, quick, before ...'

'Cal hasn't vanished. He wouldn't.'

It was Lily's voice, rising out of the crowd. She lingered behind, while the rest of the Forsyths marched on, rounded up by the stage managers to be ushered into the wings. 'Last call!' someone was shouting. 'Last call for the Forsyth Varieties!'

329

Evie's eyes fell on Lily. 'What do you mean, Lil? What do you know?'

Lily shook her head. 'I just know he wouldn't leave us. Not this time. Not now. He wouldn't. He couldn't. He's got too much riding on tonight to walk away from it. It's everything to him.'

'Everything to him?' asked Evie. There was something here that she didn't understand – but then she remembered: Cal and Lily, appearing in the crowd outside the Seagate; Cal and Lily, sharing their whispered words, their secret looks. 'Lily, if you know where my brother is . . .'

Ed nodded ruefully. 'It wouldn't be a show without a drama backstage. After him, Lily. Bring him to stage. The night of our lives is about to begin.'

Carnaby Street was awash with journalists. By the time Cal limped past Liberty, all he could see were flashing camera lights. There would be no getting near the front of the theatre, for the red carpets had been rolled out and ladies, lords and stars of the screen were taking their turns to address the spectators fawning over them at the rails.

The stage door was closed, locked shut to the night. His fists hammered on it, until at last it opened up. The same security guard who'd needed persuading to release Cal now blocked his way like a Roman wall. Cal reached for the Polaroid picture, flashed it in his face, but at first it seemed to no avail. 'Look,' he snapped. 'It's me!'

'It doesn't look like you, sir,' said the officer – and, of course, he was right. Cal's lip was split open now, his face grazed and smeared in dirt.

'Give me a lick of stage paint, and I'll be good as new,' said Cal. 'Sir, I'm due on stage. Sir, please.'

Somewhere in the Palladium, a cheer went up. Waves of

applause rolled through the building like a sea wall being burst, finally finding release in the open stage door.

'That's another act coming to its close!' Cal implored. 'They'll need me in the wings! Don't you see? They're waiting. Sir, you've got to let me inside!'

Evie and Lily surged towards Cal's dressing room. They were only halfway there when Lily saw it was hanging ajar. 'See?' she said proudly. 'I told you he'd be here. He's just ... taking a moment. He won't let us down.'

And indeed he was – for, when Lily pushed open the door, and Evie tumbled in behind her, it was to find Cal standing there, his face red raw, his eye socket crusted in crimson where it had been torn open, his lip bloody and bulging.

Lily gasped. 'What happened? Did they find you? Are they here?'

But it wasn't the strangeness of this question, the mystery it revealed, that shocked Evie the most. Lily's eyes were trained on Cal, but hers had drifted below – to the foot of the dresser, and the body lying half naked there, stripped to the waist except for the gold watch around his wrist and the heavy medallion lying in the thick thatch of chest hair

Around Bill Martin's head pooled a halo of blood, fresher still than the wounds that marked Cal's face.

'I think he's dead,' came Cal's guttering voice. 'Bill Martin is dead!'

18

Showtime!

Evie took two faltering steps. She stopped. One more step, and she could go no further. 'Cal, what happened here?' Her eyes flashed between the bloody marks on Cal's face and the dead man sprawling in front of him. 'Cal?'

'I d-don't know. Evie, he's—'

Cal seemed frozen, like an untested performer taking his first step out onto the stage. He was stammering still when Evie plunged to her knees, her head bowed above Bill, and listened for some strangled breath. 'There's no pulse,' she said, with some desperate hope, fumbling for his wrist. 'There's no breath in him.' She looked up – and there was Lily, standing aghast. 'Go and fetch my father.'

Lily looked around. 'I want to stay with Cal.'

'Now, Lily. It was an order.'

Lily turned tail and fled along the hall. 'Rudy Cardenas,' a voice was calling out. 'Rudy Cardenas, to the stage.' Quickly, Evie closed the door behind her. Suddenly, the rest of the Palladium felt distant again. She glanced at the clock on the wall. The seconds were rushing by. How long until the Forsyths went out under the lights? Ten minutes? Fifteen?

'Just tell me,' she said, hardly daring to believe the evidence of her own eyes. 'Tell me what happened.'

Cal's eyes narrowed, as if sensing some threat. He looked harried, thought Evie – harried and hunted, and there could be only one reason why.

'It's only you and me, Cal. Just say it to me. Stop hiding.'

'I got back and he was just here,' Cal snapped. 'By God, Evie, I didn't kill him. I walked through those doors, just the same as you – and there he was, just lying here.' Cal paused. 'Maybe he fell. Maybe that's all this is. He's an old boor, a louche, a drunk, and he—'

'You're not telling me the truth.'

Cal's jaw set tight.

'I know you, Cal and I know when you're holding something back. Just look at you – you've blood around your eye! Your lip's been burst. What did he say to you, Cal? What was it about?' Evie stopped. 'If you fought him, it's better you just say. What are you expecting me to do, here? Just walk away? You look beaten up, Cal, and Bill Martin is dead!'

'If you really do know me, then you'll know I wouldn't raise my fists in ...' This time, it was Cal who faltered – because, of course, he'd raised his fists in anger only weeks ago; clubbed Bruce over the head, and felled him until he, too, was lying sprawled underneath him, just like Bill Martin was now. 'You don't believe me, Evie, I don't care. I wasn't in the Palladium until two minutes ago. There's two bullying doormen up there who'll prove it. By God, there are probably journalists lurking out by the red carpets who'll have caught me in their lens.'

The door opened up. There stood Ed, in his familiar pinstripes and forest-green bow tie, looking as if he ought to already be on stage. Lily had caught up with him only moments before he reached Bill's dressing room. 'What's happening?' he said, his voice scarcely more than a whisper. 'Lily said—'

Another figure had appeared behind Ed: John Lauder, his face as white as the ghosts with whom he liked to converse. Together, they slid into the room, pushing the door shut.

Thunderous applause rolled through the theatre, reaching them like the aftershock of an earthquake. Dickie Henderson's act had reached its climax. Somewhere out there, Norman Vaughan was returning to the stage to beguile the crowd with his patter, then introduce Rudy Cardenas, the juggler extraordinaire.

'By God,' Ed said, tottering forward, then kneeling at his old friend's side. 'Bill? Bill, are you there?'

'He's already gone, Dad,' Cal said darkly. 'He's already dead. I got here and he was lying right there, lying in his own blood.'

Ed's hands grasped forward, searching for some pulse that was no longer there. 'I don't understand,' he whispered. 'Why is he here at all? Why's he …' *Half-naked*, Ed was going to say – but then words failed him. 'Bill?' He reached Bill's head, and the sticky pool of blood. 'What happened to you?'

It was only now that Ed looked up and saw what Evie had been focusing on all along: Cal's wounds were not nearly as grave as Bill Martin's, but he'd not been sporting them just a short time ago. 'Cal, did you invite him in here? Please don't tell me you—'

'I walked in and he was here,' Cal insisted. 'Look at you all, with your accusing eyes. How could you think it of me? He's Bill Martin. I have no quarrel with Bill Martin!' *Except for what he did to Magdalene*, Cal thought, and another errant thought chased that one through the back roads of his mind – because where was Magdalene now? He'd told her she could come here, treat it as a refuge while he was gone working out some way to speak to Meredith – but instead it was Bill lying dead on the floor.

'Somebody bring the stage manager. Lily, go!'

But Lily's eyes were fixed on Cal. 'Tell them,' she blurted out. Cal withered under their collective gaze.

334

'Tell us what?' Evie asked.

'Not now, Lily,' Cal snapped. 'This isn't the time.'

'It's exactly the time!' Lily shouted. 'They think you murdered him, you stupid fool. You proud, proud fool! They think you're a killer, and you won't tell them the truth of it – all because, all because ...' Lily's own face was purpling with anger now. 'Don't you see? The secret doesn't matter any more. Bruce came for you, didn't he? Look at your face, Cal. There's no point holding on ...'

Ed was still bowed over Bill's body, but everyone else looked at Cal. John Lauder pottered forward, to bow like his old friend Ed with the corpse. 'I saw it in my dream,' he whispered. 'A body, right here in your dressing room, Cal. Only ...' He cast his mind back to that bitter, blood-soaked image. In his mind's eye, a blade had been buried in the man's breast. He hadn't known it would be Bill. 'I was so afraid it was going to be you,' he said. And then – because Abel Wright had once taught him the true meaning of dreams, that the premonitions they hold expose truths the waking world does not so easily reveal – he whispered, 'This was no accident. Somebody did try to murder him. See?' And his fingers danced above Bill's face, without touching his eye. 'Somebody struck him, right here in the jaw. He fell.' John closed his eyes to the horror – but, for a man with second sight, that only made it more intense. 'He hit his head again, when he landed.' He started trembling, for the scene was playing now against the backs of his eyes. He saw the fist flying out, to connect with Bill's face. The old singer had been laughing until then, but he wasn't laughing any longer.

'Well, Cal?' Lily cried out. 'If you're not going to tell them, I will!'

'Tell us what?' Ed demanded.

'Not now, Lily.' Cal was seething.

So Lily poured it out. 'Cal didn't get that bloody lip fighting with Bill Martin. He got it fighting with a man named Bruce. It wasn't Cal's fault. Bruce is from somewhere up north. He'd been beating up his girl. Cal couldn't stand it, so he put a stop to it. But now they're after him. They're after him, and if he doesn't pay them off, they'll . . .'

'STOP IT, LIL!' Cal thundered.

'. . . they'll go after Meredith,' Lily yelled. 'They'll go after Sam.'

There was silence in the room as different worlds collided, one truth crashing into another.

'What's the meaning of this?' Ed asked, rearing up from Bill's side.

'It means he didn't kill Bill Martin,' Lily declared. 'But somebody else here did!'

A voice was halloing in the hallway without. Another act was being summoned to stage. 'The stage manager,' Ed said. 'Lily, *now*, before this goes any further. I'm still your employer, Lily – I haven't hung up my hat quite yet – and you'll do what I say, or you'll be out on your ear. On with you, now!'

Hardly chastened at all, Lily fixed Cal with a piercing look before she left. *Tell them the rest*, she seemed to be saying. *It's for your own good.*

'Well, Cal?'

That tone – Cal hadn't heard it in his father in five long years. It was the tone of a man who would brook no dissent. Cal drew himself up, looked his father plain in the eye and said, 'I don't know where to begin, but it's all true. What Lily said – every last bit of it. It's why I came back, if truth be told. I don't want you to think I hadn't been longing for it for years, but that's the simple truth of it: after I floored Bruce, they ran me out of town. They've been extorting money out of me ever since. Five hundred pounds, to make it all go away, or . . .' He had to finish the sentence, but he didn't know how. 'Or they'd take it out on my wife,' he declared. 'They'd take it out on my son.'

There was silence in the dressing room. News like this could only be absorbed in lasting silence. In the end, it was Cal who had to go on, picking up the threads of the story Lily had started to weave, telling them about London, about Meredith and Sam – until, finally, having spilled the story of Bruce and Faye and how one moment of righteous fury had got the better of him, he felt spent.

And still, Bill Martin lay beneath him.

'I didn't touch Bill,' he said. 'This time, I barely laid a finger on Bruce. They left me on the cold stone of St Anne's Passage, and when I woke up the Royal Command was already on. I heard Cliff Richard playing in the pub they'd dragged me into. And now – now I'm here, and...'

The door opened up. There stood Lily, with one of the stage managers – a moustachioed man in his middle years, with a belly portly enough to balance drinks upon, in braces and a smart black tie – beside her. 'Step aside, gentlemen. I worked in a field hospital during the war. Leave this to me.'

Ed lifted himself from the body. 'Sir, I believe Mr Martin is beyond any help you can give.'

Shell-shocked at the side of the room, Evie looked her brother up and down, trying to decide if she really knew him at all – trying to decide how it felt, to know he had a secret life, to know she was an aunt, to know that, somewhere in the north country, there was a sister-in-law in hiding and vicious thugs intent on doing her harm. A sudden thought occurred to her. 'Cal, why was Bill in your room at all? Why not his?'

'Magdalene,' Cal gasped, and started to run.

Bill's dressing room was only a short stride away. Cal crashed through the doors, with Evie hurrying behind – and there was Magdalene, trying desperately to cover her tears with makeup. It was a futile battle; every time she applied more makeup, her tears washed it away, revealing the bruises around her eyes like a retreating tide.

Cal stopped.

There was no way those delicate hands had slapped Bill with enough force to send him sprawling backwards, was there?

'Get out,' Magdalene sobbed, seeing Cal and Evie in the mirror. Cal looked around. A magnum of champagne, one of the Moët delivered to every dressing room backstage, sat empty on the dresser. The dregs of the last glass stood beside it, smeared in Magdalene's vivid scarlet lipstick. 'Cal, for God's sake, why are you here?'

Cal's mind whirled. 'You went to my dressing room, like I told you.'

'Yes,' she screamed. 'Yes, and look at me now!'

At last, she turned around – and Evie could take in the full horror of her face. Cal saw it too; the bruises around her eyes were old, but those around her neck were new – as if some grasping hand had been holding her there, pinning her in place, refusing to let her leave.

Cal realised. 'He followed you there, didn't he?'

'He was prowling for me, looking for me all over the Palladium. When he burst in, he said he knew it was where I'd be all along. Waiting for you – as if, as if… as if we were in love, and I was doing the dirty on him behind his back.' Evie had rushed to her side, seeking to console her like she would any one of her dancers, but Magdalene did not want to be touched; she cringed away from Evie, whirling her hands that she might be left alone. 'Bill's a good man, but once he—'

'A good man?' Cal raged – but then the thought of Bill lying in the dressing room, and the fact he might be looking at the culprit, swamped all other thoughts.

'He just needs a little handling, that's all. He can be like a caged animal. You caught a glimpse of it, back at the Seagate. He just needed to calm down. It's what he does before every performance. It's like an anxiety, with Bill. It gets like he's terrified of the crowd. But if he, if he…'

She brought her hand to her mouth, as if unable to give it voice – but neither Cal, nor Evie, needed her to give voice to it. Neither needed John Lauder's second sight to understand what Bill had wanted of her – nor why he'd been stripped to the waist, nor what those bruises around her neck might mean.

'Oh, Magdalene,' Evie whispered.

'I just didn't want it. I didn't want to. But it's a woman's duty, isn't it? It's what I'm here for. It's why I'm… kept.' She looked up, her tears suddenly beginning to dry. 'I just want to go home. As soon as the show's over, I'll tell him I'm sorry. We'll get on our plane, and we'll be back in California – and then? Then I can work out what's next.'

Cal and Evie shared a disbelieving look.

'Magdalene,' Cal ventured. 'When did you last see Bill?'

A voice sailed through the hallways without. 'Last call for the Forsyth Varieties! Last call for the Forsyth Varieties!' There was fever in that voice. There was the panic of every stage manager's bad dream, that he was missing his most feted act.

'He didn't follow me out of your dressing room,' she said. 'I told him I'd scream. But Bill wouldn't want me screaming. Not if it damaged his *perfect* reputation.' For the first time, she realised that Cal and Evie had fallen strangely silent. 'Why are you staring at me like that?'

Cal's heart was sinking. He was still summoning the courage, and presence of mind, to tell her what had happened, when he heard footsteps behind him. There stood John. Further along the corridor, two of the stage managers gathered at Cal's dressing room door, their heads bowed in contemplation with Ed.

'There's an ambulance coming,' John whispered. 'But he's long past help now. The police are on their way. I've known, since summer began, that tragedy was hoving into view for the Forsyth Varieties. All of those dreams, of portents and storms. Oh, Cal, I've been so fearful it would be you, lying dead in that chamber – a knife buried deep in your breast.'

'I didn't do this, John.' Cal's voice, already a whisper, lowered further when he said, 'But I don't think Magdalene did this either. She has reason enough, but she doesn't have the strength for it. And...'

'She doesn't seem to know what happened to him,' Evie whispered. 'Unless... it's a ruse? Magdalene's lying? Who else has reason to want Bill Martin dead?'

The trio retreated from Magdalene's doorway, even as another of the stagehands – oblivious to the calamity – cantered down the hall. 'Miss Forsyth, Mr Lauder.' He glanced further and called for Ed too. 'It's five minutes until you're on. Mr Cardenas is nearly finished. The hour has come.'

'Cal,' Evie whispered. 'I don't know if we can...'

Evie looked down the hall. Her father's face was a stark mask marching towards them. Soon, she could hear the scurry of other footsteps, as – the last to head for the wings, as always with an animal act – Davith Harvard hurried along with Tinky and Tiny and a column of corgis. What a sight it would make: the London Palladium, suddenly spawning corgis from its every shadow. She wanted to believe in the magic of it, to perhaps even catch a glimpse of Her Majesty marvelling at how it was done, but every thought kept dragging her back to the vision of Bill lying dead in the room.

Ed reached them at last. 'Cal,' he declared, in such a wearied voice that Evie felt suddenly thrown back six years in time, to the aftermath of their mother's death. 'You'll have to sing.'

'Dad,' Evie ventured. 'Are we still to perform?'

The idea seemed incalculable, and yet still Ed said, 'What other choice is there? There's a full theatre out there. Her Majesty, up in the royal box, waiting for us. We didn't miss a beat after your mother died. We were on stage the next night, you in your mother's dancing shoes, and we put on a show. Nothing changes.'

'The Company don't know, and they've no need to know,' Ed said. 'Cal, you took Bill's part once before. You know these songs, and you know your own better than any. Get yourself dusted down. You've a few moments yet. Then just stride out there, like you belong. The rest, we'll deal with later.' He paused. There were too many revelations tonight. 'You should have come to me, son. I could have helped. If you'd been honest with us, we would have.'

'It wasn't that easy, Dad. I'd been gone five years. What was I to do, come back home with a price on my head and ask you for a fortune?'

'We'll find a way.'

'I have my way, Dad. But . . .' Cal looked back. If Bill Martin did not take to the stage tonight, if it was not his voice singing 'Runaway Lovers', did it have any value at all? Those fools on Denmark Street had rejected the song so many times; if it was sung by an icon of the world's stage, sung for Her Majesty and all of her guests, there was every chance they could change their minds. Was there any hope, if it was Cal on that stage tonight? Would 'Runaway Lovers' really be able to save him?

'Valentino's already prepared to take the piano for "Runaway Lovers",' Ed hurriedly whispered. 'Evie, you'll deal with the dancers – if any ask where Bill is, he's been taken sick. Say nothing more. We'll deal with the fallout after we've finished. Until then,' and at once he became the Ed Forsyth who would soon step out on stage, the debonair man with a thousand gags and the kind of buttery charm that could seduce both socialites and rogues, 'the time is now. Follow me, Evie. Her Majesty awaits.'

Before Evie hurried after their father, to join the Company already waiting in the wings, Cal said, 'How bad do I look, to go on stage in front of the Queen?'

Evie was not sure why – perhaps the tumult of emotions in the last hour was just too much – but she dared to smile. 'You've looked more handsome, Cal, but ...' She looked into the room. She stopped. 'Run,' she said, urgently now. 'To the dressing room. Dad has his spare suit hanging. There's makeup enough to conceal those bruises.'

Brother and sister stared at one another.

'I'll see you under the lights,' said Evie.

Cal didn't wait to watch her go. Moments later he crashed into the Forsyths' dressing room and searched for his father's spare suit.

As he struggled into it, he heard the applause reverberate through the Palladium: Rudy Cardenas was reaching the pinnacle of his act. He forced one leg into the trousers, then another, and all the while he was thinking: why was Magdalene still here? He'd heard of people performing superhuman feats of strength when they were desperate – so perhaps there really was a way that Magdalene had struck Bill Martin. But if that was so, why was she still here? Why hadn't she already run?

Cal was ferreting through Evie's dress-up bag, producing his mother's old clutch and taking out the stage makeup inside, when, somewhere beyond the doors, there came a single scream.

He stopped dead.

But no, he realised, that wasn't Bill Martin's killer, striking again. That was Magdalene.

They'd told her what had happened.

It only made Cal more certain that it hadn't been her.

With the makeup roughly applied, he tumbled back into the passageway. Faces were appearing from the other dressing rooms now, each of them summoned there by Magdalene's scream. Cal cantered past – even while some other stagehand, his voice muffled by Magdalene's sudden, hysterical sobbing, called out, 'Mr Forsyth, you're wanted in the wings!'

The stagehand took him by the arm, started wrestling him forward. As they passed Bill Martin's open dressing-room door, Cal saw that Magdalene herself had plunged to the floor. Stagehands crowded her, variously trying to help her back to her feet, then to mollify her sobbing, in case some echo of it reached as far as the stage.

The stagehand delivered him into the dark wing of the stage. There stood Evie, surrounded by her dancers. Only Lily understood why Cal was suddenly among them. All the others looked at him with bewildered eyes, even as, out on the stage, Rudy Cardenas soaked up the wild applause.

Cal drew Evie aside. 'She didn't know. She's in pieces back there. It isn't the sound of a woman who knows...'

'Cal, you're not thinking straight,' she whispered. 'You can't be. Because, if what you're saying's true – if Magdalene really didn't kill Bill Martin – it would mean somebody else here did. It would mean there's an assassin, right here in the London Palladium – and that, some time tonight, they're going to take to the stage!'

19

By Royal Command

'I just can't believe it,' said Jim, sandwiched in the middle of the stalls. All of this day had been a dream: John Lauder meeting him at the stage door, then beckoning him through the Palladium's back halls; the tour he'd taken around the Palladium's nooks and crannies; the way John had drilled him again in the specifics of the illusion, and how it had to be rejigged to fit the Palladium. 'No illusion can stay the same, from venue to venue, Jim. That was one of the first things Abel Wright taught me. Now, I'm teaching it to you.'

Now here he sat, in a crowd of people with faces he'd only ever seen gracing the television screen: men in black dinner jackets and capes; glamorous ladies bedecked in pearls and fur stoles. A day of missed school, the eventual wrath of his father – all of it would be worth it, just to sit here, and, yet, in but moments, he was going to be up there, on that stage, where Mr Norman Vaughan was now bewitching the audience with more patter.

Then, finally, Norman Vaughan declared, 'Ladies and gentlemen, the next act needs no introduction – or, if they do, they'll introduce themselves, for they're led tonight by a long-time idol of mine. Please, put your hands together and welcome the Forsyth Varieties – featuring, for one night only, the vocal talents of the incomparable Mr Bill Martin!'

344

Jim had seen his name on the posters bedecking the front of the Palladium – and knew, in his heart, that he'd been right all along; Bill Martin had been due to appear at the Seagate Theatre, but the rumour had got out of control and plans had been changed at the very last minute. Well, now they'd see. By the time he got home – *if* he got home, for wasn't a door opening, tonight, to a different world, as if he might step into that cabinet as Jim Livesey, undertaker's lad, and emerge from it a stage illusionist's apprentice? – everyone would have seen Bill Martin standing, triumphant, among the Forsyths. Then they'd know he hadn't been lying all along.

The woman at his side snorted at the name 'Bill Martin'. Jim had been introduced to her some time before the show – partnered with her, in fact, all as part of John's ruse. 'People would not expect a young man like you to be attending the Royal Variety alone, Jim – so we must find you somebody suitable, someone who might be portrayed as your companion for this evening.' A grandmotherly figure, she was not dressed as exquisitely as some among the audience tonight, but her neck and wrists were laden with pearls and, until Bill's name had been mentioned, she'd perched on the edge of her seat with something approaching childhood delight.

'Have you seen them before?' Jim whispered. 'When I saw them, it was the most—'

'My grandson dances with them,' she replied, and Jim could see the burning pride in her eyes.

To Jim, this was every bit as amazing as the idea he would soon be stepping onto the stage, summoned by John Lauder's hand. He could feel his insides fluttering already; for the first time in his life, he truly understood the feeling of having butterflies in the stomach.

'Oh yes,' the elderly lady beside him went on, 'he's going to be a great man. A star.' Then she paused. Up on stage, Norman Vaughan was retreating, and the curtains were parting once again to find Ed Forsyth standing in a single spotlight. 'You don't get many stars these days – not true stars. Good men, I mean. Stardom turns weak men into monsters, but my grandson isn't going to be one of them. I raised him right, you see. I raised him to stand up for what's good and proper.'

Jim only heard every other word she was saying, for his attention – like the entirety of the Palladium, as the welcoming applause faded away – was focused on Ed Forsyth.

'Yes, trust me, young man – I lost my daughter to one of these *song-and-dance* men. Oh, he drove her to it – you can be certain of it. He destroyed her, bit by bit, and all because he could. You can't believe in men like that. You can't believe in the love songs they sing.'

She said something else after that, but Jim didn't hear it. The first great laugh of the Forsyths' performance was crashing over the audience like a wave – in the spotlight, Ed Forsyth dazzled – and, after that, all that Jim heard was the joy.

The projectors burst into life, Valentino struck up the band, and all across the stage, the shadow dancing began.

'Is this even right?' Evie whispered. 'Should he be out there, right now?'

They'd watched their father march out together, a true showman, only moments before. Already, he held the audience in the palm of his hands.

'What can we do?' Cal whispered. 'Drag him offstage ... in front of a crowd? In front of the Queen?'

The performance tonight would mirror, as closely as it could, the one they'd given in the Seagate – but every theatre had its idiosyncrasies, and the Palladium was no different. Half the

Company was gathered in the wing on the left of the stage, the other hidden behind the proscenium offstage right. Lily was waiting, now, on the opposite side of the stage. Beyond the shadow dancers whose can-can was beginning to accompany Ed's routine, Evie saw her frantically waving her hand back and forth.

'You've come to the wrong wing, Cal,' Evie whispered. Yes, this wasn't quite like the Seagate at all – except that, just like the Seagate, they were going to have to pull this show back from the jaws of defeat. Then, with a sudden decisiveness, she declared, 'Go, Cal. For Dad. For his Company. Whatever else is happening tonight, this – *that*,' and she gestured out onto the stage, where their father, surrounded now by the shadow dancers, was regaling the audience with tales of music hall's earliest days, 'is the moment he's been building to all these years. The performance of his life.'

'For Dad,' said Cal, haltingly. He'd forgotten what a showman his father was – how inspiring it was to see a man control a crowd, especially such a haughty and refined one like this, with just his patter, just his smile. 'I promise, Evie. I know the cues. I'll be there on time.'

'We'll talk afterwards,' Evie said, as he slipped away. 'I want – I need – to hear it all, Cal. Meredith and Sam. My nephew, Sam! And … we'll find a way to help you. We'll work out how to stop those thugs. So sing your heart out, Cal.'

Cal nodded. 'I always do.'

As he picked his way around the back of the stage, he tried to summon up the showman spirit of old – but all he could see was Bill Martin, lying sprawled at his feet. It was only as he reached the stage's opposite wing, and Lily appeared suddenly beside him, that he came out of those dark, tormented thoughts.

Lily looked up at him with glimmering eyes. 'We're still going to dance,' she whispered, disbelieving. 'After everything that happened, we're still to dance!'

Cal quelled her with a sudden glare. 'Don't let it spread, not before we go on.' He lowered his voice. 'The police are on their way. Lily, Bill Martin didn't fall. Somebody struck him. It really was a—'

'Murder,' she whispered.

Cal lifted a finger to his lips, quietened her with another glare. 'They're going to say it's Magdalene. Bill was…' He didn't know how to say it. By the time he settled upon, 'Cruel to her,' it almost seemed cowardice – because, of course, Bill had been so much more than that. Benefactor and jailer, tyrant and lover – it beggared belief that a man could be all those things at once. 'She has motive enough. She'd be free. But…'

'But what, Cal?'

'But I know people, and it doesn't feel right. The police can't work on feelings, of course. Dancers work on feelings, singers and songwriters – but not officers of the law.' He curled his hands into fists. 'They're going to take her away.'

Out on stage, the final laugh broke over Ed. Tipping his hat to the audience, he vanished into the shadows on the opposite side of the stage. Cal could just about see him falling into Evie's arms.

Then the music changed in tempo. A flurry of horns, and it faded into a swirl of eerie flutes and a bassoon's low moan.

The lights dimmed.

The shadows turned to ghosts.

John Lauder's vanishing cabinet was wheeled on, into the pockets of darkness.

Beyond the stage, a reverential hush had fallen over the Palladium – but, beside Cal, the whispers went on.

'If not Magdalene,' Lily breathed, 'then who?'

*

'Dad, you *charmed* them. You bewitched them, Dad.'

The moment Ed came off stage, the smile he'd been wearing disappearing the moment the spotlight was no longer upon him, Evie rushed to him. 'It's still going to be a triumph,' she whispered in his ear. 'Cal will make it so. Believe in it.'

Behind them, John Lauder had already tottered out on stage, the persona of his act – the frail old magician, still dabbling in seance and sorcery – rapidly becoming one with the man he was off-stage. The ethereal lights gave him a ghostly glow as he began. 'Old friends,' he called across the audience, 'we meet again.' All his talk of immortality, the experiments he'd been pursuing at the farthest edges of magic, had soon bewitched the audience – but, backstage, there seemed something terrible about it; to speak of life never-ending, when backstage a man lay bloody on the floor, never to sing again. Ed had to close his ears to it, even as John started scouring the stalls for a volunteer to join him on stage.

The boy from Seaford had been perfect in the role – starry-eyed, disbelieving, and just about anxious enough as he entered the cabinet to make it all seem real – but, when John had announced he was summoning him to the Palladium (and risking some reputational fallout by wresting him away from his undertaker father), Ed hadn't been sure. Would that same starriness, the same disbelief, be manifest a second time round? Would being under the lights of the London Palladium, with all that expectation – rather than in the familiarity of his home town – spook the boy somehow?

He'd been worried about the corgis, too. So many untested elements, threatening to upend the perfect balance of the show he'd devised. And yet – none of those thoughts were weighing on him now. The moment he'd come off stage, and the persona he'd been adopting his entire career – cheeky, wise, wry Ed Forsyth – sloughed off him, his thoughts returned, not just to Bill Martin, but to the thorny issue of his son. 'Why didn't he tell us, Evie?' he whispered, careful that the waiting dancers did not hear. 'To come back to us like he did, to have that shadow on him, and not to say?' Ed took a breath. 'To have a wife, a son…'

'I think he just needed sanctuary, Dad. I think he came to the only place he knew he might be safe. He just… didn't know he'd be welcome. He didn't want anyone to think he'd come back to extort money from the Company.' She sighed. 'Can we help him, Dad? Can we save Cal from it?'

It was one of the questions that had been preying on him. A company like the Forsyth Varieties might have drawn crowds every night, but that did not make it a treasure trove. Tonight the Company was almost forty members strong; there were wage packets to pay, vehicles to keep running, lodgings to be found and paid for. There was magic to be woven on stage, but so too was there magic needed in the ledgerbooks and balance sheets that kept the Company afloat. Five hundred pounds – it was as much as he paid some of his troupe for four whole seasons.

And yet that wasn't the worst thing that preyed on him either.

He took Evie by the hand and led her into the shadows on the edge of the wing.

'Evie,' he whispered. 'After tonight, I'm not sure there's any helping Cal.'

She gasped. 'Dad, Cal wasn't even here!'

'You misunderstand me,' Ed replied, and drew her closer. 'Evie, if Bill Martin was murdered on our watch, then there's not only no helping Cal, but also no helping any of us either. Reputational damage – it's sunk companies before. One bad headline can change the story of a company. If it's murder, better it was Magdalene than any among us. With one twist of a knife, the history of the Forsyths could be over. I'd planned tonight as my retirement, Evie. It wasn't meant to be the night variety itself came to an end.'

'Me?' Jim mouthed, his eyes darting around in feigned disbelief. He lifted his hands to his mouth. '*Me?*'

A more cynical guest might have seen Jim gasping like that and thought him a dreadful old ham (indeed, up on stage, John fervently hoped he would tone down the mock surprise, before people started getting suspicious). Lucky, then, that tonight the Palladium was not filled with cynical souls, only those ready and willing to be swept up in the wonder of the occasion. They applauded merrily as Jim joined the master illusionist on stage.

'Tell me, young man – are you prepared for the Infinite?'

At least, now, Jim didn't have to feign the awe, verging on terror, that he felt. He had to keep reminding himself not to look upwards – it was John's first rule: don't look directly at the royal box, sitting up above – and then he had to keep quashing the feeling that he might any moment fall over his own feet.

Into the cabinet, he told himself. *Secret latch up above, and into the cavity beyond.*

Into the cabinet, and into his future.

The photographers who had swarmed the Palladium before the curtain went up started regrouping. For most of the journalists out here, hurriedly scrawling shorthand into their notebooks, this was dead time – the moment to compose their pieces for tomorrow morning's editions, ready to dictate them to one of the secretaries waiting patiently at the office. Others stood shivering under the lamplights, warmed only by the hot tea in their flasks (and those other, secret flasks they kept in their back pockets).

But something very peculiar had started happening at the bottom of Argyll Street, on the approach to the Palladium itself. Two police cars had just screeched to a halt outside the doors of Liberty's of London. The grand department store had already closed for the evening, so surely there was not some emergency going on inside – unless, one of the reporters began thinking, a burglary of some kind, in progress even now?

Then an ambulance joined the police cars on the corner and, moments after that, the officers who poured out of the cars began marching up Argyll Street itself, flanking the ambulance-men as they came. Soon they were on the edges of the light spilling out of the Palladium. Then they were slipping through the stage door, pretending they were completely oblivious to the reporters who suddenly descended, the camera lights that were suddenly flashing on and off, the lone question that some wit in the crowd called out to them as they vanished within.

'What's happened? Has somebody died?'

The moment the first corgi appeared in the stalls, gambolling forward with its nose in the air and its tail up high, a strange silence spread around the auditorium. The moment the second appeared, prancing out of the shadows on the other side of the auditorium, the cooing began. But it was the third corgi, which had mysteriously appeared at John Lauder's side – and then, with a single bark, summoned two others from seats quickly vacated by stooges in the audience – that prompted the applause. After that, the mimed panic of both John Lauder and Davith Harvard, as they rounded up the corgis, hustled them into the wardrobe, only to multiply them, one after another, provoked gales of laughter of which Bob Hope himself would have been proud.

In the wings, even Ed joined the applause. How John had

done it, he was still not certain – but tonight, as the corgis abounded, it would have been tempting to believe in real magic itself. It was tempting, too, to risk a glance upwards, at the box where Her Majesty was watching. Imagining her delight at the magically multiplying dogs was the only thing that had lifted him from his dark thoughts, and the image of what was happening, even now, backstage. How long had passed since he walked into that bloody dressing room? Thirty minutes, perhaps? An ambulance crew were surely here by now. The police, no doubt, declaring Cal's dressing room the scene of a heinous crime.

'Ladies and gentleman, pray with me now!' declared John. 'Pray for this brave young man's safe return, and the end of this most meddlesome magic!'

When the spotlight had found Jim Livesey back in the stalls, he was wearing one of the little dogs' collars. After that, the applause had grown and grown, to such a pitch that, even when the lights changed, the new music struck up, and the first sally of dancers fanned out, it had not yet died.

Now Cal stood in the wing, watching as Evie marshalled her troupe. The way they moved in concert with the shadow dancers coming from John's projector was sublime. The audience, lulled into its majesty, watched as tall pyramids were made, as stars and other shapes came together and then blew apart.

Shielded from the audience, Cal started sashaying forward, the dancers rolling around him. Betty and Verity screwed up their eyes at him as they whirled past; Max kept his head bowed, as if lost in concentration at the task in hand. Meanwhile, every step took him closer to the big reveal. Every note was heralding 'Unforgettable', 'You Belong To Me', 'Can't Help Falling In Love' – and, 'Runaway Lovers' to come. He ought to have been feeling the music. On any other night, he would have been letting it swell up inside him – until, by the time the first note came, he was a living embodiment of the song itself.

But not tonight.

Tonight he was thinking …

Somebody else, here, had a motive to want Bill Martin dead. If Magdalene hadn't confronted him in that dressing room – and Cal was quite satisfied that she'd fled from it, leaving Bill semi-dressed in a rage of his own – somebody else must visited it after him.

The thought was niggling at Cal: how could his father not have known the kind of possessive, controlling animal Bill was? Cal himself had known Bruce was a wrong one from the start. Of course, there were plenty who didn't. Bruce was surrounded by cronies who practically championed him for his malice. People, it seemed, were the same in the pit towns of the north and the gilded palaces of Hollywood. There were good men all over, but there were animals too.

Motive and means. Magdalene had motive enough, but certainly she didn't have the means. There was somebody else here. Somebody with a punch strong enough to knock Bill Martin clean off his feet.

And somebody with venom enough to actually do it.

The faces of everyone backstage cascaded through his mind's eye. From performers to stagehands, musicians to dancers, comics to the cleaning staff he'd seen picking through the theatre earlier that day …

Too late, Cal realised he had lost his footing. That was what came with not being committed to the performance, not living with the moment as it unfolded around you. Too much thought was the enemy of performance. Performance needed feeling.

It was Evie who caught his eye. She was dancing past him,

the column pushing him almost to the very edge of the stage, when she whispered, 'Cal! Cal, you're almost up!'

He came out of his reverie.

The dancers fanned apart. The lights hit Cal.

He started to sing.

20

Unforgettable

'Unforgettable' filled the Palladium. In the stalls, still bursting with pride (and no small modicum of disbelief) at his moment on stage, Jim suddenly sat bolt upright. The whispers of confusion were beginning to rise up around him as well. 'I thought it was ... Bill Martin?' somebody was saying. 'I thought the Forsyths were singing with Bill Martin?'

'It's just Cal Forsyth,' Jim whispered to the lady sitting beside him. 'It's the same as it was at the Seagate – Cal Forsyth standing in for Bill Martin!'

Beside him, the old dear put a finger to her lips and shushed him into silence. 'Well,' she said, 'it looks like the old rotter finally got upstaged. And on the biggest night of his life. How about that?'

Cal's voice soared. He hadn't reached the second chorus before the whispers had long since faded away. Bill Martin, the audience had been expecting. But there was something an audience loved more than old, familiar talent.

They loved a surprise.

And here was the best one – for, after Cal had led the Company through three majestic, but familiar, songs, his voice broke free with a stirring ballad none of them had ever heard before.

It lifted hearts, then broke them and put them back together again.

'Runaway lovers ... running for cover ...'

The Palladium had never heard anything like it.

The song just burst out of him, as some songs will. He'd picked his way through the old standards capably enough, he'd managed to set aside the labyrinthine thoughts in his mind and commit himself to each song – but it was only in 'Runaway Lovers' that he sang with the full force of his heart. This was for Meredith. It was for Sam. If he sold the song strongly enough, perhaps it wouldn't matter that Bill Martin wasn't the one up here singing it. Perhaps his plan might still come to fruition – and, by tomorrow morning, he would be a free man, Bruce and his thugs paid off, Meredith and Sam finally on their way back into his arms.

'Runway lovers ... running for cover ...'

A sudden thought picked him up and dragged him out of the song.

Bruce.

Cal hadn't any personal connection to Bruce, and yet it was Cal who'd knocked him to the ground that day, Cal who – by some strange fortune – had been lucky not to have killed him when he'd fallen. Cal had done it not because he had been personally attacked; he'd done it because to leave it unchecked would have been a blot on his conscience, a stain on his soul.

There was something in this, something he couldn't quite put his finger on. If only he possessed just a fraction of John Lauder's second sight. Perhaps, then, he could identify what this feeling was. Perhaps, then, he could see ...

Somebody knew what Bill was about. Somebody thought they couldn't let it rest. Somebody who couldn't bear to let his behaviour go uncontested, who couldn't bear the blot on their soul.

'And when I ... look at you every day ... that's when I know ... I'm your runaway ...'

The answer was here. He felt like he could pluck it out of the air, and yet every time he reached for it, the song got away from him and he had to recapture his focus. His mind was being torn in two directions.

'Secrets don't die ... they just hide away ...'

Secrets never die. Yes, that was it. That old lyric, it seemed to drag him even closer to the truth of it. Perhaps there was an old secret, something buried in Bill's past.

But everybody here loved Bill.

Didn't they?

In the same moment that the song came to its conclusion, and Cal flung his arms open wide as if to embrace the audience – or perhaps to cast the song out, directly into their hearts – it struck him. Everybody here didn't love Bill; they only seemed to. Somewhere along the way, hate had been disguised as love – just as Bill himself disguised power, brutality, control as adoration of his new wife.

It was easy to do.

How often did a songwriter do it – substitute one feeling for another, all the better to wrongfoot the listener, the better to evoke a response?

Words meant one thing in a certain tone of voice, but something quite different in another.

He'd seen it for himself, plain as day.

He just hadn't truly known what he was looking at.

The motive was clear, to every upstanding person who knew the true nature of Bill's personality.

And, somewhere in the back of his mind, in that unconscious

dreaming part of the imagination – the part responsible for soliloquies and songs, for bold new dances and illusions to stupefy an audience's senses – he thought he could see who among them had the means as well.

The moment the lights cut out, and the applause erupted, Cal turned into the darkness and hurried off stage, scarcely keeping his footing as he tumbled among the dancers. In the wings, the dancers were embracing each other. Lily and Verity held each other tight. Max and Betty raised their hands triumphantly together. Out on stage, Norman Vaughan was already marching out into the freshly illuminated spotlight to introduce the next act. Stage managers were beckoning the Forsyths away from the wings, hurrying them into the backstage darkness beyond.

As they went, Cal reached out and caught Evie by the arm.

She whirled around to face him in the shadowy darkness.

'Cal,' she whispered. 'You were incredible. Just completely incredible.'

But that didn't matter to Cal, not in this moment, not now the performance was done.

'Evie,' he murmured. 'We have to talk. I think I know who killed Bill Martin.'

21

Unmasking A Murderer

Sophie Tucker was already holding the audience rapt with the first song of her set by the time the Forsyths reached the dressing rooms. The ovation she got echoed through the theatre, filling even the backstage halls where the dancers and musicians stalled, their faces etched in surprise – and not a little consternation – at the officers of the Metropolitan police who crowded Cal's dressing room.

Most of the troupe had already reached the chorus dressing room when Evie turned the corner, her cheeks marked in dark smudges where the tears – of despair, of rage, of disbelief – had cut rivulets through her stage makeup. Cal hurried in her wake, his own face set in a mask that might have either denoted sorrow, or else agony. 'Evie,' he kept saying, 'I don't want it to be true – but tell me, tell me how it happened any other way? Tell me I'm not right?'

'You don't know him like I do, Cal. You've been away. You weren't here when—'

'I know,' said Cal; he'd be carrying the apologies for it the rest of his days. 'But I'm here now, and I know what I saw. Family or not, Evie, it's . . .'

They reached the first of the police officers, but it was not the constable's dead-eyed stare that stalled them – for, in the same moment that Cal reached for Evie's arm and tried to turn her around, hoping that he might win her over with the sheer simplicity of what he had to say, their father came around the corner. The eyes that had glimmered with cheek and wit out on stage now sat dully in an ashen face. He'd scrubbed the stage make-up off the moment he reached the dressing rooms. Now he looked every one of his sixty-six years. 'They're confining us to dressing rooms,' he said, with quiet determination, 'until they're certain what happened here…' And his eyes drifted back over his shoulder, to Cal's dressing room. 'Come on, kids,' he said, and both Cal and Evie felt a strange shudder, as if with those three words they were being cast back decades in time: to an age where their father could make any trouble go away, to an era when he himself was king. 'The Forsyths are waiting. We'll see it through together.'

He turned, as if to lead them on. Only when he was no longer looking at them did Cal and Evie turn to one another. 'It can't be,' Evie said. 'I trust him, Cal. I trust him with my life.'

'It isn't your life he needed to be trusted with. Evie, I'm sorry.' Cal might have said more, but when he set off after their father he saw movement in one of the doors further along the hall. There, flanked by another pair of police officers, stood Magdalene. He tried to catch her eye, a questioning look to ask her if she had yet been placed under arrest – but then he saw that there were no handcuffs at her wrists, and he knew there was still time.

'Mr Bob Hope!' came the voice of some stage manager, flurrying down the hall. 'Mr Bob Hope and Miss Edie Adams, to the stage!'

It was the final act of the evening. The Royal Variety had reached its very height.

Their father was already banking around the corner. Evie and Cal hurried after him.

'You have it wrong,' Evie said. 'Magdalene was there with him. She had reason to want him dead. Any jury in the land can see that. One mad moment, and a plane back to California – she'd have been free.'

'She would have run,' said Cal, as Evie paused outside the dressing-room door ahead of him.

Evie looked back. He could see, in those simple words, that he'd cut through some layer of her disbelief. 'She didn't know, Evie. But I do. And, in your heart, so do you.'

In the silence that stretched between them, some fresh understanding was being born. Cal took her hand. 'Together,' he said, and, when Evie nodded, he felt as if all the old wounds were healed, that there was only honesty between them now; that, whatever was going to happen in the precious few moments before the curtain calls began, they would be in it together.

They walked through the door.

Ed wasn't sure what he was supposed to say. There'd been tragedies in the Company before. There'd been deaths – even, in his younger days, a death on stage, when old Abel Wright had entered the secret compartment of his vanishing cabinet and been removed from it only hours later, when rigor mortis had already set in. That had been a dark day – the master illusionist gone, an audience unnerved, the entertainment press uncertain if it was all part of some grisly spectacle, an illusion to be realised over the weeks to come – but its feeling was nothing like this. Staring into the eyes of his Company, he felt incapable for the very first time in his career.

He watched as Cal and Evie came into the room, closing the door behind them. At least, now, he could pretend that it was just the Forsyths here. That gave him strength – to pretend, if only for a moment, that he was the one in control.

'My friends,' Ed began, in a tremulous voice none of the Company had ever known. 'I should be standing here to congratulate you all on a performance that will define your lives. And let me say now: you shone, my friends. You did your Company, and not to say your Queen, proud. But events have overtaken us. It cannot have escaped your notice, those of you who weren't forewarned, that Cal took Bill's place tonight – just as he did for the Seagate Spectacular. But tonight it was not because Bill feared for his safety here in the Palladium. If only he had,' Ed sighed, and mopped at his sodden brow with the back of his sleeve, 'for Bill Martin was killed tonight, only a few doors away from where we now stand. Murdered, before he could take to the stage. The police officers you see swarming the halls are here for this very purpose. Because one of us, in the theatre tonight, is a killer. They killed my old friend – and they'll hang for what they did.'

The gasps in the room were as loud and wrought with emotion as the best performances out on stage. Betty and Verity buried their faces in Lily's shoulder. John threw back his head and focused on his breathing, while Davith dropped to his haunches to console his dogs, who had started to whimper.

Then the voices began.

'They can't think it's one of us!'

'They didn't even stop the show!'

'But right here? Right *here*, Mr Forsyth?'

Ed lifted his hands. 'My friends, I don't have the answers we need. Right now, nobody does. All I know is that, out there, Bob Hope is bringing the house down. Norman Vaughan is waiting in the wings, to lead us all back out there to the ovations of the crowd. The journey we embarked upon is still unfolding. We have a duty to it, and we *shall* live up to it – no matter the pain and bewilderment we're going through right now. We're the Forsyths. We have the strength to do it. And afterwards, when the lights go up, then we'll face what happened here. Right now, nobody knows what happened – so we must stay calm and let the police officers…'

Ed had thought, at last, that he had control of the panic in the room. He was rallying them to the last duty of performers – the moment when they would step out to meet their audience, not as characters on a stage, but as themselves – but, in a moment, everything changed.

It was Cal's voice that cut through the tension in the room. He spoke clearly, as declaratively as he always did on stage – but the tremble in his tone betrayed a performer desperately nervous of the crowd.

'But we *do* know.'

Then he reached out for Evie's hand.

She was, it seemed, loath to take it, but, after a moment, she relented. 'Cal,' she whispered, 'I can't.' But her brother's eyes held hers, as if spellbound. They urged her on. It seemed to Ed that they were children again, about to take their first forays onto stage – except, of course, for the fact that his children had never had stage fright. They had been eager for it, from the first.

But they were not eager for this. Whatever it was, it was as heavy as a death.

Evie tightened her hold on her brother.

Then she turned around.

'Max,' she said, brokenly. 'How long have you known your father was Bill Martin?'

*

364

In the Palladium stalls, Jim's face ached from laughing. All it took was a word from Bob Hope, an arch look, some self-deprecating whisper that had the crowd in stitches. The truth was, Jim wasn't altogether certain he understood half of the act – it was just too fast – but the laughter in the room was infectious.

But then he noticed another note in the chorus of laughter, one altogether at odds with the mirth in the room. On his right hand side, the elderly lady, it seemed, was not laughing at all.

She was weeping. Tiny shudders moved through her body. Tears rolled, one by one, down her cheeks, to be dabbed daintily away by the corner of a handkerchief.

'Please,' Jim whispered, suddenly guilty that he'd been enjoying himself quite as much as he had, 'has something happened? What's wrong?'

The elderly lady merely patted the back of his hand. 'Don't worry, dear,' she said. 'I'm quite all right. I'm just... I'm just so proud of my little boy.'

Jim wondered if his own parents might have wept with such pride, to have seen him up on the stage today. 'He's a beautiful dancer,' he said, for he could think of nothing else.

'Oh yes,' said the lady. 'That and everything else...'

In the dressing room, every eye turned on Max. He looked so lost, thought Evie. He looked so alone. The moment the words left her lips, she regretted saying them. She opened her mouth to take them back, but something stopped her. He wasn't lost, she thought. He'd been *found*. This was the look of a man caught with blood on his hands. He looked ready to run – but all about him were the other members of the Company, and beyond that only the bricks in the wall.

She'd always known he'd trained as a boxer, as well as a dancer.

She'd just never imagined he might throw a punch that ended a man's life.

'What do you mean?' he asked, but the incredulity was surely feigned. He couldn't even look her in the eyes. He'd looked her in the eye so often before, in so many secret, intimate moments. The fact he couldn't now betrayed something she had desperately wanted not to believe. 'Evie, you know me. Bill Martin? Bill Martin, my father?'

Nor could Evie look him in the eyes. She had to summon every ounce of her strength just to say, 'Don't lie to me now, Max. You've been lying too long.' She had let go of Cal's hand, for something told her it was important that she stand on her own. The Forsyths had always stood together, but there were moments in life you had to absorb for yourself – just to know that you could. 'You've never been shy, speaking of your mother, of what your father did to her.' She turned to the other Varieties, if only for the hope that their presence would buoy her up. 'Max's mother was a dancer. We all know that. Dancing's in the blood. It passes down through the generations. But Max wasn't raised by his mother. His grandmother took him in, after his mother died. After she—'

'Don't say it, Evie,' Max warned, and for the first time there was some element of true menace in his voice. Then he regained control of himself. 'My mother took her own life. There – I've said it. And why should I be ashamed of it? She was driven to it. Abandoned by my father, the moment she fell pregnant. Told to get rid of me, in some backstreet parlour. Well – here I am, and it's all because of her. All because she was brave enough, and proud enough, to do it alone.'

'And your father was never seen again, was he, Max?' Cal said. 'And perhaps that would have been OK, if it had stayed that way. Perhaps your mother really did have the strength to raise you alone, and forget about the scoundrel she'd fallen in love with. Except for the fact that he didn't stay hidden, did he? He didn't just take off, never to darken her doorway again. Soon enough, he was on the billboards in Piccadilly Circus. He was singing at the Hippodrome and Alexandra Palace. He was capturing hearts and making us all swoon in the cinema. He was right here, singing *Sunday Night at the Palladium*, on every television screen in the country…'

'So the shame started to bite, didn't it, Max? That she'd been left behind, all her dreams shattered, while this man became a colossus.'

'Stop talking about my mother,' Max said with a snarl. 'You've no right to talk about my mother. I told you it in confidence, Evie. I told you it because I love you. I didn't tell you it to parade it in front of everybody, to hang out my dirty laundry, to make a mockery of it all. *How dare you!*' He was shouting now but something in his expression told Evie that the outrage was feigned too. He was flailing, flailing for purchase while the world unravelled around him.

'How long,' said Evie, returning to the old question, 'have you known?'

'Evie, why are you doing this? You're going to be my wife!'

It might have been a minor revelation compared to the accusation Cal had levelled at him, but still it ricocheted through the crowd. Lily looked astonished. The other girls, taken aback. On another day, this might have been news to provoke cheers and applause – not to mention, to set a few tongues wagging – but today it was received with stunned surprise.

'I know it hasn't been easy, Max. Just tell me. Tell me when you found out.'

But Max remained impassive.

'You've never frozen under an audience's glare before, Max,' said Cal coldly. 'Why are you freezing now?'

'You don't know anything about me,' Max snapped, in what could only be a desperate attempt to change the course of this conversation. 'You've been keeping secrets of your own, haven't you, Cal? The runaway brother, coming back to steal hearts, to wrench the Company away from your sister. The man who abandoned his family, then came back like some dethroned king, trying to take control? Yes, Cal, that's it – I've had your number from the start, even if you've charmed every last one of them.' Here his eyes fell on Lily, who looked incandescent on Cal's behalf. 'So don't come throwing accusations at me. Bill Martin, my father? My father was a phoney. Just some song-and-dance man who left broken hearts wherever he went...'

'It sounds like Bill Martin to me.' Cal seethed, thinking of those bruises Magdalene had been trying to hide.

'Then prove it.' Max's gaze fell on Evie again. 'Evie, he's filled your head with poison. You know me. You *know me*! I haven't changed. I'm just Max. *Your* Max. Don't listen to him. He's been a fool all of his life, and he's being a fool now. He can't prove a bloody thing!'

And Evie whispered, 'But he can.'

'What?'

'He can prove it. Can't you, Cal?'

Cal could feel the weight of expectation on him, like the harshest of audiences' eyes. 'I think I can.' He had crossed the room, to the place where his brown leather jacket had been flung. Now he reached into the pocket and started ferreting around the old receipts and lint in there. 'Sometimes the things you see aren't as simple as they appear.' He paused. Out of the pocket he had drawn a small leaf of paper, folded into a square and weathered around the edges. 'I made the same mistake as you, Max. I looked at this,' and he unfolded the paper, revealing a half-written letter of sorts, 'and I saw something that wasn't there.'

And he started to read.

The moment the words left Cal's mouth, something changed in Max's expression. He'd quite forgotten about the letter he had been writing to his grandmother, back in those early Seagate days. He'd quite forgotten how it had been left there, on the seat, as he went onto the stage to help Evie.

Quite forgotten Cal had been there too.

'"Dear Nana",' Cal read. '"Preparations for our appearance at the Royal Variety have begun in earnest! Nana, it is the legend of the Forsyths that our Company leader, Ed, sang at the very first Royal Command show. Now, it is to be me who dances for the Queen."' Then his eyes flashed onward, roaming the letter until he found the passage he needed. '"Nana, there is something else. We are to combine with a Special Guest for the performance at the Palladium. Nana, I did not expect this. Never in my wildest dreams did I think I would ever cross paths with this man. I am not even certain I should tell you this, but Bill Martin is to sing with us in London..."' Cal folded the letter again and returned his gaze to Max. 'Just the letter of a fan, I thought. The letter of somebody in awe, as all of us were, at the prospect of performing with Hollywood royalty. But I was wrong – wasn't I, Max? Because, with Bill Martin lying dead on the floor through there, this letter takes on an altogether different meaning. "Never in my wildest dreams did I think I would cross paths with this man." Because you were in awe of him, Max, or because you were full of hate for the man who drove your mother to her death? "I am not certain I should tell you this..." because it was a closely guarded Forsyth secret, or because it might give your grandmother such heartache, to know that that man had crossed your path?'

Max just stared. 'You're clutching at straws, Cal. You're a worse detective than you are a brother. A worse lawyer than a son. My grandmother loves the old singers. She's proud of me. She'd want to know if I was dancing with—'

'No, Max.'

It was Evie this time. She had spent the last moments steeling herself for this, and now came the killer blow.

'I was there in your grandmother's house. I looked through her records. Tommy Dorsey, Benny Goodman. Bing Crosby and Nat King Cole. A few Sinatras in there, Max – but not a Bill Martin.'

Something changed in Max's eyes. Until now, they'd been filled with mounting fury – but now they started shimmering, as if he was suddenly on the brink of tears.

'Max,' intoned Ed, from the heart of the Forsyth crowd, 'you'd better start telling the truth now, son. It's now or never – and there's a platoon of police constables out there who'll tear it from you, if you don't give it up.'

'Max?' whispered Evie. 'Max, please?'

22

The Final Curtain

As Norman Vaughan rushed back centre stage, Jim flew to his feet. The whole auditorium was standing now. Arms were raised in appreciation. Hands beat out a rhythm every bit as powerful as the war drums of old. Jim hardly heard Norman Vaughan rounding things up, preparing the audience for the curtain calls to come, but that didn't matter. In his head, he too was about to canter onto the stage to hear the crowd roaring for him. He too would hold his arms aloft and take his bows. He too would bask in the fever, the romance, the adulation.

His heart was telling him to race up there as soon as the Forsyths arrived – for wasn't he as much a part of the show as any? – but his feet rooted him to the spot. No, he told himself, the magnificence of the illusion would be dispelled if he was to be invited on stage. Only by staying here, cheering like all the rest, could he serve Mr Lauder's finest hour.

But some day soon…

Some day soon, it would be Jim taking his bow. From this moment forth, he was an illusionist's apprentice – and, some day soon, an illusionist in his own right.

Seaford was too small, now, for little Jim Livesey.

Jim wanted the whole world.

It was his for the taking.

*

Max had tried to speak three times before he found the courage. His nerve had failed him; so too had every breath that left his body. He could not form any words. All he could do was stammer, then falter, then look at Evie with pleading eyes. 'None of you know,' were the words he finally said. 'Not one of you knows what it was like, to grow up like I did. I was eight years old when she first told me. Eight years old when my grandmother took me on her knee and said: *That's the man, Max* – pointing at the cinema screen, as she was. *There he is. Bill Martin. That's the man who killed your mother…*'

Some of the dancers had turned away from Max now. Among them, only Lily had nerve enough to keep looking as he went on. As for Evie, every tear that had been leaking out of her suddenly dried. She was not certain whether she felt some pity for him, or whether the love she'd felt was curdling, being corrupted, changing its shade. Part of her wanted to put her arms around him, and listen to him talk about the desolation of that childhood moment – but the other, greater part of her, held itself rigid, not certain if she could hear what was about to come.

'What was I supposed to do?' Max gasped out. 'Sixteen years I've lived with that knowledge. Bill Martin, feted star, worshipped as a god – and he's the one who pushed a roll of banknotes into my mother's hand, told her to visit some back-street quack and get rid of me. He's the one who stole her career and left her with nothing. He's the one who ground her down, who filled her with shame, who turned her own father against her. *He's* the one who was singing on the radio that night she, that night she…' Now, the words had filled Max up. He swallowed them down, but it did nothing to contain his rising panic. 'I couldn't just let it go, could I? Not when I was to dance for that bastard. Now when he was to bask in the applause while I fanned around him, like it was *me* worshipping him for all he'd done!'

'But kill, Max?' Evie blurted out. '*Kill?*'

'You have me wrong,' Max said, words slurring together in his desperation to get them out. 'I mean – I couldn't just ignore it. I couldn't just dance and play along. This was my chance. My chance to tell him, face to face, what kind of man he was. My God, he didn't even know! He could scarcely even remember. "There've been a lot of dames," he said – *dames*, like he was born in Hollywood, like this whole past was a mirage. I promised my grandmother, Evie. I promised her I'd go to him and confront him – tell him what he did, fill him with the shame of the moment, make him understand what his selfishness, his malice, had cost. Then he'd see the price of his glory. *You look him in the eye, Max, and you tell him that he's a killer. Then, for ever more, every time he opens his mouth to sing, he'll know in his heart who he truly is.*'

'But it didn't go that way – did it, Max?' Cal interjected.

Max refused to look at Cal as he replied. It seemed that, no matter how many eyes were upon him, his confession was for her alone.

'He just didn't care. He called me a grifter. He said I wasn't the first. Said there were probably others like me, out in the world, but he didn't owe us a thing. He thought I was coming after his money, Evie. Money and favours! But no – all I wanted was for him to finally know the kind of man he truly is. But it didn't work. He wouldn't see. A man like Bill Martin doesn't think like the rest of us. There had to be a different motive. It couldn't just be that I wanted him to look me in the eye and tell me the truth. "You want to call me *Daddy*, boy, is that it?"'

As soon as Max said those words, in his best imitation of Bill's adopted Californian airs, Evie could picture how it had been. How that sneer had sent a single surge of anger rushing through Max. How all the years of shame, the bitterness of his grandmother, the injustice of Bill Martin being on the silver screen while his mother was six feet under the earth, had rushed out of him.

He'd spent all his life honing his body. Practising his balance and poise, in pursuit of the perfect dance.

All the lost evenings and weekends of his youth, in the boxing ring, finessing the perfect punch...

'I lashed out. There he was, bared to the bloody chest, and laughing at me. Laughing at my mother. And then, before I knew it, he was lying on the cold floor in that dressing room. I caught myself almost straight away. I went to help him up. But...'

But the halo of blood was already spreading around his head, where he'd hit himself when he fell.

But his last breath had already been spent.

His heart had beat its last.

There was silence in the dressing room. As Max had spoken, the Forsyths had shrunk away from him. Now they ringed the edge of the room, holding one another in groups of three, four, five and six.

Still sensing the depth of disquiet in the room, the corgis had started to whimper.

Evie turned away, seeking comfort in the arms of her father. 'What now?' said Max, still shaking. 'What... now?'

There was a knock at the dressing-room door and Ed let go of Evie to answer it. There stood one of the stage managers, his own face an ashen grey. 'Curtain calls are coming,' he declared. Sweat was beading on his brow; the stress of the evening had clearly infected all who worked here. 'Mr Forsyth, I need you at the stage.'

Every eye in the room started darting from corner to corner, uncertain what came next. At last, it was her father who declared, 'Rally up. You deserve this moment. Listen, my friends, you're feeling weak in your hearts. So am I, after all we've just heard – after everything that's happened in this theatre tonight. But this is still your moment. None of you, save for one, are responsible for the tragedy that's occurred in the Palladium.' His eyes fell on Max. 'We've heard two stories tonight, of old angers being spilled.' Then his eyes flashed, momentarily, at Cal. 'But only one of them ended in...'

The stage manager was back at his side. 'Mr Forsyth, you *have* to come. They've already begun.'

'Hurry,' Ed called to his Company. 'One more time, for the Forsyths.'

Most of the Company couldn't wait to follow Ed through the doors. Beached among them, there Max stood – until, at last, the stage manager's eyes lit up in desperation, perhaps even fury at being disobeyed, and he said, 'All of you! All of you, come on!'

Perhaps it was just his terror at not knowing what to do that compelled Max to join the flock of performers hurrying through the door and back to the Palladium stage.

Cal jostled Evie along. She felt so weak against his shoulder. 'I was going to marry him,' she kept whispering. 'Cal, I was going to be his wife.'

Cal had no words for her; he only held her tighter.

How easily it could have been him: if the punch he'd thrown had landed differently, if Bruce had fallen more awkwardly, perhaps Cal might be in a prison cell, even now. So he was not without sympathy as they reached the edge of the stage. He was not without feeling as he heard the roar of applause and the Forsyths waited to take their turn. Life could be a fractured, complicated thing – but there was still beauty.

He tried to hold on to that idea as the Forsyths rushed out to meet their royal crowd.

The Palladium were on their feet. Now, into the spinning spotlights, came the Forsyths – Ed Forsyth, leading out the Company that bore his name, throwing his arms open wide.

Jim Livesey had been cheering throughout, but now his cheers grew even louder. He raised his arms, hopeful he might even catch John Lauder's eye – and yes, he was quite certain that the old illusionist had seen him. Those deep, grave eyes seemed to find Jim among the stalls – and, for a moment, to sparkle just a little more.

Jim was still cheering when he realised the woman at his side was strangely still. Until this moment, she'd joined in the applause. Now, her arms fell at her sides and she scoured the stage with an inscrutable expression.

'What is it?' Jim asked. 'Is something wrong?'

'It's my grandson,' she whispered, in a mounting frenzy. 'I – I can't see my grandson...'

The cheers had been thunderous when the Forsyths rushed out, but the most thunderous cheering of all came for the moment when the prize Welsh corgis emerged from the throng to prance, at Davith's command, across the very edge of the stage.

The applause came in joyful waves. When the dancers moved forward to take their bow it reached a new pitch – which only became shriller when the dancers parted, to usher Cal and Evie to the centre of the stage. Cal felt himself pulling on Evie's arm, as if some part of her was going to resist the moment, but his sister was a consummate performer, a professional with more dedication and respect for the moment than even Cal himself, and soon she was rushing forward with him, taking her applause proudly. It did not matter that her smile was feigned, nor that her heart was in such tumult; this moment belonged to the audience, as much as to Evie herself. By the time she and Cal stepped back into the ranks of the Company – and their father sallied forward to accept the final applause for himself – she was exhausted, spent, drained of all emotion, but not a soul in the audience could ever have told.

'Maybe there's another way,' Cal whispered, through the smile still plastered to his face. By now, the Company had joined in the applause as well. Cal and Evie joined hands in a long chain, and together the Company lifted their arms skyward. The lights were dazzling, the audience just an amorphous blur – but there was no denying the euphoria in the room; there was no denying the magic that had been woven, right here, in the space of three short hours.

'What do you mean?' said Evie, from behind her jubilant mask.

'If he confesses, if he tells them how it went – if he tells them how Bill provoked him, that it was an accident, that he lashed out but he didn't mean to kill. There was a tussle, it was an accident, none of it was premeditated or meant to happen.' Cal was still thinking of how Bruce had looked, spreadeagled underneath his feet. 'Bill's history would have to come out. Magdalene's back there right now, sporting the bruises of it. It's evidence, Evie. That Bill...'

Deserved what he got? thought Cal – but that idea only took him back to Bruce as well. No, then, not *deserved*... but was it, at least, understandable? That a man might think 'enough', and take matters into his own hands?

Not for the first time, he was reminded of how Meredith had

sobbed when she'd found out what he'd done. 'You're a father, Cal. There are other ways...'

Well, she'd been right then – and, if she was only standing here, she would have been right now. Max had made a mistake. He was going to have to pay for it, just like Cal – in the tumult of this evening he'd quite forgotten about the bruises on his own face, the reckoning he was going to have to face tomorrow – but perhaps there was *another way* for this moment as well. 'Magdalene can't take the blame for it, but if Max was only to...'

It was then, with the applause fading and the Forsyths preparing to retreat so that the great American acts could return to the stage, that Cal and Evie glanced around.

They had hoped to find Max standing there, hidden behind his own mask, held in check by his terror and the shock of his confession.

But, of course, the terror must have got control of him some time before – because, if Max had been swept up onto the stage with the Company at all, he was no longer among them.

The murderous dancer was nowhere to be seen.

23

The Queen's Company

Outside the Palladium, anticipation was high. If the unexpected appearance of the Metropolitan Police had piqued the interest of all the waiting writers and photographers, the sight of the acts taking their curtain calls on the television sets in the waiting vans and shop-windows galvanised them to action.

The curtain calls were not yet over. That meant there would be fifteen minutes, at least, before the doors opened up. Cameras still needed to be set up. Lighting rigs still needed to be hoisted into place.

Then the stage door, tucked to the side of the main entrance, opened up.

The Metropolitan Police had been too circumspect to leave officers stationed outside the door – the Palladium was, of course, swarming with protection, though none of it in uniform plain to the eye – but, when the doors flew open, the journalists could quite clearly see the two heavy-set officers who had been stationed within. Burly fellows, in crisp uniforms and heavy truncheons at their sides, they had evidently been keeping guard since the officers first streamed through those doors – ready to deal with any intruders who threatened to break within.

Or anyone who tried to step out.

It was only now that the journalists truly understood something terrible had gone awry in the Palladium tonight – for, between the two officers, a young man, a performer by the looks of him, struggled to break free. The moment he'd lurched for the doors, throwing them open, the officers had tackled him. Perhaps they'd thought a man of his stature would be easy to contain, but dancers' bodies were trained, their strengths often hidden, their agility at its absolute peak.

So when this young dancer tried to battle past the officers' arms, he was not as easy to contain as he had seemed. He shook off their grasping hands with relative ease; he squirmed out of their grasp by relying on the suppleness that had been drilled into his body since he'd first donned his dancing shoes. In moments – though not without some hint of a tussle – he was through the barrier they'd tried to put up, then sailing down the road with a dancer's grace, hurtling towards the light still spilling from the shop displays at Liberty's.

'Pictures! Pictures!' one of the newspapermen cried.

The photographers leapt to it. Now, it wasn't just the police officers giving chase; it was writers and lighting men too. Though they did not yet know it, the pictures that they took would be spread across the front pages of tomorrow's newspapers: *Metropolitan Police Tackle Palladium Killer! Dancer of Deceit! Spurned Son Slays Wayward Father!*

And the most famous of them all, of a promising young dancer with his face in the dirt of a Carnaby Street gutter – two officers of the Metropolitan Police looming above him with a knee in his back and handcuffs just sliding over his wrists – would be emblazoned with a headline to be remembered through all time: *RUNAWAY LOVERS, RUNAWAY KILLER.*

*

In the same moment that Max was being flung to the cobbles of Carnaby Street, the lights of the late-night cafés spilling over him as all the mistakes of his short life flashed before his eyes, the Forsyth Varieties gathered backstage. The whisper of an arrest had not yet reached them when the stage manager arrived at the dressing room door and, beckoning Ed towards him with a slight incline of the head, said, 'We're going ahead with it – under the strictest conditions, of course. Her Majesty herself insisted.'

Some moments after that, Ed had rallied the Company to a backstage hall, where every act who had graced the stage tonight was already gathered. Ed tried not to let his eyes gravitate to Bob Hope, to Eartha Kitt, to Cliff Richard and his Shadows, standing proudly with their guitars slung over their shoulders. Instead, he formed his Company up around him. 'After tonight, when we look back, let us acknowledge the torment we have seen – but let us not forget what we accomplished here.' He turned, directing their gaze to the doors at the end of the long, narrow hall. Two security men were standing there, as yet more stage managers – and palace officials, by the look of them – hurried back and forth. 'There they are,' said Ed. 'Preparing the way, just as they did fifty years ago.' And his mind flashed back in time: fifty years ago, he had stood with the Company in a corner much the same as this, his heart more a-jitter than it had been when he'd strode out onto the stage.

The doors opened. Officers of the Metropolitan Police appeared, then stepped aside, no doubt waiting for the moment when the night came to its end. There would be statements to make, interviews to conduct; they would want to know all about Seaford, and the Spectacular, and Max's history with the Company. If any of the Company got any sleep tonight, it would be a blessing. But all of that could wait. Ed meant to let his players have this moment. They, each of them, deserved the fire in their heart. After it was done, he would go to Evie and let her rest upon his shoulder, as he once had had cause to rest upon hers; he would shake Cal's hand and, together, they would work out how to unpick the problems that had beset his son's life. He would guide them through whatever the fallout of this death might be.

But that was for later.

The doors were opening again.

He took his place among the players.

'Don't speak until you are spoken to,' he declared. 'Present yourself only when invited to do so. Introduce yourself by name. You may address her as "Your Majesty" in your introduction, and then as "ma'am" thereafter.' Ed paused. 'My friends.' He beamed. 'Ready yourselves for your proudest moment.'

A platoon of palace officials were striding through the doors. Ed had told the Company not to stare, but of course he couldn't help his own eyes from flitting there. A murder, there had been. John Lauder's prophecy had come true. But the funny thing about prophecies was that they only ever foresaw the bad. Nobody ever prophesied the good in the world. There was darkness all around you, if you dared to look, but there was goodness too. There was magic and light. Sometimes, even when you'd faced terrible things, it only served to make the wondrous more life-affirming yet.

In the moment that the Queen stepped through the doors, to meet her players one by one, Ed felt it more keenly than ever.

This was why he had stayed with the Company all these years.

This was why he was a player.

In moments like these, it felt as if it was all worthwhile.

Her Majesty was working her way up the line, meeting each performer in turn, with Prince Philip standing loyally at her side, himself extending a hand to each of the entertainers who had given them such a rousing night. But as soon as she reached the Forsyths, and looked upon Davith Harvard, standing proudly in a sea of dogs, something changed. In the corner of his eye, Ed saw how her face began to glow, how the formality of the occasion melted away in the fascination she had for these noble creatures. Davith himself was flushed bright red, trapped somewhere between embarrassment and enormous pride, when the Queen asked if she might bow to the dogs and show them some affection.

'Oh, you may,' said Davith, with delight, 'but I've found them to be rather ... slobbery, Your Majesty. That is to say,' and here he started floundering over his own words, 'they do like to show one how much they love one, ma'am.'

In the corner of his eye, Ed was half convinced that Davith had performed a little curtsey as the Queen moved on.

She greeted the dancers, one by one. Prince Philip crooned about how much he'd fallen into the performance. 'Of course, the music hall was the heart of the nation,' Ed heard him saying.

But after that there was silence, for Her Majesty stood before him now.

'Mr Forsyth,' she began, looking yet more radiant than she had on the day of her coronation, 'I'm told you sang, once upon a time, for my grandfather.'

And Ed, who felt that he was bursting with even more pride than Davith and his dogs, found that all the terrible feelings of Max, of Bill Martin, of the challenges he was yet to face, had faded clean away.

'Fifty years ago, almost to the day, Your Majesty. The Palace Theatre, the very first Royal Command.'

'Fifty years,' the Queen said. 'And you returned to play for us again. Perhaps, in another fifty ...'

A smile was playing on her lips. Ed would be long gone, of course, but a little piece of him wondered if Her Majesty might sit on the throne in that far-flung future, if it might be Queen Elizabeth who guided her people into a brave new century.

'I should like to believe the Forsyths are still going strong, ma'am. And I know they will, for my beautiful daughter, my precious son, are going to be carrying the torch.' Ed stepped back, opening his arms as if to encompass both Cal and Evie, standing at his side. 'Your Majesty, might I introduce my daughter, Evie, my son, Cal.'

'Very few needs for introductions, Mr Forsyth. I was delighted to make their acquaintance up on stage tonight.'

It was almost time for her to move on. Ed felt his back straighten. His chest puffed out.

'Mr Forsyth,' the Queen continued, 'you made the nation very proud this evening. Keep up the good work, sir.'

After that, she passed on. There were yet a dozen other performers to greet, and bless with a few heartfelt words. But, for the second time in his life, Ed Forsyth felt the singular pride that came with having played for your monarch.

24

Night of Revelations

DAILY MAIL

30th October 1962

DANCE OF DEATH

The Royal Variety Performance, ordinarily a beacon of all that is joyous in the entertainment industry, reached its half-centenary last night. Yet, though its roster of outstanding talent delivered a show as memorable as the greatest performances of the last fifty years, the night will not be remembered for the feats of juggler Rudy Cardenas, the appearance of Sophie Tucker in her pomp and Bob Hope in his prime – but for the untimely death of star singer Bill Martin, who was found dead in his dressing room just as the curtain went up. By the end of the evening, Palladium sources were confiding in the journalists amassing outside the theatre that the death was being treated as suspicious by the Metropolitan Police – and our exclusive pictures reveal the moment that Max Everly, a neophyte dancer in the Forsyth Varieties, was arrested on suspicion of murder. Mr Everly, 24 years old, had been due to take to the stage with Bill Martin in the centrepiece of the show. Now, he languishes behind bars as an investigation into the deplorable backstage act begins in earnest...

'Well,' said Mr Brownlow, with some element of smugness still marring the newfound respect in his voice, 'it didn't quite go according to your proposition, did it, Cal? I was promised a new hit song, being unveiled by none other than Bill Martin. But of course...' He shrugged, rolling up the newspaper in his hands and tapping it forcefully on the desk of his Denmark Street office. 'In the light of last night's unexpected tragedy, I can quite understand that plans had to be amended at the very last moment. But it gives me something of a headache. Yes, the song is a good one – better than I had countenanced, in your own Denmark Street days. But the moment of its revelation, the moment that ought to have been rhapsodized in every broadsheet this morning, has rather been undermined, wouldn't you say? Nobody's talking about "Runaway Lovers", Cal. What they're talking about is Bill Martin – and how one of your dancers took the old star's life.'

Cal had woken that morning with the feeling that none of it could be true, that it had all been some horrifying dream. There had been the relentless questions of the Metropolitan Police, the news of Max's arrest and incarceration, the terrible feeling as the truth of what had happened backstage at the Palladium echoed around the theatre halls. When Cal had emerged from his lodgings this morning, his father's face had been riven with deep lines. He'd been in one of the local cafés, head bowed over black tea with Evie, when Cal had walked past. They'd looked like ghosts, so far gone only John Lauder could reach them.

'It's a great song,' said Cal. 'You can't deny the crowd.'

'That's true,' said Mr Brownlow. 'But what you're not seeing, Cal, is that it isn't a hit record any more. It's a... murder ballad. The song Bill Martin was meant to sing, before some scheming dancer came and...' Cal's fists had been bunching, his face purpling – so, at once, Mr Brownlow ceased to protest. The fire Cal felt wasn't for Max, languishing in some police-station cell while lawyers worked out what must be done with him; it was for Evie, whose world had been upended for a second time. Whose future had been stolen in Max's single, rash act. Cal could forgive him for what he'd done to Bill Martin; it was what he'd done to his sister that felt the bigger crime. 'You see the bind I'm in, don't you, Cal?'

Cal stood. 'No,' he snapped. 'I see opportunity for you. The song Bill Martin was meant to sing? What kind of a salesman are you, if you can't sell that?'

'It's rather ghoulish, Cal.'

'The song will shine. If you don't want it, there's others that will.'

He was already at the door when Brownlow called out, 'Now, Cal, don't be so hasty. I didn't say I didn't want it. I just said – well, the game's changed. We've got to be more cautious now. It isn't a sure-fire thing. That song of yours – it already broke the rules. Cal, it's seven minutes long. It's practically an opera. It's not for the old-timers, but it's hardly for the new, is it? Things are changing in the musical world. Things are afoot. Now, if Bill had really sold it, well, I'd have a clearer vision. But as it is . . .' He was still prevaricating as he reached for his desk drawer and drew out a chequebook.

Now, at least, Cal understood what this was all about: just a stalling tactic, just another part of the salesman's dance. He turned around.

'I want the song, Cal, but I can't throw everything in for it – not after the upsets of last night. I can't piggyback a hit off the Royal Command, no matter how much I'd like to. You gave it a good showing, but you don't come with the star quality an *ambush* like that needs. So I'll have to let the dust settle, let this story die down, and start exploring the song again. Build its reputation. Find just the right artist to match it with. Then we'll get it on the circuit, out in the clubs. Who knows – once we've built up a head of steam, we might turn it into a hit after all.' Brownlow paused. 'What you'll be wanting, of course, is a down payment. How does … fifty pounds sound? Something to tide you over, quite happily, until we've tested the song in real-world conditions, out in clubs with real people, hoi-polloi, not those nobs in the Palladium last night? Once it's out there, we can start talking about the kind of cut you'll need to take. A proper songwriter's cut, just like the old times. Well, Cal, what do you say?'

'Fifty pounds.' In his mind's eye, Cal was already at the Coach and Horses, Bruce and his thugs hoving into view. He was handing over the cash to them, and they were counting it out – and, for every pound missing, there was a fist sent flying at his jaw, another promise made against Meredith and Sam. 'I wanted five hundred.'

Mr Brownlow's eyes widened. Cal watched as he tried to control the laughter rising up his gorge. 'Now, Cal, be serious …'

'I know the kind of money you deal with, Brownlow.'

Mr Brownlow made to close the drawer. 'Well, now you're just being disrespectful.'

'It's worth much more than that,' Cal said, storming towards the desk.

A little voice in his ear told him to simmer down. He reined himself back, prowled the edges of the room.

'I'm giving you a chance, Cal.'

'No,' snapped Cal. '*I'm* the one giving *you* the chance.'

'One hundred,' said Brownlow. 'I can't say fairer than that.'

Cal just stared.

'I'm standing, Cal, and you try to judge an offer – you don't know how fair I'm being.'

'Four hundred,' said Cal, through gritted teeth. Maybe Bruce and his cronies could be appeased, if just for a while. Four hundred now, and a hundred by Christmas. Yes, that might work. They wouldn't like him to renege on their deal, but the sight of their blood money might appease them for a time.

Brownlow looked at him and shook his head.

'One seventy-five...'

The cell was scarcely ten feet by five, lit only by a buzzing electric light and the thin sliver of window that looked out onto the hall. They'd been gentle with him, Max supposed, after they'd ground his face into the cobbles of Carnaby Street; gentler than he had been with Bill Martin at any rate. But there was nothing gentle about a night in the cells. At some time in the smallest hours, he'd started crying – and that had been the worst of all, because a strange cheering had erupted through the walls, the other lags awaiting their fates taking joy in this new arrival's baptism of fire.

There was so much to feel sorry for. There was his grandmother, of course; he'd promised to confront Bill Martin, to expose the old bastard for what he really was, but she would not have wanted this. Now she would have to watch her grandson hang – or, at best, languish in prison, so that they might never meet again. She'd already watched her daughter die; the thought of putting her through it again was enough to make Max wish he'd never been born.

Then, of course, there was Evie...

He was still thinking of her, later that morning, when the door of his cell opened up and a solicitor was shown in. Bespectacled and greying, he had a faintly grandfatherly air about him – but this only filled Max with more emotion still. It would have been easier if nobody had shown any understanding at all. 'The problem,' he explained, 'is you have cause. All this story of hidden parentage, and the blame you levelled at him for your mother's unfortunate end. None of it can be proven, of course, but it's the mere fact that you believed it. And there's a dozen people from the county competitions who can testify to the effectiveness of your mean right hook. It shows how you might want to kill.'

'But I didn't,' Max said. 'I swear to God that I—'

'You'll have to swear to God, if it goes to a trial, of course. But a jury might not be so forgiving on the boy who killed Bill Martin. A jealous, scheming manipulator, that's what you'll be. No, I think it will be altogether better if we can talk about a confession. How an argument bubbled up into an unfortunate altercation. How it was all a terrible accident. What do you say?'

'But that's how it was…'

The solicitor looked at him dully. 'Good show. Let's keep to that from now on. Now, is there anything else you need to tell me, before we begin?'

Max had started shaking. 'I should like it if you could pass on a note.'

'A note?'

He was already handing Max a pen and paper. Max accepted them gratefully.

'It shan't be long,' said Max. 'I don't quite know what to say.'

Dear Evie, he began to write.

Across the boarding houses of Soho, the Forsyths were packing up. Lily, Betty and Verity were already standing with their suitcases, waiting for the black taxicabs to pick them up; Davith Harvard had employed Hugo to help him exercise his pack of corgis across St James's. John Lauder, having returned to the Palladium at dawn to supervise the packing of his vanishing cabinet and other stage-show paraphernalia, was drinking silently in a café on Golden Square.

And Ed and Evie walked back together from the café where father and daughter had spent all morning in companionable silence, each trying to measure the wonder and devastation of the night before.

The letter was waiting for Evie when she arrived, delivered by a bicycle courier who had no idea of the import of the missive. Evie was slow in opening it up. She could feel her father's eyes on her.

'Do you want me to leave you to it?' Ed asked. She spoke no words in reply, only took her father by the hand and walked together into the common room at the bottom of the lodging house. A teapot with heavily stewed, dark tea sat on a table between two armchairs. There they settled down.

Dear Evie, Max had written. *I don't have the words to express my sorrow...*

It was almost as much as she could read. Out poured Max's heartache, his sorrow for letting her down, his regret at the future they were not to share. *For one moment really can change the course of a life. How I wish it had gone differently, and that last night had been the dream we had all hoped for. How I wish last night was the beginning, and not the end. Evie, I don't believe I ever felt more at home among the Forsyth Varieties. They had become my family. And family is everything, is it not?*

Evie was afraid that, if her tears began, she would not be able to stop them.

'*What now?*'

And Ed caressed her hand. 'I remember asking you the very same thing.' He remembered it so vividly it hurt. *What now, when the world you thought you knew, the world you thought* you'd live in for many precious years to come, suddenly no longer existed. 'Do you remember what you said?'

Evie shook her head.

'You told me to count all the beautiful things I could see. To remember that, in the midst of all the bad, there is still the good. And, Evie, you are so very good...'

Evie returned to the letter. The thing that wrenched at her most of all was that she didn't know what was proper to feel. Max was a killer. She supposed she ought to feel disgust. But the real feeling that percolated inside her was just a hollowness. As if she'd been emptied of all the joy she'd been feeling. As if she was simply a shell, with nothing left to give.

'These feelings pass,' said Ed. 'You told me that as well. And... I'm going to help you, Evie. You're a grown woman, but I haven't stopped being your father.' He paused, wondering if that was quite true. 'Perhaps I stopped for a time. I lost myself, a little while ago. But I'm here now, and... you're still young. You've still such a life to live. And one day, when you're old, you'll look back and know how wise, and strong, and good this made you. But your spirit's being tested now. Just march through the darkness, Evie. There's such light on the other side.'

It was at this point that Evie looked up from the letter. Her father sat, sorrowful but steadfast, facing her across the table.

'Max is right about one thing,' she said, retracing the words. 'Family *is* everything. And... Cal.'

'I know,' said Ed. 'I've been thinking on it myself.'

'What can we do for him now?'

Ed was silent.

'It's his song,' said Evie. 'It's his soul. He's selling it, right now, so he can go back to Meredith and Sam.' She stopped. 'Dad, what if he didn't have to go back? What if he didn't have to sell his soul for it?'

Their eyes met and, in that moment – when all the wonder mixed with the tragedy, when all the joy and heartbreak intermingled – an idea was born.

Two hundred and twenty pounds: in another time, in exchange for any other song, it would have been a king's ransom. But the cheque crammed into Cal's pocket did not even cover half of the blood money he owed Bruce. Perhaps there'd be another beating in this, or perhaps he'd be able to convince Bruce that a down payment was enough for a stay of execution – either way, he was going to have to try.

The Coach and Horses was heaving, even at 3 p.m. on a Tuesday afternoon, but Cal managed to find a back booth that had just been abandoned by some railway worker and his friends. There he sat, nursing a pint of Mackeson's, and trying to ignore the curious looks he got from the other drinkers in the room. Lots of them wore abrasions and scars too, so the bumps and grazes he was still sporting from yesterday did not look particularly aberrant. Perhaps it was only the hunted look he was wearing that drew their stares.

One moment, he was sitting there alone, brooding on the value of his soul; the next, Bruce was sinking into the seat opposite him, barring him from leaving the booth, one of his thugs looming on each shoulder like the sore cankers they were.

'You got a sing-song then, Cal,' said Bruce. Cal was momentarily thrown because, for the first time, it seemed as if there was no true malice in Bruce's voice. There he sat, the victor, reigning supreme. Here to collect his winnings, he had no need to threaten or gloat.

'I'm surprised you watched. I never thought variety theatre was something you'd be interested in.' *No*, he added silently. Only cockfighting and pigeon racing, drinking down at the dogs and fights outside the Taverner's Arms on a Saturday night.

'Well, I had a vested interest,' said Bruce. 'I wanted to hear my little canary singing. And there you were...' He grinned. 'Horrible business, this Bill Martin. But just think how much more horrible it could have been, if you weren't there to save the day. Who'd have sung for him, then? Your father? The old man lost his voice, didn't he, somewhere outside Reims?'

Beneath the table, Cal's hands clenched into fists. It seemed, then, that Bruce had not left all of his ability to taunt and provoke behind after all.

'You have my money, Cal?'

'I sold my song for you, Bruce.'

Bruce nodded, vaguely satisfied. 'I don't care where the money comes from. I just care where it ends up. Hand over then, Cal.'

Now was the moment. Cal reached into his back pocket. Then, ever the showman, he stalled. 'I need your word, Bruce. Now, sitting where I am, most people would think your word's worth nothing. But I know you. I know that, sitting here with these boys of yours, you wouldn't want to be proven a liar. So I need you to promise me you won't lay a finger on Meredith or Sam.'

Bruce shrugged. 'Show me the money.'

So Cal did.

The cheque had been made out to cash, just as Cal instructed, but he kept a careful hold on it as he revealed it to Bruce. 'Now, Bruce,' he said, before he slid it across the table. 'There has been a momentary hiccough in our agreement. It's fleeting.' Cal saw Bruce's eyes darken. 'Five hundred was just too much for a month, Bruce. So what I'm paying you now buys me another two. By New Year, we'll be even – but only on the proviso that nothing happens to my family in the meantime. I'm sorry for what I did to you, Bruce. You won't know why right now, but I am – and from the bottom of my being. I shouldn't have attacked you.' Cal's eyes widened as he warmed to his theme; a kind of wild glee spread across him. 'I should have made sure you were exposed as the bastard you are.' *Just as Max and Magdalene should have Bill Martin.* 'I should have done everything in my power to see you locked up.' *Just as everyone who'd known the real Bill Martin ought to have done.* 'But I didn't, and now I'll pay for it.' He opened his hands, to reveal the detail on the cheque. 'It's all I have.'

For a moment, Bruce was discombobulated. The barbed insult, the fire of Cal's words, had not yet penetrated him. When it did, he lifted himself from his seat, hand reaching out in a claw as if he might wrestle Cal across the table, there and then. 'Forsyth, did you come here to tell me you didn't have my money by *insulting* me to my face?'

Cal just stared at him. On reflection, perhaps it had been a foolish gambit – but, by God, it had felt good. 'The only way you'll get the rest of your money, Bruce – and, against all that's right in the world, I *will* give you that money – is if you give me more time. I'm showing willing, aren't I? I need the song to fly. By Christmas, if I'm right, you'll have the rest of what I owe.'

Bruce leered. 'So *my* money's to rest on Cal Forsyth – failed singer, failed songwriter, *past-it* entertainer – having a hit record, is it? Forgive me, Cal, but where's the sense in this? Where's the reason? You're not a horse I'd bet on, Forsyth. I'd rather have my blood—'

Bruce reared up onto his feet, making a snatch for Cal – but, in the same moment, unseen arms wrapped around him from behind, wrenching him backwards and flinging him onto one of the tables behind. There, in the place where Bruce had been standing, was Cal's father, Ed. His face had turned crimson with the exertion, but his expression was defiant. 'Put the cheque away, Cal. You'll take it back to Denmark Street once we're finished here.'

Ed turned. In the moments he'd been speaking, Bruce was back on his feet, bawling at his thugs to grab the old man.

Yet, the moment they lunged for him, other faces appeared in the bar. Valentino threw himself between Ed and the brutes. John Lauder brandished his cane. Davith Harvard's two dogs had set up a ruckus, while other musicians and the male dancers formed a tight line. Beyond them, Cal could see Evie. He sensed others standing with her – Lily, Betty, Verity and all of the rest.

'You're not selling your song, Cal,' Ed declared. 'Not like this, not for a pittance. It's a piece of your soul, and it's going to stay with you.'

'Dad, you don't understand – it's for Meredith, for Sam...'

'So they can stay up north, and you can go back to them?' Ed gave him a soft, fatherly smile. 'Well, where would the fun be in that? No, Cal, *you* have a choice – and Evie and I, we'll love you whatever you decide. Pay these ruffians off, if you want. Go back to Meredith and Sam and live the life you'd imagined. Or...' Ed's eyes swivelled, to take in Bruce. The fool was still standing there, his features bunched, the veins throbbing in his beck. 'Or send for them, right now, while you can. Come back to the Company for good, and bring your family with you. They'll go where we go. They won't need protecting from the likes of him, because they'll be with us – and the Forsyths stick together.'

Evie had come to Ed's side. In the way she looked at him, he knew at last that he was understood, that the travails of the last weeks hadn't been for nothing – because he had rediscovered his sister again, and she had rediscovered him.

Cal stood.

He looked at Bruce, and for the first time he realised: *you have nothing. You held a knife to my neck for so long, but only because I had nowhere else I could turn to. All your power is withered. There's nothing to bargain for any more.*

So I'm free.

In a second, the cheque was folded and in his back pocket.

'There's a number I need to call – before these louts find out where she is.'

Ed nodded. Such was the miracle of the modern age: Meredith might be here even before Bruce and his cronies made it back to the north.

'Bruce,' said Cal. 'We'll call it even now.' And he fingered the abrasions on his face, before his hand fell again to the older wound in his side. 'But if I see you again—'

'If *any* of us see you again,' interjected Ed.

Bruce staggered backwards. There was only one thing more wounding to a man like this than a fist in his face – and that was the humiliation colouring him right now.

He stepped back, swallowed by the crowd. 'This isn't over, Cal. This isn't done.'

But, in the moment that his thugs followed him out of the pub door, Cal felt a strange weight lifting off his shoulders, and knew in his heart that – bravado and tough words aside – it really was over. All those weeks of torment, of secrecy and pain, had been undone in moments – and it had not taken money, to see it done. All it had taken were the kind words of family.

'Are we agreed then, son?' Ed asked, as Cal picked his way across the table to join them.

'If you are?' he said, eyes flitting between Evie and Ed.

'I think it's important,' Ed said, and folded his arms around them both. 'I don't think there's any one of us doesn't need the other. We're Forsyths,' he smiled, 'and Forsyths is how we'll stay.'

*

Jim Livesey had so rarely visited London. He'd certainly never spent a night in a Soho hotel, nor been woken by a professional chauffeur so that he could be driven all the way back to Seaford town. The last twenty-four hours had passed in such a whirlwind that, by the time the sea air started streaming through the canary-yellow car's open window – and the outskirts of Seaford came into view – he was quite certain it had all been a dream.

Good fortune meant that, as Jim stepped out onto the seafront road and said his goodbyes to Hugo (who had kindly delivered him both to and from his destiny), he had not yet heard the unnerving news about Bill Martin.

After some time, kicking his heels along the sands and dreaming of John's last words to him – 'it might be your first time on this stage, lad, but work hard and it won't be the last' – Jim made his way home. The dark of night was curdling over the ocean, dusk settling itself like a shroud across Seaford – and there, framed in the kitchen window, were his mother and sister, the voice of his father rumbling somewhere behind.

When he stepped through the door, his family turned to face him. That single moment lasted forever. It was as if, Jim thought, they didn't recognise him any longer, as if some piece of him had been indefinably changed. Could a single day really do that to a person? He knew that he *felt* changed – but could others see it too?

'You missed hard graft down at the yard, son.' His father was seething. 'And all for this frippery and nonsense.'

His father's words might have been venomous, but they were quickly forgotten – for, within instants, his mother and sister were wrapping themselves around him, Amy squealing in shrill delight. 'You were on the television!' she kept chanting. 'The television!'

The pride of a little girl was such a simple, beautiful thing

– but the pride Jim saw in his mother's eyes was deeper and richer somehow. After she had embraced him, she drew back and kept stroking the hair out of his eyes, as if trying to perceive the little boy in the young man he'd just become. 'My Jim,' she said, 'at the London Palladium. On stage, in front of the Queen.'

At this last remark, even Jim's father's face changed, as if to suggest some grudging respect.

'You were wonderful, darling,' Jim's mother said. 'Just wonderful.'

Jim beamed. 'And I'm going to do it, Mother. I'm going to go where they go. Mr Lauder said he'd send word as soon as they were ready. A Christmas season. The spring. I think I can do it.' He looked at his father, because some part of Jim still needed his respect. 'I really do.'

Jim's father gave the stiffest nod of his head. To Jim, that meant every bit as much as the tears his mother was now dabbing away, or the way Amy was leaping around in circles.

Jim Livesey had taken his first step on the road to the sorcerer he would one day be, and his mother was going to champion him every step of the way.

It was a long drive back from Seaford.

The night had grown old while Hugo had been on the road, crawling forward through London's relentless traffic, but the red double-decker and the flotilla of black taxicabs that formed the Forsyths' fleet were waiting in a ring on the old aerodrome west of Ealing. What a sight that was: the true sight of a homecoming. The lights were on in the vehicles, and the blue-and-white microbus was buzzing, serving up hot food for the journey ahead. A night on the road with the Varieties – was there ever anything more beautiful to savour than this?

Apparently so, thought Hugo as he drew into the flotilla and stepped out to see the Company gathered around, because there stood Ed, with both his son and daughter at his side. The whole troupe was gathered in front of him, the chill of the October night leavened by the way they stood in such close ranks, arms tight around each other.

Hugo drifted into the throng and listened.

'My friends,' Ed was saying, 'what a strange, long journey we have been on together – and what a night we have lived. In the days to come, we will begin to understand it better – but I am going to say something to you, now, that my dear daughter Evie said to me in my own blackest hours.'

Evie looked up, her expression inscrutable. She'd said so many things in those days, anything to help him get through the night, he knew she would be surprised to learn that it had lodged in his mind, to be summoned back like this, so many years later.

'Day always follows night,' Ed said. 'The curtains fall, but so do they rise again.' He paused; his smile was for Evie primarily, but in truth it was for them all. 'And, when we stay together, we are stronger than we are apart.' This last had been for Cal. Ed touched his arm now. For the first time in years, the three of them stood side by side, like a bulwark against all that was wrong in the world. 'My friends, when we returned from Monaco, I held two secrets in my hand: the first, that Bill Martin would join us in our night of glory. The second: that I would end my career as it had begun – by Royal Command.'

The hush among the Forsyths was interrupted only by the sound of the wind. Evie and Cal shared a look.

'My friends, I was reminded of something last night – not just the majesty of the theatre, nor the joy of performing in front of that kind of a crowd. I was reminded that, in our darkest moments, there is still light – and that that light is all around us, in the family we have, and the family we create. Once upon a time, I imagined a retirement with my dear Bella: the rolling countryside of Suffolk, and local theatre, and grandchildren with us every summer we had left.' He paused, as the wistfulness of the memory came over him and, in turn, sailed out across everyone else. 'My friends, I have been clinging on to that idea because it was the vision I shared with my wife. But the thing I have seen, in the last days, is that the future changes. The river rolls on. My family is all around me – not just in Evie, not just in Cal, who has come back to us at last, but in every one of you. In you, Valentino; in you, John, my oldest friend; in you, Davith, with Tinky and Tiny; in you, Lily, Verity and Betty; you, Hugo. All of you standing in front of me now.' He paused. 'So it seems that two paths branch out in front of me: the loneliness of Suffolk, and a future I once craved; or the company of the present, and going on with you all.'

There was chatter among the Company now. Eyes flashed at one another, in expectation of what Ed was about to say. Then they looked over their shoulders – for, even now, another set of headlights was approaching, another car sweeping into the great yard where they were gathered.

'My friends, three weeks separate us from the start of our Christmas season in Colwyn Bay. Between now and then we will flock out to see our loved ones, to visit mothers and fathers, brothers and sisters and others we have not seen in too long. I had imagined that, when you regrouped for the season, I would attend only as a loyal member of the audience. Instead, I would like to ask if you would care to put up with me for a little longer.'

A spontaneous cheer broke out between the vehicles. Evie and Cal's expectant look turned to confusion, then to something approaching delight, relief, understanding.

'I am not yet ready, my friends, to let you go. And, though I may begin to need some help in marshalling this fine Company of ours – just as my father once did before me – I believe I have that help alongside me. In you, Evie – and, in you, Cal. My children, it gives me such strength to think you will be together again. And to think that, soon – very soon – I might meet my grandson.'

Cal had been watching the car as its headlights arced around the yard. At first, he had dismissed them as lost travellers, just looking to lap around and rejoin the motorways that fanned out from here – but no, now he was certain; the car was coming to a halt, and a familiar figure was bowing out of the driver's seat, brawny arms covered in freckles, a mane of red hair falling about his stubbled face.

'You might get your wish sooner than you think,' said Cal, and started to run.

'Jack!' Cal called, and the red-haired man looked over his shoulder with a beam.

By the time Cal reached the car, Jack was opening up its back door. Cal shouldered him out of the way, then opened it for himself.

Across the yard, the rest of the Company watched as Cal reached in, then came back with a baby in his arms. In the next moment, a slender woman, with striking red hair cut short around her chin, emerged. With the baby in the crook of one arm, Cal embraced her. The kiss they shared lingered long enough that, in the gathered throng, Lily and the others had to look away. Then, coming up for air, Cal took her by the hand and brought her to the troupe.

'Dad,' he said. 'Evie,' he went on. 'Everyone.' He spun around, to take in every last member of the Company he was ready to embrace again. 'I want you to meet the love of my life. My wife – Meredith.'

If Meredith looked daunted, it was not because of the faces

now looking at her – for they were welcoming her, every one. It was only because the last weeks had tested every ounce of her strength – and now, without warning, it seemed to have come to an end. Life moved fast.

Ed had stepped out of the crowd, with Evie at his side. It was, perhaps, the first time Cal had seen his sister smile since the devastation of the day before.

'Meredith,' Ed began, 'you come to us in strange times, but I promise, things won't always be like this. If you'll have us, there's a home for you here – a home for you both...' Ed's eyes dropped, to the baby in Cal's arms. 'May I?' he asked.

Soon, it was Ed holding the child. He gazed into the infant's beautiful blue eyes and wondered if there was, perhaps, some whisper of Bella in him. And of course there was, because the Forsyths went on, from one generation to the next – and, if his time was not yet done, there would still come a day when the next generation took the Company into the future, then the generation after that, on and on into whatever the future might bring.

'Sam,' he said, and held his grandson to his shoulder with all the memories of his life rushing through him: his own boyhood days, lingering at the side of the stage; Cal and Evie, barely knee high and learning every trick of the trade. 'Welcome to the family, Sam. Welcome to the Forsyth Varieties.'

Acknowledgements

To my wife, Hannah, my children, George and Henrietta, and my family. Thank you for supporting me in everything I do. I love you!

To my manager and friend, Melissa Chappell, thank you for your loyalty and endeavour and for listening to all my ideas. I love that I can now say I'm a dancer, a judge and an author!

A huge thank you to Kerr MacRae, my literary agent. Thank you for always being there. Without your guidance and expertise none of this would have happened.

A big shout out also to my Orion publishing team: to Sam Eades and Lucy Brem for their editorial expertise, to Lynsey Sutherland and Brittany Sankey for their marketing magic, and to Francesca Pearce and Frankie Banks for pulling together a brilliant PR campaign. Thank you also to the Sales team for promoting my books with such energy, and to Paul Stark and Jake Alderson for another stunning audiobook edition.

To Lou Plank and the team at Plank PR, thank you for your endless support and enthusiasm. To Yvonne Chappell, thank you for always picking up the phone and always knowing what I'm meant to be doing. And to Scott and David at Bungalow Industries, I appreciate all your hard work, support and positive feedback more than I can say.

Thank you as ever to booksellers and my readers all over the world, for being such fantastic advocates for my books. I am so grateful for all your support, and I hope you love this one just as much.

I started working on this story in 2022, around the time of Queen Elizabeth II's Platinum Jubilee, which was such a joyous and momentous occasion, in which the whole country came together to celebrate her life and legacy. This novel is my personal tribute to her Majesty, and her steadfast presence in our lives.

Much love,
Anton

Credits

Anton Du Beke and Orion Fiction would like to thank everyone at Orion who worked on the publication of *The Royal Show* in the UK.

Editorial
Sam Eades
Lucy Brem

Copyeditor
Suzanne Clarke
Francesca Brown

Proofreader
Sophie Wilson

Audio
Paul Stark
Jake Alderson

Marketing
Lynsey Sutherland
Brittany Sankey

Contracts
Dan Herron
Ellie Bowker
Alyx Hurst

Design
Charlotte Abrams-Simpson
Joanna Ridley
Zane Dabinett

Editorial Management
Charlie Panayiotou
Jane Hughes
Bartley Shaw
Tamara Morriss

Production
Ruth Sharvell

Finance
Jasdip Nandra
Nick Gibson
Sue Baker

Publicity
Francesca Pearce
Frankie Banks

Operations
Jo Jacobs
Sharon Willis

Sales
Jen Wilson
Esther Waters
Victoria Laws
Toluwalope Ayo-Ajala
Rachael Hum
Anna Egelstaff
Sinead White
Georgina Cutler